Ebon
Moon

Dennis McDonald

EBON MOON

dennismcdonaldauthor.com

ISBN: **1495426459**
ISBN-13: **978-1495426452**

DEDICATION

To John Ferguson (aka Count Gregore),
from a young boy who sat wide-eyed
before a flickering black-and-white television
in the dead of the night.

"In the 15th and 16th centuries, the belief in were-wolves was, throughout the continent of Europe, as general as the belief in witches, which had then come to resemble in many respects. It gave rise to the persecutions almost as frequent as those for witchcraft, and these usually ended in the confession of the accused, and his death by hanging and burning. It was calculated to inspire even greater terror than witchcraft, since it was believed that the were-wolves delighted in human flesh, and were constantly lying in wait for solitary travelers, and carrying off and eating little children."

The International Cyclopedia (1898)

Ebon (eb'an) *a:* black like ebony. *(Old world term)*

Webster's Dictionary

PROLOGUE

"Are you sure we're alone?" Michelle Carlson asked the man sitting next to her in the front seat of the pickup truck. Light from the full moon shining through the windshield highlighted his lean face and dark brown eyes. She thought his name was Doug but wasn't sure. Or was it Dave? The night spent at the karaoke bar left her memory in a beer-induced fog.

"We're way out in the middle of fucking nowhere. Nobody's going to see anything," replied Doug/Dave. His gaze focused on her chest like an anxious child waiting to unwrap a birthday present. "Now get that shirt off and show me those big boobs."

She slid the T-shirt over her head and dropped it on the dash.

"You want to see these, cowboy?" She reached for the clasp of her bra.

"Fuck yeah," he replied, taking a sip of his longneck beer.

Friday night and another horny redneck, she thought while undoing the clasp. *What the hell? The guy's got gorgeous brown eyes.*

She tossed the bra on the dash.

"Ooooeeeee!" the Doug/Dave guy whooped. "You got some fine tits."

"Thanks."

Her pregnancy with Missy two years before had left her breasts rounder and fuller. Every Friday night, she slipped on her tightest T-shirt and got her mother to watch her daughter. Her next stop was the honky-tonk for a night of partying and a possible hookup with some fortunate cowboy. Being a single mother at twenty-three, it was her best chance for sex. The rest of her week consisted of long shifts at the convenience store and changing diapers at the house alone.

"You like?" She threw aside her long brown hair.

"Fuck yeah." Doug/Dave took another sip of the longneck. "Titties and beer. Two great tastes that taste great together."

He poured a swash of beer across her breasts causing Michelle to gasp from the sudden cold liquid on her nipples. Handing her the bottle, Doug/Dave smiled and then leaned in to lick up the spilled Budweiser. Enjoying the man's lapping tongue, she settled back in the seat.

At least he's creative. Not like the last asshole who wanted nothing more than a quick blow job. I think I'll give this cowboy the grand tour tonight. I just hope he lasts longer than eight seconds in the saddle.

With half-closed eyes, she gazed out the front windshield. They had parked on the side of a country road near a tall stand of trees. Overhead, in a starlit Oklahoma sky, the hazy full moon transformed the rolling countryside into a two-tone palette of silvery light and dark shadows. A late August breeze, whispering with the smell of freshly cut hay, blew through the open passenger window. The night had been as perfect as the weather. Doug/Dave licked up the spilled beer like an expert. A pleasant warmth spread through her body, and she laid her head against the back of the seat.

Something growled outside the truck.

Michelle opened her eyes. "What was that?"

"Waat wooss whaat?" Dave/Doug said with his face still buried between her breasts.

"I heard an animal growl." She sat up and stared out the side window where the shoulder of the road ran close to the grove of trees. She sensed something waiting there, something watching from the shadows … *something evil.*

Wiping his chin. on the sleeve of his pearl-snap shirt, Doug/Dave said, "It's probably just a coyote." He took the beer bottle from her hand.

"I think someone's watching us over there." She pointed toward the trees.

He peered out through the front glass. "Bullshit. I don't see a damn thing. There's not a soul out here." After taking a long swig of the beer, he added, "Besides, it could be a bobcat or a bear. Or it could even be Bigfoot. Yeah, Oklahoma's got him here, too. I've got a friend I go hunting with, and he swears he saw the damn thing in the woods near McAllister one night. Bigfoot watched them from the trees for a while and then took off running when they drew near."

"You're trying to scare me."

"Why would I want to scare such a stacked piece of ass?" He leaned in for another kiss.

"Doug, listen to me, I don't feel safe here." She grabbed for her T-shirt and bra off the dash. "Let's just go."

"My name's Larry, by the way." He let out a frustrated sigh and took a last sip of the beer before flipping the bottle out the open driver's window. "Don't be afraid. You ain't the only one that's got a rack." He reached up and patted the hunting rifle nestled on the gun rack in the back window of the truck cab. "This baby can drop a bear dead in its tracks. Don't worry."

"Is it loaded?"

"Fuck yeah. All I got to do is throw the safety off and jack a round into the chamber."

She studied the black hunting rifle. The weapon looked intimidating and dangerous in the dim light. *Nobody's going to screw with someone armed with that thing,* she decided.

"All right." She smiled and touched his chin. "Let's take it from where we left off."

"That a girl, I knew you weren't no wuss, babe."

She lifted up her breasts with both hands. "Come and get 'em, cowboy."

Larry leaned face-first into her cleavage and made a motorboat noise while he shook his head from side to side. The antic caused Michelle to laugh ... for the last time in her young life.

Out of her peripheral vision, a large shadowed shape rushed from the trees. Something heavy landed in the truck bed shaking the vehicle with its sudden weight. Michelle caught a glimpse of a dark hulking form in the moonlight. Wolflike fangs and fierce red eyes flashed a second before the creature leaped up on the roof.

"What the fuck?" Larry said, forgetting about her breasts.

"Something jumped on the truck!"

They both looked up in dismay. Black claws punched through the roof as if constructed of cardboard instead of sheet metal.

"Son of a bitch!" Larry grabbed the hunting rifle off the rack and jacked the bolt of the weapon. "What the fuck is it?"

"I don't care. Let's get out of here!" Michelle pushed the button to raise the side window before realizing there was no power without the truck running.

The growling horror tore open more of the rooftop. Through the jagged hole in the metal, a silhouette of something with canine fangs looked down at both of them.

"Goddamn!" Larry said, handing her the rifle. "Hold this! The safety's off, so be careful."

"Let's get out of here!"

"Fuck yeah!" He reached for the key in the ignition.

With a deep animal snarl, a clawed hand grabbed through the open driver's window causing Larry's head to snap back. He turned to Michelle with a look of surprise and terror in his brown eyes. Mouth working silently, he tried to speak, but no words came out. In horror, Michelle realized why. There was now a bloody meat hole where his throat had been a second before.

She screamed.

Claws reached in again and snagged Larry's shirt and yanked him out through the driver window. The heels of his cowboy boots were the last thing Michelle saw before he disappeared into the dark. She glanced at the ignition. The keys were gone.

Larry had taken the keys with him!

More animal snarls sounded. Michelle looked through the front windshield and watched multiple humanoid shapes move in a loping gate across the moonlit road. The creatures descended upon Larry's struggling form and fed like a pack of wild animals, ripping apart his pearl-snap shirt and blue Levi's to get at the flesh beneath. His cowboy boots twitched from the violent feeding. For the moment, the terrible beasts had forgotten about her. Breathing in short gasps, she stared down at the hunting rifle in her shaking hands and thought of her daughter.

She had to escape … to live to see Missy again.

Michelle studied the weapon. Larry had said the safety was off. *Did that mean the gun was ready to fire?* Her trembling finger slid around the trigger. *Oh God, please let me live.* Raising the rifle to her shoulder, she pointed it toward the passenger window and listened for sounds outside. The violent snarls had died down. She dared a glance out the windshield. Larry's remains lay sprawled in the center of the road, reduced to a bloody mangle of half-eaten bone, exposed organs, and ripped clothing in the moonlight. He still held the truck's ignition key in one outstretched hand. The terrible creatures had retreated back into the shadows.

Or had they?

She fought back the tears blinding her vision and focused on the truck keys. *Fifteen feet to the keys. If I could just reach them and get back to the truck, I can drive away from here. I would live to see my little Missy again.*

She decided to go for it and unlatched the passenger door handle. In the next instant, an inhuman face leaped up into the side window. Michelle glimpsed fangs dripping gore and red eyes filled with a primal hunger. Reflexes driven by fear took control and she swung the rifle around and pulled the trigger. With a thundering flash, the weapon bucked in her hands as the recoil knocked her down across the front seat of the truck.

Michelle lay still and waited. Her ears rang from the gunshot. *Did I kill it?* She concentrated on listening. No more growls. The night had grown quiet. Even the constant noise of the insects went silent, as if they were waiting for what would happen next. The only sound was her desperate breathing and the pounding of her heart. Hands slick with sweat gripped the rifle across her bare chest.

She prayed the things had returned to the world of nightmares where they belonged. Agonizing moments of silence passed until she could no longer contain her need to look.

She sat up.

They waited in front of the truck. Four large hunched forms covered in bristling dark fur studied her through the windshield. In that instant of terror, Michelle realized the creatures reminded her of something from a bad horror movie. At the time, she only paid half attention to the film. Her constant day-by-day drama of raising a baby daughter and searching for a decent man was more important than a crappy monster movie. Now the beasts hungered for her with red eyes and sharp fangs dripping drool in the moonlight.

Werewolves!

"No!" Michelle screamed.

One of the monsters jumped up against the driver's door and reached in to grab her. In panic, she threw herself to the side while claws ripped across her bare shoulder blades. Michelle kicked open the passenger door.

Run!

She leaped out of the truck and fled into the dark countryside toward the stand of trees. Her tennis shoes pounded through tall grass and reeds while low inhuman growls filled the night air behind her. Running on an instinctual fear, she dared not turn around to see the things chasing her beneath the light of the full moon. To do so would shatter her mind with terror.

In the center of the circle of dark trees, a hazy fog hung between the shadowed trunks and curled about her running form. Michelle stopped in the clearing and fought to catch her breath as she turned. Just beyond the edge of her vision, the snarls of the creatures grew louder in the mist.

She realized she still held the rifle. Her hands fumbled along the sides of the weapon. *How did he load it?* Finding the lever of the bolt, she slid it back. A piece of cylindrical metal dropped to the ground at her feet as the bolt snapped back in place. *Is the gun loaded? Oh God, I don't know.*

A hoarse animal grunt broke the silence. Michelle looked up. Black hunched shapes moved through the misty spaces between the trees. Shaking with fear, she brought the rifle to her shoulder and slid her finger around the trigger.

"The gun's loaded," she shouted. "I'll shoot anything that comes near me. Please go away. I don't want to hurt anyone. I have a two-year-old daughter who needs me."

A tree limb snapped and she swung the rifle toward the sound. A misshapen humanoid form with a doglike snout hunched down on all fours and licked its teeth. With a guttural growl, the monster leaped as she pulled the trigger. The muzzle flash lit the clearing, and the shot echoed across the countryside. In the next second, the beast knocked her to the ground. Claws tore the rifle from her grasp. She screamed and fought against the nightmare with bare hands pounding thick fur. Snarling, the thing clawed again and ripped away the flesh of both her breasts, leaving only raw torn meat in their place.

Michelle stopped struggling. She was going to die. In numb horror, she watched the head of the creature lean back revealing a maw of fangs. A red tongue lapped out for a brief second before its mouth dropped to bite her on the side of the neck. The beast's hot breath burned against her flesh as its teeth rendered and tore out her jugular. Michelle lay very still and looked up through the trees at the full moon. Blood poured from the bite wound. While the rest of the pack of werewolves moved in to feast, her final thoughts were of her daughter.

I love you, Missy.

The last thing Michelle heard before death was a piercing howl echoing through the moonlit night.

THIRTEEN MONTHS LATER

WEDNESDAY

CHAPTER ONE

Jessica Lobato reached across the picnic table and used a napkin to wipe the white ice cream from her five-year-old daughter's chin. "Baby, you're getting more on you than in you," she said with a smile.

"Thanks, Mommy," Megan replied, promptly taking another lick of the vanilla cone.

"You're welcome, sweetie."

Jessica returned to studying her surroundings through dark sunglasses. She had decided to stop and buy Megan an ice-cream cone at a roadside Tastee-Freez on the outskirts of a small town in northern Oklahoma. The steel water tower rising out of the center of the rural community announced its name as Hope Springs.

Hope springs eternal, Jessica thought to herself. *And hope is the one thing I need now.*

She glanced back down the highway taken to reach the little town as a rusted old pickup topped a hill and rattled toward them. She studied the face of the driver as it drove past: an elderly man with long gray hair and beard. Jessica let out a nervous breath.

Not my husband. Thank God.

Thinking of Blake made her adjust the sunglasses. The three-day-old black eye was still noticeable. She surmised it would take one more day before she could hide the bruising with makeup and ditch the shades. Thanks to her abusive marriage, she had a lot of experience covering over her injuries.

The lunch-hour rush buzzed while the two of them sat at a weathered picnic table in front of the little drive-in. Locals hurried in and carried out white paper sacks filled with greasy burgers.

Amidst the confusion, no one paid attention to them, and Jessica was glad for it. She let the familiar knot of paranoia subside in her stomach.

It's so peaceful and normal here. Nothing like the hell I left.

She turned back to Megan. In appearance, her child was a smaller version of herself with sunlit honey-blonde hair and precious blue eyes. Everyone recognized them instantly as mother and daughter. The only trait Megan carried from her father was his strong chin. At least, Jessica prayed it was the only thing she inherited from the monster that sired her. In the noon sun, the bruises on her daughter's right arm were ugly blue-green stains that would take more time to disappear than a black eye. She feared the bruises on her daughter's soul were permanent, however.

"What do you think about this town?" Jessica asked.

"It's nice," Megan replied with a nod of her head.

"Baby, we might see if we can find a place to live here."

"Do you think Daddy will find us?" Megan took another lick at the ice cream.

"I pray to God he doesn't, sweetie." An icy chill ran down her spine at the thought.

Megan ate her cone in silence. Jessica knew her daughter was too quiet and withdrawn for a five-year-old girl. Often she wondered what went through her mind in quiet times like this. *Is she thinking of her sick father? What damage has the cold-hearted bastard done to the psyche of his own innocent child?* Megan's eyes tried to hide the pain she carried, but the hurt was still there like a jagged rock beneath a layer of thin blue ice.

A terrible memory filled Jessica's thoughts.

"Do you still love me, Jess?" Blake asked, loading the single bullet into the .357 magnum pistol. He spun the chamber.

"Please, don't do this." Jessica struggled against the duct tape trapping her

15

in the chair. The black eye where he punched her had already swollen shut. With her good eye, she watched in terror as he stepped beside Megan sleeping peacefully on the couch. He placed the barrel of the gun against their daughter's head.

"What's the answer, Jess?" His eyes burned with an insane glint. "Yes or no?"

"Please, don't," Jessica pleaded while tears ran down her face. She spoke in a soft voice so as not to wake Megan. "Do me. Not our daughter. Please, Blake."

"Not so much fun, Jess." He showed his evil smirk, signaling he was about to do something very bad. "Do you still love me, Jess?"

"Yes."

"You lie."

Click.

"Lovely day, isn't it?" A voice asked causing Jessica to jump and turn.

A large woman stood outside the front door to the Tastee-Freez. Dressed in a grease-spotted white apron with an equally stained work shirt, she lit a cigarette and smiled. Jessica looked around. The rest of the cars in the lot were gone except for her silver 1974 Camaro. The lunch rush had ended with her locked in memories so painful she didn't notice.

"I'm sorry, what did you say?"

"I said it's a beautiful day."

"Yes, it is," Jessica replied.

"It's very warm for it being the last week of September." The woman blew out a puff of smoke. "Indian summer is what they call it."

"Indian summer," Megan muttered before putting the last of the cone in her mouth. She crunched down, causing white ice cream to squirt down her chin. "All gone, Mommy."

Jessica handed her daughter a napkin. "Wipe your face, baby."

The Tastee-Freez woman continued with an Oklahoma twang to her voice. "The weatherman says there's a cold front coming, though. It should be here by the end of the week. You have a lovely daughter. Will you look at those big blue eyes? How old is she?"

"Five."

Megan cleaned the ice cream from her chin and hid her bruised arm under the picnic table. *Five years old and already knows to hide her abuse,* Jessica realized.

"Are you from around these parts?" The woman's presence hovered just beyond the edge of the table. Jessica felt the paranoia return. *Don't get all spooked. It's just a bored working woman wanting to make small talk after the lunch rush. Besides, she might be able to give me some information.*

"Just passing through."

"I'm Marjorie, by the way."

"Jessica, and this is my daughter, Megan."

"Hello," Megan said with a smile.

"Welcome to Hope Springs." The woman smelled of cooking grease and fried burgers.

"Thank you," Jessica replied. "Perhaps you can help us. I'm thinking about settling in a small town like Hope Springs. We come from a larger city. Is this a place for a single mother to raise a daughter?"

"Oh, honey, it's a wonderful place. You couldn't find one better. It's a town of good church-loving people. Hope Springs is a very quiet community of softball games, weekend cookouts, and Sunday meetings. Just plain peaceful country folk around here." Marjorie took the last pull on her cigarette. "There's just one drawback."

"What's that?"

"It's a small town, dear. Everybody knows everybody."

"So everybody knows everybody's business," Jessica added.

"That's correct, and what they don't know, they try to guess." Marjorie chuckled. "Not many new people move into town. A pretty woman like you won't be a stranger long."

"If I decide to live here, how would I go about finding a place?"

"The *Gazette* only comes out on Monday," Marjorie said, stepping on the cigarette butt. "If I was you, I'd try the post office. There's a community bulletin board where people advertise houses for rent and things for sale."

"Thank you. I'll do that." Jessica stood and said to her daughter, "Let's go, baby."

"Okay."

"It's nice meeting you," Marjorie called out. "I hope you decide to stay. Lord knows we can use fresh faces about town. If you drop by and see me again, Megan, the next cone's on me."

"Bye." Megan waved back before climbing into the passenger side of the Camaro.

Jessica slid behind the wheel and reached under the front seat to touch the loaded .357 magnum. The feel of the pistol gave her a small sense of security. She stole both the car and gun from Blake before escaping her home. If he found her now, he would do more than beat her.

This time he would kill her.

Jessica put the key in the ignition, and the Camaro's large engine roared to life.

"This is a pretty town, Mommy," Megan said. "I like it. Are we going to stay here?"

"If we can find a place," she replied, backing the Camaro out onto the highway and angling the car toward the town.

*   *   *   *

Like a Rockwell painting from the forties, Hope Springs was a little postcard-perfect community. The highway served as Main Street running through the center of town to the one traffic light. They drove past a church, dollar store, Laundromat, and courthouse before coming to the small post office.

Jessica parked the Camaro. "I'm going in to see if there's a house to rent. You wait here," she said.

"Okay, Mommy."

Jessica closed the driver door before remembering the pistol under the front seat. She decided against leaving Megan alone in the car.

Opening the passenger door, she leaned in. "Why don't you come inside with me, baby."

"Okay." Megan slid out of the seat.

Taking her daughter by the hand, Jessica entered the post office and removed her sunglasses to see better in the fluorescent light. On one wall in the lobby, she found the community bulletin board covered in tacked-up flyers and notices. Most were ads for used cars and trucks, auctions for farm machinery, garage sales, etc. Pinned to the board were three rental notices. She wrote down the phone number of each across her palm.

"Who is that, Mommy?"

Jessica glanced up. Megan pointed to a flyer showing a picture of a pretty brown-haired young woman in her early twenties. The heading at the top of the yellowed paper asked: *Has anyone seen Michelle?* Jessica leaned closer to read the text that stated Michelle Carlson had vanished over a year ago. Beneath her picture was a phone number for anyone with information on her whereabouts.

"It's a notice about a missing girl," she answered.

"She looks sad."

Beneath the missing person flyer, Jessica noticed a gold

thumbtack that pinned a business card to the board. Printed across the face of the card were the words:

Waitress Wanted
$5 an hour plus tips
Roxie's Roadhouse
Karaoke, Cold Beer, Good Times
5 miles east on Highway 133

Jessica stuffed the card in the pocket of her jeans.

"Let's go, sweetheart." She took Megan by the hand and left the lobby for the sunshine outside.

Once she locked the seat belt around her daughter in the passenger side of the Camaro, Megan asked, "Is she dead, Mommy?"

"Who?"

"The girl in the picture."

Jessica paused for a second. "She's just missing. Maybe she ran away from home like we did."

Megan shook her head and looked down at the bruises on her arm. "I think she's dead."

CHAPTER TWO

Opening the door to his workshop, Jasper Higgins kicked out the empty whiskey bottle. It rolled end-over-end before coming to rest against an old tire sitting in the weeds. He squinted up at the sunlight with bloodshot eyes and a hangover pounding in his head.

He had spent the night with Jack Daniel's, the only companion he had left now.

Together, they painted a new sign.

Rubbing calloused hands across the gray stubble on his face, Jasper selected a hammer and nails from a workbench and dropped them into the pockets of his overalls. He bent down to grab the sheet of plywood, sending a deep pain shooting through his back. He used to carry the signs, but in the last year, his body had succumbed to painful arthritis. Now he could only drag them to their destinations.

Grunting and cursing under his breath, he pulled the plywood across the overgrown grass toward the others he posted over the last two years. The handmade billboards stood in a line along the stretch of his farmland bordering Highway 133 and were intended for the drivers traveling between Hope Springs and the larger town of Morris, seven miles away. The words scrawled across the scabby pieces of wood told of the beast who murdered his wife one horrible night. The signs served as a warning to the unbelievers of their impending doom. God's judgment was at hand, and the wolf was waiting at their door.

Reaching the pole he erected the day before, Jasper stopped to catch his breath. The sun beat warm upon his brow, and he wiped sweat away with the sleeve of his grimy work shirt. He took a moment to look back over the farm he worked for the last fifty years. The clouds broke the sunlight to cast shifting shadows over the rusting tractor, the overgrown fields, and the peeling paint of the house and barn. When Emma was alive, golden wheat fields surrounded the property. The farm died when Satan murdered his beloved wife. Its only crop now was the signs he made.

Jasper located the aluminum stepladder against the fence running along the front of his property. Just a few yards beyond, cars and trucks raced down the two-lane blacktop of Highway 133. None slowed to read his scrawled words of innocence and doom. A few passing drivers honked, but he did not wave to them. To most of the locals, he was a crazy Bible-spouting drunk who murdered his wife.

He unfolded the ladder, grabbed the painted plywood, and hefted it up the pole. Once in place, he pounded nails through the sign. Every hammer blow became more intense as he recalled why he hung the words in the first place. No one believed what he saw the night of Emma's death. Not the sheriff. Not the papers. They tried to pin the murder on him, but there wasn't enough evidence. After a thorough search of his farm, they never found Emma's body.

He became their number-one suspect.

Jasper had no doubt who committed the vicious crime. The Beast of Revelations murdered his wife. He remembered waking that night to see something looming over their bed, a hideous hunched shadow against the glow of the moonlight from the open window. The creature's red eyes burned like fire. Before he could cry out, the demon grabbed Emma with black claws and fled leaping through the window. Her horrible screams faded away as the thing carried her off into the darkness beneath a full moon.

He pounded in the last nail as tears moistened his eyes. Tucking the hammer in the loop of his greasy overalls, he descended the ladder and stared up at his latest handiwork. The sun shone across the words he had spent all night painting on the plywood. He read them one more time:

> I did not commit any crime.
> Satan in all of his wickedness
> took my wife from me.
> I've seen the Beast of Revelations
> It comes like a thief in the night.
> The descent to Hell is easy.
> Find God and the love of Jesus.
> For the end-times are here.

"I love you, Emma," Jasper whispered with a tear in his eye.

Tires squealed from behind. He turned to the sound. A late-model gray pickup had parked on the shoulder of the road. Two teenage boys exited the vehicle and walked toward him. One of them he recognized: Terry Newman, a young man who had been a member of his youth ministry group at the Southern Baptist Church of Christ in Hope Springs before Emma's death. Since that time, the boy had put on a few extra pounds around the belly. The other was a skinny teen whose face was covered in pimples. He walked next to Terry holding the last three cans of a six-pack of beer wrapped in plastic rings. Neither of them was of legal drinking age.

The two stopped just on the other side of the fence.

"What are you doing, Mr. Higgins?" Terry asked. "Putting up another sign?"

"Yep." He nodded. "It's nice to see you again, Terry. You've grown so much I nearly didn't recognize you."

With apprehension, he studied the other youth with the pimples and the beer. The boy looked like trouble. Jasper once loved spreading God's word to the young men in the area, but since Emma's death, he didn't trust teenagers. When he went into town, they would honk and call him cruel names while racing by in their fancy cars or trucks. He also suspected a group of teenage boys were responsible for shooting holes through his signs in the middle of the night.

"I don't think I've met your friend, Terry." Jasper started folding the aluminum ladder and placing it on the ground.

"Oh, this is Sid Granger."

"You want a beer, old man?" Sid asked, pulling a can from the plastic ring of the six-pack.

"I don't drink with minors."

"Really?" Sid chuckled. "You're already shitfaced. I can smell it on your breath. Your ass is drunker than both of us combined." He chuckled handing the beer to Terry.

"Don't be a prick, Sid." Terry popped the top. "Mr. Higgins used to be my Sunday school teacher."

"Is that right? I hear he's a crazy bastard that murdered his wife and says the devil did it. He's a fucking psycho, but that's cool."

"If he said the devil murdered her, I believe him," Terry replied and said to Jasper, "You didn't do it, did you, Mr. Higgins?"

"I'm innocent." He couldn't count how many times he had said those words to anyone who would listen.

"There. Mr. Higgins is innocent. Enough said," Terry replied, looking at the row of signs running along the fence. "You sure put a lot of work into your signs, Mr. Higgins. I bet there are over thirty of them."

Sid squinted up at his latest message in the sunlight. "Hey, what does that mean, you've seen the Beast of Revelations? So this beast is the one who broke into your house and killed your wife, right?"

Jasper nodded but said nothing.

24

"That's awesome, man. So what the fuck did it look like?"

He described the horror to them: the black hunched shape, the claws and fangs, and the eyes that burned with hellfire. Even in the hot sun, the recollection brought a chill down his spine.

"Sounds like a werewolf to me," Sid commented after taking a long drink of beer. "I don't think you got the right monster, old man. It's not the Beast of Revelations; it's a fucking werewolf."

"A werewolf? Are you saying it was some kind of wolf?"

"You mean you don't know what a werewolf is?" Surprise showed on Sid's face.

Jasper thought to himself. It seemed one of the arresting detectives used the term, but he wasn't sure. Not after a night of hard drinking. "I guess not."

"Didn't you ever see the movie *The Howling*?" Sid asked.

"I don't own a television. Emma always said it was a tool of the devil. We just listen to a Christian station on the radio."

"Fucking boring." Sid tossed away an empty can into the ditch.

Terry spoke up. "Well, a werewolf is a man who changes into an animal form when there is a full moon. It'll run around killing people and change back to human after the night of the full moon is over. It's only a myth, though. No one's ever seen one for real."

"There was a full moon the night of Emma's murder. Maybe it was a werewolf I saw in my house that night."

"You know how you kill one of those fuckers?" Sid popped the top of the last beer.

Again, Jasper shook his head no.

"You got to shoot him with silver bullets. The only way you can kill one."

"Silver bullets?"

"Yeah, silver does a fucking number on them. It kills them deader than shit. Any other wound they can heal, but not one from a silver bullet. You shoot one and he turns back to a naked man lying on the ground and all fucked up."

Terry laughed and said, "You got to have silver bullets, Mr. Higgins. That'll kill any werewolves coming around your house."

"Thank you. I'll keep it in mind."

"No problem, Mr. Higgins." Terry finished his beer and crumpled the can.

For a moment, Jasper remembered the boy he knew three years ago. Terry had been an eager participant in the Bible classes he taught to the young men before the murder accusations. Afterward, many of the parents pulled their kids out of the youth ministry because he had become an embarrassment to the little church. Looking at him now, Jasper fought back a deep sadness.

"Terry, when was the last time you went to church?" he asked.

The boy's eyes looked down to the ground. "I haven't gone back since you stopped teaching the youth classes. I hang out with Sid now."

"Don't turn away from God, son. Don't let what happened to me keep you from church and the love of Jesus."

"I guess I just don't believe like I used to," Terry said in a barely audible voice.

"Don't stop because of me. You were saved, son. I was the one who was your witness before God."

"I know." Terry nodded.

Sid shoved the boy against the shoulder. "You're going to take preaching from a whacked-out old drunk? The fucker killed his wife, dumbass.

Jasper ignored him and continued, "Remember the things we talked about in Bible class? How Jesus died for our sins and only through him can one reach salvation?"

Sid began walking back to the truck. "It's all bullshit. Don't pay any attention to the old fucker. Let's get out of here."

"Please go back to church, Terry. Don't turn your back on the love of Jesus. Do it for me."

"Here's what I think about your Jesus, fuckhead!" Sid spun around pitching the half-empty can of beer. It struck the new sign splattering all over the words in a spray of foam. "Now, what do you have to say, preacher man?"

"Jesus loves you, too, son."

"Stick it up your ass!" Sid flipped him the finger and turned to Terry. "Are you coming or not?"

Terry gave Jasper one last look before walking to Sid's truck.

"Terry, don't forget the love of our savior," he called out to his back. "He died upon the cross for you."

Terry remained quiet and climbed in the passenger seat.

"No one listens to you anymore, old man," Sid said.

The pimple-faced youth let out a long doglike howl before jumping in the truck cab. With a heavy heart, Jasper stood by the fence as the pickup gunned its motor and spun its tires, spewing grass and mud behind it. Once on the highway, the vehicle sped away toward Morris. He whispered a prayer for God to protect Terry's soul and walked back to his lonely farmhouse. Along the way, he came to a stark realization.

He had hung his last sign.

No one believed the words he painted. Nothing he said convinced anyone of his innocence in his wife's murder. He remembered what the police interrogator asked over and over. "What did you do with the body, Jasper? Why did you do it, Jasper? Did you lose your temper and kill your wife? Is that what happened, Jasper? Did you just snap? Did you get drunk and hit your wife with something and then hide the body? You can tell us, Jasper."

He never confessed to something he didn't do.

When he told them how the beast had killed his precious Emma, the investigating officers shook their heads. He knew they doubted his sanity. Sometimes, he doubted it himself. In the end, when no corpse was ever found, the police reached an impasse. They would not press charges until the discovery of more evidence, but the accusation turned him into a pariah to the locals and congregation at the church where he and Emma attended for over thirty years. Even his family and closest friends shunned him. Two years later, nothing remained in his life but the whiskey bottle and the sign making.

But he would do no more. His body ached from seventy-three years of shuffling on the earth. His weary soul longed to see the creator.

Tonight he would end it all and join Emma in heaven.

CHAPTER THREE

"What's the matter, Mommy?" Megan asked.

With her pocketbook open, Jessica turned to her daughter in the passenger seat of the Camaro. "We're running out of money."

Jessica counted the bills again. Less than four hundred dollars remained. From a side pocket in her purse, she removed Blake's credit card. Her husband may have already put a stop on the card, but she doubted it. Either way, she couldn't dare use it unless in an absolute emergency. Blake would be able to trace the purchase and, eventually, find her. She slid the card back.

"Mommy's going to have to get a job," she said, stuffing the purse in the glove box.

Megan looked out the passenger window. "Are you going to dance some more?"

Jessica shook her head. "No more dancing."

A year ago, Blake had forced her to work strip bars for extra money to feed his voracious coke habit. The only thing Megan knew was Mommy danced like the women she watched on *Dancing with the Stars*. She didn't know Mommy's job entailed taking her clothes off and giving sweaty lap dances to old perverts.

"Am I going be home by myself?"

Jessica let out a sad sigh. Working as a stripper meant leaving her daughter in Blake's care. Many times after the club closed, she came home to find Megan, alone and crying, on the couch.

"Listen, sweetie, I've got to go to work to make money, but I promise I won't leave you by yourself. I'll find a babysitter, okay?" She took the child's hand. "You understand, don't you?"

"I understand."

She kissed Megan on the forehead. "Good girl."

"Where are we going to live?"

"I'm going to call around and see if we can find a house to rent." Sliding on her sunglasses, Jessica popped the door latch and climbed out. "I'll be using the phone right outside."

"Okay, Mommy."

She had parked before a pay phone outside a Jiffy Trip located a block from the Highway 133 and 71 junctions in Hope Springs. Jessica fished some change from her jean pocket and dropped the coins into the phone. She dialed the numbers jotted earlier on her palm in the post office. The first one said the house was already rented. The second one didn't answer. On the third call, she got a reply.

"Hello?" a mature woman's voice answered.

"I'm calling in regard to the two-bedroom trailer house you have for rent. Is it still available?"

"Yes, it is."

"How much is the rent?"

"Two hundred and fifty dollars a month."

The low rent amazed Jessica. In Chicago, she couldn't rent a one-room slum hole for two fifty a month.

"Is there a deposit?" she asked, praying there was none.

"A hundred and fifty."

Jessica winced. She barely had enough money to cover both rent and deposit. There wouldn't be anything left after that.

"I'm a mother with a five-year-old daughter. I want to settle here in Hope Springs, but I don't have much money."

The woman chuckled on the other end. "You want to waive the deposit?"

"That would be great, but just until I can earn enough to pay it." She hated asking a favor from a stranger, but desperate times required desperate measures.

"It's difficult to talk about such matters over the phone. I tell you what. Come out and look the place over. We'll discuss it then. How does that sound?"

"Wonderful."

"My name is Nelda Olson."

"Jessica Lobato."

"Well, Jessica ..."

"Call me Jess."

"Well, Jess, do you know how to find the house?"

Jessica said she didn't. The woman on the line gave her the address, and she jotted it down on her palm.

"I'll be right out there," Jessica said.

"I look forward to meeting you. Bye now, dear."

She hung up the phone just as someone let out a loud wolf-whistle from behind. Jessica cringed at the sound. Accustomed to men's whistles while topless and dancing on a stage, she didn't welcome such attention outside of a strip bar. Her anger flared but quickly cooled when she turned around and faced the offender. A tall, broad-shouldered man dressed in a brown khaki uniform stood on the passenger side of the Camaro. The ball cap on his head read "Sheriff." Jessica glanced over to see a white patrol car parked next to hers.

"Hello." She stepped up to her driver door hoping she didn't sound as nervous as she felt.

"The Camaro is yours?" he asked in a strong voice, surprisingly minus an Oklahoma drawl.

"Yes." Jessica prayed he didn't ask for registration or insurance verification. Blake may have reported it stolen.

The sheriff let out another whistle. "She's a real beauty. What is she, a '74?"

"Correct." She put her hand on the door handle and prayed for the officer to go away. Instead, he walked around to the rear of the car. Jessica couldn't tell if he was admiring the rear taillights or reading her license plate.

"She's a real classic. I love the silver paint job," he said. "It's fine."

"Thank you." Jessica's heart began to race. What if the sheriff searched the car and found the unregistered gun under the seat, or worse, some of Blake's coke in a hidden stash? She sensed the man walking around to her.

"They don't make them like this anymore. I'm a bit of a car aficionado, myself."

"Really?" Jessica adjusted her sunglasses and turned to face the sheriff. For the first time, she noticed his medium-length sandy-colored hair, tanned skin, and blue eyes. He reminded her of a young Robert Redford. She guessed his age to be about thirty-five.

My God, if they grow men this fine here in Oklahoma, why the hell was I living in Chicago?

"The name's Dale Sutton," he said with a white smile while tipping the brim of his cap. Jessica could tell he had an easy confidence around women.

"Jessica Lobato," she replied, nodding toward the interior of the car. "That's my daughter, Megan."

"Hi, Megan." He waved.

"Hello." Megan waved back.

"Lovely girl." He turned his attention back to Jessica. His gaze paused for a second on her face. She realized he saw her black eye and bruised cheek through the sunglasses.

"Thank you," she replied, turning her head slightly.

"Are you visiting Hope Springs?"

"Are you asking as a sheriff or just an interested citizen?"

"Both," he said with a low chuckle. "I couldn't help noticing your Illinois plates."

"Actually, my daughter and I are thinking about settling here in your little town, Sheriff."

His eyebrows arched a bit. "That's great news. Let me be the first to welcome you to our fair community. We don't get new people often. Where are you staying?"

Jessica hesitated. The man had such a calm demeanor it was hard to tell if he was friendly or flirting with her. She had to watch her words and not give too much information. The last thing she needed was a police officer hanging around, even one this attractive. She glanced down at his left hand. No wedding ring and no pale band to show there ever was one. The idiots at the strip bar who took off their wedding rings before entering never realized the white band around their finger still showed. She had become an expert at spotting married men, because they tipped the best.

"I just got off the phone with a Nelda Olson about a rental home. Do you know where it is? I wrote down the address on my palm." She extended her hand for him to read the scrawled words and realized she still wore her gold wedding band. The sheriff must have noticed it by now.

He stepped closer and gently touched her palm to better read the writing. A pleasant smell tickled her nose, causing her pulse to quicken.

Is it his cologne?

"The Olson farm," he said. "It's about a mile and a half out of town. I know where it is."

"Could you tell me how to get there?"

"I can do better than that. I'll show you. Just follow my car."

"I wouldn't want to keep you from your law enforcement duties, Sheriff."

"This is Hope Springs. Not much in the way of crime on a Wednesday afternoon." He flashed his white smile again. "Or any afternoon, for that matter."

"Okay." She smiled back. "You lead the way."

He returned to his car as she climbed in the front seat of the Camaro.

"Are we going to jail?" Megan asked with a worried tone.

"No, honey." She started the engine. "He's going to show us the way to the new house we may be living in. Isn't that nice of him? He's giving us a police escort."

*   *   *   *

Leaving the outskirts of Hope Springs behind, she followed the patrol car another couple of miles before turning down a lane of broken asphalt. Under the golden glow of the afternoon sun, farmland and rolling fields stretched to the horizon on both sides of the road. The landscape only served to remind her how far she had come from the crowded streets of Chicago.

"Look, Mommy, cows." Megan pointed out the passenger window. "And more cows."

"Even more cows." Jessica nodded to the fields on the other side of the road.

"I think Oklahoma is one big cow farm."

"It's called a ranch, baby. We've certainly seen a lot of cows since coming here, haven't we?"

She nodded her head.

The left turn signal on the patrol car flashed ahead and the vehicle turned into a drive. Jessica followed as gravel crunched beneath the tires of the Camaro. She parked beside the sheriff's car in the front yard of a beautiful two-story white clapboard farmhouse and got out. The air smelled of freshly mowed grass. Large elm trees swished in the breeze, providing a shifting shade to the lawn. A fabricated metal barn and a toolshed stood beside the house.

Sheriff Sutton climbed out of the patrol car as the front door opened. A slim middle-aged woman in jeans, a T-shirt, and a cooking apron stepped out of the house. She had graying brown hair and gold-rimmed glasses. Jessica guessed the woman was in her midfifties but still very attractive.

"Sheriff Sutton, don't you be giving anyone a ticket in my front yard," she called out.

"I'm not issuing a traffic ticket, Nelda."

33

Jessica shut the Camaro driver door. "He's just showing me the way here."

"That's fine then. We have too few visitors at the farm and don't need Wyatt Earp here running them off."

Jessica chuckled. She already liked the woman.

"You must be the Jess I spoke to on the phone," she said, wiping her hands on her apron before offering a handshake. "I'm Nelda Olson."

She smiled and shook the woman's hand, which was soft and damp. *Just finished washing dishes,* Jessica guessed.

The passenger door to the Camaro opened and Megan climbed out. In the stark sunlight, the bruises on her daughter's forearm showed in blue-green blotches against her pale skin. Jessica was certain both Nelda and the sheriff saw them.

"Do you have any cows?" Megan asked shyly.

"Sure do." Nelda nodded. "Horses, pigs, and chickens, too."

"This is my daughter, Megan," Jessica said, pulling her close.

"She's so pretty," Nelda said. "An absolute angel."

"Can I go play on your tire swing?" Megan asked, pointing to a black tire swing hanging on a rope under one of the elm trees.

"Sure, honey, if your mother doesn't mind."

"Can I, Mommy?"

"Go ahead. I've got to talk to Nelda here."

Megan ran toward the swing and jumped upon it, sending it spinning in circles.

Sheriff Sutton cleared his throat. "If you ladies will excuse me, I'm going to be on my way."

"Sure you don't want to stay, Sheriff? I got a fresh-baked apple pie cooling on the stove."

He patted his stomach above his gun belt. "Sounds tempting, Nelda, but I better get back to work. Don't want the taxpayers to think I'm loafing on their money."

"Before you take off, Sheriff, answer me one question," Nelda said when he was about to climb back into the patrol car.

"Sure."

"How come a good-looking man like you isn't married?"

"It's because you're already taken, Nelda." He flashed another smile before closing the car door. The two women watched him pull out on the blacktop and head back to Hope Springs.

"Mmm-mm," Nelda muttered. "That man is as handsome as the day is long. It's a sin no woman has tied him down yet. How about you, Jess? Are you married?"

"Separated."

"Well, you can do worse than a handsome man like Dale Sutton. Come on, I'll show you the rental."

CHAPTER FOUR

Fifty yards from the farmhouse, the double-wide trailer sat on a permanent stone foundation with a redwood deck jutting out on one side. Flowery curtains hung in all the windows, making the home look cozy. Atop a small hill, the trailer provided a panoramic view of the farm. To the west, a tractor plowed furrows in a brown field, turning up a cloud of red dust in the afternoon sun.

Jessica, with Megan at her side, followed Nelda up the worn path through the grass leading to the trailer. She got another sense of being in a different time or another world. The scenic beauty of the farm was the polar opposite of the graffiti-covered slum projects of Chicago.

"That's my husband, Sam, out there on the tractor," Nelda said, pulling a door key from a pocket on her apron. "Sam and I lived in this trailer until we got the farmhouse built. It's nothing fancy, mind you, but I think it'll suit you and your daughter."

"Where do I park my car?" Jessica asked, looking around and seeing no drive leading to the trailer.

"You can pull it around the barn and park it here in the grass, as long as there's no heavy rain and the lawn isn't too muddy."

Jessica liked the idea of hiding the car from the highway.

"Look, Mommy," Megan suddenly said, racing forward to where a fat tabby cat slept under the redwood deck. The cat tried too late to escape before Megan grabbed the animal up in her arms.

"That's old Tig," Nelda said with a chuckle. "He used to be a good mouser when he was skinnier and younger. Now he just lies around all day getting fat." She walked up to Megan and scuffed the top of the cat's head. "You don't look too happy, Tig. What's the matter? You miss Rocky?"

"Rocky?" Megan asked.

"Rocky's our hound dog. He chased Tig all the time. I'm sure old Tig is enjoying the peace and quiet of not having that big mutt around."

"Where did Rocky go?" Megan asked.

"I'm not sure exactly. A couple of nights ago, he ran off barking at something in the woods. We haven't seen him since." Nelda ascended the three steps to the redwood deck and put the key in the trailer door. "He probably found him a girl dog and is out making puppies. He'll show up again soon." Turning the key, Nelda added, "You'd better leave Tig out here, honey. He's not an indoor cat. He's used to staying outside."

Nelda opened the door to the trailer, and Jessica followed her in. Megan remained on the porch petting Tig.

"This is nice," Jessica commented, looking over the interior of the trailer.

The front room consisted of a couch, recliner, coffee table, and glowing light fixture mounted on the ceiling. Sunlight shone in through the paisley curtains a warm homey glow. Adjoining the living room was a small dining area with a bay window overlooking the farm's acres.

"Down that hall you have two bedrooms and a restroom with a shower." Nelda pointed. "The kitchen is beyond the dining room with a working refrigerator and stove. It's small, mind you. I'll have to tell Sam to fill the propane tank before you can use the stove, though. There is also a utility room with a working washer and dryer. It's not much, but we called it home for twenty years."

"It's lovely," Jessica replied. "How much is it a month?"

"Two hundred and fifty."

"That's pretty cheap for such a nice place."

"Well, it is off the highway and kind of isolated. It's without a cable or satellite hookup, so no TV now that everything has gone digital. Some nights you might wake up with a cow mooing out your window."

"We talked over the phone about letting the security deposit go until I can pay it.

"We did." Nelda smiled. "You and you're daughter don't look like the type to tear the place up. I can let the security deposit slide until you can pay it later."

"Then I'll take it."

"Great," Nelda replied. "When do you plan to move in?"

"We're moved in now.

"You don't have any boxes or furniture to move?"

"Nothing." Jessica shrugged. "Just me and Megan."

A perplexed look crossed Nelda's face. "Jess, can I ask a couple of questions first before I rent to you?"

"Yes," she replied, feeling nervous inside.

"Are you hiding from someone? You're husband, perhaps?" She looked down at her wedding ring.

"Why do you ask?"

"Well …" Nelda hesitated and glanced out the front door where Megan played with Tig on the porch. "You and your daughter look like you've been through a prizefight judging from the bruises on her arm and the black eye you're trying to hide with those sunglasses. I don't want to pry, and I'm not one of those small-town biddies who like to spread gossip. I just need to know if there's going to be a problem with your husband."

Jessica slid back her sunglasses. "Blake physically abused me. Unfortunately, Megan got in the way of one of his violent episodes and was hurt, too. That's when I ran out on the bastard." Tears filled her eyes. "I couldn't let him hurt my daughter."

Nelda reached forward and hugged her tightly. The smell of fresh cooking permeated the woman's hair. Jessica accepted the embrace with memories of being hugged by her mother after falling down and scraping her knee.

"Poor girl," Nelda said.

Jessica wept in Nelda's arms. The emotion she had held inside for the last three days released itself in wracking sobs.

"Are you okay, Mommy?" Megan asked from the front porch.

Jessica broke off from Nelda's hold and swiped tears from her eyes. "I'm fine, baby."

Turning to a nearby cabinet, Nelda removed a box of Kleenex. "Here you go, girl." She handed one to her.

Jessica wiped her eyes and blew her nose. "I guess I needed a good cry."

Nelda chuckled. "We all do from time to time."

"Do we get to rent?"

"Does your husband know you're here?"

"He doesn't even know I'm in Oklahoma."

"So you're from out of state?"

"Chicago."

"That's good."

"I'm not going to contact him or call him. He's never going to find us. I just need a place to hide out until I get my feet back on the ground."

Nelda nodded. "Then you're welcome here, Jess."

"Thank God. You don't know how much this means to me." Jessica reached into her jean pocket and removed the money she set aside to pay the rent. She counted out the amount into Nelda's hand. "Two hundred and fifty dollars. I'll get the deposit as soon as I can." Amidst the bills, she found the white business card taken from the bulletin board at the post office. "Oh, and one more thing. Can you tell me where I can find this place?"

Nelda took the money and read the card. "Roxie's?"

"Yes."

Nelda handed the card back. "You know the street light in Hope Springs?"

Jessica nodded.

"That's Highway 133. Just turn left and head out of town for five miles. You won't miss it."

"What kind of bar is it?"

Nelda chuckled. "It's the greatest place in the world if you like rednecks, beer bellies, and bad karaoke."

Jessica laughed. "That classy, huh?"

"Sam and I used to go there occasionally on a Friday night. We stopped going about two years ago after the new owners bought the place." Nelda studied her face for a second. "Why do you ask?"

"I've bartended before. Since they need a waitress, I'm going to see if I can get a job and make some quick money."

"You won't have any problem getting hired as pretty as you are."

"I hope."

"Here's the key." Nelda placed the trailer door key into her hand. "You and Megan can come over for supper tonight. I promise it'll be as good a meal as you've ever had. Supper's at six. I've got a pot roast cooking in the oven and the apple pie Sheriff Sutton passed on. If he only knew what he was missing."

Jessica chuckled. "We'll be there."

CHAPTER FIVE

Once settled into their new trailer home, Jessica loaded Megan into the Camaro and drove back to Hope Springs. At the traffic light, she turned left, taking Highway 133 out of the little town. The bank clock showed the time was a little after four in the afternoon.

"Where are we going, Mommy?" Megan asked.

"I have to see if I can find a job." Jessica glanced sideways at her daughter. "Do you remember when I told you I had to find work and make money?"

"Yes." Megan nodded her head. "Are you going to dance there?"

"No dancing, baby. I'm just going to wait on tables."

Highway 133 was a two-lane blacktop rising and falling over rolling hills. To either side of the road, fields created a quilt work of greens and browns broken only by the occasional farmhouse. Megan watched quietly out of the passenger window. A road sign announced the town of Morris lay seven miles ahead. Jessica switched on the radio, scanned through the channels, and settled on a country station out of Tulsa. In contrast to the blues and hip-hop she listened to in Chicago, the drawling vocals of George Strait seemed to fit for rural Oklahoma.

"Mommy." Megan sat straight up in her seat. "Look at all the signs."

The Camaro topped a hill. On the left side of the road lay a run-down farm of overgrown weeds. Alongside the fence bordering the highway stood dozens of handmade signs constructed of plywood mounted on poles. Jessica tried to read the painted words as she drove by. Some were biblical passages about the end-times; the others relayed the sign maker's innocence in the murder of his wife. The bizarre scene was quite odd and out of place in the beautiful countryside. One sign in particular caught her eye. It gave a warning about blood and the Beast of Revelations coming in the night.

"What do they say, Mommy?"

"They are about the Bible, baby. Like your coloring book."

Two days ago, she had stopped in a convenience store in Missouri and picked up a coloring book and crayons for Megan. The book illustrated the story of Jesus from his birth to the crucifixion.

"About baby Jesus?"

"Yes."

Jessica glanced in her rearview mirror, watching the strange vista disappear from view. She couldn't fathom what would drive a person to work so hard to warn the public with such rambling obscure messages.

Two miles farther down Highway 133, she came upon a professional billboard advertising Roxie's Roadhouse. A painting of a sexy black-haired woman holding two bottles of beer filled most of the advertisement. A red arrow below the woman's breasts announced: "Turn Here for the Coldest Beer in the State." Jessica slowed the Camaro and eased into a gravel parking lot surrounded by thick green trees and tall brush. At the far end sat a one-story fabricated building with a vinyl banner announcing karaoke and happy hour beer specials hanging above the front door. Only two vehicles occupied the parking lot.

Jessica parked the Camaro. "We're here.

Megan leaned forward in her seat. "Is this where you want to work, Mommy?"

"Yes." Jessica checked her look in the car mirror. The black eye still looked bad and she wouldn't be able to wear her sunglasses in the dark bar. *Please, God, let me get this job,* she prayed silently. *I need the money badly.*

"Can I go with you, Mommy?"

"No, sweetie, this is a place for grown-ups only." She took her daughter by the hand. "I want you to stay in the car and wait for Mommy."

"I don't want to."

"Please, baby. Mommy will only be gone for a short time." She reached into the backseat and pulled up the Bible coloring book and box of crayons. "You stay here and color another pretty picture of Jesus. Can you do that for me, sweetie?"

"I guess so."

"Good girl." Jessica leaned forward and kissed her on the forehead. "I'm going to lock the car doors. You don't open them for anybody but Mommy. Okay?"

"Okay."

While Megan colored in her book, Jessica slipped the .357 from under the seat into her purse without her daughter seeing. She exited the Camaro into the bright sunlight and used her key to lock both doors. She hated leaving her daughter alone. Too many times Megan had been left by herself, but it couldn't be avoided this time. She didn't know the bar or the type of people inside.

Brushing back her blonde hair with her hands, Jessica walked toward the roadhouse. She took one last look back at Megan concentrating on her coloring before opening the front door. A nervous flutter rested in the bottom of her stomach. Her daughter looked so alone and vulnerable sitting in the passenger seat. *She'll be all right,* Jessica told herself. *It's the middle of the afternoon and no one is about. I locked the car doors.*

Fighting back her fears, she stepped inside the bar.

Her eyes needed a second to adjust to the dim light as she glanced around the interior to get her bearing. Round wooden tables and empty chairs filled the place. In one corner, a darkened karaoke stage bordered a hardwood dance floor scuffed by the heels of countless cowboy boots. A lit jukebox played a low country song in the other corner. The air smelled of cheap beer and stale cigarettes. Adorning every bare space on the walls, advertising posters promoted various brands of beer using beautiful half-dressed models.

Directly across from the front door, two people chatted to themselves at the bar. They both looked up when she came in. One was a portly middle-aged man spread out on a bar stool. His thick shoulder-length steel-gray hair and equally gray mustache highlighted a wide tanned face. On the other side of the counter, a very pretty young woman leaned in to talk to the gray-haired man. She was near Jessica's age with raven-black hair falling straight to the middle of her back. A tight black T-shirt and a pair of even tighter blue jean shorts hugged every curve of her lean body. Jessica guessed this was the sexy female represented on the billboard standing out by the highway.

"Hi," Jessica said, walking up to join them.

The girl straightened up. "You need a beer?"

"No." Jessica placed the business card taken from the post office on the bar top. "I need a job."

The woman picked up the card. "You here for the waitress position?"

"Yes."

"Hire her," the gray-haired man said loudly. "Lord knows we can use another hottie working this place. The last girl you hired only had half her teeth."

"Hush, you old drunk!" the girl snapped over her shoulder. She turned back to Jessica. "That's Uncle Johnny. Just ignore him. He sits here from open to close." The girl extended her hand across the bar. Jessica noted the girl's black-painted fingernails and the tattoo of a pentagram inked on the inside of her forearm. "I'm Roxie by the way. You can call me Rox, though. Most people do around here."

"Jessica, but you can call me Jess." She took the hand and shook it. "Are you the owner?"

"I share ownership with my brother, Collin." She nodded toward an open door behind the bar serving area. "He's in the back room stocking up beer."

"Is the waitress job still open?"

"It is. Have you had any experience working in a bar, Jess?"

"I tended bar in college," she lied, but she didn't want anyone to know her real bar experience came from stripping.

Roxie's gaze centered evenly on Jessica's face. "That's a nice shiner you're sporting. Who gave it to you? Husband or boyfriend?"

"Softball," Jessica lied again. "Family reunion ball game last Sunday. I tried to catch a fly ball and missed."

"I know a girl who got her front teeth knocked out just like that," Uncle Johnny spoke up.

"Again with the teeth thing," Roxie said. "Keep quiet, you old drunk. I'm trying to hold an employee interview." Rolling her eyes, she continued, "You better get used to him if you're going to work here. We try to run a nice place, Jess. Good times. Good beer. Most of the customers are local farm boys with a few bikers thrown into the mix. Crowd can get a bit rough sometimes, especially on nights with a full moon. That's when all the crazies come out. If you think you can handle it, I could use a pretty girl like you waiting tables. I will still have to clear it with my brother. He makes final decisions on who gets hired."

"I can handle it." Jessica's stomach fluttered at the realization she might have gotten the job.

"Hey, Collin," Roxie called out. "Come out here. I got someone I want you to meet."

The door to the back room opened and a tall man stepped through. He had piercing dark eyes and shoulder-length black hair parted in the middle. Ruggedly handsome, in a tough biker-grunge rocker sort of way, the man stood a good head and shoulders over Jessica. The sleeveless blue jean vest he wore showed off well-defined muscles lined with various tribal tattoos in black ink running down his arms.

"What?" he asked in a low voice.

"This is Jess." She nodded in her direction. "She wants a job."

The man's dark gaze raked her up and down. A chill centered in the bottom of Jessica's stomach. The man's eyes reminded her of Blake.

Before he could speak, the front door swung open, letting in a shaft of brilliant late-afternoon sun. Jessica turned. Sheriff Sutton entered holding Megan by the hand. The chill sitting in the bottom of Jessica's stomach spread through the rest of her body.

"Mommy," Megan called out in her stressed voice.

"I think this little girl belongs to you." Sheriff Sutton let her daughter go, and she ran to her arms. "She was too scared to come inside."

"What's wrong?" Jessica took Megan in her arms.

"I got to go pee real bad."

Jessica sighed in relief while everyone in the bar chuckled.

"Where's the restroom?" Jessica asked with embarrassment reddening her face.

"Over there." Roxie pointed to the other end of the room.

"Come with me." Jessica led Megan to the restroom. Once inside, she shut the door behind them. "I thought I told you to stay in the car," she said in a quiet voice.

"I had to go pee."

"You should've told me before I left." She undid the fly on Megan's jeans and helped her up on the toilet.

"Sorry."

"Didn't I tell you not to open the car door for anyone but Mommy?"

"The policeman showed up. He knocked on the window and I rolled it down. He was nice."

"What did he say to you?" Jessica asked. Low voices came from the occupants in the main room of the roadhouse, but she couldn't make out what they were saying.

"He asked what I was doing by myself. I told him I had to go pee real bad."

"Next time you do what your Mommy tells you."

"Sorry."

"Wash your hands when you're done."

Jessica exited the restroom. The voices grew quiet as she returned to the bar. Sheriff Sutton now stood to one side of Uncle Johnny. All eyes were on her.

"Thanks for rescuing Megan, Sheriff," Jessica spoke.

"No problem." The man showed his perfect white smile. Jessica decided he was just too handsome for his own good.

"How old is your daughter?" Roxie asked.

"Five."

"She's a doll."

"Thank you."

"About the job …" Roxie popped the business card against her painted nails. Jessica waited for the shoe to drop. They weren't going to hire a battered single mother dragging around a five-year-old daughter. "I can handle waiting on the bar tonight and Thursday. Business is pretty slow during the week. You show up about five thirty Friday night and I'll put you to work."

"Okay."

"You work the floor and I work behind the bar. You get paid five dollars an hour plus you keep your tips. I pay you out of the till each night. It's easier then filling out employment forms and state tax papers. You show up. You work. Understand?"

Jessica nodded.

"One bit of advice. Wear something sexy. The more skin you show the more tips you make. You're very attractive so I don't think you're going to have much of a problem in that area."

"I understand."

The restroom door opened, and Megan came into the room.

"I washed my hands, Mommy."

Everyone laughed.

"Good girl." Jessica drew her daughter to her.

"One more thing," Roxie said. "I need a phone number if I want you to fill in one night when I can't make it."

"I just moved to Hope Springs. I don't have a phone yet."

Sheriff Sutton stepped up. "Aren't you staying at Sam and Nelda Olson's trailer?"

"Yes." Jessica felt a tinge of worry. She didn't want her address revealed to a room full of strangers.

"Rox, you can get the Olson's home phone out of the book. I'm sure Nelda will relay any message you want to give," Sheriff Sutton stated.

"Works for me."

"Friday night at five thirty then," Jessica said while backing out of the bar toward the door. "I'll be here. It was nice meeting everyone."

"We'll see you then." Roxie waved her hand. "Bye, Megan."

"Good-bye," Megan called back.

Jessica stepped outside into the late afternoon sun and noted the sheriff's patrol car parked once more beside her Camaro.

"Did you get the job, Mommy?"

"I did, baby."

Behind her, Sheriff Sutton exited the roadhouse.

"Go get in the car, sugar." She opened the passenger door and belted her daughter in. "Mommy needs to talk to the policeman."

"Okay."

Once Megan was inside, she closed the door and crossed her arms. "Are you following me, Sheriff?"

"Not intentionally, if that's what you mean." He took off his uniform cap and ran his hand through his sandy hair. "I came out to Roxie's to get more information on a fight here last Saturday night."

"So it's just a coincidence I've encountered you twice in four hours?"

"It's a small town." He put the hat back on his head and smiled. "Since we seem to run into each other so much, don't you think we should be on a first-name basis?"

"Okay, I'm Jess."

"Dale."

"Well, Dale, I won't hold up any more of your time. I better get back to my new home." She opened the driver door and climbed in. "I'll see you later."

He leaned in before she closed the door. His nearness caused all her senses to go on edge. Jessica breathed his scent, and her pulse raced.

"One of my most enjoyable duties as the town's law enforcement representative is heading up the Welcome Wagon."

"Welcome Wagon?" Her voice sounded nervous and far away.

"It means I get to officially welcome all new citizens to Hope Springs."

"Is that so?"

"Why don't you meet me for lunch tomorrow?"

"I don't know." Her voice sounded unsure.

"You can bring your daughter."

"Okay." She nodded.

"It's a date then. Meet me at Dottie's Diner. It's in the center of town one block off Main Street. Everyone in Hope Springs knows where it is."

She started the Camaro.

The sheriff stepped back. "I'll see you tomorrow at twelve."

Jessica shut the driver door and pulled out of the parking lot. In the rearview, she spotted Sheriff Sutton standing beside his patrol car watching her leave. She couldn't believe she agreed so quickly to go on a lunch date with the man. *Why the hell did I say yes? I just got rid of one man. The last thing I need is another hanging around. Especially a law man.*

CHAPTER SIX

After living on nothing but fast food for the last three days, Jessica found Nelda's home-cooked supper was everything she had promised. Megan, who hadn't had much of an appetite in months, ate two plates of pot roast, carrots, and potatoes. The warm meal seemed to brighten her spirits as well. She talked more, going on and on about Tig and her new home.

Nelda's husband, Sam, joined them at the table. A tall man with a round belly stuffed in a faded pair of blue bib overalls, he sported short gray hair, hazel eyes, and skin tanned to the texture of book leather. Jessica imagined what the Olsons might have looked like when they first married thirty years ago. She guessed the two were the best-looking couple in the county back then.

During supper, Megan and Sam quickly became good friends.

"Do you have any horses, sir?" Megan asked.

"Little girl, I'll call you Meg if you call me Sam."

"Okay, Sam."

"Well, Meg, to tell the truth, I've got a little foal out in the stable. She's too young and high-spirited for you to ride, but you could pet and feed her. Maybe you can think of a name for her." Sam winked at his wife beginning to clear off the dirty dishes from the table. "I haven't been able to think of a name for the little filly yet, have I, Nel?"

"No you haven't, dear."

"Tomorrow, after I get my winter wheat planted, you can meet her, Meg. But I can't introduce her properly if she doesn't have a name. Maybe you can think of one for her. Would you like that?"

"Mommy, can I?"

"I don't see why not, honey," Jessica answered, picking up the remaining dirty dishes from the table.

"Okay!" Megan said back to Sam.

"Good, we'll do that tomorrow afternoon," Sam stated with a broad smile.

Jessica placed the dirty dishes on the counter by the sink and grabbed up a towel to help dry.

"Sam and I never had children," Nelda stated while washing a plate.

"Never?"

Nelda shook her head no. "When I was seventeen I had a car accident. It ruined my baby-maker. Sam knew I could never give birth when he married me. It's just been us two all these years." She glanced over to Sam and Megan talking. "Sometimes, I think he wishes he was a father."

"He gets along with my daughter just fine."

"He's a good man," Nelda said, rinsing off a dish and handing it over.

"Believe me, Nel, good men are a rare treasure these days." Jessica dried the plate and asked, "What can you tell me about Sheriff Sutton?"

"Dale?" Nelda's brow raised in surprise. "Why do you ask?"

"He invited me to lunch with him tomorrow."

"I'm impressed, Jess. He's a very handsome man. You'll be the envy of all the girls in the county."

"It may not exactly be a date, but he seemed interested in spending some time with me. Maybe I should've turned him down, but I just couldn't get the will up to do so."

"No surprise. Any woman would be hard-pressed to say no to him. He's a hunk."

*　　*　　*　　*

After supper, the group retired to the front porch to watch the sunset and drink a pitcher of sweet tea. Settled into a wicker chair, Jessica felt a peace and calm she hadn't known in years of turbulent marriage to Blake. The feeling seemed alien, like meeting an old friend who was now nothing more than an awkward stranger over the passage of time. Life with Blake was a constant walk along a razor's edge, never knowing from where the next verbal or physical abuse would strike. In this quaint farmhouse in rural Oklahoma, she discovered another side of life: simple joys of sharing a pitcher of tea and conversing with people void of drug abuse and domestic violence.

Jessica deeply inhaled the warm evening air, letting the painful existence she had in Chicago slip away, like the sun on the horizon.

"What is that, Mommy?" Megan asked, excited. Her daughter pointed out onto the front lawn. Little blips of glowing light danced in and out of the trees.

"Lightning bugs," Sam answered. "You never saw a lightning bug,

Meg?"

"No."

Sam eased out of the wicker chair to his full height. "Come on, little girl, let's go catch us one."

He took Megan by the hand, and the two rushed out onto the front lawn in the growing twilight.

"Wow!" Megan said, watching the glowing bugs fly around her.

Jessica couldn't remember her daughter saying wow to anything.

"Your daughter's lovely," Nelda said in a low voice. "How could any man hurt such a beautiful child?"

"He wasn't a man." The statement shocked Jessica with its truth. A real man was Sam taking time to show a little girl the wonder of lightning bugs in the front yard. The last semblance of any emotion she felt for Blake evaporated. Now, she saw him for what he really was: a violent, hateful coke fiend who made her strip in clubs while leaving Megan home alone. He abused her in front of their daughter. A sudden shame passed through her.

"God forgive me," she spoke softly. "No man will ever do that to me again."

"What was that, dear?" Nelda asked.

"Nothing." Jessica put down the empty glass of tea. "I was just talking to myself."

"Mommy!" Megan came running up to the porch with a glowing light cupped in her hand. "I caught one."

"Let me see it, baby."

She opened her hand to show the glowing bug in her palm. Her blue eyes flashed with wonder. "Isn't it great?"

"Yes." Jessica felt tears misting her eyes. She looked up at Sam standing on the porch of the steps. "Thank you."

He wiped his sweating brow on the sleeve of his flannel shirt. "I forgot how much work it is chasing lightning bugs."

*   *   *   *

The gathering dusk deepened as stars appeared in the Oklahoma night sky. Jessica walked with Megan along the grassy trail leading back to the trailer. The silver Camaro looked out of place parked in front. Earlier, she had taken the pistol inside and stuffed it between the mattress and box spring of her new bed.

"There you are, Tig." Megan charged forward and caught the cat sleeping under the bottom step of the redwood deck. The feline remained limp in her arms. She picked up the tabby and hugged him tight. "Can he sleep with me tonight, Mommy?"

"You heard what Nelda said, honey. Tig is an outdoor farm cat. He would just cry all night wanting out."

"Okay." She put the cat down on the porch. "You stay out here tonight, Tig. I'll see you in the morning."

"That's a good girl." Jessica patted her daughter on the shoulder and opened the front trailer door with the key. "Now wash up and get ready for bed."

"Okay, Mommy." Megan ran toward the bathroom to wash her face. While her daughter disappeared down the hall to the back of the home, Jessica locked the front door and bolted the chain. She went around the trailer checking every window. Convinced the trailer was secure and locked, she went to join her daughter.

"All done, Mommy," Megan said, rubbing the washcloth over her face.

"Brush your teeth?" Jessica asked with a smile.

"I did."

"Good girl." Jessica kissed the top of her daughter's head. "Now off to bed with you. You'll have to sleep in your clothes tonight. Mommy left your pajamas in our old home."

"That's okay." She bounded into her small bedroom and leaped on the bed. Jessica sat next to her on the mattress and tucked Megan under the covers.

"Let me see your arm," Jessica said.

Her daughter pulled the injured left arm from under the covers. In the light of the overhead bulb, Jessica studied the bruises.

"Does it still hurt?" Jessica asked.

"A little."

"I'm so sorry that your father hurt you. I should have taken you away sooner. When you get older, I hope you understand."

"Okay, Mommy."

Jessica brushed a strand of blonde hair from her daughter's brow. "Do you like it here in Oklahoma?"

"Yes." She nodded. "Very much."

"I'm glad, because I do, too."

"Do you think Tig will be all right sleeping outside in the dark?"

"He'll be fine. Now go to sleep, you silly girl." She kissed her daughter on the forehead. "I'm going to leave the light on and the door open. I'll be sleeping across the hall. Okay?"

"Okay, Mommy."

She stood and crossed to the door of the bedroom and turned toward Megan, who smiled back at her.

"I love you, Mommy."

"I love you, too, sweetie."

A dark frown crossed her daughter's face.

"I don't love Daddy anymore," Megan said in a quiet voice.

"Neither, do I," Jessica replied.

CHAPTER SEVEN

He stripped nude, letting the cool night air flow against his bare skin. Hiding in the line of trees bordering the partly plowed field, he watched the trailer until the lights went out, leaving one lone window lit in the back.

Mother and daughter had gone to bed.

He glanced up through the trees. The Ebon Moon was still five nights away, which meant he could control the animal inside and keep some form of his human self. An old hunger had returned tenfold upon seeing the little girl named Megan earlier in the day. He needed to quiet the raging beast in some fashion, if only to run through the countryside at night.

He thought of it as walking his inner dog.

Every fiber of his being tingled with anticipation of the thing he was about to become. He loved/hated the animal inside. On one hand, lycanthropy gave him incredible strength, agility, and superhuman senses, but on the other, there was the hunger.

Always the hunger.

Tonight, he could not be seen. Exposure risked revealing the Pack to the humans. They had taken great care to hide their kills without the locals becoming aware of the wolf in their presence. The foray was dangerous, but he couldn't fight the overpowering urge twisting both his human and animal mind.

The pain of the transformation spread like wildfire through his body. He fell to all fours with muscles twitching in spasms. Thick hair erupted from his pores covering his bare flesh as his bones elongated and shifted, causing him to gasp in agony. Sharp claws extended from the ends of his fingers and toes. The most painful part of the morphing followed; his facial bones separated to allow the wolf's face and maw to emerge. He wanted to howl but kept his torment silent. The pain receded. The transformation was complete.

In the shadow of the trees, the beast stood to its new height of eight feet. He had managed to keep his human identity, but the bestial side fought against him like an enraged animal pounding the door to its cage.

53

Do I dare approach the trailer?

The beast answered for him. It wanted to get closer ... *much closer.*

Only halfway, the human side replied.

Nose and ears twitched as his enhanced senses searched the farm. Quiet. Even the crickets were silent in awe of the supernatural creature. On canine legs, he ran out from the cover of the trees and crossed the plowed field in a loping gait under the dim moonlight. Reaching the tractor parked in the center of the field, he ducked in its shadow and paused again to sense the night air. No lights came on in the trailer or the farmhouse. No headlights on the blacktop road in front of the farm. He hadn't been seen or heard. He returned his attention to the lone light shining through a bedroom curtain of the trailer like a beacon.

Closer, the animal inside demanded.

In a leap that would have broken all Olympic records for a human, he cleared the tractor and landed on all fours in the freshly plowed dirt. Keeping low, he bounded forward and stopped in a crouch beneath the trailer window. Again no sound or activity came from within. The two occupants slept unaware of the danger outside. He pressed an ear to the trailer wall under the lit window and focused his acute hearing. The gentle breathing of a sleeping child rose and fell on the other side.

The bestial mind raged. The only thing protecting the child was a thin wall of sheet metal and insulation. It would be so easy to tear through the structure and snatch up the little girl.

No! The human side fought back the urge. *To do such an act would send the local citizens in a relentless hunt for the abductors of the offspring. The Pack would be in great danger of discovery.*

I must look at her! Peer through the window.

No!

The beast attempted to play a trick on his mind. If he saw the sleeping child, the primal hunger would be impossible to control, leaving the animal inside free to act without constraint. Instead, he contented himself to listening through the wall of the trailer. Slaver dripped in streams from the lust to feed upon the child; to taste her blood, and to rend her tender flesh.

Feed me now!

We wait until the moon darkens in five nights.

I must eat now!!

His ears sensed something hiding under the redwood deck. A fat tabby cat with hair standing up on its back hissed at him. He spun and snatched the animal up in one clawed hand and squeezed off its growl. The cat's green eyes stared for one last moment at the ravenous maw of the beast. In the next second, he bit down on the animal and felt the cat's bones crunch. One more bite and he swallowed the creature whole.

The beast inside grew still. It had tasted blood and death and could be quelled for now. Such would not be the case during the Ebon Moon. Only the flesh of a child would satisfy the animal then. He pressed an ear once more against the wall of the trailer and listened to her slow breathing.

When the moon is in shadow, you may devour her.

The beast understood and loped away from the trailer house to run free into the countryside once again.

CHAPTER EIGHT

Jessica awoke gasping in shock. She didn't recognize the bedroom. Panic took over for a brief second before she remembered the new trailer home. She settled back in the strange bed and listened.

Something had awoken her.

Megan?

She turned to the light coming in from her daughter's room.

"Mommy!"

Jessica sprung from the bed and rushed across the hall. She found Megan curled into a fetal position under the blanket.

"Mommy!" her daughter cried once more.

"I'm here, baby." Jessica pulled back the blanket. "What's wrong, dear?"

"I had a very bad dream."

Jessica sighed with relief. She brushed back the blonde hair from Megan's face, wet with tears. "It's just a dream, baby. Do you want to tell Mommy about it?"

"Daddy was here."

The words sent icy fear through her body. The thought of Blake in the trailer caused her stomach to knot. A frightening image of her husband standing in the bedroom doorway flashed in her mind. For a second, she imagined him loading the pistol with one bullet and spinning the chamber.

"Do you feel lucky, Jess?"

Pushing the terrible image away, she hugged her daughter. "Daddy's not here, baby. He doesn't know where we are."

Megan's only reply was to continue crying. Her tears soaked a spot in Jessica's T-shirt.

"Shhh," she said, patting her on the back. "Don't cry, baby, everything will be all right. How about sleeping in Mommy's bed tonight? Would you like that?"

Megan nodded but said nothing.

Jessica hefted her daughter up and carried her into her bedroom. She laid Megan down and climbed into the bed next to her. Holding her close, she continued comforting the child until the sobbing stopped.

"Everything will be all right, baby," she whispered as her daughter drifted back to sleep. "Everything will be fine. You're safe here."

But is she?

Something tugged at the edge of Jessica's paranoia. The source of the dread hovered just out of the range of her senses. Years of existing under Blake's brutal abuse had taught her how to be on guard. Once Megan was asleep, she eased out of the bed, slid her arm between the mattress and box spring, and removed the pistol.

While in Chicago, she had enrolled in a firearm class to protect herself from Blake. Without his knowledge, she trained many hours on how to use a gun. Shooting at the pistol range gave her confidence and empowerment over being a victim at home. In her mind's eye, every paper target had her husband's face on it.

She lifted the .357 magnum, which was heavier than the Glock she fired at the gun range. Snapping open the cylinder, she counted the rounds again. Six hollow points. Holding the weapon should've made her feel safe and secure, but it didn't.

Something still bothered her.

Had Blake somehow followed us from Chicago?

After he hit Megan in one of his coke-induced rages, Jessica took an aluminum baseball bat from the garage, snuck up behind her husband, and swung the bat hard against the side of his head. It landed with a loud thunk. He collapsed to the floor. While he lay unconscious and bleeding, she grabbed the pistol, car keys, and some cash before fleeing the house with her daughter.

I should have killed the bastard when I had the chance. But could he have followed me? Traced us here to our new home?

It didn't seem possible, but fear forced her to check once again.

In T-shirt and underwear, Jessica stood with the pistol ready. She moved quietly through the trailer house without turning on the lights. Every door and window was still locked. Nothing seemed tampered with. Peering out a front window, she studied the Camaro parked in the dark yard. The vehicle appeared untouched. Her gaze shifted to the line of dark trees bordering the plowed field to the west of the trailer. She saw nothing but shadows in the dim moonlight.

Is Blake out there watching me?

Jessica shook her head no. If he knew they were here, he would have busted in the front door and she would be dead by now.

Someone else?

She studied the trees. Focusing upon the shadows, she saw nothing in the dark. The hair stood up on the back of her neck.

Quit spooking yourself out. You're a city girl staying in a trailer out in the country. Of course you're going to feel paranoid. There's nothing out there watching you. Go to bed, girl.

She sighed and let the tension flow out of her body. She was too tired to deal with anything but sleep. There was nothing more she could do to protect herself tonight. Returning to bed, she put the pistol under the pillow and snuggled close to her sleeping daughter.

"I promise I won't let anyone hurt you again," she whispered in Megan's ear before falling back to sleep.

CHAPTER NINE

Jasper Higgins prepared for his suicide like he was attending church on Sunday morning. Emma would be waiting for him in heaven so he needed to look his best. After a shower and shave, he combed his gray hair and splashed on some Old Spice. From a closet he slipped on his Sunday best suit, polished the dust from his black slippers, and picked out his favorite tie. Once dressed, he studied himself in the bathroom mirror. He cleaned up nicely, he decided. Emma will be so proud.

Jasper shut off the bathroom light and entered the living room. The sun had set so he switched on a couple of soft lamps. The rest of the house he kept dark so as not to face its emptiness. Since Emma's murder, his upkeep of the farmhouse had declined. Dingy curtains covering the windows matched the dingy upholstery on the sofa. The place looked dusty, faded, and worn—much like him. He didn't spend enough time tidying up. Commiserating to a bottle of Jack Daniel's and painting the signs he erected by the roadside took up his time. He was glad Emma wasn't here to see it.

With a weary sigh, Jasper settled on the sofa. He rubbed his hands down the thighs of his suit pants and pondered what to do next. He had never really contemplated suicide before. It wasn't Christian and would only confirm he was a murderer to the people in the area. They'll say he did it out of guilt for killing his wife. Jasper didn't care anymore. No one believed him anyway. God knew the truth, and everyone else could go to hell.

But how was he going to do it? Drinking himself to death was taking too long. Hanging was one option, and there was the fifty feet of rope in the shed. All he had to do was sling it up over a beam in the workshop and step off a chair. After a couple of minutes of thrashing and kicking, the deed would be done. He didn't like the idea, though. A few days would pass before anyone found his body. By that time he would be bloated through decomposition and look like a fat balloon dangling on a rope—not the image he wanted to leave the world. Cutting his wrists was too painful and bloody. Turn the gas on and stick his head in the oven? But then he'd be found on his knees with his fat ass sticking out of the stove—another bad image he didn't want to leave for posterity.

He could shoot himself like Mack Carver did a few years back. When the bank threatened to take his land, the old farmer went into the barn, stuck a rifle in his mouth, and pulled the trigger. That would be quick and easy. The problem was that, after Emma's murder, the police confiscated his rifle and shotgun to test them with forensics. They were never returned so he had no guns left in the house.

Jasper thought for a moment.

Or do I?

The summer before Emma's murder a double homicide took place in the next county. Two escaped convicts went to the door of a farmhouse and tried to rob the place. In the process, they shot and killed an elderly woman and her daughter home by themselves. On the day of the double murder, he gave Emma a pistol to protect herself; an old snub-nosed .38 that belonged to his father when he was a deputy sheriff. It's strange he hadn't remembered it until now, but age, grief, and alcohol made him forget more each day.

He rose from the couch. The police did a thorough search of the house in their hunt for evidence. *They confiscated my rifle and shotgun,* he thought to himself. *But not the snub-nose, which means the pistol was well hidden. Where would Emma stash it? That's the question. The kitchen was her favorite room in the house. Start there.*

Jasper entered and turned on the light. The bare glow of an electric bulb lit the chipped cabinets and faded linoleum of the room. An image of Emma standing at the counter, rolling pie dough and humming a church hymn, warmed his mind. He could almost smell the pies baking in the oven. His heart ached from the memory of the woman so wrongly robbed from him.

"Emma, I can't keep living like this." His voice sounded hollow and distant in the empty kitchen. "I don't want another day without you."

He looked through cabinets and drawers. Even though it had been two years since Emma's murder, he had kept most of the kitchen the same in honor of her memory. Living alone, he only used a few pots and pans to cook with. Everything else remained untouched. Opening cabinets, he moved aside plates and glasses in the hunt for the pistol but found nothing. He stepped back and surveyed the kitchen again.

Where would she hide it?

He noticed a cabinet door above the stove he hadn't opened in years. Inside he found various dusty glasses and china, remnants from his wedding day in 1959. An old Cain's coffee can sat in one corner with "Mad Money" written in Magic Marker on the lid. It was Emma's handwriting. Jasper took down the can and felt something move inside making a clunk sound. He popped open the lid and found the pistol.

Emma hid it here for when a robber came to the door demanding money. She would tell them there was money in a coffee can in the kitchen and offer to go fetch it for them. Instead of cash, she would pull the gun. Smart girl.

Jasper removed the pistol. He snapped open the cylinder and found it fully loaded. He examined the gun. The .38 was in desperate need of cleaning. Rust spots marred the blue steel of the barrel, but it would still do the task he required. All he needed was it to fire once.

Returning to the living room, he placed the gun on the coffee table. He next found the old family Bible and sat it beside the pistol. He removed his favorite pictures of Emma from various photo albums and lovingly arranged them on the table. Once done, he settled back down on the couch and studied the black-and-white glossies. One showed a younger Emma in her summer dress, another of her leading the church choir, and yet another of her standing next to him in a long wedding gown of white when he married her after returning from Korea—a parade of the best moments of his life in faded photographs. His gut ached from the want to return to those happier times, to step into the gray images and be by her side again. The only way he could join her now was through death.

Dear God, forgive me.

He snatched the pistol from the coffee table and put the barrel in his mouth. The metal tasted cold on his tongue. His hands shook so badly he could barely pull back the hammer. Tears flowed down his face while his finger slid through the guard and nestled against the trigger.

Do it, old man. End it right here and now. His heart thundered against his rib cage as he applied pressure against the trigger. *Hurry, you old fool, before you die of a heart attack.*

He pulled the gun barrel from his mouth and laughed out loud.

"How ironic would that be, Emma?" Jasper asked the empty room. "They come to find me dead of a heart attack when I was about to commit suicide. That would be a hoot."

He looked down at the gun and decided he couldn't do it in the house. Not where he shared so much love and memories with his wife. He wouldn't profane their home with his blood. He let out a long sigh. There was only one other place he could think of—the spot where he first kissed Emma when he was just a farm boy of seventeen working on his father's land.

Jasper gathered up the gun, Bible, and photographs. He took one last look at the interior of the farmhouse before turning out the light and stepping into the night air. He shut the door but didn't bother to lock it. When whoever came to discover his suicide, he wanted them to have access to the house. They could have everything. There was nothing left for him there.

Under the partly cloudy night sky, he crossed the farmyard to his old red Ford F-150 pickup parked beside the work shed. He climbed in and placed the items he brought from the house on the front seat. The truck engine turned over, shattering the quiet of the farm. Jasper slipped the truck in gear and pulled out of the yard. Headlights cut a dusty beam through the darkness while he drove around the work shed and headed to the pond nestled in the back acres of his property. The truck bounced and bucked over the rutted road and weedy pastures of the southern section of his farm. At the edge of the pond, he put on the brakes and slid to a stop in a cloud of dust turned red by the taillights.

He shut the truck off and sat in the dark cab. While the engine pinged and cooled, Jasper stared out the front windshield where the light of the moon shone on the black water of the old cow pond. It was here, on a summer evening a lifetime ago, that he first got the nerve to kiss Emma. They were just teenagers when he awkwardly pressed his lips to hers while they sat on the bank. The happiest part of his life began that day, and it seemed fitting it would end here.

He was able to pull the trigger now. He felt it in his soul. He wasn't afraid anymore.

Jasper placed Emma's photos on the dash before him. He put the Bible in his lap while he said the Lord's Prayer. When finished, he began reciting the twenty-third Psalm aloud while picking up the pistol from the seat. No tears this time. No emotion. Just a still calm deep inside. He pulled back the hammer.

"As I walk through the valley of death, I will fear no evil."

He put the pistol barrel again in his mouth.

His finger slid against the trigger … and paused.

On the other side of the pond, a dark form stood up.

Jasper lowered the gun and focused his tired eyes on the shadowy shape. It wasn't a cow. He had sold off all his livestock after Emma's death. *What in blazes is it? A bear?*

He snapped on the spotlight mounted on the outside cab of the truck. A beam of intense white light cut through the dark sky above the pond. He adjusted the light down to illuminate the shape. A hunched form covered in dark fur stood on two legs in the bright light. Something with red eyes, sharp canine fangs, and black claws.

The beast!

Anger like he had never known swept through him. This was the demon that took his Emma away!

In the spotlight, the creature growled at the truck.

Jasper dropped the pistol and started up the truck engine. He slammed it in gear and pressed his foot hard on the gas. Tires threw up dirt and dust as the pickup raced forward. He had only one thought. Run the abomination over! The truck fishtailed but he swung the wheel around to keep the vehicle from going into the pond. In the erratic bouncing beam of the spotlight, the beast didn't flee but turned toward the pickup and charged.

"Goddamn you! Goddamn you to hell!" Jasper screamed at the top of his lungs while the truck lurched over the rutted grass.

The horrid shape closed in on the speeding pickup. Jasper caught a glimpse of a maw of wet teeth and a doglike face in the headlights fifteen feet before his grill. A second before the monster was beneath the wheels of the barreling vehicle, it jumped into the air. Clawed feet landed and dented in the hood with its weight. With another low throated growl, the creature leaped again. In the rearview, Jasper saw the beast land in the grass behind the taillights.

Stomping on the brakes, he brought the truck to a sliding stop.

Jasper scrambled for the gun in the truck seat. He kicked open the driver door and half-fell out of the cab while pointing the pistol toward the beast. In the hellish glow of the taillights, the monster growled and hunched down on all fours. Wet slobber streamed from its horrid fangs while emitting another terrible growl.

Jasper pulled the trigger and the gun bucked in his hand. The shot thundered across the stillness of the pond. Fur flew up where the bullet struck the monster's shoulder. The creature bolted away and into the dark beyond the taillight glow. He kept firing at the fleeing form until the hammer dry-clicked against the empty shells. He couldn't tell if he hit it again or not. The beast had disappeared into the shadows of the night.

Adrenaline draining from his body caused Jasper to fall against the side of the truck. A pressing tightness spread from his heart and across his chest, preventing him from breathing.

I can't die. Not now. Please, God, not now.

Slowly, the pain subsided, allowing him to breathe again. He couldn't die yet. Not until he found and killed the thing that had murdered Emma. In the dirt at his feet lay the .38 pistol. He picked it up while the conversation he had had earlier in the day with Terry Newman and Sid Granger went through his mind. What did they call the demon?

A werewolf?

He snapped open the cylinder and dropped out the warm spent shells into his palm. The words Terry said about how to kill a werewolf replayed in his mind: *"You got to have silver bullets, Mr. Higgins. That'll kill any werewolves coming around your house."*

THURSDAY

CHAPTER TEN

Jessica opened her eyes to sunlight glowing through the curtains of the small bedroom and the sound of a tractor engine outside. Shifting a sleeping Megan, she rose to look out the window facing the field. Sam sat on his tractor plowing clumpy brown dirt beneath the vehicle's turning blades.

She eased out of the bed without waking her daughter. Remembering the pistol under the pillow, she removed it and put the gun back between the mattress and box spring. She wouldn't need the .357 during the day. If Blake found her, he would attack at night. She was certain of that.

After a quick morning shower, she studied herself in the bathroom mirror. With blonde hair, blue eyes, and a figure other women envied, she still looked good at twenty-seven. Though she hated exploiting her body for money, it could make her much needed cash at the roadhouse. However, at the first possible chance, she would apply for more respectable employment. She needed to be a role model for Megan and give up working late nights pandering to men.

Sheriff Dale Sutton crossed her mind. She hadn't thought about another man in years. There were enough worries dealing with a psychopathic husband. Up to this point in her life, men were nothing but a parade of users, losers, and abusers, with Blake being the worst of the lot. She was about to give up on men altogether. The last thing she needed was involvement with another member of the male gender; nevertheless, one had entered the picture. She had a lunch date with him today.

She leaned closer and examined her black eye. It looked better. Taking makeup from her purse, she applied it over the bruised area. Soon all signs of Blake's abuse lay hidden beneath a layer of foundation. Good. She didn't need to wear sunglasses when she met the sheriff for lunch.

"Never again will I let a man hit me," she promised the mirror.

A slight rapping came from the front trailer door.

She slid on her jeans and T-shirt, crossed the trailer, and peeked out a front window. Nelda stood on the redwood deck holding a cardboard box in her arms. Jessica unlocked the front door and swung it open.

"Good morning, Jess." Nelda showed a bright smile. "Are you up?"

"Just. What's in the box?"

"Some fresh eggs from the henhouse, a slab of bacon, pancake batter, and a pot of fresh coffee. I'm going to fix you and Megan a proper Okie breakfast."

"Megan's still asleep, but please come in."

"You look better this morning." Nelda placed the box on the dining room table.

Jessica knew she referred to the black eye. "It's a wonder what a little makeup can do."

Nelda nodded. "Did you sleep well?"

"Not exactly. It's a little too quiet out in the country. I'm used to the sounds of the big city at night. You know, sirens, loud cars, and the occasional drive-by shooting."

"You'll be sleeping like a baby in no time, I'm sure of it." Nelda removed two cups and a pot of hot coffee from the box. "I perked you some fresh this morning." She next lifted out a black iron frying griddle. "You pour the coffee and I'll get the pancakes started."

Nelda placed the griddle on the stove and turned on the gas. "Damn!" she exclaimed.

"What's wrong?" Jessica looked up from pouring the coffee.

"Sam hasn't filled the propane yet. We've got no gas to cook with." She slid the griddle off the cold burner. "I told him to fill it first thing this morning."

"I heard him out plowing the field," Jessica said. "Can't we just ask him to do it now?"

"That's the problem. Once he gets on his tractor it's like pulling teeth to get him off to do anything else."

"I see."

Nelda lifted a cup and smiled. "Though, a couple of pretty women bringing a hot cup of coffee would cause any man to climb down off his tractor."

*　　*　　*　　*

Jessica followed Nelda out of the trailer and into the sunlight. The morning coolness combined with her wet hair from the recent shower created a chilly embrace sweeping away the last cobwebs of sleep. She took a deep breath of fresh country air as Nelda led the way across the dewy grass of the lawn. Together they stopped at the edge of the plowed field. Fifty yards away, Sam crouched in front of the tractor, studying something in the harrowed earth.

"Brought you a cup of coffee, big man," Nelda called out.

Sam looked up startled.

"What's the matter, hon? You look like you've seen a ghost."

"It's nothing." He stood and brushed dirt from his jeans. Crossing the field, he took a steaming cup from Nelda. "Now tell me what I did to earn two beautiful women bringing me coffee.

"It's not what you did, but what you didn't do. I don't have any propane to cook breakfast with," Nelda replied.

"I knew it was something like that." He smiled and sipped his coffee. "I'll get to it right away."

Sam walked over to a large propane tank mounted behind the barn. Jessica and Nelda followed and watched while he grabbed a canister and connected it to a hose from the tank. Turning a valve, a hissing noise followed, and Jessica smelled the odor of natural gas.

"Did you sleep well, Jess?" Sam asked while the canister filled.

"I tossed and turned. I guess I'm not used to the quiet of the country."

"You didn't see or hear anything last night?"

"No, why do you ask?"

"Well, it looks like a big dog paid the farm a visit during the night. There are tracks all over my field."

"A big dog?" Nelda asked, surprised.

"Either that or a couple of coyotes." Sam shut off the valve. "It's hard to tell. The tracks are all messed up."

"Maybe Rocky came back?" Nelda asked.

"No." Sam looked over his shoulder at the line of trees on the other side of the field. "I didn't want to tell you this, dear, but I found Rocky yesterday morning. It looked like he got torn apart. It could be the same animal responsible."

"Dear God," Nelda gasped.

"I buried him out in the trees."

"Poor Rocky." Tears formed in the corner of Nelda's eyes. "He was a good old hound dog."

"I'm going to keep my rifle close in case it returns. I don't want anything spooking the horses or cattle. My new foal is jumpy enough."

Nelda nodded. "You do what you have to, dear."

Sam carried the filled canister, placed it in a compartment on the back of the trailer, and hooked it up. Turning on the valve, he said, "All right, girls, you can cook now."

"Thanks, hon. I love you." Nelda gave him a quick kiss on the cheek.

"Love you, too. I better get back to work."

*   *   *   *

The smell of fresh cooked bacon and pancakes filled the trailer. Jessica sat back in her chair and sipped hot coffee while watching Nelda cook breakfast like a pro.

"How do you like it here so far, Jess?" Nelda asked, dropping more bacon to sizzle in the frying pan.

"I love it. Life here is so very different from the hell I left."

"Listen, girl." Nelda placed a plate of eggs, pancakes, and bacon on the table. "I don't want to get into your business, but if you need to talk, I'm here to listen. Sometimes just talking to someone can help you overcome the bad things in your life."

Jessica poured syrup over the pancakes and looked up at Nelda. "You don't want to hear the abuse I've gone through in my marriage, Nelda. Believe me."

"It's that bad?"

"Yes."

"Then tell me, Jess, why didn't you call the cops and report the bastard?"

"I couldn't." Jessica looked down at her plate of food. "Blake is a cop."

CHAPTER ELEVEN

Undercover Narcotics Officer Blake Lobato stared down at the aluminum baseball bat resting across his thighs and imagined swinging it full force into his wife's face. He pictured the club flattening Jessica's nose in a bloody splat and shattering her front teeth. She would then fall to the ground while he kept hitting her. With each new swing more bones shattered until he pulverized her into a bloody misshapen pulp. Next came his favorite part of the fantasy.

He would turn the bat on little Megan.

Blake was sick in the head and knew it. He didn't care about women. To him they were just pieces of meat for screwing or knocking around when they did you wrong. He learned that from his drunken old man. Sometimes Dad would just knock the shit out of his mom for no reason. He still remembered when he was just a child crying next to his mother sprawled out across the kitchen floor like a KO'd boxer.

The bastard had been a cop, too. When his old man was really angry, he forced his mother to play the Russian roulette game with his service revolver. One night his mom turned the gun on dear old Dad. Boom! Game over. At eleven, he witnessed the killing while sitting terrified on the couch. Dad lay on the living room carpet with his brains leaking out of the hole in the side of his head. That was when they lived in Detroit, where he spent his childhood. After he moved to Chicago and applied for the police academy, he left that charming family story out of his application.

Sitting in the recliner in the living room of their Chicago home, he replayed Jess's payback scene, over and over, in his mind. The long night passed with anger brewing inside, like a cold storm. Jessica was to blame for his failed life. Now he hated her more than anything he had ever known. Everything was her fault.

The bitch took his backup pistol. She stole his car and the last of the money. He didn't care that she took his daughter. She could have the whiney brat, but she should have never taken his coke money. He had snorted his last line and was coming down from the high. He needed more but had no way to buy any. His old man had been right when he told him women were nothing but backstabbing whores.

Blake's head throbbed where Jessica had hit him three days before.

Putting aside the bat, he made his way through the house to the bathroom mirror. Since his hair started receding a few years before, he shaved his head every day. Leaning into his reflection, he examined the swelling on the right side of his bald head. A dozen butterfly bandages held his scalp together where the aluminum bat had left its mark. It was a miracle she didn't kill him in the attack. He wouldn't make the same mistake when he found her. The bitch would pay for hurting him.

He studied himself in the mirror. Strong features with dark, expressive eyes and a constant five o'clock shadow made it easy to find women. The problem was they were all the same—traitorous whores just like Jessica. He still couldn't believe she grew a set of balls and ran out on him.

His cell phone suddenly rang, and he snatched it out of the belt holster.

"Blake," he said to the person on the other line.

"The rat squad's coming for your ass." It was his old partner, Detective Mark Rudman, the closest thing he had to anything resembling a friend in the department. "They are bringing you in for questioning this morning."

"Why? What more do those assholes want? I'm already under suspension from the force. They got my badge and gun."

"Ortiz ratted you out about murdering a dealer in cold blood a couple of years ago. He said you lifted all the money and coke."

"Fuck."

"You're going down, buddy. I can't help you anymore. Ortiz cut a deal, and the assistant DA is convening a grand jury. Internal Affairs is going through your case logs with a fine-tooth comb. You're up to your neck in shit. You were a good cop when we were partners before you went to narcotics. That's the only reason I'm sticking my neck out for you now."

"Okay."

"One more thing?"

"Yes?"

"You told me to let you know if I had any information about Jess's location."

Blake froze. "You got something?"

"Since you reported your Camaro stolen, I flagged it to see if it came up on any BOLO check. It seems some small-town sheriff ran the plates on your car."

"Where?"

"Hope Springs, Oklahoma."

"Oklahoma?" Blake swallowed hard. "What the hell?"

"Just thought you'd like to know."

The line went dead.

Blake put his cell on the bathroom sink and returned to gazing at his cold eyes in the mirror. He wanted to start a new life in the Windy City; to prove he could be a good cop and forget about his old man. Instead, he discovered cocaine on the streets, lots of it. Dealers out of Columbia moved it through the street gangs of Chicago. He and his partner, Robert Ortiz, began taking down scum and confiscating their drugs and cash. All of the drugs didn't end up in the evidence room, however. Most of it went up their noses. Stolen drug money purchased more. His life had become one of good cop, bad cop. During the day he was a respected undercover officer who had commendations for drug arrests. At night, he patrolled the back alleys of Chicago's South Side with his partner, skimming blow from dealers and getting high.

Then the bastards in Internal Affairs had gotten wind of the scam. Someone gave them an anonymous tip. He suspected it was Jessica who had turned him in. They took his badge and suspended him from the force. His regular channels for scoring coke had dried up. No one wanted to deal to a dirty cop on suspension.

Now Ortiz is spilling his guts to the rat squad. The little fuckhead was telling them everything about the night they popped a seventeen-year-old punk in an alley. Rudman was right. He was going down and looking at serious prison time. He knew what they did to dirty cops in prison. He wasn't going to go out like that.

His life had turned to shit, and it was all Jessica's fault.

White-hot anger pounded at his temples, and he punched the mirror with his right hand. Glass shattered sending splinters cascading to the sink and floor. He looked down. His hand bled from several shards of glass embedded in his flesh, but he didn't feel any pain. Not anymore.

Returning to the living room, he picked up the bat leaning against the recliner. Morning's arrival lit the curtains in a dingy glow, and he looked about the room in the growing light. Various photographs from his fucked-up marriage lined the banister and walls, each one so lovingly hung by his wife—family portraits of the three of them smiling at the camera.

"Bitch!" he screamed to the empty room. "You're dead!"

Swinging the bat, he shattered the glass in the frame of their wedding photo. Another full swing and he hit a home run, clearing the banister of family pictures and knickknacks in a shower of glass and broken ceramics. He continued through the house smashing every vestige of his fucked marriage: Megan's toys, Jessica's family heirlooms, pictures in frames, etc. Everything lay shattered and broken by his brutal swings. He stopped when his arms got too tired.

He needed to get out of the house, leave before the officers showed up to take him in for questioning. His boots crunched across the debris littering the floor as he went to the garage. Grabbing up a container of gasoline, he returned to the living room and splashed the pungent liquid across the walls and furniture. He continued throughout the house until the can was empty. Before leaving, he put on his favorite jacket, a black floor-length leather duster that buttoned in the front. He tore a hole in the inner lining and slid the baseball bat inside. The jacket hid the bat beautifully.

Standing in the open back door, he paused. The house he had shared with Jessica and Megan represented the last remnant of normality he had in his world. Once he torched it there would be no turning back. They would add arson to his list of felonies. He didn't care. His only purpose now was to find Jess and make her pay for what she had done to him.

"I'm coming for you, bitch," Blake said to the quiet house.

From the kitchen table, he grabbed a newspaper and rolled it tight. He lit the end with his Bic lighter and tossed the makeshift torch on the kitchen floor soaked in gasoline. Flames made a whooshing noise, rushing along the liquid to engulf the rest of the home. Blake shut the door and crossed the backyard in the early morning light. His next course of action would be to get out of Chicago before the police arrested him. He didn't have any money or a vehicle, but he knew where he was going.

Hope Springs, Oklahoma.

CHAPTER TWELVE

Jessica parallel parked the Camaro behind the sheriff's car in front of Dottie's Café. The diner was a small whitewashed building like something out of a photograph from the fifties. Words painted across the front picture window announced breakfast and lunch specials in a yellow text.

"Are we here, Mommy?" Megan looked up from coloring a new picture of Jesus.

"It looks like this is the place." Jessica checked her look in the rearview mirror. The makeup covered the black eye to the point one had to look hard to see the bruise. She quickly applied some lip liner. *God, look at me,* she thought to herself as she finished. *I'm fixing myself up like a virgin on a first date. Get ahold of yourself, girl. This is just lunch.*

"I'm hungry, Mommy."

"I know, baby. We're getting something to eat here. We're meeting the sheriff. You remember him, don't you?"

Megan nodded and returned to her picture.

"He invited us to have lunch with him, so I want you to be good." Satisfied with her look, Jessica grabbed her purse.

"Is he going to be my new daddy?" Megan asked innocently while coloring Christ's robe with a white crayon.

Jessica stopped and turned toward her daughter. "No, he's not. Why would you ask such a thing?"

"Because he's nice."

"He invited us to lunch. I said yes, so that's why we're here. Now come on, we're late."

"Can I bring my coloring book?"

"Okay."

Jessica exited the Camaro and helped Megan get out on her side. She bent down to look into her daughter's face. "Now you got to promise Mommy not to say anything about the sheriff being your new daddy. Do you hear me, baby? You promise?"

"Yes, Mommy."

"Good, let's go in."

Taking Megan by the hand, she opened the diner's front door. The interior design, consisting of a lunch counter and line of booths running along one wall, reaffirmed her initial impression that the establishment was a throwback from the 1950s. Black-and-white photographs showing faded pictures of old softball teams, cars, and homecoming queens from years past covered every available space on the walls. With lunch well in progress, the air smelled of cooked food and hummed with the clatter of plates and people talking.

Sheriff Sutton, dressed in his khaki uniform, stood up by the back booth. He smiled and motioned for them to join him. Jessica's heart jumped. Though she couldn't put her finger on the reason, she hadn't felt such attraction for a man since meeting Blake seven years ago. The sheriff was handsome but definitely not her type. She had always been attracted to the urban bad boys that she grew up with in Chicago. This small-town hick sheriff was definitely different. What was it that drew her to him? The only thing she could think of was his scent when he was close.

I'm here because of the way a man smells?

Aware that everyone was watching her, she continued to the booth with Megan in tow.

"Sorry we're late," she said breathless while helping Megan into the seat.

"No problem." He smiled. "I'm just glad you showed. I was beginning to think I got stood up."

"We spent all morning searching for a cat named Tig. He turned up missing last night, and Megan just wouldn't give up looking for him." She settled into the booth. "That's the reason we're running late."

"Did you find the cat?" Sheriff Sutton sat in the booth across from her.

"No." Jessica shook her head. "It seems pets have a way of disappearing on the Olson farm."

"I see." He turned his attention to her daughter. "Hi, Megan."

"Hi." Megan did a little wave. "Mommy doesn't want me to talk about you being my new daddy."

"Megan!" Jessica jumped and turned toward her daughter. "I told you not to say anything like that. It's so rude. We don't even know Sheriff Sutton."

"Sorry, Mommy."

Jessica faced the sheriff with her cheeks burning from embarrassment. "Oh, God, I'm so sorry. I apologize."

"No need." He chuckled. "I'm honored."

"Maybe this is a mistake. Now that my daughter has embarrassed the hell out of both of us, I should go." She grabbed Megan by the hand. "Come on, baby."

"Don't leave." The sheriff reached across the table and placed his hand on hers. "Please stay."

All resistance evaporated instantly, and she settled back down in the booth.

"Okay," she said in a weak voice.

"Let's start over." He removed his hand and held it out for a shake. "My name is Dale and I would enjoy you and your lovely daughter's company for lunch."

She took the offered handshake. "I'm Jess and I accept."

He smiled. "You're in for a treat. Dottie's has the best lunch in the county. I suggest the grilled ham sandwich with fried okra."

"Between this and Nelda's cooking, I've probably gained five pounds since moving to Hope Springs."

"It certainly doesn't show."

"Thanks." Her face flushed again.

They gave their order to a pudgy waitress with dyed red hair. He introduced her as Dottie, and the woman shot her a cool glare. Jessica concluded Nelda was right. Other women in Hope Springs had their sights set on the sheriff.

While waiting for the meal, they engaged in sporadic small talk about the town, weather, and local events. Jessica got the impression they were talking about everything but what they really wanted to discuss. Each had questions to ask the other but didn't know how to approach the subject. During the wait, Megan concentrated on her coloring book and remained quiet.

The food arrived and they ate in an awkward silence. Jessica turned her attention to the ham sandwich and fried okra, a delicacy she had never heard of before coming to Oklahoma. Nelda had fixed her a big breakfast, so she just picked at her plate. Megan, however, devoured her two chicken strips and a cup of corn before returning to coloring. Finally, Sheriff Sutton looked at her over his cheeseburger. Their eyes met for a second.

"So what are you, Jess?" He glanced down at the ring on her finger. "Married? Divorced? Widowed?"

Jessica sighed. "It's complicated."

"Complicated." He picked up a french fry and looked at her again. "How complicated?"

"I'm separated. My husband was an abusive asshole. Let's just leave it at that."

"Sound's fair."

"What about you? In a relationship? Married? Divorced?"

"None of the above."

"Why is that? There are at least six women in this place who are jealous of me sitting here with you."

"And every man wishes you were sitting with them."

"You didn't answer my question."

"I'm not from Hope Springs. I transferred here about two years ago and took the sheriff post. Small-town girls are nice and all, but I'm looking for someone with a little more depth and edge to them."

"I don't mean to be abrupt, but I don't like playing head games. I went through that with my marriage. What is it you want with me and my daughter?"

"Right to the point. I like that." He reached out and placed his hand on top of hers. "You're very attractive, Jess. I want to get to know you better."

His touch sent her heart racing. It took all of her willpower to slowly pull her hand back. "I'm a battered wife with a five-year-old daughter. That's a lot of baggage for a single man unaccustomed to a long-term relationship to handle."

"Understood."

"I'm not going to lie to you. I find you very attractive, Dale, but what I need from a man is something supportive for me and my daughter. My inability in the past to find a good one has left me nothing but heartbreak. I don't know you yet. Let's just start at friends and see if anything else develops. Agreed?"

"Agreed." He returned to his plate and finished his meal.

Surprised at her strength in resisting his first advance, Jessica glanced over at her daughter. Intent on coloring a picture of Jesus preaching the Sermon on the Mount, Megan's tongue stuck out between her lips as she concentrated on staying in the lines with the crayon.

I have to think of her now and what is best for the two of us.

"Excuse me, Sheriff. Sorry to interrupt your lunch."

Jessica glanced up. A husky middle-aged man now stood beside the table with a stained ball cap in his hands.

"What is it, Ernie?" Sheriff Sutton wiped his mouth with a napkin.

"It's Elmer Grosslin up on Route 23. He showed up on my farm talking all excited and ranting about Bigfoot killing one of his cows last night. Says he's got proof this time. Wants you to come out and see him real bad. He doesn't have a phone so I told him if I saw you, I'd tell you. Can you swing by and pay a visit?"

"Okay, Ernie, I'll drop by this afternoon."

"Thanks, Sheriff."

The man nodded politely to her before leaving.

"What was that about?" Jessica asked.

"Elmer Grosslin is a crazy old coot who lives by himself out in the country. He's always thinking that UFOs and the CIA are trying to abduct him. I get a call out to his farm every couple of months. I hate going out to speak to him because he's covered in lice."

"He's not the one responsible for all those signs I saw yesterday along highway 133?"

"No. That's Jasper Higgins. I arrested him for the murder of his wife a couple of years back just after I became sheriff. He claims the devil stole her away in the middle of the night. The guy thinks he can convince others he's innocent by putting up all those signs. He's guilty as hell, though. The only reason he hasn't gone to prison yet is because they haven't found his wife's body. County DA is attempting to put a circumstantial case against him. It's just a matter of time." He chuckled again. "Old man Grosslin is the kind of crazy who ends up wearing a tinfoil cap. Sometimes I think there's something in the local water supply that breeds nutcases in this county."

"Remind me to drink bottled water," Jessica replied.

"Either that or get fitted for a tinfoil hat."

They laughed together, and the tension hanging between them vaporized.

Megan looked up from her coloring book. "Mommy, you're laughing."

"Yes, baby."

Megan hugged her. "I like that."

"I do, too." Jessica said to the sheriff, "I guess she hasn't heard me laugh in a while."

"I'm glad to be of service," he replied with a wink.

She released Megan. "Keep coloring your pretty picture, baby. I'm going to talk to the sheriff for a bit."

"Okay," she replied, picking up a crayon.

Jessica smiled. "Thanks for a lovely lunch, Dale."

"The pleasure's all mine. I enjoyed sharing lunch with the two prettiest girls in town."

"Anyway, it was fun."

"We'll have to do it again sometime." He leaned back against his seat. "So you're starting work at Roxie's tomorrow night?"

"Yeah, I need the money."

"Well, would you like to go out there tonight? They're open and they shouldn't be too busy. Just a friendly outing, nothing more. Drink a couple of beers and get to know the bar before you start working there."

"I've got Megan. I don't think I can go."

"I understand." He stood and picked the ticket up from the table. "It was just an idea."

She exhaled. "Write down your phone number and if I can find someone to watch Megan, I'll give you a call. How does that sound?"

"Good enough." He scribbled the number on a napkin and slid it across the table. "I'm off duty after six. If you can make it, come out."

"Look, Mommy, all done," Megan announced and held up her coloring book. The picture showed Jesus standing on a mountaintop with arms outspread over the heads of a crowd of people. Megan had colored the Messiah's skin a bright orange.

"Pretty," Jessica said. "Grab your book and crayons. We're leaving."

They followed the sheriff out of the diner to the sidewalk.

He shifted his gun belt and stated, "I think I ate too much, but I enjoyed every minute of it."

"We did, too."

He stepped closer to her and their eyes locked. For a frightening second she thought he was going to kiss her. *Not here. Not in front of everyone watching through the windows of the diner. Not now.*

Instead he put his arm around her shoulder and gave her a friendly hug. Jessica breathed in the man's aroma, which caused her heart to race.

What kind of cologne is he wearing?

"If you want to go out tonight, call me." He released her. "Okay?"

"Okay." Her head felt giddy as if she was speaking in a dream.

He bent down and shook Megan's hand. "You be a good little girl for your mother."

Megan suddenly reached up and hugged the sheriff around his neck. The move surprised Jessica. She had never seen Megan do the same with her own father. "Good-bye," Megan said.

"You're a sweet girl," he replied awkwardly. He pulled back from her daughter and said, "Talk to you later."

They both watched in silence as he walked back to his patrol car.

CHAPTER THIRTEEN

Sheriff Sutton drove down the country road leading to the Grosslin farm on Route 23. A trail of red dust kicked up by the tires hung in the still air behind the vehicle. A couple of miles from the farm, he radioed in and told Wanda, his dispatcher, he was paying a visit to Elmer Grosslin's place.

"What's the nature of the visit?" Wanda asked.

"One of his cows got killed last night."

She chuckled over the speaker. "Knowing that crazy coot, he's probably going to tell you aliens did it."

"You're close. He claims Bigfoot's responsible."

"I'm not surprised."

"I'll call you when I get done with him."

"Roger, Sheriff."

Grosslin's farm came into view, and he slowed the vehicle. The place consisted of a run-down farmhouse and dilapidated barn missing much of its roof. High weeds grew around the junk trucks and cars littering the front yard. The place lacked running water or electricity. Turning the car into the open front gate of the fence, the tires bumped over a rusted cattle guard before coming to a stop in the middle of the yard. The cloud of red dust followed him into the lot.

The front door of the house burst open and Elmer Grosslin came out on the rickety porch. The old hermit had unruly gray hair, a dirty beard, and worn overalls slick from grime. He squinted toward the patrol car and swung up a double-barreled shotgun.

"Is that you, Sheriff?" he called out.

Sheriff Sutton unclasped his pistol and buzzed down the driver window. "It's me, Elmer. Put down the gun."

"My eyes ain't as good as they once was. Step out of the car so I can see you."

He opened the door and slid out with his hand still on the pistol at his hip. "Put down the gun, Elmer."

He squinted. "Okay, I see it's you, Sheriff." Lowering the shotgun, he added, "You can't be too careful these days. Damn CIA sends spies to watch me all the time."

Sheriff Sutton shut the door to the patrol car. "I heard you got a problem out here, Elmer?"

The old man spat tobacco into the dirt off the porch. A stream of spittle remained in his dirty beard. "It got my cow last night. Butchered it and ate it alive."

"Who did?"

"Bigfoot, that's who." Elmer spat another stream of tobacco. "Poor Lisa's tore to shreds."

"Lisa?"

"My cow." Elmer's eyes looked like they were about to weep. "My beautiful cow."

"Show me where."

"Come with me, Sheriff." Elmer stepped off the porch with the shotgun carried in the crook of his arm. "She's out back."

Sheriff Sutton followed him around the house. The body odor coming from the old man caused him to breathe through his mouth. They reached the backyard where the rotten smell of death competed with Elmer's stench. Ahead in the tall grass, the legs of a dead cow stuck up toward the sky.

"It's not a pretty sight, Sheriff." Elmer nodded toward the body. "Damn Bigfoot tore her to pieces."

Flies buzzed when they walked up on the kill site. The cow lay ripped open with organs spilled out and scattered about in bloody sinewy strips around the carcass. Huge bite marks, visible on the throat and neck, left gaping holes in the flesh.

"Look what that bastard did to my Lisa." Elmer shifted the shotgun to wipe a tear from his cheek.

"How do you know it was Bigfoot, Elmer?" Sheriff Sutton crouched to inspect the body closer. "It could have been coyotes or a mountain lion."

"Coyotes didn't do that, and there ain't been no mountain lion in these parts for fifty years."

"Tell me what happened." Sheriff Sutton stood again.

"I heard a commotion last night. Lisa was bawling like a young calf. I run out of the house with my shotgun and lantern and come upon the monster. It was right there ripping apart my Lisa with its fangs."

"I never heard of Bigfoot having fangs or eating a cow."

"Well it does, 'cause I seen them." Elmer spit another stream of tobacco juice. "It was too involved in eating my cow to see me standing right where I'm standing now. It just kept tearing off pieces of meat and swallowing them whole."

"Why didn't you shoot the monster?"

"I did but not with my shotgun." Elmer reached into the pocket of his grimy overalls and produced a small disposable camera with flash. "I shot him with this."

"You carry a camera, Elmer?" Sheriff Sutton asked perplexed.

"Sure do. Bought it at the Dollar Store in town. I keep it for when I see a UFO or one of those CIA men in black suits that drive by my farm all the time. I know they're spying on me. Might be watching us right now. Last night, the camera flash sent the creature running off into the night. I guess old Bigfoot is a bit camera-shy, but I got him bigger than life this time. Now people will believe me and won't think I'm nuttier then bug shit."

"That picture is evidence, Elmer. You're going to have to turn over the roll of film to me."

"Can't, Sheriff."

"I promise to give it back after it's developed but, for now, it's evidence of a crime."

Elmer shook his head and spit tobacco. "I don't got it anymore. I gave the film to old Jasper."

"Jasper Higgins?" Sheriff Sutton asked in shock.

"Yeah. He came around this morning. He heard of my murdered cow. Said he saw something last night, too, on his farm. His property is only a couple of miles from here."

"You're kidding."

"No, he took the roll of film to develop it. Said he'd bring it back. Told me I might have gotten something important. They might want to put the picture up on television or in the papers."

"Jasper is a suspect in his wife's murder. He's looking for a way to pin the murder on anyone or thing but himself."

Elmer paused for a second and looked down at the rotting carcass. "He says what I saw last night was a werewolf."

Sheriff Sutton's gut tightened. "A werewolf?"

"That's what he says. He claims there's a werewolf running around and it's the same one that killed his wife. I told him I know Bigfoot when I see one." Elmer laughed. "I think he's the one crazier than bug shit."

"He was probably drunk."

"Stone sober. The first time I had seen him such since Emma's death. I liked her, by the way. She was a nice lady and came over and read the Bible to me on some days."

"Something did kill your cow last night, Elmer. I'm going to have to file a report and mark off the crime scene." He removed a pair of latex forensic gloves from his back pocket and slid them on each hand. "Right now I'm going to check those bite marks."

"When Jasper returns with the photographs you can use them as evidence."

"I'll need those, too." He pointed at the shotgun Elmer held in the crook of his arm. "That's a nice firearm, Elmer. Where did you get it?"

"This old double-barrel?" He shifted up the weapon for the sheriff to look closer. "Belonged to my grandpap, and then my pappy, and he handed it down to me."

"What is it? A 12 gauge?"

"Yep."

"Do you mind?" Sheriff Sutton extended his hand.

"Not at all." Elmer handed it over to the sheriff.

"Thanks." He whistled softly and hefted the weapon. Unlike himself, the old hermit kept the double-barrel perfectly clean. "She's a beauty."

"I keep it loaded for when the CIA or aliens show up to abduct me."

"Good plan," Sheriff Sutton said, sticking the shotgun under Elmer's beard and pulling both barrels. The surprised man's head exploded in a shower of blood, bone, and chunks of brain matter. The shot echoed across the farm while the headless body fell to the ground beside the carcass of his beloved cow. Bending down, he placed the smoking weapon on Elmer's chest and curled a dead finger around the trigger to make it look like he committed suicide. It wouldn't pass any real forensic test but would do on a cursory examination.

"Elmer, you stink worse dead than alive," Sheriff Sutton said, standing back up and peeling the gloves off his hands.

Walking back to the patrol car, he pulled out his cell phone and pressed dial.

"Roxie's Roadhouse," Roxie said on the other end after three rings.

"We need a gathering," Sheriff Sutton said. "Call the rest of the Pack together."

"This afternoon?"

"Yes, before the bar opens."

"We're all hungry. Collin says you must find us some meat first."

Sheriff Sutton cursed under his breath. "I don't know if I can on such short notice. It's very risky."

"Dale," Roxie spoke in a quieter voice, "the hunger is intensifying due to the upcoming Ebon Moon. I know you feel it, too. We need to feed."

"I'll see what I can do."

He ended the call and climbed into his car. For a second he stared at the run-down farmhouse of the recently deceased Elmer Grosslin. Everything he had worked so hard to keep secret for the last two years was unraveling. The night of the Ebon Moon was just a few days away. Roxie was right. The Pack was starving. They needed to satiate their hunger by devouring human flesh and blood. This was the nature of the curse each lycanthrope bore within his or her soul. The feeding had to take place before the next full moon or the primal side would take control to the point where nothing would stop them from feasting on any human at hand. Sheriff Sutton knew this, for the same hunger gnawed at his soul like a thing alive. But now a complication had come out of left field by someone he thought powerless.

A hunter had emerged.

Jasper Higgins needed dealing with once and for all.

CHAPTER FOURTEEN

"I get to see the pony now." Megan slammed the passenger door of the Camaro and ran headlong across the grassy lawn in front of the trailer house.

"Young lady, you wait for your mother," Jessica called out, exiting the car.

Megan stopped. "Please, Mommy, hurry." She shifted to one foot and then the other.

"Okay, okay." Jessica joined her daughter's side.

From the shadow inside the barn, a smiling Sam stepped out into the bright sunlight. He wiped his hands blackened with grease on an oil rag.

"Anxious to see my little filly, are you?"

"Can we now?" Megan asked, running the distance to the barn entrance.

"Well, I'm changing the oil in the old tractor. Give me a minute."

Jessica glanced over her shoulder. The field bordering the trailer was brown with freshly furrowed earth. "You got the plowing done?"

"I just finished." Sam walked back into the barn to where the tractor waited. The air smelled of engine oil and freshly plowed dirt. "I'm getting the tractor ready for winter now."

"Then we can go see her?" Megan asked.

Sam reached out and patted the top of her blonde curls. "We sure can, sweetie."

"She has done nothing but talk about that since leaving the diner." Jessica laughed. "I've never seen her like this. Please forgive her, Sam."

"There's nothing wrong with a child being a child." Sam shut down a panel covering the tractor engine. Jessica noticed a hunting rifle leaning against the driver's seat.

"Are you expecting Indians, cowboy?" Jessica quipped.

"Coyotes," Sam replied. "I think they've been harassing my livestock lately. I've got a very excitable filly, and the last thing I need is some vermin terrorizing her."

"Can we go see her now?" Megan pleaded.

"I guess you're not the only one who has an excitable filly," Jessica remarked.

Sam laughed. "I guess not." He bent down and said to Megan, "Hop on, Meg, and I'll give you a piggyback ride to the stable."

"Okay." Megan climbed up on Sam's back laughing with joy. He stood and walked out of the barn while Jessica followed.

As they passed the back door to the farmhouse, Nelda stepped out on the patio. Her graying hair was swept back into a ponytail.

"What are you doing now, you old fool?" Nelda called out to her husband.

"Taking Meg to see the foal."

"Well, don't hurt your back in the process."

"Nonsense, woman," Sam called back. "My back is as strong as when I married you."

"Just remember you said that when I'm rubbing Bengay on it tonight."

Nelda joined Jessica, and they followed a short distance behind Sam and Megan toward the stables.

"How did lunch with the sheriff go?" Nelda asked.

"Perfect." Jessica laughed. "Well almost. Megan asked him if he was going to be her new daddy."

"Out of the mouths of children," Nelda replied. "What did he say?"

"It was so embarrassing I wanted to leave right then and there. He asked me to stay, though."

"That's a good sign. At least he didn't bolt for the door."

Jessica stopped and turned toward Nelda. "Can I ask you something woman-to-woman?"

"Sure."

"Have you ever been around a man who smelled so good it just makes you melt? I mean, Dale's scent just takes my breath away. I just lose it when he's near."

"Is it his cologne?"

"I don't think so."

"Well, if it's the aftershave he's wearing, I'm going to have to get a bottle for Sam, for sure."

They both laughed.

"I don't think its aftershave. It's like a natural male scent. Something his body gives off."

"Pheromones." Nelda said.

"I don't follow you."

"I saw something on Animal Planet about it. Animals and humans give it off. It's an odor used to attract the opposite sex for mating purposes."

"Well, the sheriff's got it in spades."

They walked up to the white rail fence surrounding the stock pen connected to the stable. Megan leaned on the fence and waited anxiously while Sam went inside.

"Sam has gone to get the little horse, Mommy," Megan said while her eyes never left the double doors to the stable.

"Are you excited, baby?"

Megan bobbed her head. The next moment the stable doors burst open and the foal came scampering out into the pen. The animal was beautiful with a black coat and a long white stripe on its snout as if someone took a brush and painted it on. She kicked up her back hoofs sending brown turf flying into the air. Sam came out of the double doors throwing a bridle on the ground.

"Damn it, I tried to get a bridle around her head and she bolted."

The young horse continued scampering around the pen and keeping her distance from Sam.

"She's beautiful!" Megan shouted with eyes wide with amazement.

"And a little too high-strung, if you ask me. Now I'll never get her to calm down." Sam walked over to where they stood on the other side of the fence. He winked at Jessica. "But maybe you can, Meg."

Megan looked up at him. "Me?"

Sam reached into the pocket of his coveralls and pulled out a carrot. He winked at Jessica, who almost laughed. It reminded her of Mr. Green Jeans from *Captain Kangaroo*. "Perhaps you can make her come over with this, but wait until I get over the fence." Sam hefted himself over the railing and dropped to the other side. "I don't want her knocking me down trying to get to the carrot."

"Okay." Megan took the carrot and stuck it through the railing. "Will she come and eat it?"

The foal continued kicking up more turf while staying away from their side of the enclosure.

"You have to give her a name first. She's not going to come over by calling her horse," Sam said.

Jessica reached out and stroked the back of her daughter's blonde curls. "What are you going to name her, sweetie?"

"Princess." Megan nodded. "Her name is Princess."

"Princess it is then," Sam replied. "One princess to another."

The foal slowed her cantering back and forth and stopped across the pen. She eyed the carrot Megan held out and snorted.

"Here you go, Princess." Megan waved the carrot. "Come and get it."

The animal took a few cautious steps toward the offered treat.

"Come on, girl. I won't hurt you. Pretty Princess, I've got a carrot for you."

She lowered her head and walked up to the carrot.

"That's a girl," Sam said under his breath.

The foal snuffled the carrot and began taking bites.

"You can pet her now," Sam spoke in a soft voice.

Megan reached out and stroked the horse's nose.

"Wow," she said, almost breathless. "She's beautiful."

"Just like you," Sam said, petting the mane between the animal's ears.

*   *   *   *

For over an hour, Megan sat at the railing admiring Princess in the pen. Jessica retreated with Nelda to the patio where they shared a pitcher of cold tea and watched her daughter. Sam had gone into the stable to care for the other livestock.

"You're a lucky woman, Nelda," Jessica said after taking a long sip of tea. "Sam is a wonderful man."

"Yes he is." Nelda leaned forward and poured another glass. "We've made a good life here on this old farm."

"I've totally screwed my life up from day one."

"You're young and beautiful, Jess. Plus, you have a wonderful daughter. You still have time to fix things and find happiness."

"Sheriff Sutton asked me out again."

Nelda leaned forward in her patio chair. "He did?"

"He wants to take me to Roxie's tonight to get an idea of the place before I work there."

"What did you tell him?"

"I told him I couldn't because I don't have a sitter for Megan."

"Sam and I would love to watch your daughter. She has brought such joy to this empty house."

"I've imposed on you enough, Nelda."

"Nonsense." Nelda shook her head. "You go out with that man and have a great time. We'll watch Megan."

"I hate not taking her. When I left her with Blake, he would just up and leave the house. Megan was home by herself many times."

"She'll be fine with us."

"Okay." She stood up. "I'll give him a call. Do you have a phone I can use?"

"There's one on the wall in the kitchen next to the refrigerator."

She bent down and hugged the woman's neck. "Thank you so much for everything you've done for us. You're an angel, Nel."

Nelda returned the embrace. "Thank you for bringing Megan into our lives."

CHAPTER FIFTEEN

Studying the short skirt of the cheerleader walking in front of him, Terry Newman exited the Morris High School building. The swaying hemline belonged to Becky Warren, his current eleventh-grade crush. He followed her down the exit stairs while she chatted to a group of booster girls. Morris High was abuzz for the big football game Friday night. To show their school spirit, all the cheerleaders showed up in their gold and maroon uniforms. Terry didn't mind. He loved how the uniform hugged Becky's tight body and exposed her perfect brown legs.

He only wished he had the nerve to tell her so.

Once they reached the sidewalk, the group of girls dispersed into their various after-school rides parked by the curb. None paid attention to him as he passed by. Becky slid into a late-model yellow Mustang with a shiny wax job. For a brief second, he glimpsed her long legs and the edge of her white panties before she shut the passenger door. The Mustang's engine revved and the car squealed out into the street leaving behind the smell of burning rubber. Word around school was that Becky had started dating a senior named Brandon Harrison. What made things worse was that the guy had both looks and money. Terry had neither.

After the Mustang drove away, he sighed and wished for a car of his own. There was no way he was going to get a girlfriend by catching rides with a dropout like Sid Granger. The slacker drove a nice pickup, thanks to the pocketbook of his grandmother. He looked up the street for Sid's truck but it was nowhere in sight. The dweeb had forgotten to pick him up again, probably due to getting high while listening to his screamo music.

Terry refused to ride the school bus. It would make him the laughingstock of the junior class. Instead, he started the two-mile hike to home as a carnal fantasy formed in his mind like a porno movie. He imagined what he would do if Becky was in the front seat of his car. In his fantasy, he would reach over and touch her silky thighs before running his hand up to feel the fabric of her soft white panties.

The sound of a vehicle shifting gears and slowing down behind him shattered his erotic daydream. He looked over his shoulder expecting to see Sid's truck. Instead, it was an old red Ford F-150 cruising to a stop. The passenger window rolled down.

"You need a ride, Terry?" a familiar voice asked from the truck cab.

"Mr. Higgins?"

"Hop in."

He stepped up to the passenger door and hesitated. He liked Mr. Higgins and even once thought of him like a father figure after his own had run out on his mother. He was fifteen years old then and attending Sunday school Bible classes. Now two years older, he wasn't so naive. Did he want to go riding with a man accused of brutally murdering his wife?

"It's all right, Mr. Higgins. I can walk home. The exercise will do me good." He took a step back from the truck.

The old man leaned over, opening the passenger door. Mr. Higgins looked tired, as if he had been up all night. White stubble jutted from his chin and a glazed look of fatigue shone in his eyes. "I need to talk to you, son."

Terry glanced into the cab. A worn Bible sat on the car seat. "Mr. Higgins, I understand you want me to go to church and—"

"I'm not here to preach."

"You're not?"

"You remember when you and that foul-mouthed boy stopped by the farm yesterday?"

Terry recalled Sid cussing the old man out and tossing a can of beer at one of his signs. He nodded and said, "Yeah. I'm sorry for the way Sid acted. He can be a real doofus sometimes."

"I'm here to learn more about what we discussed."

"Werewolves?" Terry asked, perplexed.

"Yes."

"Listen, Mr. Higgins, that was just talk, you know?"

"I need your help, Terry. You're the only one I can turn to." The old man's tired eyes met his. "Please get in."

Terry let out a long breath. Though he suspected he was going to regret doing so, he slid into the passenger seat and shut the door.

"Thank you," Mr. Higgins said, putting the truck in gear.

Terry prayed none of the other classmates saw him climbing in with the old man. An awkward silence hung between them until the truck swung into a spot at Dixie's Drive-In a couple of blocks from the school.

"How about a snow cone, or are you too old for those now?" Mr. Higgins asked, putting the truck into park. "I'm buying."

"I'll take a Dr. Pepper." Terry glanced around at the cars parked under the long awning. He spotted Becky's ride. The shiny yellow Mustang sat in the bay across from theirs.

Oh God, I hope she doesn't see me with crazy Mr. Higgins.

The old man pushed the call button and placed the order. Afterward, he turned and showed a weak smile.

"How's school?"

"Pretty good." Terry looked down at his hands. He was lying. High school wasn't going well at all. His grades were fair, but he wasn't popular and didn't have any friends. Sometimes, he would go through the entire school day without speaking to anyone.

Mr. Higgins cleared his throat before saying, "I graduated Morris High. Class of 1950. The old school still looks the same."

"Homecoming's tomorrow night," Terry replied. He couldn't care less about the football game. The only reason he brought it up was that he wanted to ask Becky to the dance afterward, even though it was a stupid idea with zero chance for success.

"The Morris Maroons. I remember my homecoming. I bet you didn't know I played football when I was there. I wore a letter jacket and was even the quarterback in my senior year. God, that was so long ago. My old heart wouldn't let me do anything like that again."

"It's a stupid name for a team."

"The Morris Maroons?"

"It sounds like Morris Morons." *Considering some of the jocks on the team, the name fits*, Terry thought to himself.

Mr. Higgins chuckled. "I guess it does."

The carhop brought their order, and Terry recognized the skinny girl with frizzy brown hair and thick glasses as Jenny Painter from his homeroom class.

"Hi, Terry," she said, handing Mr. Higgins the drinks through the driver window. She smiled showing a mouthful of braces.

"Hi," he replied and looked away. He had no interest in Jenny Painter. His one true love sat in the yellow Mustang across from him.

Mr. Higgins paid for the order, and Jenny took her tray and left. She waved one last time before disappearing into the main building of the drive-in.

"Nice girl." Mr. Higgins handed him the Dr. Pepper. "Do you have a girlfriend?"

"Nope." He took a long slurp at the straw. "Not at the moment."

Another lie. He never had a girlfriend.

"I drink coffee now," Mr. Higgins said, removing the lid from his Styrofoam cup. "I gave up the Jack Daniel's."

"That's good." Terry wondered what the old man was leading to with this conversation.

"By the way, I saw it again last night."

"It?"

"The horrible beast that killed my wife." His tired eyes looked across at Terry. "That's why I came to talk to you, son. I need you to tell me what you know about these werewolf creatures."

The old man has gone crazy, he decided. *Best to humor him until he drops me off at the house.*

"Mr. Higgins, those things only exist in the movies. They're not real. We were just pulling your leg yesterday."

"They're real, all right, son. I shot one last night on my farm. Hit him in the shoulder before he ran off howling."

"You're kidding."

"Nope. The way I figure there's been one in the area for a while. It killed my Emma two years ago. Do you remember when Michelle Carlson mysteriously went missing last year? They say she disappeared without a trace. She just up and vanished leaving a little baby behind for her mother to bring up."

"I heard a rumor she ran off with her boyfriend."

"I think the werewolf got her."

"A werewolf in Oklahoma," Terry said and chuckled. "Sounds like a bad movie to me."

"I'm serious, son. You said you believed I was innocent of murder yesterday, or were you just pulling my leg then?"

Terry contemplated the question for a moment. Mr. Higgins had always been a simple, straightforward man. He remembered the unconventional way he taught Bible class by taking the boys out of the church to sit under the shade of an elm tree. There he would talk to them about life and read passages from the scriptures. It was the closest he had ever felt to a spiritual God.

"I don't think you killed your wife," Terry replied.

"God bless you, son." Mr. Higgins straightened up with a look of relief showing on his face. "Then you have to believe me about the thing I shot last night."

"Okay." Terry nodded. "Let's say for the sake of argument you shot a werewolf. Where did it go?"

"I have no idea."

"Do you know who it is? I mean a human has to transform into a werewolf. Do you know the identity of the human half?"

"No, but I do have proof it exists."

"You do?" he asked, surprised.

Mr. Higgins took a sip of his coffee. "Open the Bible in the seat."

Terry reached down and lifted the front cover of the book. A Motophoto packet rested inside. Picking it up, he removed the first picture. It was an amateur photo shot at night showing the darkened shape of something bent beside the body of a cow. Fierce red eyes and sharp fangs were the only facial features picked up by the flash.

"Did you take this?"

"Not me. Old Elmer Grosslin did. Last night he came upon the monster killing his cow. He managed to take a photograph of the beast before the thing ran off."

"You mean Crazy Elmer, don't you?" Terry shook his head. "I've heard stories of him since I was a kid. We used to say, 'Watch out or Crazy Elmer's going to get you.' He's not the best source for reliable proof."

"I understand, but when I heard his cow got killed last night, I checked on it thinking it was probably the werewolf's doing. He told me how he came upon the monster and snapped a photo of it. He thinks he got a picture of Bigfoot." Mr. Higgins chuckled. "I don't know who's crazier. I'm searching for a werewolf and he's seeing Bigfoot. Whatever the thing is, there is a monster running wild killing people and animals in the county. The picture is proof of that."

Terry thumbed through the rest of the pictures in the packet that were all taken during daylight. Most showed airplanes in the clouds and vehicles driving by on a dirt road.

"What are all these pictures of planes and cars?"

"Stuff Elmer shot. God knows why."

Terry returned his attention to the photo of the monster. "It could be a guy in a werewolf costume. You can buy them, especially this time of year around Halloween."

"You see that dent on the hood of my truck? I tried to run the thing over and it practically jumped over my truck. I don't think it's someone in a costume."

"Why don't you tell the local sheriff?"

"Sheriff Sutton has done his best to pin a murder on me. He didn't believe me when I told him Satan killed my wife. Do you think he's going to when I tell him a werewolf did it?"

"So what do you plan to do?"

"I have to prove this monster is real. You can help by giving me information about these creatures. When I was younger, I used to hunt deer all over the countryside. I know the lay of the land. I just need more info about what I'm hunting. I don't know what I'm up against here. Until yesterday, I didn't know what a werewolf was."

"You need to talk to Sid about that. He knows everything about werewolves, vampires, demons, and all that stuff."

"Sid's your friend who was with you yesterday?"

"Yes."

"Take me to him then."

"Okay, I'll do it, but I don't know if he'll help you. Sid's an asshole sometimes."

"I've noticed, but I'll take my chances." Mr. Higgins started the truck. "Let's go see him now."

"Okay."

Terry turned his attention back to the photo. In the grainy picture, the creature stared back with evil red eyes highlighted by the camera flash. *Can it be real? A werewolf? The idea seems absurd and impossible. Monsters don't exist. Or do they? Isn't proof right here in my hand?*

Terry glanced up at the yellow Mustang as the pickup backed out of the drive-in stall. *If the werewolf is real, maybe I should help Mr. Higgins hunt the monster. What would Becky think about me then? Would she think I was cool or insane? Probably the latter since my hunting partner is Mr. Higgins and our inspiration is a picture taken by Crazy Elmer.*

But what else is there to do in a small town, anyway?

Terry Newman, werewolf hunter.

I like how cool it sounds.

Maybe Becky would, too.

CHAPTER SIXTEEN

After leaving Elmer Grosslin's property, Sheriff Sutton raced his patrol car back down the dirt road, turning toward I-35. Anger fumed inside at the thought of Jasper Higgins having a photograph of a werewolf. He wasn't sure what the picture showed, but he knew one of the Pack had been reckless and got caught on film. He intended to find out who, though he had his suspicions. Only Collin would be so bold. But why? What drove him to take such a risk?

The patrol car turned up the paved ramp leading to I-35 and merged with the traffic on the busy highway. The late September sun created cloud shadows flowing across the four lanes of the interstate while he headed north. Searching the road ahead, he struck pay dirt twenty miles later. A shabbily dressed hitchhiker walked along the shoulder with a rucksack on his back. Sheriff Sutton hit his lights and pulled over behind the homeless man. Turning off the dashboard cam, he climbed out of the patrol car.

"What is it, Sheriff?" the man asked. "Am I doing anything wrong?"

Sutton studied the hitcher for a second. He was in his late twenties and poorly dressed in faded jeans, a dirty T-shirt, and an old army jacket frayed at the sleeves. The suntanned face bore several days worth of grime and unshaved whiskers.

"Hitchhiking is a crime in this county, son," Sheriff Sutton replied.

"I'm not hitchhiking. I'm just walking along the interstate. I'm not thumbing for a ride."

"You got ID?"

The hitcher dropped his rucksack to the ground. Reaching into his jean pocket, he pulled a wallet of faded leather. He handed it to the sheriff. "I don't have a driver's license. I just got a military ID."

"Take it out so I can see it."

He removed the identification card.

"Your name is Russell Norris?"

"Yes."

"You're in the army?"

"I was. Served two years in Iraq until an IED killed my buddy and took out my left knee. It's been replaced by an artificial joint, which works well considering I've been walking on it for several days now."

"What are you doing out here on the interstate, soldier?"

"I'm just trying to reach Wichita, sir. My ex-girlfriend lives there."

The windy wake of a semi truck roaring by made Sheriff Sutton realize he had to get off the highway. The longer they stood out in the open, the more chance someone would remember them talking together.

He handed back the military ID. "Okay, Russell, it seems I've got a bit of a problem here."

"Problem?"

"Did you stop at the Conoco Travel Plaza about five miles back down the highway?"

"Yeah, but only to use the restroom and fill a water bottle."

"They reported someone fitting your description shoplifting there."

"I did no such thing. It's a lie."

"Turn around and put your hands behind your back," Sheriff Sutton commanded, reaching for the handcuffs in a holster on his belt.

"What the fuck?" Russell shouted above the roar of another passing 18-wheeler. "I didn't take anything."

"Listen, soldier, do as I say and maybe we can clear this thing up." He reached up and grabbed the hitcher by the shoulder of his army jacket. "Put your arms behind your back."

Russell bent over the hood of the patrol car, and Sheriff Sutton locked the handcuffs around his wrists. "Are you arresting me?"

"Not yet." He straightened the young man up and walked him toward the rear car door. "I'm just going to take you back to the store, and if they don't identify you as the shoplifter, I'll personally drive you to the state line."

"Okay."

Sutton opened the door. "Watch your head." He eased the man into the backseat and then picked up his rucksack and placed it in his lap. "We can clear this thing up. If you're not the perpetrator, you'll be free to go."

"Can't a wounded vet get a break?"

"Not today." Sutton closed the car door.

Once behind the wheel, he shut off the lights and eased the patrol car out onto the interstate. Crossing the grassy median to reach the lanes on the other side, he headed the car back south toward Hope Springs.

"This is just great," Russell said behind the mesh grill separating the front seat from the back. "You fight for your country and how do they repay you? First they replace your blown-off knee with a steel joint and then send you out into the civilian world with a medal and a handshake. While you're in the hospital, the bitch you're supposed to marry runs off with your best friend. It's all fucked up. The shrinks say I suffer from some sort of posttraumatic stress because I choose to live homeless and sleep under bridges. Fuck them. Life is much simpler that way."

"You could be right," Sheriff Sutton replied, driving past the exit leading up the Conoco Travel Plaza.

Russell peered out the back side window. "Hey, wasn't that the travel plaza we passed back there?"

"Change of plans."

"What? Where are you taking me?"

"You'll see."

Sheriff Sutton put his foot on the gas and accelerated the patrol car down the interstate. His nostrils breathed in the smell of fear emanating from his backseat passenger. The intense hunger churned in his gut. The car sped the miles back to the turnoff exit for Highway 133. He took the off-ramp and headed down the two-lane blacktop toward Morris and Hope Springs.

"Where are we going?" Russell leaned forward, asking through the steel mesh.

"Just sit back and be quiet." Sutton cleared his throat. "Let's talk about something in the meantime. Russell, do you believe in fairy tales?"

"What the hell?"

"Answer the question."

"You mean like nursery rhymes? That kind of shit?"

"Something like that."

"No."

"Can I tell you a story? You fought for your country, so I owe you that much."

"Whatever." Russell sat back against the backseat. "If you're arresting me, you need to read me my rights."

"You have the right to listen to what I'm about to tell you." He glanced in the rear view mirror. His prisoner stared back at him with a perplexed look. "It's funny you should mention nursery rhymes, Russell. Can I call you Russ?"

"I don't give a shit."

"Russ, you know the story of Little Red Riding Hood and the big bad wolf?"

"Yeah."

"That story is actually referring to a werewolf. Do you believe in werewolves?"

"No, should I?"

"You might want to start." Sheriff Sutton chuckled. "No one knows where lycanthropy came from. Some claim it was a curse placed by the Church on some heretic. That's bullshit, Russ. Werewolves predate Christianity. The supernatural world is real, by the way. It hides in secret from the mundane world. Werewolves fall into that category. They've existed since before recorded history and are the stuff of legends and myths. During the Dark Ages, the Wolfkin, as I refer to them, hunted in packs in the mountains and forests of Europe. A plague known as the black death killed millions of people in the thirteenth century. Perhaps, you've heard of it. The sick were everywhere, and the Wolfkin grew strong in numbers culling the human herd."

"What does this have to do with me?"

"I'm getting to that." Sutton turned the car down a rutted dirt road with thick trees bordering each side. "During the black death, the Wolfkin developed an unquenchable hunger for humans, especially for the taste of their young offspring. Thus, they became the stuff of fairy tales and nursery rhymes told to children at a time when man feared the creatures of the dark. During the Church's rise to great power, religious zealots hunted the Wolfkin to near extinction and burned them at the stake along with witches during the Inquisition. To be sure, many of the victims of the burning weren't werewolves at all, but just poor souls suffering from schizophrenia and other mental disorders. The method by which the Church determined one a heretic was not always exact."

"Why are you telling me this history bullshit?"

"Humor me."

"Due to the persecution, the Wolfkin learned to keep their numbers small and live among the mundane world. They organized into Packs and hid their kills from the humans for fear that discovery would eradicate the bloodline forever. They moved from one hunting ground to the next when the human threat became too great. In other words, they adapted."

"Are you telling me there are werewolves living around here today?"

"I'm afraid so."

"This is crazy. You're whacked." Russell slammed his face against the mesh screen. Sheriff Sutton could smell his fear rising. "Where the fuck are you taking me? You haven't read me my rights or told me what I'm being charged with. I want out now!"

"Sorry."

"Fuck!" Russell threw himself hard against the backseat.

Sheriff Sutton removed his cell phone from a holster on his hip. He speed-dialed the number.

"Yes?" It was Roxie's voice on the other end.

"I'll be there in two minutes." He ended the call.

$$* \quad * \quad * \quad *$$

The place where the Pack assembled was in an old wooden hay barn located a quarter-mile behind Roxie's Roadhouse. This was their killing floor where they could feed in private. As he approached in the patrol car, Sheriff Sutton saw two large barn doors open. He drove in, leaving a cloud of dust in his wake. Shutting off the car, he surveyed the interior. Holes in the roof of the structure let in sporadic beams of the afternoon sun. Beneath a loft brimming with old hay, the rest of the Pack stood naked in the shadows. There were three: Uncle Johnny, whose portly body showed flab and wrinkles in the dim light; Roxie, whose trim figure highlighted her small but perfect breasts; and Collin, exposing a hardened lean body covered in various tribal tattoos.

Sheriff Sutton exited the patrol car as Roxie stepped forward. Her dark eyes centered hungrily upon the passenger locked in the backseat. From inside the car, Russell screamed a stream of obscenities and slammed himself against the side window.

"There's not much time," Sutton stated, unbuttoning his shirt. "I'm still on duty."

"I've got to open the bar soon," Roxie replied and nodded toward the backseat. "Your passenger is the excitable type."

"Ex-soldier. Wounded in Iraq," Sheriff Sutton replied, unhooking his gun belt and dropping his pants. He placed all items of clothing on the front hood.

"Too bad," Roxie replied, returning to join Collin and Uncle Johnny.

Once he was completely naked, Sheriff Sutton went to the rear car door and opened it.

"What kind of kinky fucking shit are you planning to do to me?" the vet screamed, letting loose a spray of spittle. "Stay away!"

"End of the road, soldier."

He reached in, grabbed Russell by his army jacket, and yanked him out of the backseat. With his hands still cuffed behind his back, Russell struggled to get free from the sheriff's grip. Sutton dragged the prisoner to the center of the barn and dropped him to the dirty floor.

"Lunch is served," he said coldly to the others.

In unison, the Pack began to shape-shift into their true bodies. They growled in pain as their bones popped and elongated. Like the others, Sheriff Sutton fell to his hands and knees. Thick hair covered his exposed flesh, and claws emerged from his feet and hands. In less than a minute, the transformation was complete.

"Fuck no-o-o-o!" Russell screamed in terror at the sight of the four huge werewolves surrounding him. He struggled to get to his feet and run. "Stay away from me!"

The Pack leaped upon their prey in a frenzy of tearing teeth and ripping claws. Blood and entrails flew into the air as the creatures ripped Russell apart. Starved by the lack of human meat, they consumed the ex-soldier whole. Claws tore flesh as fangs crunched through bone to get at the marrow inside. The Uncle Johnny creature chomped down on the titanium steel knee replacement and spat it out. The bloody steel prosthetic went rolling along the barn floor before coming to a stop.

When the feeding finished, nothing was left of Russell except shredded clothing lying on a bloody patch of ground. One by one, the Pack resumed their naked human forms now covered in slick blood. The pangs of hunger Sheriff Sutton felt earlier had receded. He could control it now. Walking over to an old water trough in the back of the barn, he washed the bits of flesh and blood from his body. The rest of the Pack joined him.

"Which one of you went roaming last night?" Sheriff Sutton splashed water into his hair.

Collin's dark gaze looked up and met his own. "It was me."

"You endangered the Pack."

"I was restless," his deep voice replied.

"You killed Elmer Grosslin's cow, and he got a photograph of you."

"No one's going to believe that crazy old coot," Collin replied.

"Is that right? Jasper Higgins believes. He's got the picture now and is talking about a werewolf in the area."

"No one will listen to that old bastard, either."

"Why did you go out last night? You were looking for something more than a cow to eat."

Collin showed an evil smile. "I went to the little girl's home."

"Little girl?"

"The daughter of our new employee." Collin's tongue licked his lips. "To eat her flesh would be so tender, so succulent."

A chill embraced Sheriff Sutton's insides. Collin spoke of Megan, the sweet little girl who had hugged his neck in front of Dottie's Diner. "You stay away from her."

Collin's eyes hardened. "Humans are our cattle, or did you forget that?"

"I said to stay away from her."

Roxie stepped forward and placed a hand against the sheriff's bare back. "Why should we? You told us Jess is from Chicago and hiding from her abusive husband. If she and her daughter went missing, no one around here would be suspicious. They would just say she went back to her husband again in Chicago."

"It's too damn risky." Sheriff Sutton walked over to the hood of his car and began putting on his uniform.

Uncle Johnny shook his head. "It doesn't make sense, Dale. We need to feed again during the Ebon Moon, which is coming in three nights. It is the way of the Clan. She and her daughter are perfect for the feast. If we're careful and cover our tracks, no one would miss them. They would think they moved to someplace else."

"I've told you many times we can't kill a child," he replied, buttoning up his shirt. "To do so will cause the humans in the area to triple their efforts to find the killer. It's too dangerous, so take her off the dinner menu."

"What are we supposed to eat?" Collin interjected. "We need better fare than dirty hitchhikers. Our kind has fed on children in the past during the Ebon Moon. The life force of a devoured child strengthens the bloodline."

"You can eat Jasper Higgins." He stuffed his shirttails into his uniform pants. "He's become too suspicious and needs to be taken care of."

"That tough old bastard …" Collin replied.

The sheriff's cell phone rang on his belt. He picked it up and flipped it open.

"Sheriff Sutton."

"Dale, this is Jess."

"Hi, Jess."

"I asked Nelda to watch Megan tonight so I can go out if the offer is still available."

"It is." He looked at the rest of the Pack putting on their clothes and watching him at the same time. "I'll meet you at the bar around eight tonight. That'll give me time to get off work and get cleaned up."

"Eight tonight. I'll see you there. Bye."

"Bye." Sheriff Sutton closed the phone and said to the others, "Jess is meeting me tonight at the bar."

Roxie slid her tight shirt over her round breasts. "Maybe that's the reason you're protecting Jess and her daughter. You got more than a passing interest in the two."

"I'm just maintaining my cover as a small-town sheriff. Nothing more."

"If you say so."

Sheriff Sutton buckled on his gun belt. "Everyone listen. No one is to harm Jess or her daughter. After the bar closes tonight, we will have another meeting to discuss ways to handle the Jasper Higgins situation. Do you understand?"

The Pack nodded in agreement.

"Good." Sheriff Sutton climbed back into the patrol car and began the drive back to Hope Springs.

CHAPTER SEVENTEEN

Sitting at his computer desk with Marilyn Manson screaming in his iPod earphones, Sid Granger rolled another joint in preparation to go online to his favorite porn site. He thought he was alone in the garage apartment connected to his grandmother's house until a hand patted him on the shoulder. He jumped, sending the bag of weed spilling to the floor. Yanking the earphones out, he spun around expecting to see his grandma but blinked in disbelief when he discovered Terry Newman and the crazy old sign maker standing behind him.

"Dude, you scared the holy shit out of me!" he said to Terry.

"We knocked, but no one answered."

Sid stared at the old man as if he were a ghost standing there. He grabbed Terry by the front of his shirt to pull him close.

"What the hell is that old fart doing in my room?" he whispered.

"Mr. Higgins wants to talk to you."

"Is he pissed about yesterday?"

"No." Terry shook his head adding, "Oh, by the way, you forgot to pick me up, you asswipe."

"Sorry, man," Sid replied. "Why did you let that crazy murderer into my house? Not cool."

"Just hear what he has to say."

Mr. Higgins bent down and picked up a DVD from the shelf by the bed. "Is this the movie you spoke of yesterday? *The Howling?*"

Sid stood and crossed the room. Taking Mr. Higgins by the elbow, he said, "Sorry, but my grandma doesn't allow me to have visitors, especially those who fall under the creepy-old-man category. You'll have to leave."

Mr. Higgins ignored him and turned the DVD case over. "This is the one with the werewolves in it?"

"Man, we were just bullshitting you yesterday about werewolves. They're not real." He took the movie case from the old man's hands. "Now, I have to clean my room, so you'll have to go."

"Show him the photo, Mr. Higgins," Terry said.

"What photo?" Sid asked.

From a pocket in his overalls, Mr. Higgins pulled out a photograph and handed it to Sid. "Does this look like a werewolf to you?"

Sid looked down at the picture. The grainy photo showed something dark looming over the body of a dead cow. He studied the shadowy shape caught in the flash. The hair on the back of his neck rose. The creature did look exactly like the way he imagined a werewolf.

"Who took the picture?" he asked.

"Elmer Grosslin on his farm last night," Mr. Higgins replied. "The thing killed his cow."

"I heard of this Elmer guy. He's fucked up." Sid returned to his computer desk and switched on a lamp. He leaned into the light to take a closer look. "What makes you think this picture is real and not a hoax?"

"Elmer's so poor he hasn't got a pot to piss in." Mr. Higgins joined Sid and Terry at the computer desk. "Nor does he have the money or the smarts to pull off an elaborate hoax. He thinks he took a picture of Bigfoot."

"Is it Bigfoot, Sid?" Terry leaned in close to study the picture.

"No." Sid turned to the keyboard of his computer and typed in a few search tags. A picture of a hairy bipedal creature came up on the screen. Taken in broad daylight, the image showed a creature looking back at the cameraman. "This is the most famous picture of Bigfoot ever taken. Some guy named Patterson took it back in the sixties. As you can see, Bigfoot is a big, hairy, apelike creature. The monster in your photograph has canine features and fangs."

"So it's a werewolf," Mr. Higgins stated.

"You wish." Sid studied the photo up close. "It's a guy in a fucking suit. Probably running around trying to convince everyone there's a werewolf loose. Both of you are dumbasses for falling for it."

"The thing in that picture killed my wife," Mr. Higgins said in a weary voice while sitting on the corner of Sid's bed. "It's my only proof it wasn't me."

"If that's the case, let me scan the picture into my computer. Keep it on file. That way we will always have it saved." Sid put the photograph in his scanner.

"Go to the sheriff, Mr. Higgins," Terry said. "Show him the picture."

"He'd never believe me."

"Bad idea, anyway," Sid stated, handing the photograph back to Mr.

Higgins. "Sheriff Dickhead stopped me one night when I was returning from OKC. He just hit the lights and came out of nowhere. He pulled me over and searched the truck for pot. Luckily, I smoked it all at the ICP concert, so he didn't find any. He scared the hell out of me, though. We were out on a country road in the middle of the night. The guy had a weird look in his eyes. I swear he was smoking something, himself. The sheriff's a real prick. I'd go over his head and call the highway patrol."

"Do you think they'll believe me?"

"No, so you're just basically fucked."

"Unless I can find and kill the creature myself."

Sid chuckled. "Not as easy as it sounds. Let's suppose what you're up against is a real werewolf. Do you even know how to kill it?"

Mr. Higgins shook his head. "That's the reason I came to you."

Sid smiled and leaned back in his chair. "Well, I'm no expert or anything. I just know what I've seen in the movies." He put his hands behind his head and pondered for a moment. "You can't shoot or stab a werewolf with conventional weapons. If you do that they'll heal just like Wolverine does. I even saw a movie where the fucking thing was blown to bits and formed back together just like liquid metal. Is any of this making sense to you?"

Mr. Higgins shook his head no.

"Okay, let me try again. Only a weapon made of silver hurts a werewolf. Things like silver bullets, knives, swords, etc. In one movie Lon Chaney Jr. killed one with the silver end of a cane."

"Silver weapons kill a werewolf. I got that."

"There's another way to kill one. That's by fire. It kills both werewolves and vampires."

"So they don't come back after being burned?" Terry asked.

"Hell no. Fire is the great equalizer when it comes to supernatural creatures. Except, of course, if you're a demon and fire doesn't hurt you."

"Let's not get off subject and stick with werewolves for the moment," Mr. Higgins said and asked, "How do I find it?"

"You see that's the fucking beauty of this monster. Most of the time a werewolf remains in human form. You can't tell who it is. It could be anybody. They're not like vampires who can't run around during the day."

Terry pulled up a chair and sat next to Sid. "Do they only come out on a full moon?"

"Some do, some don't. Some can shape-shift at will, day or night."

"I saw the monster last night and there was no full moon," Mr. Higgins said. "By the way, I shot the damn thing in the shoulder with my .38."

"Did you use silver bullets?" Sid asked.

"No."

"It healed just like that." Sid snapped his fingers.

"Why would a loving God put such an abomination on the earth?"

"You'll have to take that up with him. As for me, I think it's kind of cool. Supernatural monsters running around in the dark makes the world a lot more interesting. Changes everything we believe in."

"So you believe in the monster now?" Terry asked.

"Fuck no, but I'm having fun watching you two dweebs falling for it."

"Terry, you mentioned a full moon. I checked the *Farmer's Almanac* earlier. There's a full moon starting tomorrow night. Oh, and another thing, on Sunday night we are going to have a total lunar eclipse," Mr. Higgins said.

"We talked about the upcoming lunar eclipse in science class today," Terry replied.

"I wonder if it means something," Mr. Higgins said, turning to Sid.

"I don't have a fucking clue." He shrugged.

"Is there anything else I need to know?" Mr. Higgins asked.

"There is one other thing. If a person is ever bitten by a werewolf and lives, he will become a werewolf himself. There's something about a werewolf's bite … it's like a virus or something. Those who are bitten can become one."

"That's an important fact."

"That's about all I know about the shit," Sid stated.

Mr. Higgins let out a weary sigh. "Tomorrow I'll make a decision on what to do next. I'm too tired tonight. I've been up for the last twenty-four hours straight." He started walking toward the door. "Thanks for all your help, Sid."

"Good luck with the hunt, old man."

"Are you coming with me, Terry?" Mr. Higgins asked before he opened the door.

"Nah, I'll let Sid take me home."

"Very well. Good-bye, boys." He closed the door.

"Mr. Higgins," Terry called after him.

The door reopened and the old man stuck his head back in the room. "Yes?"

"I still believe you."

"Thank you, son."

He closed the door and was gone.

"That guy's psycho," Sid commented as he returned to sit at his computer.

"Mr. Higgins is a good man," Terry replied.

"He's apeshit crazy if he thinks anyone is going to buy that werewolf bullshit about killing his wife." Sid returned to rolling his joint. Once done, he lit the end and took a long drag. "Are you still going to do it?"

"Do what?"

Sid exhaled a cloud of white smoke. "Ask Becky Warren to the homecoming dance."

"Yes."

Sid sputtered in the middle of another inhale on the joint. "You're nuts, dude. Brandon Harrison is going to kick your ass."

"I don't care. I love her."

"To me she's a stuck-up cock tease, but if you love her, that's cool." Sid handed the joint over. "Hit on this and you'll feel better."

Terry shook his head. "No, man, that crap makes it hard for me to concentrate on my homework."

"Isn't the homecoming dance tomorrow night?"

"Yes."

"When do you plan on asking Becky?"

"In the morning." Terry pulled out his Algebra textbook from his backpack. "If she says yes, are you still going to loan me your truck so I can take her out?"

Sid laughed, spraying out a cloud of the pungent smoke. "If she says yes, I'll give you the fucking keys, title, and all."

"She likes me, I know she does."

Sid took another puff of weed. "You're crazier than that old man who thinks werewolves are real."

CHAPTER EIGHTEEN

Blake Lobato walked up the driveway toward the two-story brick home packed in a line of similar town houses. He had crossed Chicago on foot since torching his house earlier in the day. Desperate to score some blow and find some wheels to get out of the city, the brick home before him could supply both.

He glanced up and down the quiet street. The neighborhood consisted of sidewalks and neatly edged lawns under the shadow of large shade trees. Some of the leaves had changed color signaling the approaching autumn. A cold front moving in from the north threatened the blue skies with increasing gray clouds.

When he reached the top of the drive, he peered through the windows set in the garage door. Parked inside was a Harley Night Train motorcycle. *Good,* he thought to himself. *The fucking dyke is home.*

Monique Sanders was her real name. Passion was just her stage name. She stripped in the same club as Jess and dealt drugs to the other dancers on the side. A raging lesbian, Passion rode to work on a new Harley with her current girlfriend sitting on the back. He had scored some coke off her a couple of times while waiting for his wife after the club closed. He secretly followed the stripper home one night in case he needed to bust her in the future. It was ironic that a small-time dealer like Passion lived in such a nice suburban neighborhood. Obviously, dealing drugs and stripping had paid off.

Blake slid on some leather gloves from the pocket of his duster. Next he pulled the aluminum baseball bat out of its makeshift holster and hid it up a sleeve. He could hold it there if he kept his arm straight. He walked up the steps to the front door and rang the doorbell. While waiting for someone to answer, he scanned the neighborhood once more from the porch. Everything was quiet. School had just gotten out, and a bus stopped down the street to unload students.

The front door unlocked and swung open. Passion stood there, a lithe, muscular African American girl with large expressive eyes and dark brown nipples showing clearly through the fabric of her white tank top. She unlatched the storm door and swung it open a foot.

"What the fuck do you want?" she hissed in a low breath.

"Can I come in? I need to score some blow," Blake answered, shifting the weight of the bat in his jacket sleeve.

"Fuck no. I don't deal from my front porch, and I sure as fuck don't deal to a narc. Get the fuck out of here," she said, starting to close the storm door.

"Come on, can't we just be friends?" Blake grabbed the door from her hands and swung it open. He charged inside the house while shoving the surprised girl. She staggered back a few steps as he slammed shut the door and locked the dead bolt. In a sudden move, Passion grabbed a piece of iron pipe from a table next to her.

"What you going do now, motherfucker? The last man that laid hands on me I beat his ass with this." She brandished the foot-long piece of pipe in front of her. "What do you say now, bitch?"

"My dick's bigger."

Blake dropped the aluminum bat out of his sleeve straight down into the palm of his hand. He swung, hitting the girl's right collarbone with a resounding thud. Bones snapped and the pipe clattered to the hardwood floor.

"Fuck!" she screamed in pain, holding her hurt arm.

Blake stepped forward and thrust the bat hard into Passion's solar plexus, knocking the wind out of her. He didn't want to use the bat on her face. Not yet. He needed her to be able to talk. Bending over double, she tried to catch her breath. He grabbed her up by the tank top and dropped her into a wooden chair with a resounding thump. The stripper's breath came in short gasps as he yanked a length of curtain cord from a window.

"Passion, are you still with me? Don't pass out," he said, winding the cord around the girl's wrists and tying them to the chair handles with the cord. "You got to stay with me, girl." He continued binding both her ankles to the front chair legs. "There, we can talk better now."

"Fuck you," she replied in a gasping voice.

"That's the spirit. Hang in there, girl."

He grabbed the back of the chair and dragged it into the middle of the front room. The chair's legs cut deep scuff marks into the perfect hardwood floors. He returned to the foyer and picked up the bat.

"You know that good cop/bad cop routine they pull in all those stupid police shows on TV?" He tapped the bat against his palm and stepped in front of the girl. "Well, guess what—you get only the bad cop today."

She looked up at him. "What do you want?"

"Tell me where your stash is."

"I don't got a stash."

"Wrong answer."

He swung the bat hard against the girl's left shin. The bone cracked like dried wood beneath the blow, leaving splintered pieces of bone jutting out of her brown flesh. She let out another terrible howl of pain.

"It hurts, doesn't it?" Blake leaned in close to the girl's sweating face. "I know, because my wife used the same bat against the side of my head. See the bandages where the bitch hit me?"

"Jess should've killed your punk ass," Passion replied in a barely audible voice.

"You still got one shin left, you ugly dyke." He placed the bat against Passion's right shin. "You want to dance again, or not? Tell me where your stash is."

"Please, don't."

"Wrong answer." He pulled the bat in preparation for another swing.

"I'll tell you … I'll tell you. Under the kitchen sink … the garbage disposal is fake … the shit's in there."

"See, that wasn't so bad." He patted the side of her face. "Now don't pass out on me. I may want to play some more."

Taking the bat with him, Blake rushed from the living room into the small kitchen. He had to hurry. At any moment, Passion's girlfriend could show up. Stopping before the double sink, he located the switch to the disposal and flicked it. Nothing happened. Reaching into the drain hole, he felt around with his fingers finding nothing. He decided to check the engine housing under the sink. Opening the cabinet doors, he removed several bottles of cleaner to study the unit. *Some of these dealers are real smart in hiding their stashes,* he thought to himself. *I doubt Passion's one of them.*

He reached up and pushed against the iron casing of the disposal engine. The unit shifted. He twisted again and it dropped. Inside, he found two plastic bags of pure coke. Removing the stash, he also discovered two wads of bills wrapped in plastic in the bottom of the hollow engine housing. Blake thumbed through the cash and guessed the amount at about fifteen thousand. Things were starting to turn for the better.

He popped open a coke bag and snorted a line. The blow burned in his nose and coursed through his body. He stuffed both drug bags and money in the pockets of his duster knowing time was running out and he needed to leave. Picking up the bat, he returned to the front room.

"You still with me, baby?" he asked. The girl's head hung limp to the side with eyes closed. Blood ran from the compound break of her shin. "Damn, girl, I thought you were tougher than this." He felt for a pulse to see if she had died of shock. She was still alive. "I told you I was coming back to play some more."

He walked back into the kitchen and retrieved a bottle of ammonia cleaner he saw under the sink. Returning to the bound girl, he passed the open bottle under her nose. She quickly regained consciousness.

"Don't hurt me anymore," she said in a weak voice.

"I got your stash, girl. The coke is primo, by the way. You always had good shit," Blake replied, gripped the girl by the chin, and turned her face up to look at his. "Now tell me where I can find the keys to your bike and I'm out of here."

"Not the bike," she pleaded with tears running down her face. "Don't take my baby."

He looked down at her broken leg. "I don't think you're going to be riding for a while."

"If I give you the keys, you'll leave?" she asked and coughed.

"I promise."

"On the hook by the door leading to the garage."

He released her chin and stepped back.

"One last thing before I go. I need a little batting practice for when I run into my bitch wife again." He pulled back the bat as if preparing to swing a home run. "Batter up!"

"Motherfuck—"

The bat hit the girl on the side of the head with a loud thud. The impact sent a jolting vibration up his hands and arms. He swung again and again until nothing was recognizable of what was once Passion's skull and face. He stepped back for a second to admire his handiwork.

"A preview of what's going to happen to you, Jess," he said aloud to the corpse in the room.

It was time to get out of the house before someone discovered the murder. He needed distance from the crime. Finding the bathroom, he turned on the sink and washed the blood, bone, and brain matter from the aluminum bat. Next, he did the same from his face and the front of his duster. He was leaving behind a very messy murder and knew he didn't clean up all the evidence. So be it. By the time the Chicago homicide detectives started to piece everything together, he would be long gone and in Oklahoma.

He slid the bat back into the hole in the lining of his duster and grabbed the Harley keys hanging by the door leading into the garage. Descending the steps to the garage floor, he studied the Harley Night Train. The brand new bike had a black paint job and shiny chrome, making it an evil-looking ride. No wonder Passion loved it so much.

Blake slid his leg over the saddle seat and turned on the ignition. He rose up and kicked down on the start pedal. The metallic monster rumbled into life with a low throb of the idling engine. A thrill went through his body as he applied the throttle. The pipes roared from the power of the 96 V-Twin. Dismounting, Blake yanked up the garage door, letting in the light of day, and returned to the idling bike. He climbed back on and noticed a leather sunglass case attached to the center of the handle bars. He removed a pair of men's Oakley sunglasses as black as the paint on the bike.

After sliding on the dark glasses and checking his look in the mirror, he let out a low whistle. The shades fit perfectly and became the crowning touch to his new look. He was Blake Lobato no more. Completely garbed in black with shades and bike to match, he had become a dark Angel of Death. He reached into his pocket, pulled out the bag of coke, and snorted another line. His new ride idled between his legs with the low-throated rumble of a monstrous creature.

A long road to Oklahoma stretched before him, and the police would put out an APB for his arrest soon. He didn't care. They wouldn't stop him. He was on a one-way ride to Hell knowing in his soul he would see Jess one more time before he went down in flames.

"The Angel of Death is coming for you, baby," he said to no one but himself.

Popping the clutch, the bike roared out of the garage and onto the streets that would eventually lead to Oklahoma.

CHAPTER NINETEEN

Jessica took a deep calming breath of the cool evening air. Nervousness fluttered in her stomach from the anticipation of meeting Dale Sutton again. This time he would be off duty, and she didn't have Megan. Though she disliked leaving her daughter behind, she felt good about her in Nelda's care. Megan didn't seem to mind, either. She just smiled when Mommy left and returned to coloring in her Bible coloring book.

Leaving the Camaro, Jessica crossed the gravel parking lot toward the front door of Roxie's Roadhouse. Several cars and trucks already lined the parking lot, and the sounds of muted music came from inside. Jessica checked her watch: 8:38. The party starts early at Roxie's, she realized. As always, she was running late. Like a nervous schoolgirl, she couldn't decide on what to wear since most her clothes were left in Chicago. Nelda came to the rescue, providing a nice retro-looking blouse to go with her Levi's denims. Not too tight or low-cut, it still highlighted her figure in all the right places.

"Never show too much the first time," Nelda commented after Jessica tried the top on. "Always leave them wanting more."

Before entering the front door, she checked her blonde hair tied back into a loose ponytail. Another life was opening up for her in Oklahoma, one very different from the nightmare of her marriage. She wanted desperately to put the terrible memories of Blake behind her, to start anew and discard the years of physical abuse, like a shabby old coat. She opened the door and stepped through.

The noise was the first thing to hit her. Though the bar was not full and some tables were empty, the patrons made enough noise for a crowd twice its size. Amidst the smoky lights of the small karaoke stage, a pretty middle-aged brunette woman held a microphone and sang Patsy Cline over the sounds of customers talking among themselves. Jessica glanced over to the bar. Collin worked behind the counter popping the lids off beer bottles. He looked up with his dark piercing eyes in her direction. She attempted a weak smile and wave. His only response was a slight nod before going back to serving up the beer.

"Oh, hey, there you are, Jess," Roxie called out, pushing her way expertly around the customers and tables while holding a serving tray in one hand. "The sheriff's been waiting for you."

"I know," Jessica replied back. "I'm late."

"He's over at the corner table with Uncle Johnny." She nodded in the direction. "Do you see him?"

"Yes."

Roxie brushed past her and went to the bar to pick up more beer bottles. Dressed in a black tank top and blue jean shorts so tight they appeared painted on, the dark-haired beauty had dollar bills jutting out of every pocket. Roxie had the look that, at any moment, she would be up dancing on the bar like one of those Coyote Ugly girls.

Jessica made her way to the table where Dale sat across from Uncle Johnny. The two men were talking intently about something as she approached.

"Can a girl find a seat in this place?" she asked above the singing coming through the speakers situated throughout the bar.

Both men looked up surprised. Uncle Johnny's eyes sparkled with approval while Dale flashed his white smile.

"Sure can," Uncle Johnny replied. "Especially one as pretty as you."

"Hey, you old wolf, she's my date," Sheriff Sutton responded, standing up to pull a chair out for her.

Jessica settled into the seat. "I'm sorry I'm late."

"No problem." he replied. "The karaoke is just getting started."

For the first time, Jessica noticed the woman on the stage was finishing a great version of Pasty Cline's "Crazy."

"She's pretty good," she commented as sporadic applause sounded throughout the bar.

"That's Pearl singing. She won a few karaoke contests in Oklahoma City and Tulsa. She's also running the machine tonight. If you want to sing something, you tell her."

Uncle Johnny pushed a large binder across the table in her direction. "The song lists are in here."

"Oh no, I'm not singing. Just going to drink a couple of beers and relax."

As if on cue, Roxie came over to the table. To Jessica's surprise, she held a pot of coffee and refilled cups in front of Sheriff Sutton and Uncle Johnny.

"What are you drinking, Jess? It's on the house for you," Roxie said.

"Budweiser in a bottle will do."

"Bud, it is then."

Roxie retreated from the table toward the bar.

"No alcohol for you guys tonight?" Jessica asked.

"Not on any night," he replied. "It wouldn't look good if the town's sheriff drove home after having a few. As for Uncle Johnny, he's on the wagon again."

"Cheers." Uncle Johnny raised his cup and winked at her.

"I feel bad about drinking in front of you two."

"Don't." He placed his hand over hers. "You look really pretty tonight, Jess."

"Thanks." She gave his hand a light squeeze. "You look pretty good yourself, cowboy."

From the stage, Pearl announced to the audience the next singer would be Uncle Johnny.

"What song are you butchering now?" Sheriff Sutton asked as the older man left his chair.

"'Hotel California,'" Uncle Johnny replied and left the table for the stage.

Sheriff Sutton grimaced and said to Jessica, "This is going to suck. We went from the best to the worst singer in the house."

"Is he that bad?" she asked above Joe Walsh's long opening guitar intro while Uncle Johnny took the mic.

"I always tell him if you get near the melody, grab hold."

Jessica laughed. Uncle Johnny started to sing, and she knew instantly what Sheriff Sutton meant. The poor man was tone-deaf, but he pushed on fearlessly off-key through the song. What notes he couldn't hit, he made up for with raw determination.

Halfway through the painful rendition of the Eagles' classic, Roxie came over and put down a cold bottle of Bud on the table and noticed the sheriff holding her hand.

"There you go, Jess."

"Thanks, Rox."

Before she left, Roxie's eyes met the sheriff's for a second. An instinctual female alert went off inside Jessica. There was a connection between them. The two may have been lovers in the past, she decided. *Are they still? How many others has he had?* She probably didn't want to know. Taking a draw from the longneck, she let the cold liquid wash down her throat. She never was a beer drinker. While stripping in Chicago, she downed mixed drinks to loosen her up before she went onstage to undress in front of strangers. Somehow, the cold beer and the karaoke went together.

"Good stuff," she said after taking another sip.

"I hope you weren't talking about Uncle Johnny's singing."

"No." She laughed. "Just the beer."

Mercifully, the song ended and Uncle Johnny returned to his chair. "How did you like it?" he asked Jessica.

"The Eagles are hard vocals. You sang it from the heart."

"Oh God, don't encourage him," Sheriff Sutton whispered in her ear.

Uncle Johnny smiled. "I like this girl."

Jessica leaned back in her chair and studied the rest of the bar. The customers consisted mostly of the type of men she had come to see during her few days in small-town Oklahoma. The collective fashion sense in this part of the country consisted of worn shirts, cowboy boots, and faded blue jeans with tobacco can rings on their back pockets. The most common form of headgear was the sweat-stained baseball cap, most with OU or OSU logos, since the college football season was under way. Women came in all shapes and sizes, most in blue jeans and wearing various tops ranging from those that showed half their bellies to men's plaid shirts with pearl-snap buttons. Gone was the urban street ghetto look young people tried to emulate in Chicago. No flashy bling and caps turned the wrong way.

Sheriff Sutton squeezed her hand. "Hey, are you still with me?"

She turned and smiled. "I was just getting a feel for the place. I'll be waiting tables here tomorrow night."

"What do you think of Oklahoma so far?"

"It's very different from Chicago."

"You haven't experienced Oklahoma until you've danced the two-step." He stood and pulled her up from her chair.

"Oh no, I'm afraid I don't know how," she stammered in protest.

"You will now."

He swept her on the dance floor in front of the karaoke stage while a young man sang a George Strait song about his exes being in Texas. He held her close, pressing her body against his.

"Just follow my movements," he said, beginning the dance.

"I'll do my best."

She joined in the step. He was an excellent dancer, and in moments she was in tune with him and the music. For her, dancing up to this point entailed using a pole or cavorting on the stage floor like a slut. It never involved moving in unison with another male. Sheriff Sutton spun her left and then right before bringing her up close again to his chest. His scent filled her nostrils, and the blood rushed to her head. The mix of beer, smoky lights, and his overpowering male scent made dancing almost like having sex. She fought back the urge to kiss him on the floor in front of everyone in the bar.

The song ended.

"How did you like it?" he asked, looking down into her eyes.

"I'll let you know when I catch my breath."

He laughed and released her from his arms.

"Excuse me, everyone," Roxie's voice boomed over the speakers. She was on stage holding the karaoke mic. "I have a special announcement, so listen up. We have a beautiful new girl starting tomorrow night. I want everyone to give Jess a warm Roxie's Roadhouse welcome."

The crowd cheered and clapped, and a few even whistled. Jessica waved and smiled. She returned to her chair next to the sheriff. This time he put his arm around her shoulders, pulling her closer.

"I think they like you," he said.

"I hope so."

The rest of the night progressed in a blur of dancing, country music, and Sheriff Sutton's subtle flirting. She drank too much beer and staggered a bit when she walked from the dance floor. After midnight, Roxie came to the table and poured her a cup of coffee. Jessica looked up, perplexed.

"Sheriff's orders," Roxie said with a smile.

By the last song, she had drunk coffee until she was sober again. The bar began to clear out in a slow progression. The sheriff had not kissed her yet. She had the impression he was waiting for the right moment.

"I'll walk you to your car," he said, taking her hand. "Are you okay to drive?"

"I've drunk enough coffee to float a battleship," she replied.

He laughed and guided her to the door.

"Tomorrow night, Jess," Roxie called out. She was behind the bar figuring tabs. Jessica realized she hadn't seen Collin in a while.

"I'll be here."

In the next moment she was out the door in the cool night air. Sheriff Sutton had his arm around her waist as they walked to the Camaro.

"Hold me close, I'm cold," she said, leaning against him.

"Not a problem." His strong arms wrapped around her waist, and she snuggled her face into his shirt. She breathed in the smell of him.

"Did you have fun tonight, Jess?"

"I really did."

"That's good."

"Dale, can I ask you a few questions? I mean, I know so little about you."

"What do you want to know?"

"How come a good-looking lawman who is polite and can dance is not married? I mean, you have never been tied down by a woman?"

"Let's make a deal. I won't ask about your past if you don't ask about mine. Is it a deal?"

"Deal."

He kissed her. She absorbed his mouth's embrace hungrily with her own. The intensity increased, and she pulled him in closer by grabbing the hair at the back of his head. Their mouths opened and tongues found each other. The deep kiss continued until he finally pulled away.

"I better stop," he breathed huskily against her mouth. "We keep this up and I won't be able to."

"Okay." She pulled away and looked up. His eyes seemed to have changed color and were much darker. It might have been a trick of the moonlight shining through the clouds, she decided. "I better get home, anyway. I told Nelda I wouldn't be out this late."

He released his hold around her waist. "You'll be here tomorrow night, so I'll come by and check on you."

Jessica nodded and brushed a loose strand of blonde hair back from her face. What had started with so much passion had ended in something awkward. As a stripper, she had gotten good at reading men, but she couldn't decipher Sheriff Dale Sutton. Some invisible wall stretched between them, something she hadn't learned yet. Was it because she was still married? She didn't think so. She was about as far removed from being married as a woman could get. She hated her husband and almost killed him. No, it was something else—Roxie, perhaps, or some other woman from his past.

She turned and put her key in to unlock the Camaro's driver door.

"See you tomorrow, Jess," he said, walking away into the night.

"Bye," she called out to his back.

She settled into the driver's seat and slammed the door. *What the hell just happened?* Reaching under the seat, she unconsciously felt for the .357 magnum pistol. Since Nelda decided to watch Megan in the trailer until she got home, Jessica snuck the pistol out in her purse so her daughter would not find it by accident under the bed mattress. Jessica's fingers touched the cold steel of the gun.

Relieved, she settled back against the driver's seat. She licked her lips, still wet from the sheriff's kiss. She tasted something else. *Blood?* Turning on the interior dome light, she examined her tongue in the rearview mirror. A raw red scratch was on the tip.

Did he bite me during the kiss? I don't think so. I must have scratched it against a sharp tooth. The kiss was more intense than I realized.

She started the Camaro and drove back toward the trailer.

CHAPTER TWENTY

Collin stepped out the back door of the roadhouse while lighting a cigarette. All night he had watched Jess and the sheriff together at the corner table. *If the mother was here,* he asked himself, *where was her daughter?* He turned his gaze toward the Olson farm, which lay miles away. Even though he shared in the feeding of the hitchhiker earlier in the day, his interest in the little girl had not waned. The beast inside twisted at the thought of devouring the human child. So much time had passed since he had tasted such flesh.

The moon peaked from behind a dark cloud, bringing a strong longing for home in British Columbia. There the Clan had survived hidden from the eyes of the world. History and the Inquisition had taught the Wolfkin a hard lesson. They needed to camouflage their existence from humankind. Toward the end of the nineteenth century, the enclave transplanted itself from the forests of Europe to a remote corner of the Canadian wilderness. For over a hundred years, they lived in harmony with the wolves and the surrounding forest. In secret stock pens, they bred and raised humans like cattle. No longer forced to hunt for human flesh, the Clan thrived. They substituted their diet with the raw meat of elk, moose, and cows, choosing only to partake of human flesh when the hunger demanded. In time, the twentieth century encroached upon the enclave. Increasing numbers of loggers and hunters threatened the Clan's borders. The wolf became endangered and scarce. The elders of the Clan decided that, for the Wolfkin to survive, they needed to blend in with human civilization or risk extinction. The Clan devoured the last of the livestock and broke up into smaller units known as Packs. Agreeing to meet in their tribal home every ten years during winter solstice, they scattered.

The back door of the roadhouse opened, bringing Collin's thoughts back to the present. He smelled his sister on the night breeze. Stamping out his cigarette, he turned as she rushed to his arms and planted a kiss upon his lips. Their bond went much stronger and deeper than that of siblings or lovers. They were Pure Born, descendants from true Wolfkin parents. Lycanthropy had been theirs since birth.

"The bar is empty," Roxie stated, looking deep into her brother's eyes. "What are you doing out here in the dark, my love?"

"Missing home."

"I do, too. You know what I miss most? The tall trees of the great forest." She placed her head against his chest. "There aren't enough trees here in Oklahoma."

"I sometimes wonder what we're doing here." He rubbed his hands across her back. "I hate pandering to these human fools. They should learn they're nothing but food on our plate."

"It is dangerous to entertain such thoughts, my brother. We are superior, yes, but our weaknesses are easily exploited. Our best chance of survival is to stay hidden among them."

"In the midst of plenty we should starve to death?"

"We fed today. Dale says we may do so again during the Feast of the Ebon Moon."

"What will he provide for such a feast? A drunken old man or an illegal Mexican? I want more succulent flesh during the Ebon Moon. The devouring of a child has been our tradition for many centuries. He is only one of the Bitten and not a Pure Born like we are. He does not fully understand us."

"Dale has taught us the ways of the humans so we may hide among them. Without him we would have been lost, or have you forgotten?"

Collin turned his back to look once again at the light of the moon. "I think it is all for nothing. We are a dying breed. I no longer feel the other Wolfkin Packs in my blood, sister. Do you sense them?"

"They are silent to me, as well. We will know their number at the next gathering in seven years." Roxie placed her arms around his waist. "Come back inside, my brother. Dale has called a meeting of the Pack. Let's hear what he has to say."

She took Collin by the hand and led him back into the roadhouse. With the lights turned down low and the jukebox shut off, the quiet of the place seemed haunted after a night of raucous noise. Uncle Johnny sat at the corner of the bar drinking coffee while Sheriff Sutton closed the window shades to hide the meeting from the outside world. Both men turned as Roxie and Collin entered.

"We're here," Roxie announced.

"Good," Sheriff Sutton replied, stepping away from the window. "We need to discuss what to do with this Jasper Higgins situation."

"Refresh my memory," Uncle Johnny replied. "You said Elmer

Grosslin took a picture of Collin killing his cow last night. Where's the picture now?"

"Jasper Higgins has it and suspects it's a werewolf." Sheriff Sutton walked over and took a place at the bar. "Don't worry about Elmer Grosslin, though. I took care of him."

"You did?" Roxie asked.

Sheriff Sutton chuckled. "Let's just say he committed suicide over the loss of his beautiful cow."

"So all we have to do is worry about Jasper," Collin said. "It shouldn't be a problem. Everyone suspects he's crazy and guilty of murder. No one's going to believe him."

"I wouldn't be so sure. The photograph is evidence of something going on. He might be able to convince others."

"So what do you propose to do about it?" Uncle Johnny asked.

"I haven't received a call from anyone discovering Elmer's body yet. Early in the morning, Johnny, I want you to go to the farm and clean up the crime scene. Dump Elmer's body someplace where it won't be found. I suspect Jasper Higgins will show up tomorrow at the Grosslin property to return the picture. I want you to sit and wait for him. There's an abandoned oil site right across the road. Hide your truck there until Jasper shows up."

"And what do I do if he does show up?" Uncle Johnny asked.

"Eat him. I'm tired of dealing with the old man."

"He's armed with a pistol, so be careful," Collin said. "He shot me in the shoulder last night."

"He's as good as dead," Uncle Johnny replied.

"Fair enough," Sheriff Sutton stated.

Collin cleared his throat. "What is your plan for the Feast of the Ebon Moon? I think we need more succulent flesh than dirty hitchhikers and some old drunk."

"Who do you propose?" he asked giving him a stern look.

"Jess and her daughter, Megan, would make a fitting sacrifice in honor of our ancestors."

"I told you they are not to be harmed," Sheriff Sutton said, walking toward the door of the bar. "I've had my last say in the matter."

FRIDAY

CHAPTER TWENTY-ONE

The mornings were the worst.

Jasper Higgins awoke to the same empty house every dawn since Emma's death. Yesterday, after his meeting with Terry Newman and Sid Granger, he returned home to collapse on the bed without bothering to change out of his clothes. He slept hard until the first light of dawn glowed through the windows.

He sat up and put his feet down on the cold wood floor. A northern front had blown in sometime during the night and the frigid wind rattled the window screens. The weather change had also fired up his arthritis again. Grasping the bed post, he eased himself off the mattress and stood on painful legs. A flutter shook his weak heart between beats. He knew it was just a matter of time before the big one would end it for good.

God, at least, had granted him one more day.

After turning on the heat in the house, he sat at the kitchen table with a pot of coffee brewing on the stove. He stared at the items he brought in from the truck the night before. The .38 pistol resting atop the family Bible reminded him how he wanted to end his life two nights ago. The Lord had intervened by giving him another glimpse of the unholy creature responsible for Emma's death.

Anger as cold as the morning chilled him inside. The sudden feeling of rage surprised him. Why did God allow his wife's murder? He had been a good man and a devout Christian his whole life. Emma was the most loving and gentle woman one would ever meet, yet she died a horrible death in the jaws of a beast of the Devil. He picked up the pistol and placed it aside. Tears formed in his bleary eyes as his hand ran over the chapped cover of the Bible. In the past, he would have gained comfort from reading the scriptures before the start of each day, but this morning no such peace was available.

"Why did you do this to my Emma, Lord?" Jasper asked in a hoarse voice to the empty room. "I'm old and my body is failing. I needed her in my last days, and yet evil took her away. I can't imagine the terror she suffered at the hands of that monster. It's not fair. She didn't deserve that."

He broke down and cried with his head bowed. He had never known such weight upon his soul.

The coffee began to percolate in the pot. Jasper wiped away his tears and opened a cabinet door. A forgotten half-empty bottle of Jack Daniel's waited amidst the coffee cups. Taking the bottle, he returned to his seat at the table and twisted off the top.

"Give me a sign, Lord. What is it you want me to do?" For the first time in his life, his connection with God slipped away from his heart. Not only had he lost his most beloved Emma, he started losing his faith. A loving and caring God would not have had Emma suffer such a horrible fate at the hands of a monster. He knew such thoughts were blasphemous, but he couldn't change his feelings. "Show me a sign or I'll climb into this bottle and never climb out. I'll drink the pain away until my last day. This I vow to you."

His only answer was the hiss of the burner and the percolating coffee.

"To hell with you then!" he shouted, sweeping the pistol and Bible from the table. The items clattered to the floor.

Tipping up the bottle to take a long swig, he stopped when the whiskey touched his lips. His gaze centered on the items he had thrown to the floor. The Bible lay spilled open amidst a scattering of photographs. The pistol rested across two pictures—the grip upon a black-and-white glossy of Emma when she was twenty years old, and the barrel upon the photo taken of the werewolf by Elmer Grosslin. Jasper lowered the bottle. In an instant his heart knew what the symbolism meant.

God wants me to kill the werewolf.

His purpose was now crystal clear.

He stepped over the photos on the floor and poured the Jack Daniel's into the sink. No longer would he deaden his pain with alcohol. Instead, he would sharpen his remorse and hone his resolve to do the last important act of his life.

Picking up the Bible, pistol, and photographs, he returned them to the table. He clicked open the tarnished cylinder of the .38 and dropped out the six spent shell casings into his palm. To perform the task set before him he needed silver bullets. But how does one make them? First, he needed silver. He rubbed his hand over the gray stubble on his face and remembered the cabinet where Emma stored the good dishes and silverware. Inside, he found a fine leather box that was a wedding gift from her parents. Emma was so proud of the expensive set because the silverware was pure sterling silver. Opening the case, he found compartments of knives, forks, and spoons. He sat the box on the table next to the pistol. That solved the first step. Silver he had, but how could he melt it?

He thought he had an answer.

Jasper grabbed up the items and walked out the back door of his house. The cold wind buffeted him as he crossed the farmyard to his workshop in the back. Stepping inside the cluttered room, he switched on the fluorescent shop lights overhead. Everything was a mess. A jumbled collection of farm equipment parts, pipes, tools, wiring, power cords, etc., covered the two workbenches. As of late, he used the shop to cut his signs, which left the floor covered in thick sawdust. He cleared a space on one workbench and pinned a black-and-white picture of his beautiful Emma on the corkboard over the bench.

She would oversee his new project.

CHAPTER TWENTY-TWO

"No!" Jessica screamed as she struggled against the gray duct tape holding her wrists firmly in place to the arms of chair.

"Don't fight it, Jess." Blake's voice came from a shadowy silhouette in a dark hall. Though she couldn't see his features, she knew it was her husband. Megan stood before him. A look of total fear shone in her eyes as tears ran down her face.

"Blake, what are you doing?" she called out.

"Do you still love me, Jess?" He asked, producing the .357 magnum pistol and placing it against Megan's temple. "Do you?"

"Don't do this, Blake!" Jessica tore at the tape holding her in the chair.

"You didn't answer the question, baby." His face had become a dark void. In a voice distorted to something guttural and animal-like, he asked again, "Do you still love me, Jess?"

From somewhere beyond the nightmarish scene, she heard, "Mommy, wake up."

Jessica opened her eyes. She lay on her bed in the trailer with Megan softly nudging her shoulder. The terrible dream about Blake faded like broken cobwebs into the shadows of her mind.

"I'm awake," she said, turning her head. Megan, dressed in a T-shirt, was on the bed next to her.

"You were talking in your sleep, Mommy. Were you having a dream?"

"Yes." She reached out for her daughter. "Just a bad dream, baby."

"I'm cold." Megan nuzzled up close.

Jessica pulled the blanket over her. The interior of the trailer had turned much cooler through the night. She glanced at the window. A pale gray light lit the curtain and the walls of the bedroom. Her watch said it was 7:38.

"Why is it so cold, Mommy?"

"I guess summer is over and fall is here." She hugged her daughter to her under the blanket. "Mommy will keep you warm, baby."

"Did you have fun with the sheriff?" Megan asked.

Jessica thought about the events at Roxie's the night before. Everything seemed surreal as though it, too, was part of a vague dream. She recalled meeting him, dancing the two-step, and kissing in the parking lot after the bar closed. She touched the tip of her tongue to the roof of her mouth. The end still felt raw and scratched.

"I had a good time," she replied. "Did you like being here with Nelda?"

Megan nodded. "Uh huh, she let me color and we made hot chocolate. It was fun."

"Sounds like it." She tickled her daughter, who giggled under the blanket. "Now let Mommy up. I'm going to go turn on the heater and warm the trailer."

Jessica slipped out of the bed and pulled on her jeans. The achy tinge of a slight hangover pounded at her temples. Running her hands through her blonde hair, she walked barefoot into the living room and opened the panel over the heater controls. Turning up the thermostat, the heater rumbled into life under the trailer. Warm air began blowing through the vents.

"How about breakfast, baby?" she called down the hall at her daughter.

No answer.

"Megan?" Jessica asked again. Still no reply.

A sense of dread centered in her stomach.

"Baby, how come you didn't answer Mommy?"

She quickly returned to the bedroom and froze in shock.

Sitting on the bed, her daughter held the .357 magnum pistol in her hands. Jessica forgot she had hidden it under the pillow last night. Megan looked up at her with innocent blue eyes.

"Is this Daddy's gun?"

"Megan!" Jessica shouted. "Put it down!"

Shocked by the fear in her mother's voice, Megan dropped the pistol to the carpeted floor where it landed with a thump. Putting her hands over her face, she cried.

"Listen to me, baby," Jessica said in calmer tones. "Don't ever play with Daddy's gun again. It's dangerous. Do you understand?"

"I'm sorry, Mommy," Megan replied through her sobs.

Jessica sat on the bed hugging her close. "I didn't mean to scare you. It's just that the gun could have gone off and hurt you. Never touch it again. Do you understand?"

She nodded and sobbed in her arms. "Daddy let me play with it."

Jessica pulled her daughter away. "What do you mean?"

"Daddy played a game with me."

"With the gun?" Jessica asked as her blood turned to ice.

Megan nodded. "Uh huh, he showed me how to play."

"When Mommy was gone?"

"Uh huh." She nodded again.

Hot anger flared inside Jessica. Blake had played Russian roulette with his own daughter just to get some sort of sick thrill in his psychotic mind. A horrid memory flashed from the dream she had before waking.

"Do you still love me, Jess?"

"Your daddy did a bad thing, baby. He is sick in the head. You must promise me you'll never play with the gun."

"I promise."

"Good girl." Jessica stood and picked up the pistol. She slid it under her T-shirt into the waist of her blue jeans. The steel of the .357 felt icy cold against her bare stomach. "How about breakfast, baby?" she asked, attempting a weak smile toward Megan.

"Okay."

"You stay here under the blankets and keep warm. I'll call you when it's ready, sweetie."

Megan nodded and pulled the blanket up to her chin.

Jessica returned to the front room of the trailer. Through the windows, the scenic farmland lay gray beneath an overcast sky. She didn't see Sam on his tractor or any activity in the barnyard. A light layer of frost covered the windshield of the Camaro.

She pulled the pistol from the waistband of her jeans and placed it in a cabinet high above the stove, safe from Megan. It would do until she removed it to her car. She thought of the chilling words Megan had said about Blake and the gun game. It was just like the son of a bitch. Though he could be physically abusive, terrible mind games were a specialty of her husband. But this was a new low, even for him. She thanked God she had gotten out of the house when she did.

Nelda had left the frying pan used to cook breakfast the day before. In the almost-bare refrigerator, she grabbed some eggs, pancake batter, and bacon left over from the same meal. She fired up the stove and soon had the trailer smelling of cooking bacon and eggs. Megan padded into the room on bare feet, perched herself at the dining table, and watched her mother.

"Smells good, Mommy," she commented.

"Ready in a couple of minutes." She smiled back.

A sudden clattering noise sounded outside the trailer. Jessica, in the middle of picking up the frying pan from the stove burner, dropped it back on the flame in surprise. Hot grease splattered her forearm.

"Shit!" She cursed before remembering her daughter sitting at the breakfast table.

"What was that noise, Mommy?" Megan asked, looking around.

"I'm not sure." It sounded like someone had tripped over something outside the trailer. Jessica glanced toward the cabinet where she put the gun. *Blake?* she asked herself. *Is he outside?*

Another crashing followed. The sound came from below the kitchen window. With her heart racing, Jessica rose up on her tiptoes and looked outside, half-expecting to find a strange man moving around the trailer house, or worse, Blake staring back at her. Two metal trash cans lay over on their side. From the second one, the head of a raccoon popped out from spilled garbage.

"Come here, baby," Jessica said with relief. "Quick."

"What is it?" Megan hopped out of the chair and ran to her mother. "Did Tig come back?"

Hefting her up to sit on the kitchen counter, Jessica pointed outside. "It's a raccoon making the noise. Do you see it?"

As if on cue, the animal backed out of the garbage and began chewing on a piece of bread crust.

"I do, Mommy," Megan answered. "Wow."

"Isn't he cute?"

They watched the comical animal for a couple of minutes as it perused through the trash looking for tasty tidbits to eat. Megan was quiet and observed with rapt fascination.

A knock sounded at the front door. Jessica glanced through a window to see Nelda wearing a heavy jacket standing on the outside deck.

"Good you two are up," Nelda said after Jessica let her in. "It turned cold last night. I came over to see if you got the heater going."

"I started it earlier," Jessica replied.

Nelda nodded toward Megan sitting on the kitchen counter and staring out a window. "What's going on?"

"A raccoon is outside in the garbage."

Nelda chuckled. "Welcome to life in the country. If Rocky was here that old coon would be running for the hills."

"I've got some breakfast on the stove. Care to join?"

"Sure. Sam took the truck and went in to Stillwater to get some things. I was just sitting over at the house by myself." She waved to Megan. "Hi, sweet pea."

"Hi, Aunt Nel."

Jessica laughed. "Aunt Nel?"

"Sam and I have made both of you part of our family. I hope you don't mind."

"Not at all." Jessica removed the pan from the stove and scooped out the eggs and bacon. "I hope you like it."

"It'll be fine," Nelda said, settling into a chair. "I don't think anyone has fixed breakfast for me in years. I feel privileged."

"Wait until you taste it first. I'm not as good a cook as you are."

Megan jumped off the counter. "The raccoon ran off."

"Well, come over and eat, baby," Jessica replied and placed her daughter in a chair before a plate of eggs and bacon. To Nelda she said, "Megan told me she had fun last night while you watched her."

"Oh, we had a ball. We colored in her book and made hot chocolate. She was a perfect angel." Nelda took a sip of coffee and looked up. "How did your night go?"

"Well, I learned a new dance called the two-step and met some people at the bar." She paused for a moment and thought of the awkward exchange between her and Dale. "In the end I got a good-night kiss and went home."

"By the sheriff?"

"Yes."

"Aren't you the lucky girl."

Jessica shook her head. "I don't know, Nelda. Dale Sutton is a gorgeous man who seems passionate and fun, but there is something else about him I can't put my finger on. My gut tells me he is holding something back or keeping something from me. It's almost like he is secretly married and doesn't want me or anyone else to know about it."

"It wouldn't be the first time that's happened; but to tell the truth, something like that would be hard to keep secret in a small town."

"Doesn't it seem strange he's been single all this time?"

"A stone-cold bachelor, I'm guessing." Nelda laughed. "He's got the Marshall Dillon syndrome."

"Marshal Dillon?"

"Marshal Dillon on *Gunsmoke*."

"*Gunsmoke?*"

"A television series before your time. It came on in the sixties. He was the Dodge City marshal on that damn show for many years, and I don't think he ever once kissed a woman."

"I didn't know that."

Nelda put down her coffee cup. "I got a great idea. Sam's gone so let's have a girls' morning out. We can go into town and do some shopping at the Dollar Store. Both of you need clothes, and the refrigerator can use some groceries."

"I don't have a lot of money, Nel."

"Nonsense, I'll pitch in and you can pay me back with what you make in tips at the bar tonight."

"Can we, Mommy?" Megan looked up from her finished plate.

"Sounds fun, so why not?"

"That's the spirit. Sam's taken the truck so we'll have to drive in with your car, Jess."

"Not a problem."

CHAPTER TWENTY-THREE

Through the night, Blake Lobato drove the Harley on the edge of a cold front blowing south. Behind him, dark clouds gobbled up the stars and sent the temperature plunging. The land before him slept in the last vestiges of summer. He told himself he was the herald of fall, the harbinger of the season where green things die.

In the glow of the one cyclopean headlight, the interstate raced underneath the motorcycle tires. The cold wind burned the flesh on his face and bald head raw. He didn't care. He had his coke and hatred of Jess to keep him warm. When the approaching dawn brightened the sky to the east, he crossed from Missouri into Oklahoma, laughing like a madman. Jess was in this state somewhere. He knew it.

The engine rumbled between his legs as he searched for any highway patrol or law enforcement. He didn't know how long it would take Chicago PD homicide detectives to link the arson of his house and the murder of the dyke stripper. He had a short window of time to find Jess and take care of her; two or three days at best by his estimate. No matter, there was no way he would go to prison. He was on a one-way highway to hell.

At an all-night travel stop he had purchased an Oklahoma road atlas and searched for Hope Springs through the various regional maps. He didn't know what part of the state to look at. Only after checking the index did he find the listing "Hope Springs: Population 1168." The town was a fly speck on the map well off the main highways.

Is the bitch still there?

His anger and hate had pushed him this far, but he hadn't really contemplated what to do once he got there. He knew the sheriff in the small town had run her plates two days ago. He would have discovered she was driving a stolen car and probably threw her in jail. Without his Chicago police connections, he had no way to know. Once he arrived in town, he would take it one step at a time, observe and carefully find his wife to pay her back with the end of a baseball bat.

He smiled to himself and rode like a man possessed, crisscrossing northern Oklahoma under a pallet of gray clouds pushed by a cold wind. The countryside blurred past on each side of the roaring bike as he chose two-lane asphalt highways over the interstate. Following the back roads, he drove past a continuous loop of farms, plowed fields, and narrow bridges. Occasionally, he entered a small town; most were nothing but a few buildings and a co-op station in the shadow of a lone grain elevator. He kept his vigilance for any highway patrol or local law enforcement, but saw none.

It was ten in the morning when he turned on Highway 71. His heart raced at the sight of a road sign announcing Hope Springs thirteen miles ahead. He throttled the bike up to sixty-five and thundered down the ribbon of blacktop toward the small town. The cold bit at his face and hands beneath the leather gloves. He gritted his teeth against chapped lips and bent to the wind. When he thought he couldn't take the freezing wind anymore, he topped a hill and discovered a small town waiting in the valley below. The water tower rising out of the community had "Hope Springs" painted across its face.

He had made it at last.

From his approach, he noticed the asphalt highway ran down the center of town. He decided to drive through Hope Springs first and get a lay of the place. Afterward, he would look for any sign of Jessica and any trail she left. He gunned the motorcycle and sped toward the outskirts.

*   *   *   *

"Hold still, baby, so I can zip it up," Jessica said, sliding the red winter jacket over Megan's outstretched arms. Zipping up the front, she asked, "Do you like it?"

"I do, Mommy." Megan spun around to display the coat. "It's pretty."

"Okay, let me have it back." Jessica unzipped the coat and handed it to Nelda standing by the shopping cart in one of the aisles of the dollar store.

"I guess we'll take it. I'm in your debt, Nel. I promise I'll pay you back."

"I know," Nelda replied, placing the jacket on the other items they had selected. "Don't worry about it, Jess. You and your daughter are like family now. She needs something warm to wear. I'm more than glad to help out."

"Thank you." Jessica felt someone watching her and looked around the discount store. The place had a few customers moving about. Two old ladies in the next aisle were discussing curtains. She glanced toward the cash registers. A couple of college-age girls were chatting to each other behind the counter. They took turns glancing in her direction, and Jessica sensed that she was the subject of their conversation.

She leaned in close to Nelda. "Do you know the two girls working the counter?"

"Only one by name," Nelda replied. "Alicia is the daughter of the coach at Morris High School. The other one is Debbie, I think." She raised her eyebrow. "Why do you ask?"

"I think they're talking about me."

Nelda smiled. "You're the new girl in town and you've been seen with Sheriff Sutton. I'm not surprised."

"I don't like it. I think it's rude."

"It's called life in a small town."

"Mommy, can I get this?" Megan asked, pulling a coloring book from the shelf. "Please, Mommy."

Jessica took the book and looked it over. It was the *Illustrated Coloring Book of Fairy Tales*. The cover showed a picture of Red Riding Hood walking down a lane in the forest with the Bad Wolf spying on her from around a tree.

"It's not up to me, baby. Aunt Nel is the one with the money."

"Please, Aunt Nel." Megan looked up with her pleading blue eyes.

"Now how can I turn down such a pretty face?" Nelda tossed the book into the cart. "Anyway, you've almost got your pictures of Jesus all colored. We can work on this one tonight."

Jessica pushed the shopping cart toward the checkout stand. "What do you say, Megan?"

"Thank you, Aunt Nel."

"You're welcome, sweetie," Nelda replied, giving her a hug.

"Did you find everything all right?" the first checkout girl asked when they reached the counter. She could have lost a few pounds but was still pretty. A nose ring stuck out of one nostril. The other girl was skinnier, sporting brown hair with blonde highlights. She smacked on some gum while watching Jessica with green eyes surrounded by too much mascara.

"Just fine." Jessica started putting the items on the counter.

"Your name is Jess, isn't it?" the checkout girl asked while scanning the items. Her name tag said Alicia.

"Yes. How did you know?"

"I was out at Roxie's last night."

"I see."

"I heard you're working there." The skinny girl suddenly piped up between smacks of her gum. Jessica glanced at her name tag and read Debbie.

"That's right." Jessica continued unloading the shopping cart on the counter. "I start tonight."

"You're dating Sheriff Sutton?" Debbie asked with eyes darting to the wedding ring on Jessica's hand.

"Why do you ask that?"

"Well …" Debbie hesitated and smacked her gum before continuing. "Word around town is that you've been seeing a lot of each other. I know it's none of my business and I'm not trying to cause any drama."

"Then don't. We're just friends."

"That's good to know because he's been asking me out. He wants to take me fishing with him out in the country." She smacked her gum. "All alone."

"He said that?"

Debbie nodded her head. "Yeah, that's the reason I thought you'd like to know, if he's been asking you out, too."

Jessica's anger rose. "He's a grown man and can do whatever he wants."

The girl smiled. "My name's Debbie Miller, by the way."

"Jessica Lobato." Their eyes met for a second, and she read the jealousy in the girl's gaze.

"I might be out at Roxie's tonight," Debbie stated. It sounded more like a warning than a casual comment.

"Then I'll see you there," Jessica replied.

"Sixty dollars and thirty-eight cents," Alicia said to Nelda, who placed four twenty-dollar bills in her hand. "Thanks, Nel." Once she made change, Alicia nodded toward Megan and asked, "Is that your daughter?"

"Yes." Jessica grabbed up the full shopping bags.

"She's so pretty."

"Thank you."

She guided Megan out the exit door to the sidewalk. The cold wind hit her in the face but did little to cool the hot anger inside. She headed toward the Camaro parallel parked in front of the store.

Nelda followed and asked, "What was that all about?"

"Apparently I'm not the only one interested in the sheriff."

"She's lying. Dale Sutton could do a lot better than that skinny trailer trash."

"I don't know him that well." Jessica opened the car trunk and placed the bags inside. She slammed it shut and shouted above the roar of a passing Harley motorcycle, "If that's the kind of girl he wants, more power to him. I've got more important things to worry about than playing immature jealous games with some small-town skank."

She's just trying to make you upset," Nelda commented as she loaded Megan into the backseat.

"Well, the bitch got the job done." Jessica climbed into the driver's seat and started the Camaro. She reached under the seat to make sure the .357 pistol was there before remembering she had left it in the trailer. Once Nelda was inside, she pulled out of the parking space and into the main street. At the corner, she waited behind a black Harley motorcycle and rider for the traffic light to change. The light went to green. The Harley turned left and she went straight.

*   *   *   *

Blake couldn't believe his luck. He spotted Jessica and Megan walking out of a retail store just as he drove through the middle of town. His heart jumped with surprise. He couldn't have planned it any better. He managed to look straight ahead and not let her see his face behind the sunglasses. At the corner, the traffic light turned to red and he stopped. He shifted the rearview mirror just enough to watch the Camaro leave the curb and pull up behind his bike at the light. Jessica talked to an older woman in the front seat and seemed upset about something. Oblivious to his presence, he realized any second she might see the Harley's Illinois plates.

A cocaine-driven rage burned inside. He wanted to put down his kickstand, grab the bat, and walk back to the car. He would then yank the bitch out from behind the wheel and beat her to death in front of everyone in the middle of Main Street.

Too risky, he decided. *If Jess saw me walking toward her, she would just slam the Camaro in reverse and drive away. I might lose her then. Best be patient and follow where she goes. Find a perfect time to get my revenge.*

He put the left turn signal on and waited.

The traffic light went to green. He made the turn as the Camaro went straight. Popping the clutch, he raced halfway down the block, swung the bike around, and returned to the intersection. Again, he had to wait at the traffic light. The Camaro was two blocks away and soon would be out of sight. He thought about running the red light and glanced up and down Main Street. As if on cue, a sheriff patrol car cruised down the center of town toward the intersection. Blake's heart sank. He didn't dare pull out in front of the sheriff and risk having his plates read. In desperation, he looked to the right as the Camaro disappeared over a hill.

Jess was gone for now. The sheriff represented a more serious threat. The patrol car slowed and the driver, a man with sandy-colored hair, glanced in his direction. Blake didn't look at him directly but watched him through shades as the car continued through the intersection. A block farther, the patrol car turned off on a side street. Blake's internal warning signal went off. The sheriff could be circling back to check on him. Small-town cops were very suspicious about strangers in their jurisdiction. He needed to get out of town but had to find where Jess had gone. Obviously, she was still in Hope Springs, which meant she was staying someplace other than jail.

The light turned green and he went straight, turning down the first alley behind the stores along Main Street. He parked his bike behind a Dumpster and waited. Less than a minute passed before the sheriff's car cruised past the mouth of the alley and continued down the street. Blake knew the longer he stayed in town, the more risk he took of encountering the sheriff.

But where is Jess?

He needed more information. Years of experience working undercover narcotics had taught him how to get it.

Leaving the bike, he walked out of the alley and down the sidewalk in front of the storefronts. He scanned up and down the street. No sign of the sheriff. Very aware the long black jacket and sunglasses were conspicuous to the locals, Blake quickly stepped into the dollar store where Jess had exited a couple of minutes earlier. Behind the register, a young brown-haired woman rang up two old ladies. All three looked up with curious faces as he entered. Another thin blonde girl stocked product in the candy aisle. Blake decided to approach her; the clip-clop of his riding boot heels sounding on the floor tiles as he walked to the girl.

She looked up, smacking on a piece of gum. "Can I help you?"

"Maybe you can." He paused to look at her name tag. "Debbie."

The girl smiled. "Sure, what do you need?"

"Do you have any ChapStick? I've been riding all morning in the wind."

"I have some right here." She walked down to the end of the aisle. "You've been riding in this weather?"

"My Harley's parked down the street." Blake followed her and picked up a tube of cherry-flavored ChapStick from the shelf. "I wasn't expecting the weather to turn so cold."

"Weatherman said it's a record-breaking cold front for this time of year."

"That's Oklahoma for you."

"It sure is." Debbie smacked on her gum for a second and then asked, "So you got a Harley?"

"Yes."

"I always wanted to ride on a Harley."

"I'm just passing through or I'd give you one." Blake contemplated for a second on how to approach the next subject. In Chicago, he could offer money for information. He had plenty, thanks to the stash from the recently deceased Passion. A stranger passing out hundred-dollar bills and asking questions would raise too much attention in a small town. He needed subtlety. "Debbie, maybe you're the one who can help me with something. When I was driving into town, I saw a young woman and a little girl just leave here. I could swear she went to school with my sister. I haven't seen her for years. She was a family friend. Does she live around here?"

"You mean Jessica?"

"That's her name."

"No. She's new in town."

"The last I knew she was living in Tulsa," Blake lied.

"I don't know where she came from, but I don't like her, though."

"Oh?" Blake leaned in a step closer. "Why?"

"She's dating my man."

"Really? You're kidding."

Debbie nodded her head. "She shows up in town, and the next thing I know, she's going out with Dale Sutton. He's the local sheriff here in Hope Springs."

"That sounds like Jess." Blake smiled, causing one lip to crack. The iron taste of blood seeped into his mouth. "She always had a thing for cops."

"Your lip is bleeding," Debbie pointed out.

"Sorry," Blake replied. "I guess I better pay for this ChapStick."

They walked together to the register. On the way, Blake spotted a shelf with hunting supplies. A set of camouflaged field binoculars caught his eye, and he picked them up as well. They could come in handy for spying on his whore of a wife and her new lover.

"Do you know where Jessica is staying?" Blake asked.

"Not sure," Debbie said between smacks of her gum. "I know she starts work at Roxie's Roadhouse tonight."

"Roxie's?"

"Yeah, it's a karaoke bar about five miles out of town. Continue down Highway 133. You can't miss it."

"If I'm still in the area I might drop by there." He smiled. "Catch up on old times."

The brown-haired girl behind the checkout counter asked, "Did you find everything all right?

"I sure did." Blake put the ChapStick and binoculars down and pulled a fifty from his wallet. To Debbie, he said, "Thanks, you've been most helpful."

"You're welcome." She smiled.

Blake paid for his purchase and walked out of the store. Jessica had only been gone for less than a week, and the bitch was already fucking another man. The local sheriff, no less! The sandy-haired man he had seen driving in the patrol car earlier at the light. No wonder she wasn't in jail for stealing his Camaro. She had a get-out-of-jail-free card between her legs. He remembered what his old man taught him about women. They were all backstabbing whores.

His boots pounded on the pavement as he returned to his bike. Anger throbbed at his temples and caused his vision to blur. He had to leave town, find a place to clear his head, and think of what to do next. With the sheriff involved with his wife, the longer he stayed, the more dangerous it became. He started the bike and turned south on Highway 133. A road sign said Morris lay seven miles ahead. He throttled up to the speed limit and checked the rearview to see if the sheriff was coming up behind him. No sign of the bastard.

His purpose for coming to Hope Springs had changed since Jessica was fucking the local sheriff.

Now, he had to kill them both.

The Angel of Death smiled and leaned into the wind.

CHAPTER TWENTY-FOUR

Because of the homecoming football game, Morris High School only had a half-day on Friday. Elated for getting out early, Terry Newman followed the other students down the hall and through the exit doors. He didn't catch sight of Becky Warren until he was out of the building. She stood at the curb, a teenage vision of beauty dressed in a tight sweater-and-jeans combo. Terry's pulse quickened. All morning he had built up his nerve for what he was about to do next. With his heart pounding, he knew it was now or never. He swallowed hard and stepped up beside her.

"Hey, Becky."

She half-turned with green eyes showing a hint of confusion. "What's up?"

"Are you excited about the game tonight?" *Stupid question,* he told himself. *She's the cheer captain.* Becky nodded but said nothing. He decided to press on. "I heard you got homecoming queen. You deserve it. You know there's a dance afterward?" *Another stupid question.* He swallowed hard again, and his tongue felt like an old washrag. "I'm asking because I was wanting …" His voice began to break, but he wasn't going to stop. "I was wondering if you'd like to go with me to the dance."

A look of surprise flashed in her eyes. "With you?"

The next words he blurted out. "Sid, my friend, said I can borrow his truck so I'd be able to pick you up."

"I already have a date."

"You do?" He felt his heart drop into his shoes. *She's Becky Warren; of course, she's got a date to the dance.*

"Sorry." She turned away to look again down the street.

"No problem," he said, knowing it was time to make his exit. In fact, he wanted to run away like a screaming idiot. "I'll be seeing you."

Someone grabbed him from behind and shoved him up against the chain-link fence surrounding the football training field. Brandon Harrison's face filled his vision. Two other members of the football team gawked over the star quarterback's shoulder. All wore maroon letter jackets.

"Are you hitting on my girl?" Brandon grabbed the front of his shirt.

"Let go!" Terry squirmed out of the hold. "I was just talking to her about the dance tonight."

"I've seen you checking out my girlfriend, you little dork."

"He didn't mean any harm." Becky's voice came from behind the wall of maroon jackets surrounding him.

"I better not catch you talking to her again." Brandon pointed his finger.

Terry tightened his fist. "Screw you."

"What did you say?"

"I said to go screw yourself." He knew he was about to get an ass kicking, but he didn't care.

One of the jocks at his side chuckled. "I'd say he's looking for a fight."

"You want some of me, dork?" Brandon shoved him hard once more against the fence.

Terry replied by bouncing back and throwing his best right. The punch connected to Brandon's jaw with the sound of meat being slapped. In an instant, the fight was on. Everything became a blur as he threw punches and took them in return. From out of nowhere, Coach Lawson appeared and yanked them both apart.

"Goddammit, Brandon," the coach growled. "You want to get suspended right before the big game tonight?"

"This dork started it, Coach," Brandon replied while dabbing at a bloody scratch on his cheek. A couple of other bruises on his face were evidence Terry had landed more than one punch to that area.

"You shoved me first!" Terry snapped back with the taste of blood in his mouth from a split lip.

"Stay away from my girlfriend, creep!"

"Okay, you two," Coach Lawson interjected. "I'm not going to turn this into the office. I can't have my starting quarterback suspended for fighting right before homecoming tonight." He nodded in Terry's direction. "Just leave and go on home, son."

Terry spit out a stream of blood and wiped his lips with his sleeve. "Fine."

Putting his hands in his pockets, he walked away down the sidewalk. *Screw them all,* he thought to himself and spat more blood. *At least I stood my ground against that moron Brandon Harrison.* He looked up to see Sid's gray truck rounding the corner. Screaming rock music seeping from inside the closed cab heralded the stoner's arrival from half a block away. The truck pulled to a stop, and he climbed into the passenger seat.

"What the fuck happened to you?" Sid asked, turning down the deafening music. "You look like shit."

"I got in a fight with Brandon Harrison."

"Let me guess, you tried to ask Becky out?"

"You got it." Terry opened the window and spat more blood.

"I hope you gave more than you got."

"I think I did."

"That's them up ahead, isn't it?" Sid nodded down the street where Brandon, Becky, Coach Lawson, and the other two maroon morons stood talking to each other on the sidewalk."

"Yeah."

Sid buzzed down the driver window. "Take the wheel."

"What?" Terry asked, surprised, and grabbed the steering wheel.

Sid undid the front of his pants. "Just watch."

Terry guided the truck down the road toward the group. As they drove near, Sid yanked down his jeans.

"Hey, you assholes," Sid shouted out the window. "Here's one more for you to look at."

He mooned the surprised group, who stood in open-mouth shock at the sight of his skinny bare ass hanging out the driver window. Dropping back down into the seat, Sid flipped them a double bird and yelled, "Have a nice day!"

They sped away in the truck howling like a couple of crazy lunatics. Laughing so hard that tears streamed down their faces, they pulled over into the Wal-Mart parking lot until they got their composure. When the laughter died down to the point that they could look at each other without going into another outburst, Terry said to Sid, "Thanks, man."

"I couldn't let those douche bags dis you like that."

"You're a good friend." Terry smiled. His split lip had finally stopped bleeding.

Sid looked out the front window toward the store. "You're my only friend, dude."

"You're kidding!"

Sid shrugged. "No one else puts up with me, I guess."

Terry knew he was the only one who would hang out with the pimple-faced loner.

"So what do we do now?" he asked.

Sid nodded toward the retail store. "The other day when I was in Wal-Mart with Grandma, I saw a boxed DVD set of twenty horror movies. I got some cash, so why don't we go buy it and spend the weekend getting high and watching crappy monster flicks."

"I got a better idea."

"What's that?"

Terry turned in the passenger seat toward Sid. "Why don't we help Mr. Higgins hunt the werewolf?"

"You're shitting me. You don't really think the thing is for real?"

"He's too old to do it by himself."

Sid shook his head. "He's a fucking senile nutcase."

"Come on, dude. It's a werewolf hunt. How cool is that?"

Sid shrugged his skinny shoulders. "There's a full moon tonight."

"So let's do it?"

Sid nodded. "Might be good for a few laughs."

CHAPTER TWENTY-FIVE

Jasper Higgins spent the morning casting silver bullets but soon found the job was not easy. To get started, he cleaned the .38 pistol to make sure it would fire correctly. Next, he had to find some live ammo. Luckily, he discovered a near-empty box of rounds in a cabinet above his workbench. There were nine shells inside. He took the pistol out on his property and fired two of the rounds into a bale of hay to make sure the gun worked properly. That left him with seven rounds. He could go buy more, but he would have to drive some distance. If he bought his ammo locally, the seller might tip off the sheriff to his purchase. He was still under suspicion for murder. The seven rounds would have to do. If he couldn't kill the werewolf with seven bullets, so be it.

He returned to his workshop and contemplated his next step. He didn't have to make the entire shell casing silver; only the bullet needed to be cast in the metal. To do this he had to separate the lead from the brass shell. He pulled the dusty cover off his old bullet reloader. Once he removed the bullet from the casing, he placed it on the workbench to examine it under a shop light. If he was going to make the same thing in silver, he needed a mold of the original bullet. He found a bag of plaster in his tool shed and mixed it in a bucket. Next he made a mold by placing the bullet in plaster. While waiting for the plaster to dry, he removed the other six bullets from their casings.

Fatigue began to set in, but the obsession to kill the monster who took his Emma drove him on. It was time to smelt the silver. He removed pieces of silverware from the luxurious leather holding case and placed them on the workbench. Firing up an acetylene torch, he applied the flame to a silver butter knife. The metal began to soften and liquefy. He poured the molten metal into the top of his plaster mold. The silver bubbled and disappeared into the hole. Once the metal cooled, he knocked apart the plaster mold and removed the casting with a pair of tongs. He further cooled the silver in a bucket of water. After filing away all metal flash, he pressed the bullet back into the live shell casing using his reloader. Once done, he removed the finished product and studied the silver bullet in the fluorescent shop light. The bullet needed to be machined to proper specifications using a metal lathe, but he had none. It was the best he could do under the circumstances. He didn't know how accurate the round would be when fired, and he prayed it wouldn't jam in the barrel. The time was twelve thirty.

Exhausted, Jasper Higgins sat in a chair and felt doubt settle in. One bullet was all he had managed to produce. He looked down at his hands gnarled by arthritis. His knees hurt so badly he could hardly keep standing. What was next? Was he going to run around the countryside after nightfall to look for a monster in the dark with his one bullet? His revenge could only carry him so far. He was old and worn out. Letting out a weary breath, he contemplated going to the liquor store instead. Drowning in a bottle of Jack would have been easier than going on a foolish hunt for a beast in the night.

He looked up at the picture of Emma he had tacked to the corkboard as tears of defeat moistened his eyes.

"Please, God, I don't have the strength to continue," he prayed aloud.

The sound of closing truck doors came from outside his workshop. Jasper stood painfully to his feet and crossed to look out a shop window. Terry Newman and the Sid Granger kid stood outside and knocked against the one door.

"Are you in there, Mr. Higgins?" Terry's voice called out.

Jasper swung the door open. "Yes."

"We want to help you on this werewolf hunt," Terry announced, looking like he had been in a fistfight due to a swollen lip.

"Thank you," Jasper replied. Elation filled his heart, for he knew God had answered his prayer. "Then you believe me about the beast?"

"Let's just say we want to believe you," Sid replied, looking around the shop. "What's that smell? Have you been burning something?"

"I've been smelting silver," Jasper replied, pointing to the box of silverware. "Been all morning trying to make silver bullets."

"Having any luck?"

Jasper held out his hand and showed his handiwork.

"Holy shit." Sid's eyes narrowed. "It's a real fucking silver bullet. You're serious as hell about this."

"Thank God you two boys showed. I was about to give up."

"We're here now, Mr. Higgins, and willing to help," Terry said.

Jasper pointed to the bullet reloader. "I've got six more to do. I know the process now and with all of us working together can make them much faster."

"This won't be as boring as the metal shop class I took one semester," Terry said with a chuckle.

They went to work. Youthful energy had now been breathed into the project. Jasper discovered Sid Granger was very eager to help, even though he had a foul mouth while doing so. The work fascinated both young men. The shop became abuzz with activity as they melted the silver, forged bullet castings, and reloaded the shells. The acrid smell of molten metal hung in the air. In four hours, they had made the other six silver bullets and pressed them into the brass casings. Once completed, they stepped back and took a moment to admire their craftsmanship lined up in a row on the worktable.

"Job well done," Jasper remarked and clasped Terry on the shoulder. "I couldn't do it without you boys."

"Thanks, Mr. Higgins," Terry replied.

"Is that a picture of your wife?" Sid nodded to the black-and-white of Emma tacked to the corkboard.

"It is." Jasper picked up the .38 pistol and began loading the chamber with the silver bullets.

"She was hot," Sid said.

"Yes, she was." Jasper clicked shut the chamber. He picked up the last bullet and tossed it to Terry. "You keep that one. It's a souvenir of your hard work."

"Okay." Terry placed the bullet in his flannel shirt pocket. "I feel like that deputy on television who kept one bullet in his shirt pocket."

"You mean Barney Fife?" Sid laughed.

"Yeah, that's the one."

"What's next?" Sid turned to Jasper.

"We've got our silver bullets," Jasper replied. "Let's go find our werewolf."

"Where do we start?" Terry asked.

"The beast was last seen at Elmer Grosslin's place. We'll start there," Jasper answered. "Besides, I promised Elmer I'd bring back his photos today."

"I'm stoked. Let's do it." Sid started walking toward the door. "Let's get this fucking hunt on the road."

"So says the one who would be the first to crap his pants if we actually encounter a werewolf," Terry commented with a chuckle.

Jasper said in a somber voice, "I've already seen the creature. It's a frightening sight, believe me. I wouldn't blame anyone for being afraid. I don't want to put you boys in danger. Are you sure your parents are going to let you go on this hunt with me? We could be out really late tonight. This is my hunt, not yours."

Sid shrugged. "All I have is my grandma. She lets me do what I want."

Terry looked at his feet and said, "My mother hasn't been the same since my father ran out on us. She just sits in front of the TV watching stupid reality shows. I'm seventeen now and am pretty much on my own."

"It's set then," Jasper said, grabbing his coat and slipping it on. "We'll take my truck." He put the pistol in one pocket and patted the other. "I've got Elmer's pictures right here."

Sid let out his best fake wolf howl. "Owwwwooo! A werewolf hunting we will go."

CHAPTER TWENTY-SIX

"You look pretty, Mommy," Megan said, standing at the open bathroom door.

"Thanks, baby." Jessica smiled at her daughter and returned to applying eyeliner in the mirror. For her bar waitress ensemble, she chose a tight black top with spaghetti straps to go with equally tight blue jeans. She was going for sexy without looking like a whore in the process. With her limited wardrobe at the time, this was as close as she could get.

"Hello." A voice came from the front room of the trailer. "Is there anyone here?"

Jessica stuck her head out of the bathroom to see Nelda standing in the middle of the living room. "We're both in here, Nel."

"Jess, I knocked but no one answered." She walked down the hallway to the restroom door.

"We didn't hear you. I'm getting ready to go to work."

"Hi, Aunt Nel." Megan ran forward and gave her a big hug.

"Hi, sweet pea." Nelda returned the embrace. "Are you ready to have fun tonight? I brought some stuff to make chocolate chip cookies and hot cocoa."

"Yeah."

"It doesn't sound like I'm going to have any problem leaving Megan with you." Jessica said with a smile.

"No." Nelda shook her head. "We have a lot of fun together."

"You don't mind watching her in the trailer?"

"Not a bit. You forget I lived here for twenty years. This feels like home to me. Sam wants to watch some college football game, so we girls will just stay here until you get home."

"I don't know how late I'll be."

"No problem."

Jessica adjusted her hair and asked, "Well, how do I look?"

A smile crossed Nelda's face. "Like I did thirty years ago. You're going to knock 'em dead tonight."

"I hope so. I can use the tips. Thanks for letting me borrow the top." Grabbing up her purse, Jessica walked into the kitchen. She glanced over her shoulder. Neither Nelda nor Megan was looking her way. Jessica quickly reached into the high cabinet door, removed the .357 pistol, and stuffed it in her purse before turning around.

"She doesn't have a bedtime tonight, Nel," Jessica said. "Keep her up as late as she wants. That way she won't be waking me up first thing in the morning and I can get some sleep."

"Did you hear that, baby?" Nelda rubbed Megan on the top of the head. "No bedtime."

"Yeah."

"Come give your mommy a good-bye kiss." Jessica knelt as Megan ran into her arms and planted a messy wet kiss on her lips. "Now you do what Aunt Nel says and be a good girl."

"Okay, Mommy."

"Bye."

Jessica left the trailer and stepped out into the brisk air of the approaching night. As she descended from the wood deck to the driver's side of her Camaro, she checked her watch. It was just after six thirty, which meant she had just enough time to make it to Roxie's. Once behind the steering wheel, she removed the pistol from her purse and placed it under the driver's seat. Starting the car, she pulled out of the front yard and drove around the barn and back to the road.

As she cruised through the center of Hope Springs she noticed the town seemed emptier than normal. Nelda had mentioned something about a big high school football game in Morris tonight, which could account for the lack of activity. One thing she learned since coming to Oklahoma was that people loved football here.

At the one stoplight she turned on Highway 133 and headed toward Roxie's. As often happened when Jessica was alone, a deep paranoia tugged at her insides. She constantly checked her rearview. Something felt wrong, but she couldn't define its source. Everything about the world around her seemed normal, but it was like looking at it through a fogged window. If she could just wipe away the fog, she would get a clearer vision of reality. It troubled her that she had gotten away from Blake too easily. If she had known it was that simple, she would have run a long time ago. Of course, Blake had other issues to deal with than just his wayward wife. When she left, he was about to go down for being a corrupt cop. He could be in jail instead of looking for her, but she doubted it. He knew the system and wouldn't be incarcerated long.

Then there was Dale Sutton. The sheriff seemed genuine, but her intuition said there was something hidden beneath the surface. He seemed like a walking cutout of a man, as if she could pull apart a layer of his skin only to find cardboard instead of flesh. Granted, some men were emotionally distant, but the sheriff seemed so to the point of hiding something. What was it? Other women? Probably. Her run-in with the skinny blonde in the Dollar Store this morning was evidence of that. Whatever the case, she needed to tell him to forget about her. Emotional entanglements she didn't need at the moment. Megan was her focus now. But could she do it? If he made strong advances, could she turn him away? She seriously doubted it.

She topped the hill overlooking the farm with all the handmade signs. The setting sun caused long shadows from the makeshift billboards to stretch across the highway. The place intrigued her, and Jessica entertained the idea of stopping to read the jumbled messages but decided not to be late for work. She did notice one thing out of the ordinary. In earlier drive-bys, she saw no activity whatsoever and thought the overgrown farm abandoned. This time an old red Ford truck pulled out of the property and onto the highway a hundred yards ahead of her. In the setting sunlight, she made out the heads of three passengers through the back glass. She followed the truck until the parking lot entrance of Roxie's. The truck continued on as she made the turn.

The lot wasn't as full as the night before, just a few pickup trucks and a couple of motorcycles—surprising since it was a Friday night, but she suspected the cause might be the football game. She parked the Camaro, checked her look one last time in the mirror, and then locked the car before crossing the gravel to reach the front door. In case she needed to refresh her makeup during the night, she brought her purse.

"Hey, Jess, glad to see you," Roxie called out from behind the bar when she entered. At her side, Collin counted out bills from a bank bag before placing them in the register. He glanced up with emotionless dark eyes and grunted something like a hello.

"I hope I'm not late." Jessica checked the rest of the place. A group of four occupied one table in the middle of the floor while a couple of bikers, members of a local riding organization by the cut of their leather, sat drinking beer at the bar. Beyond that, the roadhouse was empty. Low music wafted out from the jukebox in the corner.

"The real craziness hasn't started yet." Roxie let out a low whistle. "Chick, you look hot. I'm jealous now. I know who's going to make all the cash tonight."

"Thanks."

Motioning for her to come behind the bar, Roxie said, "Back here, girl. Let's get you acquainted to the place and how we do things."

Jessica joined her side. "Where do I put my purse?"

"I'll show you."

Roxie stepped through the open door leading to a back room. Jessica followed to discover the room bigger than she thought. To her right was the walk-in cooler used to store cold beer; to her left stood a series of three metal school lockers. A broken exit sign hung above the back door leading to the outside. The most intriguing feature of the room was a sleeping cot in one corner. Taped to the wall above the bed were various hand-drawn pieces of art. Most showed scenes of forested mountains and a full moon shining in the sky, all drawn by an artist of considerable talent.

"Here's your locker," Roxie said. "You can store your things in there."

Jessica put her purse away. "Who sleeps back here?"

"Collin," Roxie replied. "We had a break-in a few weeks ago, so he sleeps here when the bar's closed."

"And who does the drawings? They're incredible."

"Those are Collin's, too. He's always been able to draw."

Jessica leaned closer, examining one of the pictures. It showed a forest of tall trees with high mountains in the background. "They don't look like pictures of Oklahoma."

"They're not. Those are scenes from home."

"Colorado?" Jessica asked.

Roxie shook her head. "Canada."

"You and your brother are from Canada?"

"Yes."

"I had no idea."

"I better show you the ropes and get you trained before the crowd gets here." Roxie smiled. "There's a full moon tonight so who knows what can happen."

CHAPTER TWENTY-SEVEN

Uncle Johnny sat in his truck waiting for Jasper Higgins's arrival. From his vantage point behind the oil tank on the abandoned lease site, he had a good view of Elmer Grosslin's farm. Earlier in the morning, he had hidden Elmer's decaying body by carrying the rotting headless corpse down to the bank of a creek and camouflaging it under broken limbs. Once done, he returned to his truck for his long vigil watching for Jasper's F-150. The sheriff had provided him information on the make and tag number.

The afternoon stretched into dusk, and hunger gnawed at his insides. He wanted to devour the old man's aged flesh, to rip sinew with teeth and taste hot blood flowing down his throat. After hours passed with no sign of Jasper, he was about to give up his watch and return to Roxie's.

The sky darkened and the first stars pierced the twilight when a dust trail signaled the approach of a vehicle on the dirt road. Minutes later, a Ford truck rounded the bend before the Grosslin farm. Removing a pair of binoculars from the dash, Uncle Johnny focused the lens on the cab to see who was driving. Jasper Higgins sat behind the wheel with two teenage boys riding in the front seat. The sheriff hadn't said anything about others accompanying the old man. Who were they? He put down his binoculars in disgust. He wanted desperately to feed, but now things had changed. Two teenage boys who suddenly disappeared would be hard to hide from the locals.

Disappointed, he looked out through the windshield. The full moon appeared over the horizon in a darkening sky. Magnified in size, the orb showed blood red due to the setting sun. The sight of it wracked his body with the need to release the beast.

Feed me! The beast raged inside his mind. *The sheriff promised you this kill. Now you can eat all three!*

No! he screamed internally back at the monster. *Too risky. Best to retreat and talk to the rest of the Pack.*

Feed me now! Let's feast upon the flesh of the young and the old.

No!

He fought against the monster inside, but the magnificent rising full moon proved too strong an influence. Hair began growing on the back of his hands.

"Goddammit!" he cried out in a voice already changing into an animal growl.

Uncle Johnny threw himself out of the truck cab and landed on the gravel of the lease road. He crouched down on all fours as the fire of transformation swept through his body and distorted his physical form. His clothes ripped from his body. In less than a minute, he became the beast. Now covered in gray fur, he stood on two canine legs. His enhanced senses picked up voices and movement at the Grosslin farm across the country road. With animal eyes, he took in the beauty of the full moon and, though he tried to fight it, the beast was in control now.

The monster threw back its head and released a long howl.

*   *   *   *

"This place is giving me a serious case of the creeps," Terry said as he shut the door of the truck and took in the view of Crazy Elmer's dilapidated house and barn. The yard was a cornucopia of broken refrigerators, old tires, and useless junk cars rusting among tall weeds. Weathered paint peeled in flakes like dried skin from the outside walls of the house. In the fading orange light of dusk, the property took on an eerie and haunted appearance.

"You could film fucking *Texas Chainsaw Massacre* here," Sid remarked as he took in the same view.

Jasper shut the driver's door and yelled, "Elmer! It's Jasper Higgins. I brought your photos back! I got them all developed. A couple of friends came with me."

No reply.

"I don't think anyone's home," Terry said.

"Where else would he be? He doesn't have a vehicle and his bum leg won't let him walk very far." Mr. Higgins looked toward the barn. "He's here somewhere."

Sid peered closer at the house. "The front door is open."

"Then he's home," Jasper remarked. He repeated his call to Elmer.

Again, no answer.

Sid leaned into Terry and whispered, "When I was a kid, I heard stories about Crazy Elmer, which scared the shit out of me. He would run around naked grunting like a pig. On Halloween night, if he caught any kids on his property, he would cut their dicks off with a knife."

"I know," Terry replied. "I heard the same stories."

"He's just a poor decrepit old hermit," Jasper commented. "He never harmed anyone."

"Well, it doesn't look like he's home," Terry replied.

"Let's move up to the porch."

They crossed the distance to the front of the house and stood together on the creaky porch boards. Terry peered into the dim interior. The front room was a cluttered mess of old furniture and peeling wallpaper. Magazines and newspapers placed in well-ordered stacks created a maze about the room for anyone walking in the house. Broken windows with sheets of plywood nailed over them allowed very little light in to illuminate the room.

"This place is creepy," Terry whispered to the others.

Mr. Higgins knocked against the door frame. "Elmer, are you here? Only silence.

"He's not home," Terry stated. He stuck his head through the open doorway. A stack of UFO magazines were on the floor just inside the door. "Maybe he got abducted by aliens."

"Maybe he's out …"

A piercing howl stopped Mr. Higgins's reply short. The terrifying noise grew in intensity and rolled out over the property, sending hundreds of blackbirds flying out of nearby trees. In a noisy erratic cloud, they circled overhead, cawing and dipping in the darkening sky.

"Tell me that was a coyote," Sid said with an edge of nervousness in his voice.

"No coyote," Mr. Higgins replied.

"Fuck, I was afraid you were going to say that."

Terry turned around and glanced over the front yard. The sunset created deep shadows on the high weeds and rusting junk. The hair on his neck stood on end. Something was very wrong. "You got the pistol with you?"

"Right here." Mr. Higgins removed the .38 from his coat pocket.

"I think you're going to need it."

A deep beastlike growl sounded closer to the house. They looked in unison to see the flash of a dark gray shape dart between the rusted wrecks of two old automobiles.

"Holy shit!" Sid said. "What the fuck is that?"

"It's no farm dog," Mr. Higgins answered.

The canine growling rose louder and nearer.

"This can't be happening." Sid's eyes were wide with terror. "Things like this don't exist."

"You tell the werewolf that," Mr. Higgins replied, pointing out in the yard.

A large loping form raced toward them, cutting a path through the tall weeds.

"Into the house!" Terry shouted.

None of them hesitated. They charged into Elmer's living room, and Terry slammed shut the door. The next second something heavy threw itself against the wood, causing dust to shower down from the ceiling. The door nearly splintered from the force of the impact. A horrible bestial snarl accompanied the assault.

In a panic, Sid stepped back, tripped over a stack of *Weekly World News*, and fell to the floor. "It's going to get in!"

Terry fumbled with the locks and dead bolts on the door. "I can't hold it back!" he shouted above the growling.

Again, a heavy force threw itself against the wood, threatening to tear the door off its hinges.

"Step aside, son." Mr. Higgins took a firing stance with the pistol. "I just got to get one good shot."

Terry threw himself to the floor as the door burst open. A dark hunched shape filled the doorway a second before Mr. Higgins fired the pistol. The crack of the gunshot accompanied by a muzzle flash illuminated the beast. In a microsecond, Terry saw gray fur, canine fangs, and the red eyes of the hunched form. The nightmarish creature let out a grunt and disappeared off the porch.

"I think I hit it," Mr. Higgins announced.

Scrambling to his feet, Terry replied, "You did."

He listened for some sound that the beast was near but heard only the cries of blackbirds circling overhead.

Mr. Higgins remained in firing stance with gun pointed toward the door. "Let's just wait and see if it returns."

"No, let's get out of here," Sid said in a low voice as he regained his feet.

"Quiet, "Mr. Higgins demanded. "Listen."

Nothing growled or creaked on the porch boards. A full agonizing minute passed with Mr. Higgins keeping the weapon pointed at the broken door.

"I think it's gone," Terry whispered to the others.

"I hope," Mr. Higgins replied. His voice sounded labored, and sweat beaded upon his forehead. "Terry, take the pistol."

"What's wrong?"

"Hard to breathe." Mr. Higgins clutched his chest in pain. "My heart ..."

Terry grabbed the .38 as the old man dropped into a ratty recliner. His rheumy eyes looked up at him. "Keep the gun pointed toward the door, son. You're in charge now." His face winced again in pain. "I think I'm having a heart attack."

"This can't be happening!" Sid declared. "This can't be fucking happening now!"

"Shut up for a second." Terry tried to grasp what he should do next as he held the pistol in his shaking hand. He turned to Sid. "Call 911. We need an ambulance for Mr. Higgins."

"Okay, okay." Sid reached into his jacket and removed a cell phone. He punched in the number and began talking to a dispatcher.

"Help is on the way, Mr. Higgins," Terry said, patting him on the arm. "Just take it easy."

The old man grabbed him by the hand. "I hope I make it to then ... if I don't ... just want you to know ... how thankful I am ... for believing in me ... son," Mr. Higgins said between gasps for air.

"I understand."

"They want to know our address," Sid said, holding the phone against his ear.

Terry picked up a nearby UFO magazine and tossed it over. "Read them the mailing address on the front."

Sid returned to his conversation with the emergency dispatcher. Terry stepped slowly toward the splintered doorway. His heart pounded against his throat, and the gun felt odd in his sweaty hands. He had fired a pistol before when his dad took him out hunting, but that was back when he had a dad. His hand shook so badly now that he doubted if he could hit anything at the moment. Reaching the dark doorway, he peered out into the front yard. Dusk had turned into night, and the world outside was shadow and moonlight ... with no sign of the monster.

CHAPTER TWENTY-EIGHT

After he left Hope Springs that morning, Blake Lobato continued down Highway 133 until he reached Morris. Along the way, he drove past Roxie's Roadhouse and looked over the place. The bar's isolation made it perfect for his return during the cover of night.

On the outskirts of Morris, he checked into the Siesta Trail Motel, a run-down one-story strip of rooms with a manager's office at one end. It seemed to cater mostly to Mexican oil field workers, judging by the amount of pickup trucks with Hispanic detailing parked in the lot. When the greasy-looking man at the front desk asked for his driver's license, Blake slipped him a couple of hundred-dollar bills instead. The man said nothing and turned over the room key. Apparently, the desk clerk had experience dealing with customers unable to produce ID.

Blake backed the bike into the parking space before his room. He didn't want some flunky cop driving through reading his plates. Unlocking the door, he went inside and turned on the lights. A saggy bed, dingy yellow curtains, and a stuffed chair pitted with cigarette burns furnished the room. Nonstop Mexican music boomed through the thin walls from the room next door. When he switched on the bathroom lights, a dozen roaches ran across the tile. The place was a dump, but it would do. He only needed to stay here until after dark.

Throwing himself on the bed, he watched the ceiling fan go around. He had been up for over forty-eight hours but was too coked up to sleep. He pulled the bag of blow out of his jacket and snorted a couple more lines to keep his high going. Today had been a good day. Not only did he make it to Hope Springs undeterred but, in an incredible turn of good luck, he also encountered Jess and Megan on arriving in town. The only complication was her involvement with the local sheriff. He stared at the revolving fan while imagining coming up on both the sheriff and his wife in bed and beating them to death with his bat. Vividly, he pictured the cracking of their skulls and the blood and brain matter spraying the walls of the room with every blow. A smile crossed his cracked lips. It was a good fantasy.

Hours passed. He entered some sort of fugue state driven by the coke, exhaustion, and lack of sleep. When he focused again on the external world, dusk darkened the dingy curtains. Blake rose from the bed and contemplated doing more coke but decided against it. His mind needed clarity for what was next. Running the bathroom water, he splashed some over his head and drank heartily using his hand. Afterward, he dressed in his shirt and long black duster, pocketed the field binoculars, and slid the aluminum bat into its makeshift holster.

It was time to leave.

An unexpected occurrence interrupted the drive out to the roadhouse. Ahead on the highway, blue and red lights topped a hill accompanied by the wail of a siren. Blake pulled his Harley over to the side of the road as an EMT ambulance barreled past going the other direction. A minute later the sheriff's patrol car followed at a high speed. The man driving was the same one he had seen earlier in the day. His features looked stern as he went by in a blur of red and blue flashers.

Blake felt a little disappointed. He hoped to catch Jess and the sheriff together but couldn't if the man responded to an emergency call. He would still drop in on Jess. He throttled the bike up and continued to Roxie's.

The place was busy. The gravel parking lot was full with more vehicles pulling in. Blake steered his bike until he found a line of parked motorcycles. He backed his Harley into the end of the line, shut the engine off, and decided to sit and watch the place. Muffled karaoke music seeped out of the roadhouse, increasing in volume every time someone opened the door.

Where was his Camaro?

He searched the lot and spotted it parked under a streetlight. Sliding off his bike, he crossed over to the car and peered through the side glass. A smile crossed his lips. When Jessica ran off, he seriously doubted he would ever see the car again. He figured she would sell it for cash. He tried the doors. Locked. He hadn't thought to bring his spare key when he left Chicago. Thanks to his law enforcement training, he knew how to jimmy the door open but didn't want anyone coming up on him breaking into the car.

For now, he would just sit and wait.

* * * *

Carrying ice-cold bottles of beer, Jessica pushed her way through the cigarette smoke of the crowded bar. Customers occupied all but two of the thirteen tables. To aid her in remembering who ordered what, Jessica gave each table a number in her mind. Table two had a one-legged farmer who tipped well and smiled at her every time she went by. Eight had a group of bikers who were going to some rally in Tulsa. A young couple, more interested in making out than drinking, occupied table five.

She reached table six with their order. The occupants laughed loudly at a dirty joke as she put the bottles down in front of them. "Eight dollars."

The nearest man quit chuckling long enough to put a ten in her hand. "Keep the change, gorgeous."

"Thanks." She smiled and returned to the bar where Roxie served customers with expert efficiency.

"You're doing fine, Jess," Roxie said, taking the ten and making change. "The customers like you."

"I hope so." She put the two dollars in her steadily increasing tip jar under the counter. "It does get busy in here pretty quick." Jessica glanced over the rest of the tables. Number four would need a refill soon. The other customers had full beers and seemed content to listening to the karaoke. On the stage, Pearl sang an excellent version of a Mary Chapin Carpenter song while couples two-stepped to the music on the dance floor.

"How do you like our little bar?" Roxie asked.

"I like the tips, but I'm not used to the cigarette smoke."

"If you need to step out for some fresh air, I can watch the place for a bit."

"Okay." Jess grabbed up the bottle of cold water she'd been sipping on all night. "I'll be right back."

Crossing through the back room, she stepped out the exit door into the cool evening air. The back door closed, replacing the noisy crowd with the sound of crickets in the country. She had never seen what lay behind the building and discovered a thick grove of trees bordered the back property of the roadhouse. A worn footpath cut through the woods leading toward the dark shape of an old barn in the distance.

Jessica closed her eyes and took a deep breath of the fresh night air.

A dry crackling in the nearby underbrush caused her to reopen her eyes. Turning toward the sound, her blood froze. A dark figure stood in the shadow of the trees.

Blake! her mind screamed. *Oh God, it's Blake!*

The man stepped from the shadow into the moonlight, but his face remained half-hidden. Unnaturally dark eyes stared at her. Jessica gasped in shock.

"Who's there?" she called out in a nervous voice.

"Collin," the shadowed figure replied, taking another step closer. Moonlight shifted to show his face and shoulder-length black hair.

"You gave me a fright," Jessica stated. She had been too busy to notice he wasn't in the bar when she stepped out.

"I just came out to see the moon," he stated.

She glanced up through the trees at the hazy orb hanging in the starlit sky. "It is beautiful tonight. Is that what you call a harvest moon?"

"I like to think of it as a hunter's moon."

"I heard someone in the bar saying there's a lunar eclipse soon."

"In two nights."

Collin had never shown any interest in talking before. Jessica sensed this was a time for a little conversation. She didn't particularly like the man, but he was her boss. Best to keep things on good terms, she decided. "I saw your drawings on the wall of the back room. They're really good. You have a lot of talent."

"Just random etchings of a lost home." He stepped closer, revealing the dark pupils of his eyes were wide and intense.

He's high on something, Jessica decided. *What is it? Meth? Crack? Coke? Probably came out here to get a fix.*

"I guess I better get back to work," Jessica said, cautiously taking a step back.

For the first time, Collin showed a thin smile. "You're needed inside."

"Roxie's probably swamped with customers by now." She put her hand on the doorknob to the back door.

"Tell sister I'm going to …" He paused to step back into the shadows. His voice grew deeper and hoarse. "… take off for a while."

He turned and ran down the wooded path before disappearing into the dark.

Jessica let out a nervous exhale. She wasn't sure what to make of her awkward encounter with Collin. Obviously, Roxie's brother was strung out on something, which explained his strange behavior. She was glad he left and didn't try to come on to her. One night in Chicago, she had a crackhead try to follow her home. It scared the hell out of her. She didn't want anything like that to happen here.

Returning to the smoky environment of the bar, Jessica found Roxie running back and forth serving tables.

"I'm back," Jessica announced above a girl doing a painful rendition of a Reba McEntire song on the karaoke stage. The singer was terribly off-key and out of time with the harmony.

"Good." Roxie put four more bottles of beer on the counter. "These go to the bikers at the table against the wall. They've already paid." She next placed a bottle of water next to the beer. "Can you take the water to Pearl?"

"Sure can." Jessica gathered up the order.

"Did you happen to see Collin while you were out? I need him to bring a case of Bud from the cooler."

"Only for a second. He said to tell you he had to run off." *Literally run off,* Jessica thought to herself. *I wonder if she knows about her brother's drug use.*

Roxie frowned. "I'll just do it myself."

Jessica took the beer to the table of bikers. All were burly men over the age of fifty with gray beards and large bellies straining against leather vests. Jessica wondered what need drove middle-aged men to turn into Harley riders. Probably overcompensation for the fact that they needed Viagra as well.

"There you go, guys," she said with a smile, placing the bottles on the table.

One of the bikers reached out and put an arm around her waist. "What's your name, sweetheart?"

"Jess."

"Well, Jess, can you tell the girl on the stage to stop strangling the cat?" The rest of the table burst into laughter.

"Why don't you grab a mic and show her how it's done?"

"I could fart better singing than that."

Another round of raucous laughter shook the table. The girl on stage ended her song and gave the loud group a dirty look before returning to her chair.

"Well, here's your chance to show us." Jess nodded toward the empty stage.

One of the men slapped the biker on the back, and they roared in laughter together. Jess used the opportunity to slip out of the man's arm.

Her next stop was Pearl, who was sitting at the karaoke machine programming in songs. "I brought you some water," she said, handing over the bottle.

"Thanks, Jess." She took off her reading glasses and rubbed her eyes. "I can't see the screen without these damn things. How's it going so far?"

"Everybody seems like they're having a good time."

"Let's hope it stays that way." Pearl took a swig from the water bottle. "It's a full moon tonight, which means the freaks are going to come out of the woodwork."

"So I hear." *They'd be hard to beat what I just saw outside,* Jess told herself.

"Uh-oh, here we go." Pearl nodded toward the front door. "The circus begins."

Jessica followed Pearl's gaze. Four new people had just entered the place, all dressed in a retro style reminiscent of the eighties right down to ripped jeans and cheap black sunglasses. The one girl in the group—for some reason Jessica couldn't fathom—had her blonde hair tied so it stuck straight up on her head. They made their way to sit at table thirteen.

Jessica let out a sigh and went to wait on them.

"What would you like to drink?" she asked. All four looked up at her in unison with eyes hidden behind dark shades.

"Hi, Jess." The girl slid off her glasses to show she was Debbie Miller. "Remember me? We talked at the Dollar Store earlier today?"

The skinny trailer trash, Jessica reminded herself.

"I remember."

"I told you I'd be out here tonight."

"You did."

"Can you guess why we're dressed like this?"

Jessica shrugged. "Halloween's early this year?"

Debbie smiled an evil grin. "I'll be singing hits from the eighties tonight. You know? Joan Jett, Corey Hart, Madonna."

"You sing karaoke?"

"I do." Debbie replaced the sunglasses.

Jessica took their beer order and returned to the bar.

"Watch out for that girl," Roxie commented as she popped the tops off the ordered longnecks. "She likes to make trouble. Debbie comes in here with her posse of lowlives and stirs up drama. I've had Collin throw them out a couple of times."

"Okay."

Returning to the table, Jessica put down their order and took their money. She was about to leave when the man sitting across from Debbie grabbed her by the wrist. He was about thirty with reddish brown hair and a light goatee.

"You're name's Jess, isn't it?" The man squeezed her wrist tighter. "I'm Brody."

"Hi," Jessica said, trying to slip her wrist from his grip. "I have to get back to work."

"That's the sheriff's girl," Debbie chimed in. "You better watch it."

"It is?" He looked Jessica up and down. "He always did know how to pick a hot piece of ass."

"Please, let go," Jessica said in a more demanding tone.

"Or what? Are you going to call the sheriff on me? I'm scared now. But you know what?" He looked around the bar. "I don't see him."

"Oh, that's right," Debbie said. "He had to go on some emergency call. I saw him racing out of town doing ninety to nothing. That's why he's not here." Debbie showed another smile. "Too bad, huh, Jess?"

"You're hurting me," Jessica said in a louder voice and then kicked him hard in the shin with the toe of her shoe.

"Bitch." He released the hold on her wrist and stood to his feet. "What did you do that for?"

"Don't touch me again," she said, stepping back.

Roxie suddenly appeared at her side holding the sawed-off end of a pool cue in her hand. "Brody, I don't want any of your shit tonight."

"Sorry. I was just talking to the pretty new lady."

Pointing to everyone sitting at the table, Roxie said, "If there is any more bullshit; I'm tossing you all out. Understood, Debbie?"

Debbie nodded. "We're here to have a good time. No trouble."

"Just make sure it stays that way."

Following Roxie back to the bar, Jessica said, "Thanks."

"I saw what happened," Roxie stated, placing the sawed-off pool cue back under the bar. "You aren't afraid to fight back, are you?"

"Not anymore."

"Well, Debbie shouldn't cause any more trouble. She loves to sing karaoke and doesn't want me to throw her out. I'll wait on their table the rest of the night."

"Works for me."

"I just wish Collin was here."

Jessica thought for a moment, looking toward the stool at the end of the bar. "Where's Uncle Johnny? I thought you said he never missed a night here."

Roxie shrugged. "I guess I was wrong."

TWENTY-NINE

From the backseat of the sheriff's car, Terry Newman watched EMTs roll the gurney carrying Mr. Higgins off the porch of the dilapidated farmhouse. Strapped to the stretcher, the old man wore an oxygen mask covering most of his face. The flashing red and blue lights provided by emergency vehicles made the scene look surreal and dreamlike. They wheeled him to the back of the ambulance and loaded him inside. With sirens blaring, the ambulance pulled out of the front yard and down the country road.

"I hope he's going to be all right," Terry said to Sid, sitting beside him in the backseat.

"Me, too, but what we have to worry about now is Sheriff Dickhead." Sid nodded toward Sheriff Sutton, who had just finished talking to a couple of Oklahoma Highway Patrol officers. "We're fucked now," Sid stated.

"Just be cool," Terry cautioned.

"What are we going to say happened?"

"The truth."

"Screw that." Sid fidgeted in the seat. "We need to come up with a better story than a werewolf."

"Let me do the talking."

Sheriff Sutton opened the rear door on Terry's side and leaned his head in. The flashing police lights alternatively illuminated his grim face in red and blue.

"Are you boys going to tell me what the hell you were doing out here tonight?"

Terry cleared his throat. "Is Mr. Higgins all right?"

"He's stable, but it's touch and go. They're rushing him to County Regional in Stillwater. Now tell me what happened."

"We came with Mr. Higgins."

"Why?"

"Are we under arrest, Sheriff?" Sid suddenly asked.

"I don't know. I haven't decided yet."

"If we're not under arrest, we're free to go then. I know my fucking rights."

"Listen, you little prick." The sheriff leaned farther into the car. "I've got you on trespassing and breaking and entering. Plus, we can't find Elmer Grosslin, so you might be involved in his disappearance. If you don't answer some questions, I'm hauling your pimply ass to jail tonight."

"Let me handle this, Sid," Terry said, and then to the sheriff, "We came out here to return some photographs."

"Did you see Elmer?"

Terry shook his head. "When we got here, the front door was open, but he wasn't home."

"It looks like you boys broke in the front door when you found out he was gone."

"We didn't break in," Terry replied.

"Why would we?" Sid asked.

"To steal anything you could get your hands on."

"Like what? There's nothing in there but UFO magazines and mouse shit." Sid threw himself back against the seat. "This is really fucking stupid."

"The front door is torn off its hinges. Which one of you did that?"

Terry hesitated for a second. "The werewolf."

Sheriff Sutton's face grew tight. "Werewolf?"

"We were in the front yard and heard this howling. It came running for us so we fled into the house and locked the door. The werewolf broke it down."

"I'm supposed to believe that?"

"It's true," Terry stated. "I'm not lying, sir. I saw it with my own eyes."

Sheriff Sutton sighed. "Okay, let's move to something else." He produced Mr. Higgins's .38 pistol. "Who was carrying this?"

"Mr. Higgins. He shot the werewolf after it broke down the door."

Dropping out the cylinder, Sheriff Sutton emptied out the bullets into his hand. "One spent round. Five live." He examined one closer and his eyes grew cold. "Silver bullets." He looked at both of them. "Who made these?"

"Mr. Higgins," Terry answered. "He thinks a werewolf killed his wife."

"Where did he get that idea?"

"A picture Elmer took the other night."

"This picture?" The sheriff reached into the front pocket of his shirt and removed the photograph. "Mr. Higgins gave it to me before he left in the ambulance."

"That's it." Terry nodded. "Mr. Higgins said that the creature in the picture was the same one that killed his wife. He wanted to prove he didn't do it and asked for our help."

"So you two slackers filled his head with stories about werewolves?"

"Look at the picture. What do you think it is?"

"Just a dark shape beside a dead cow. Probably something that nutcase Elmer staged. You can get a mask like that at any Wal-Mart. They've got all their Halloween stuff out now."

"It's a werewolf, and that picture proves it."

"What picture?" Sheriff Sutton ripped the photograph into shreds and tossed the pieces into the wind.

"Hey, that was fucking evidence!" Sid shouted.

"Not anymore."

"Why did you do that?" Terry asked. "It's our only proof we weren't making it up."

Sheriff Sutton leaned back into the car. His eyes were dark pools. "I'm only going to say this once. Thanks to you two pussies and your werewolf fantasy, I've got a murder suspect on the way to the hospital and Elmer Grosslin missing. I'm probably going to be out all night walking over this shithole looking for the crazy coot. I'm letting you go for now, but if I hear any more bullshit about a werewolf, I'm throwing you both in jail. Do you understand?"

"Yes, sir," Terry replied.

Sid crossed his arms and stared out the window.

"That goes for you, Granger."

"Fine. I understand."

Sheriff Sutton tossed a set of keys into Terry's lap. "Mr. Higgins said to give you the keys to his truck and drive it back to his farm. Can you do that, son?"

"Yes, sir."

"Okay, get out of here but remember what I said. No more bullshit about a werewolf or I will arrest the both of you."

Terry exited the back of the patrol car. Sid followed. They crossed the high weeds until they reached Mr. Higgins's Ford F-150, and Terry slid behind the wheel. Once inside, he started the engine and looked out the front glass. Sheriff Sutton had shut off the patrol car lights and now stood watching them leave.

"That guy scares me," Sid stated.

"Let's just leave."

Terry put the truck into gear and backed out onto the country road. He glanced into the rearview mirror one last time as he pulled away. The sheriff stood like a stone statue in the yard.

The guy is creepy, Terry thought to himself.

*   *   *   *

Sheriff Sutton fought back burning rage as the two boys pulled away in Mr. Higgins's pickup truck. Under the light of the full moon, his body wanted to transform into his Wolfkin form and rip the two teenagers apart. If he had not fed on the hitchhiker the day before, it would have been impossible to hold the beast at bay tonight.

Once the taillights of the truck disappeared over a hill, Sheriff Sutton slid into the front seat of the patrol car. He turned his gaze to the .38 pistol laying in the passenger seat and thought about the silver bullets. The Pack hadn't faced such a threat in years. Fortunately, the old man wasn't expected to live through the night. That just left Terry Newman and Sid Granger to worry about. They convinced Mr. Higgins that a werewolf had killed his wife. The old man didn't know shit from werewolves before meeting those boys. That much was certain.

He put the pistol in the glove box and shut the door.

The Pack will deal with the two meddling teens soon if they continue causing trouble. He doubted he had scared them enough to stop spreading talk of werewolves. Teenage boys had big mouths, especially the Granger kid, but he doubted anyone would believe a couple of nerdy outcasts spewing tales of monsters in the night.

He had a more pressing concern at the moment. One of the Pack might have been shot by a silver bullet. Uncle Johnny, as he was known to the locals, was an elder of the Clan who survived with the other Wolfkin in the wilds of Canada. Something had gone terribly wrong. Uncle Johnny should have never approached Mr. Higgins if he had the two youths with him. The upcoming Ebon Moon made it harder to resist transforming to the beast inside. Uncle Johnny may have fallen victim to the moon's influence, which could have triggered an uncontrolled transformation.

Sheriff Sutton left Elmer Grosslin's property on foot. Under a sky full of stars, he crossed the dirt road heading toward the rusting oil storage tanks overlooking the farm. He found Uncle Johnny's pickup parked behind the largest tank. Sheriff Sutton stopped his approach and sniffed the night air. The tangy essence of fresh blood wafted on the breeze … *Wolfkin blood!*

Racing forward, he reached the driver's side and popped open the door. Uncle Johnny's body sat in the front seat with his head slumped against the steering wheel. Blood was everywhere—the seat, dash, and floorboards. Sheriff Sutton reached in and leaned Johnny back. The portly man hadn't completely transformed to human yet and still carried some of the Wolfkin characteristics. Gray fur still lined the edges of his face. He let out a raspy breath, spitting blood from his semicanine mouth. Clawed hands clutched a bullet hole in his chest.

"I'm dying … silver bullet," he struggled to speak. "Higgins shot me."

"I know," Sheriff Sutton replied. "He's dying, too. Heart gave out."

Uncle Johnny reached out and grabbed the sheriff by the arm. Sheriff Sutton felt the sharp nails retreating back into the flesh.

"Tell Collin and Roxie …" He coughed and spit out more blood. "They are the last … of the Pure Bloods." His breath came in barely audible rasps. "There are no others … I've kept it secret from them." He coughed again. "The last Full Bloods … must leave this cursed place … return to the forests in the north … mate again … continue the bloodline … or all is lost."

Uncle Johnny let out a last rattling cough and grew still.

"I'll tell them," Sheriff Sutton said to the dead body.

He stepped back away from the truck and slammed shut the door. The war between Wolfkin and humans had raged since before history, and mankind was winning. In this modern digital age of the Internet and cell phones, there was no place for the werewolf. The kills were becoming harder to hide and the Wolfkin teetered on the edge of extinction. If what Uncle Johnny had gasped in his dying breath was true, Roxie and Collin bore the last of the bloodline.

Sheriff Sutton stared up at the full moon. Feelings of anger and sadness fought for domination within. He quelled the want to release the animal inside, to run feral through the countryside and bring down the first warm body he found. His human side was still needed tonight. Instead, he threw his head back and released a long, mourning howl that echoed across the surrounding plains and fields.

CHAPTER THIRTY

After leaving Jess at the back door of the roadhouse, Collin shed his clothes before transforming into the werewolf. On canine legs, he raced through the backcountry leaping over barbed wire fences and crossing dark fields. Even in his beast form, he was not totally feral. His human mind still remained in control. Hunched over, he loped on all fours and kept to the shadows with acute senses constantly searching the countryside for human occupants. With miles to go, he wanted nothing to interrupt his foray into the night. An intense obsession drove him toward one destination, like a candle flame in the dark.

The mother was working.

It was time to pay the daughter a visit.

The thought of Megan consumed him. In two nights, the beast would feed on the girl's tender flesh under the darkening light of the Ebon Moon. As his ancestors have done for centuries, so it would be with him.

Though his intention was not to devour the child this night, his human side needed to know how protected she was while the mother worked. Leaping another fence, he slipped into the brush lining the bank of Skeleton Creek and followed the creek bed under the cover of the overhanging trees. He kept to the shadows hidden from sight. At one point, he waited beneath a cement bridge as a car passed overhead. Once gone, he continued following the ribbon of black water that would eventually lead him to the Olson farm.

Halfway through his journey, human voices sounded ahead and car doors slammed. He slid beneath the underbrush, sensing the area around him. Ahead lay a bend where the creek widened. Figures of several people moved against the glow of a bonfire raging on the water's bank. The sickly sweet scent of marijuana hung in the air. *A party of some kind,* Collin's mind realized deep within the body of the creature. *Teenagers celebrating a local football game victory.*

One of the boys threw a beer can and howled at the moon. The empty can landed less than twenty feet away from the spot where he waited in the shadows. He fought back the impulse to charge forward and leap amid the youths, rip into them with tooth and claw. Instead he circled around the party and continued his journey.

A couple of miles farther, he climbed out of the creek bed and approached the Olson property. On the edge of the plowed field, he studied the farm sprawled under a full moon hanging in the sky. Everything seemed quiet and peaceful. Lights were on in both the farmhouse and the trailer in the back. He focused on the trailer house. The child would be there. Running across the field, he slid into the shadow at the back of the barn. From the new vantage point he studied the lights in the trailer.

Give me the child, the beast demanded deep inside. *Let me feast upon her flesh.*

No! Collin responded. *The moon has not yet darkened.*

Give me the child!

He left the shadows and crossed to the side of the trailer house. Beneath the lighted bay windows, he crouched and listened against the wall. Through the sheet metal and insulation came the sound of movement and breathing. The child was in the room beyond. The creature's mind twisted inside at the thought of being so close.

I must see her!

It's too dangerous.

I MUST SEE HER!

The mind of the beast pushed his human consciousness aside. Now in full control, the creature slowly rose and peered in through the bay window. Lit by a fluorescent overhead lamp, the child sat at a dining room table occupied with a coloring book while a middle-aged woman knitted in a recliner in the front room. Both were oblivious to the monster watching from the darkness outside. A ravenous hunger raged at the sight of the flowing golden hair and tender young flesh of the human offspring. Its red tongue lapped at dripping saliva. From deep within the animal mind, Collin fought the creature's urge to leap through the bay window and snatch up the child with its jaws.

You cannot!

But she is so close. I can almost taste her.

In two nights you will have your feast.

The woman turned to say something to the girl. The beast ducked below the windowsill and listened intently. Human voices, woman and child, spoke within the interior of the home. A knocking sounded at the front door. Someone entered the home. A man's voice followed. Deciding to move, the creature continued along the outside of the trailer and stopped to hunch down on all fours at the back door. The child was so close. Reaching up with one clawed hand, the beast lightly scratched across the door's surface.

Come to me, child. Come see what the noise is.

*   *   *   *

Megan jutted her tongue out one side of her mouth as she concentrated on coloring Red Riding Hood's cape. Pushing the red crayon along the paper, she tried her best to keep within the lines. She wanted to show her mommy the picture when she came home from work. The overhead light above the dining room table illuminated her artwork in a soft glow. From the front room, Nelda sat in the reclining chair and knitted a sweater for fall. Megan was happy. The hot chocolate she drank earlier had warmed her tummy and the trailer house, her new home, was quiet and cozy. She missed Mommy but knew she would be home later. She didn't miss Daddy. He was a bad man who left her alone in a dark house in the middle of the night. Mommy made sure she had Aunt Nel to watch over her. Megan liked Aunt Nel, who was nice and always smelled like cookies when she gave her a hug.

Megan put down the red crayon. She had finished with Red Riding Hood's cape and turned her attention to the Bad Wolf. In the line drawing, the animal watched the girl secretly from around a tree. It was a scary picture. The Bad Wolf had sharp fangs and a tongue sticking out of its mouth. The drawn eyes of the animal reminded her of Daddy when he was angry—the kind of look he would have right before he hit Mommy.

"How are you coming with your coloring, sweat pea?" Aunt Nel asked as she put down her needles and slid her reading glasses up on her forehead.

"Okay," Megan replied. "What crayon should I color the Bad Wolf? Gray or black?"

"I think wolves are mostly gray."

"Okay." Megan picked up the gray crayon.

A sudden knocking rattled the front door of the trailer. The abrupt noise caused Aunt Nel to jump to her feet and spill the knitting out of her lap. Startled, Megan reached for the gray crayon, but it rolled off the end of the table before she could grab it. Continuing along the linoleum tiles on the floor, the crayon bumped against the bottom of the back door in the laundry room.

Aunt Nel went to the front door. "Who is it?"

"It's Sam."

Unlocking the bolt, Aunt Nel swung it open. "Jesus, Sam, you scared the hell out of me," she hissed.

"Sorry." He stepped into the light of the front room wearing a heavy jacket over his coveralls and a hunting rifle held in the crook of his arm. "Something's spooked the livestock." Seeing Megan sitting at the table, Sam waved. "Hi, Meg."

"Hi," Megan said as she scooted her chair back from the table.

Turning to Aunt Nel, he said, "I want you two to stay inside the trailer. If you hear anyone moving about outside, it's just me."

On bare feet, Megan padded across the floor to retrieve the lost crayon. From the front room came the low voices of the two grown-ups. She bent down to pick up the gray crayon at the base of the back door and stopped. Scratching noises sounded from the other side of the door.

It's Tig, she thought to herself as she remembered the tabby cat. *Poor Tig wants to come in from the cold.*

Megan reached up and unlocked the doorknob. She wasn't tall enough to unhook the chain, but maybe she could open the door far enough to let the cat inside. She turned the knob and the door popped open as far as the chain would allow, letting in light from the full moon. Something suddenly blocked the moonlight. A nightmarish form with red eyes and a horrendous maw of sharp fangs gazed at her through the space in the doorway.

Scared, Megan fell back on the floor and watched speechless as black claws reached for her through the open space of the door.

She screamed.

Aunt Nel and Sam rushed into the room, shock showing in both their faces at the sight of her curled up on the floor.

"What's wrong, baby?" Aunt Nel asked.

Megan pointed at the door hanging open on the chain.

"Something's outside, Sam," Nelda said as she swept Megan off the floor and into her arms. "I heard it growling."

"Stay." He unclasped the chain and swung open the door. "What the hell?" were his next words as he snapped the rifle up to his shoulder and fired. The shot thundered within the confines of the utility room. A second shot sounded as Aunt Nel carried her away into the light of the living room.

"There, there, sweet pea, it'll be all right." Nel held her close. "Tell Aunt Nel what you saw at the back door."

"The Bad Wolf," Megan whimpered with wet tears against the woman's neck.

CHAPTER THIRTY-ONE

"You've got a call," Roxie shouted above Debbie Miller belting out a Pat Benatar song over the karaoke sound system.

"What?" Jessica yelled back.

From behind the bar, Roxie raised the phone and motioned for her to come over. Jessica jostled her way through the crowd.

"Phone call," Roxie said when Jessica reached the bar.

"Okay." She took the portable phone and stepped into the back room to better hear the person on the line.

"Hello?"

"Jess, this is Nelda."

A tinge of fear settled in Jessica's stomach. "What's wrong?"

"Something scared Megan."

"What do you mean something scared her?"

"She heard scratching at the back door and thought it was Tig. She opened the door and something scared her. Sam and I were both in the front room. He had come over because the livestock were spooked. I should've been watching her closer, Jess. I'm sorry. I'm not used to looking after children."

"Is she okay?"

"She's pretty shook up. So am I. We're too scared to stay in the trailer tonight. I brought her over to my house. She's here with me."

"You said something scared her. What was it?"

"Sam thinks it was a big dog scratching to get in from the cold. He only saw it running away in the dark. He shot at it twice with his rifle and thinks he may have hit it."

"Is that ordinary for a stray dog to come on your farm like that?"

"We've had problems with coyotes and wild dogs in the past, but none have ever come scratching at the door."

"Can I talk to her?"

"Yeah, she's right here."

As Jessica waited for Megan to come to the phone, she glanced out at the crowded serving area. The place was too busy for her to leave. Roxie popped open a line of beer bottles and tried to wait on customers crowding the bar. Jessica knew she needed to rush home but didn't want to leave Roxie in a bind running the bar herself. Not on her first day on the job.

Damn it! Where the hell is Collin?

"Mommy?" Megan asked in her weepy voice on the other end of the line.

"Hi, baby. Mommy's here."

"I'm scared."

"I know, baby. Mommy will be home as soon as possible. Okay, sugar?"

"I saw the Bad Wolf, Mommy."

"The one in your coloring book?"

"Uh huh."

"You stay over at Aunt Nel and Sam's house until I get there. You be a big girl until Mommy comes home. All right?"

"Okay."

"Let me talk to Aunt Nel."

Silence, and then, "I'm so sorry, Jess. It's my fault. I shouldn't let her out of my sight."

"Don't blame yourself, Nel. Compared to how her bastard father used to leave her alone at night, you did nothing wrong. Keep her warm and close until I get there. I'm going to try to get off work as soon as possible. The place is packed right now."

"She's safe here. Sam is with us and he has his rifle."

"That's good."

"The poor girl has been through so much."

"Too much," Jessica said and ended the call. She returned to the main room of the bar and replaced the phone on the receiver.

"Something wrong?" Roxie asked as she readied to expertly open another beer.

"My daughter got scared by something at the house. She's pretty upset."

"Scared? What frightened her?"

"A big dog."

Roxie stiffened and the bottle she opened slipped out of her grip, spilling beer down the bar.

"Damn!" she cursed and grabbed up a nearby towel. "Are you kidding? A dog?"

"I've got to go home as soon as possible."

"Just leave," Roxie replied in a terse voice as she sopped up spilled beer. "Go ahead. Don't worry about me."

"Are you sure? Listen, Roxie, I can't afford to lose this job."

"Just go." Anger flashed in Roxie's dark eyes.

Jessica made her decision then. She could always find another place to work. Megan was more important than anything else in the world. They had been through hell together, and she knew her daughter was home crying for Mommy.

Taking the purse out of the locker, she emptied the dollar bills out of her tip jar and stuffed them inside. Without saying a word to anyone, she stepped out the front door of the smoky bar and into the night air.

A sense of paranoia gripped her as she walked briskly toward the Camaro waiting at the end of a line of vehicles facing the roadhouse. She glanced over her shoulder to see if anyone was behind her, a lesson she learned in Chicago when the crackhead followed her from the strip club. She focused on the row of parked Harley motorcycles. A dark figure in black stood by one of the bikes. A cold chill raced down her spine as she increased her step and took the keys from her purse. Reaching the side of the car, she inserted the key to unlock the driver door.

A man grabbed her from behind. *Oh God,* her mind screamed. *Blake!*

"Not leaving so soon, are you, baby?" asked an unfamiliar voice.

She pushed out of the man's hold to find it was Brody, the smartass who had held her wrist in the bar.

"Stay away from me," she warned.

"The party's just getting started, girl."

"I have to go home, so leave me alone."

"Hey, no need to get all upset." He leaned closer, reeking of beer breath. "I just want to apologize for what I said in there. Let's kiss and make up."

"Leave me alone!" she shouted, jabbing him in the face with her car key. He staggered back from the sudden attack. Shoving him farther away, Jessica popped open the car door and jumped inside behind the wheel. Before she could shut the door, Brody blocked it with his shoulder and stuck his head inside the car.

"You little tease!" Spittle flew from his lips. In the glow from the dome light, blood ran down from a deep scratch in his cheek. "You're going to pay for that!"

Jessica reached under the seat and yanked up the .357 pistol. She shoved the barrel under the man's nose.

"I said to the get the fuck away from me!" she warned again.

His eyes went wide from the sight of the large pistol in his face. He stepped back from the car as Jessica shut the driver door. Placing the gun in her lap, she fumbled with the car keys and finally got one in the ignition. With her heart racing from the adrenaline rush of the assault, she turned the engine over and backed the car out in a cloud of white gravel dust. Without a look in the rearview mirror, she drove the Camaro out of the parking lot.

She never saw what happened next to Brody.

*   *   *   *

Used to long stakeouts, Blake waited patiently in the dark for Jess to leave the bar. Intending to keep his vigil until she went home after closing time, it surprised him when the front door opened and she stormed out. Blake checked his watch: 11:38. Too early for closing time and, judging by the full parking lot, the roadhouse was too busy for a waitress to leave. Something must have happened.

As Jess walked toward the Camaro, she looked directly at him over her shoulder. Blake stepped back into the shadows. For the second time today, she didn't realize her husband watched her. Like before, something else was on her mind. With hurried footsteps, she continued to the car. He slid his leg over the Harley to start the bike. Homicidal anger burned in his gut at the sight of his wife. It was time to follow the cheating whore home and take his revenge with the baseball bat.

The roadhouse door opened again. A tall man staggered out of the bar and followed after Jess. He knew instinctively that the drunk was going to assault her.

No one touches my wife but me!

Blake slid off the bike and eased the aluminum bat out of his coat. He crossed the lot toward the two of them. Words exchanged as Jessica struggled with the assaulting drunk. Crouching down behind the bumper of a nearby truck, he risked a glance around the taillight to see what transpired between the two. Jess had his .357 service pistol stuck into the man's face. Eyes wide with fear, the drunk staggered back and she shut the driver's door. The Camaro's engine turned over and the car tore out of the gravel lot.

Blake stood up with the bat gripped in his hand.

"Hey," he called out.

The drunk half-turned toward him. Blake swung the bat and struck the man's head with a sickening thud. He collapsed against the side of the pickup and fell to the gravel. Blake contemplated a second swing, but the taillights of the Camaro disappeared down the highway. If he didn't follow her now, he could lose Jessica twice in the same day.

He sprinted toward the Harley and started the bike. The engine thundered to life and he roared out of the parking lot onto Highway 133. Turning toward the speeding Camaro, he spotted the taillights a couple of miles down the dark highway heading toward Hope Springs. Blake increased the throttle to keep the Camaro in sight. Jessica barely slowed as she tore through the center of town and continued on. Blake followed and hoped he wouldn't be pulled over for speeding. Jessica didn't have to worry about a ticket since the whore was fucking the town's hick sheriff. He would have to kill whoever stopped him.

Outside the town limits, she turned down a two-lane blacktop. Blake slowed the bike and took the same turn. He contemplated turning off his headlight but knew the loud pipes of the bike could still be heard. He had to chance a drive-by when Jessica reached her destination and hope he wouldn't raise her suspicions of being followed.

A mile down the blacktop, the Camaro turned into the driveway of a large farm. As he drew near, the car disappeared around the back of a barn. He checked out the property as he drove past. A large farmhouse, barn, metal shed, and darkened double-wide trailer on a hill made up the details he could discern at night. The only interior lights were on in the house. He continued farther down the road past the farm.

Blake smiled. Now all he had to do was sneak back. Then he would repay the bitch for what she did to him. He reached out and touched the end of the bat stuck in the gap of the handlebars. His quest to find his backstabbing wife paid off.

He had Jess now.

CHAPTER THIRTY-TWO

Jessica exited the Camaro. Sam stood at the back door of the farmhouse holding his hunting rifle.

"How's Megan?" she shouted above the rumble of a passing motorcycle on the road running in front of the farm.

"She's safe with Nel," Sam replied. "The poor girl's had a bad scare and been asking for you."

"I came as fast as I could." He held the door open to let her in. She passed through the kitchen, dining area, and into the living room where Nelda sat on the couch cradling Megan wrapped in a blanket.

"Are you okay, baby?" Jessica asked while dropping her purse into a chair.

Megan looked up with teary blue eyes. "Mommy!"

Sliding out of the blanket, she ran across the room and into her arms. Her wet face pressed against Jessica's cheek as she lifted her up to hold her close. The child shivered in her embrace.

"I'm here now," Jessica whispered in her daughter's ear.

"She's been frightened near to death." Nelda stood and crossed over to join them. She ran her fingers tenderly through Megan's blonde curls. "It scared the hell out of me, too."

"Tell me again what happened," Jessica said.

Sam laid the rifle across the dining table and entered the living room. "The livestock were spooked so I went to check things out. I stopped at the trailer to tell Nel not to be afraid if she saw or heard me moving about outside. I was talking to her in the front room when little Meg here heard scratching at the back door. I guess she thought Tig was trying to get in and opened the door as far as the chain allowed. Whatever was on the other side scared her and she screamed. We both ran into the utility room, and I fired two shots out the back door at something running into the night."

"It was the Bad Wolf, Mommy," Megan sobbed.

"Could it have been a wolf?" Jessica asked Sam.

"I don't think so. There hasn't been a wolf in these parts for a hundred years. The ranchers killed them off around the turn of the century."

"What the hell was it then?"

Sam shook his head. "I don't know. I'm thinking a large dog, black bear, or a mountain lion, something big. I only got a glimpse when it ran off, though I'm pretty sure I shot it at least once before it got away. I'd go out looking for it but don't want to hunt a large wounded animal in the dark. I'll wait until morning comes."

"I guess I shouldn't have bought her the coloring book, Jess. It's was probably too scary for her," Nelda stated.

"I think she'll be all right," Jessica replied. "Let me just hold her for a while until she goes to sleep."

Jessica eased into a reclining chair hugging Megan close. After a few minutes, the child passed out and breathed softly against her chest in blissful sleep. Jessica fought back her own tears. In less than one week, she had fled her violent husband only to find her bad luck had followed her from Chicago. Running low on money, she probably lost her job tonight. Whatever scared Megan was going to make it nearly impossible for her to leave her daughter again and go to work. Once again, her life had jumped on a runaway train barreling downhill out of control.

"Here's some hot coffee, dear," Nelda said in a quiet voice as she put the cup on the stand beside the recliner.

"Thank you."

She took a seat on the couch across from her. "You're welcome to sleep here tonight, Jess. You don't have to be alone in the trailer. This couch folds out into a bed. I think we'd feel better if you stayed here."

"That'll be fine."

"I'm glad you were able to come as fast as you did. I tried to comfort her, but there's nothing like a mother's love."

"I knew I had to be here. I could feel it in my bones." She brushed a curl out of Megan's sleeping face. "I might have lost my job, though."

"You think so?"

Jessica nodded. "The bar was packed, and Roxie and I were the only ones working. When I left she gave me an angry look before I went out the door. I didn't get the impression she wanted me to come back. I know I owe you money, Nel. I'll have to find another job to repay you. I'm sorry."

"I never did like that Roxie girl," Nelda replied, taking a sip from her coffee cup. "The roadhouse was a pretty nice place to go on Friday night back when it was called the Boggy Bottom Bar. An elderly couple owned it.

When Roxie and her brother took over the place, Sam and I stopped going. Roxie flaunted her body in clothes so tight a schoolgirl couldn't fit in them. Men were always drooling over her, but she gave me the creeps. There's just something about her. "

"I think her brother Collin's a meth head. You should have seen the wild and crazy look in his eyes tonight."

"I'm not surprised with some of the people that frequent the place now."

"Which reminds me," Jessica said. "I had to fight off a drunk when I was leaving the bar to come here."

"Who was it?"

"Some guy named Brody. One of Debbie Miller's friends, which makes me think she may have set the thing up. He followed me out of the bar and tried to come on to me, but I pushed him away and drove out of there."

"That settles it then. I don't think you should go back. It's not safe for you to work there."

"Pearl was right," Jessica said with a chuckle. "The place does get crazy on a full moon."

Minutes passed while she comforted Megan. She was about to say something to Nelda when headlights brightened the living room curtains. The crunch of tires and the stopping of an engine signaled a car had pulled up in the drive. Sam came out of the dining room and looked out the front door.

"Who is it, Sam?" Nelda asked.

"Sheriff Sutton."

"You didn't call the sheriff, did you, Sam?"

"Nope."

Nelda looked at Jessica from across the room. "I wonder what he wants at this late hour."

"Best let him in and find out," Sam said, opening the front door.

"Evening, Sam," Sheriff Sutton's voice came from the foyer.

"Can I help you, Sheriff?"

"I want to talk to Jessica."

"It's kind of late for a social call."

"I just need to ask her a few questions."

"She's right in here." Sam motioned for him to enter. Sheriff Sutton looked tired as he stepped into the room. There was seriousness cast to his face coupled with weariness in his blue eyes. His took off his hat and held it in his hands. Tipping his head toward Nelda, he said, "Evening, Nel."

"Good evening, Sheriff."

He next nodded to Jessica. "Hello, Jess."

"You want to ask me some questions?"

"I do, but it would be best in private. Can you step outside for a bit?"

"I just got Megan to sleep."

Nelda stood up and came over. "I'll take her, dear."

"Okay."

She eased the sleeping child out of her arms into Nelda's. Megan didn't even stir during the exchange.

Jessica stood, saying to Nel, "I'll be right outside if she needs me."

Once out on the front porch, the brisk night air reminded Jessica she still wore a thin spaghetti strap black top. She hugged herself to help retain body warmth.

"Perhaps it would be more comfortable speaking in my car," the sheriff suggested.

"Okay," Jessica replied.

Inside the patrol car, the sheriff started the engine and turned up the heater. In the glow from the dash lights, Jessica studied his rugged features while his musky scent filled her nostrils. Breathing in his aroma, her pulse quickened but she fought down the attraction. With her life spiraling out of control, she needed to focus on Megan and not lust for another man.

"I'm sorry I didn't make it out to the bar tonight. I had to respond to a call. Some teenage boys broke into a farmer's house," Sheriff Sutton said.

"It's okay, I understand." Jessica looked away toward the moon.

"If I had been there then none of this would have happened."

"None of what?" Jessica asked, turning toward him again.

"Well, Jess ..." Sheriff Sutton pulled up a metal chart holder and flipped it open. "I've got some questions to ask, so please answer truthfully. I want to say, first off, I've come to really like you and your daughter, but I'm here in my professional capacity as an officer of the law. It's nothing personal. Do you understand?"

"Yes." Jessica said with a sinking feeling in her gut. Something was wrong.

"I got a call to go to Roxie's and came here from there. What happened when you were leaving the bar?"

"Someone named Brody grabbed me as I was getting in my car to leave. I told him to stay away. He was really drunk."

Sheriff Sutton wrote on an incident report clipped to the metal binder. The pen made scratchy noises in the confines of the car. "He reported you pulled a gun on him."

Jessica let out a sigh of desperation. "I have a .357 magnum revolver that I keep close for my protection. It's under the front seat of my car."

"Is it registered?"

"It belongs to my husband."

"So it's registered under his name?"

"I think so. Blake Lobato is a Chicago police officer."

"I didn't know that." Sheriff Sutton's eyes met her for a second. "You didn't tell me."

"We promised not to dwell on each other's past, remember?"

"I remember."

"Is the guy trying to press charges against me?" Jessica fought back new tears at the growing anxiety. She didn't need trouble with the law. "I should be reporting him."

"How was Brody when you left?"

"I scared the hell out of him. Hopefully, he learned a lesson not to attack women."

"So he wasn't injured?"

"I didn't shoot his ass, if that's what you're asking," Jessica replied as a growing panic rose inside. "Why? Did something happen to him?"

"Someone hit him from behind and nearly caved his head in with a club. It happened right after you drove off. Almost killed him. He's on his way to County Regional to get his scalp stitched together. He says a friend of yours did it."

"I just moved to town. I don't really know anybody, yet," she stated, and added, "except for Nelda and Sam, of course, and they were here watching Megan."

"So you have no idea who might have done it?"

"None."

"Anyone pay special attention to you in the bar?"

"Look how I'm dressed." Jessica glanced down at her black top and tight jeans. "A lot of men paid attention to me."

Sheriff Sutton smiled. "Point taken."

"There were a bunch of bikers in the bar, and Brody was acting like an asshole. He could have pissed anybody off."

"Your husband doesn't know you're here in Hope Springs?"

A sudden chill went down her spine at the thought. "I don't think so. He doesn't even know what state I'm in."

"You haven't called or contacted him?"

"Of course not," Jessica replied with a tinge of anger in her voice. "I'm trying to get away from the abusive bastard."

Sheriff Sutton closed his metal report holder. "End of interrogation. That's all the information I need for now. If there are any more questions, I'll come by tomorrow." He suddenly reached out and took her hand. She looked down in surprise. "You're not angry, are you?" He emphasized the question by giving her hand a comforting squeeze.

Jessica let out a breath. "I'm just overwhelmed. I had to leave Roxie's tonight because Megan needed me here. I probably lost my job and then you show up asking me questions. I'm under a lot of stress."

"If you want, I can talk to Roxie and put a good word in for you."

"I don't know if I want to go back if it means being assaulted every time I leave."

"I'll be there next time you get off work. I'll make sure you get home safely." He showed his white smile. "Okay?"

Jessica nodded. "Okay."

He bent in and kissed her lightly on the lips. "Don't think I forgot about our dancing together last night. I had a great time."

"So did I." His face was so close it caused her to look deep in his blue eyes. His scent clouded her mind. She fought back the urge to reach up and pull him in for another kiss but knew to do so would push her beyond the brink to stop. The need to feel a man's warm embrace combined with the incredible aroma he exuded stripped away her self-control. If he wanted hot, wanton sex in the front seat of the patrol car, she would gladly give it to him if she stayed any longer in his presence. As a defense, she popped open the passenger door, letting in the cold evening air.

"I better go now," she said in a weak voice.

"I understand." He patted the top of her hand. "Get some rest. Things will look better in the morning."

"I hope."

"Trust me," he said as she exited the patrol car.

CHAPTER THIRTY-THREE

A primal rage twisted inside the beast like the coils of a deadly snake. Its obsession to see the girl child had proved disastrous again. The rifle bullet buried deep in its chest burned like a red-hot poker as it crouched on the bank of Skeleton Creek near the Olson farm.

In the full moonlight, it drew upon its lycanthropic ability to heal. Muscle and tissue knitted together, forcing the bullet slowly from its flesh. Excruciating pain made breathing unbearable. It wanted to howl in agony but kept quiet in case human hunters were tracking it through the night. With its black claws, it reached into the chest wound, dug around, and removed the blob of lead with a thick sucking sound. Once the bullet was free, the healing increased and the flesh formed together.

The rage, however, grew stronger. Gone was the mind of Collin. The layers of bestial instinct overpowered the human side deep within. There was only the animal now … and it was hungry.

Fully healed, the beast surveyed its surroundings and listened to the night sounds. Someone was moving a short distance away, walking stealthily through the trees and dead brush, littering the forest floor. The beast recognized the footsteps of another predator. It crawled out from under its cover to peer ahead into the darkness. A few yards away, the figure of a man dressed in a long black coat made his way through the woods toward the farm. Instead of a rifle, the human predator carried a large club in one hand.

A low throated growl of satisfaction rumbled within the creature.

It had found its new prey.

*　　*　　*　　*

Blake Lobato followed a rutted cow path running along the fenced fields of the farm where Jess stayed. Not wanting the loud motorcycle to draw attention in the area, he walked his Harley along the fence line until he reached a spot near a grove of trees. He hid the bike in the shadows and pulled the aluminum bat from the handlebars. If the situation proved right, he could finish the job of killing his wife tonight. His payback for Jess's betrayal would then be complete. He stretched two strands of barbed wire and propped the space open with a dead tree limb. Through the gap, he eased onto the other side of the fence.

Baseball bat in hand, he took a path leading him closer to the farm. The air about him was quiet except for the breeze whispering through the canopy of leaves overhead. He soon discovered a winding creek bed and continued along its bank to cover his approach. After trekking a couple hundred yards, he found a good spot to recon the farm. He crossed to the edge of a plowed field, crouched, and put aside the bat. Removing the pair of hunting binoculars from his coat, he focused them on the farm.

The trailer home looked dark. If Jess and Megan were home, there would be a light on. He knew his wife was too paranoid to sleep in a dark trailer without any light. The farmhouse was where he focused next. He scanned the home just in time to see a car's headlights turn in the front yard. Through the lens, he spotted the sheriff's patrol car parking in front of the house. He watched the man walk from the car and disappear inside. A cold anger settled in his gut. The bastard was here to see his wife.

A couple of minutes passed before Jess and the sheriff stepped off the front porch and climbed into the patrol car together. He focused the binoculars upon the windshield of the cruiser. Through the blurry glass the two conversed. The next thing he spied turned his anger to homicidal rage. The sheriff leaned over and kissed Jess. The filthy whore was making out with the bastard in the front seat! He lowered the binoculars and picked up the baseball bat so tightly his knuckles turned white. He had to kill them both. To catch them together and swing the bat until their heads cracked open …

A growl came from behind him.

Blake's hair stood up on the back of his neck. He turned toward the sound. A dark shape pounced from the shadows and knocked him flat on his back. An image flashed like a snapshot from a nightmare. Large canine fangs, red eyes, and a growling wolf face hovered for a heartbeat above his prone form. By reflexes and instincts honed as an undercover officer, he snatched up the baseball bat and blocked the creature from ravaging his throat and neck. The canine maw bit hard upon the bat and nearly tore it from his hands. He kicked the beast from him and leaped to his feet.

The monstrous thing attacked again. Black fur bristled on its back as it charged forward to bite with its horrendous maw. Running on pure adrenaline and instinct to survive, Blake swung the bat against the side of the beast's head. Aluminum smacked hard against fur, flesh, and bone. The creature howled in pain and fell out of sight down the bank of the creek. He knew he had only a second to escape. Panic replaced his will to fight. He flung aside the bat and ran toward where he parked the Harley.

His riding boots thudded the soft turf of the woods. Behind him, the creature snarled and climbed out of the creek bank to give chase. A memory flashed of when he was just a boy of eight watching a *Wolf Man* movie in a dark theater. When the monster showed on the screen, he covered his eyes and prayed it to go away. As he got older, he learned his abusive father was far worse than any cinema monster created of cheap rubber and makeup effects ... until now. The horror chasing him stripped away all his years as a hard-ass cop on the street. He was eight years old again, and this time he could not cover his eyes to make the monster go away.

Behind him, dead limbs and brush snapped under the charge of the beast. The creature was closing in. Its sharp fangs bit against the night air inches from the swirling tails of his long leather coat. Any second, the nightmare would pull him down.

Ahead in the moonlight, the Harley waited on the other side of the barbed wire fence. Blake ran with all his strength toward the bike and dove through the propped-open space left between the strands of fence wire. His long coat snagged, and he yanked the leather free. Unable to slow its pursuit in time, the monster ran with full force into the metal wire and got hung up in the barbs. Blake had a precious few seconds to live. He reached the motorcycle and hit the ignition button as the beast tore apart the fence as if made of balsa wood and string. The bike's engine turned over, but before he could escape, the snarling horror rose and loomed over him.

Blake screamed in terror and popped the clutch as the creature sank its teeth deep into his shoulder. The bike shot forward, tearing the beast's bite free from his flesh. He opened the throttle, sending the Harley bouncing along the rutted cow path. He nearly spilled the bike but managed to keep it up on both wheels. In the rearview mirror, the monster loped full speed behind the taillights. He increased the throttle and left the creature behind as the bike roared out of the cow path and onto the asphalt farm road.

He had escaped the horror.

Coming down from the adrenaline high, Blake fought off succumbing to shock. He drove toward Hope Springs attempting to come to grips with the nightmarish encounter. What had bit him? Some deformed farm dog or wolf? The cold air helped clear his mind. He looked up at the full moon shining brightly overhead as he passed through the center of Hope Springs. A cold chill shook his body.

A werewolf?

Blake glanced over to the bite wound on his right shoulder. Ragged flesh shone through the rips in the leather jacket, and blood ran down the inside of the coat sleeve. He weighed his options. He couldn't go to the police and tell them what happened. He was wanted for arson and murder by now. Nor could he go to a hospital emergency room for the same reason. The only option was to treat his wounds back in the motel room. Opening up the bike engine, he raced toward Morris.

Upon arrival at the Siesta Trail Motel, Blake staggered through his room door while squeezing tightly the jacket sleeve to keep from leaving a blood trail. He fought back the urge to fall upon the bed and pass out, knowing he would bleed to death without dressing the wound. Like a drunken sailor, he stumbled into the tiny bathroom and switched on the dusty light. Blood dripped upon the dirty tile floor and grimy toilet seat as he eased his arm from the sleeve. Fortunately, the loud Mexican music coming through the thin walls of the adjoining room covered his cries of pain.

He studied the bite. In the bare light of the overhead bulb, the deep rips in his shoulder flesh looked raw and torn. Blake grabbed a towel from a nearby rack and compressed the blood flow. He couldn't imagine how unsanitary it was, but he had nothing else to clean the wound. He used the towel to staunch the bleeding and tore strips from another to tie the makeshift compress to his shoulder. The cloth soon turned red with blood. Dizzy and on the edge of fainting, Blake stumbled to the bed to lie down. He stared up at the revolving ceiling fan and contemplated his situation.

A werewolf had bitten me? A werewolf! How was this possible?

The room spun as he wavered on the edge of consciousness. He concentrated on the ceiling fan to keep his bearing. Reflections of his life seeped through the dizziness. Was this the end? Bleeding to death in a filthy motel room while raucous Mexican music thumped through the walls next door? His hatred for Jess had driven him this far, but there was nothing more left in the tank. His life had become a coke-driven train wreck, and he blamed his fucked-up old man for turning him into what he was today. In the end, there was only failure. So many mistakes made. The one contingent he hadn't planned on was a werewolf attack.

He noticed something happening to his body. Instead of suffering cold due to shock, his skin burned as if in the throes of a high fever. It was too early for an infection. Something else was occurring to his physiology. Sweat beaded on his brow and chest. He tossed and turned in the bed as agonizing fire spread to every inch of his being. He lost his grip on reality. Voices and sounds rose in volume only to fade out. Faces floated in the dark corners of the room. Time passed, but he had no grasp of how much.

Finally, his mind slid into a merciful veil of cloudy darkness.

SATURDAY

CHAPTER THIRTY-FOUR

At twelve thirty in the morning, Terry Newman rode the elevator up to the ICU on the second floor of County Regional Hospital. An oppressive uneasiness weighed on his heart as he waited for the elevator to come to a stop. The ICU was where his grandmother had died the year before. Now he was here for Mr. Higgins.

The doors slid aside revealing the visitor's desk and waiting lounge. A small open chapel lay directly across the hall. Due to his grandmother's passing, he knew the place all too well. He glanced at the waiting room, which had the lights turned down. A family holding a watch for a loved one slept stretched out on the uncomfortable seats and carpeted floor. As far as he knew, he was the only one there for Mr. Higgins.

I don't think he has any family. Or any who would claim him after the murder accusation.

The double doors leading to the ICU swung open, and a nurse stepped into the hall.

"Can you tell me about Mr. Jasper Higgins?" he asked as she walked past. "How's he doing?"

"Are you family?"

"I'm a friend."

"He's sleeping peacefully for the moment."

"When he wakes, can you tell him Terry Newman is here to see him?"

She nodded. "I will."

Retiring to the dimly lit waiting room, Terry settled into the same chair he sat in the night his grandmother died of cancer. Leaning his head against the wall, he let out a weary sigh. He was bone tired and closed his eyes to drift into a troubled sleep. The awkwardness of the very uncomfortable chair forced him to wake up every few minutes and shift his body. Sleep became surreal. Each time he awoke to the hospital surroundings, he thought he was having a dream about his grandmother's passing.

"Terry?" a soft voice asked from somewhere outside the sleep fog.

He opened his blurry eyes. The nurse he spoke to earlier stood in the door of the waiting lounge.

"Yes?" He stood running his hands through his hair.

"Mr. Higgins wants to see you now."

Terry followed her out into the hall. "How's he doing?"

"I wish I had good news," she replied in a quiet voice. A sad look lined her face. "We've tried to stabilize his heart arrhythmia, but so far we've had very little luck. He's fading fast."

Her words hit him hard. "It's that bad?"

"I'm afraid so."

"Oh, man ..." Terry felt his world fall out from under him. He hadn't prepared for this. Even though their contact had been very limited since the murder, he always admired the old man. After his father had deserted his family, Mr. Higgins was the rock Terry steadied himself upon. The strange events of today had brought them even closer.

The nurse reached out and laid a hand on his shoulder. "Are you going to be all right?"

"Yeah."

"Normally, only immediate family would be let in to visit at this time, but since he's requested to speak with you, I'll let you go back for a short visit."

"Thank you." Terry straightened his posture.

"Follow me."

The nurse led the way through the automatic doors and into the unit where patients slept in darkened cubicles. The air felt cool and sanitized. Behind the monitor desk, a low beeping sounded from the bank of flat computer screens. The scene brought back memories of the last time he saw his grandmother, frail and shriveled, dying in the cubicle located straight ahead. Terry swallowed hard. The nurse nodded toward a corner unit, and the heavy feeling turned in his stomach as he walked the short distance to the room.

Mr. Higgins lay on the bed connected to a variety of IVs and monitoring equipment. A plastic oxygen mask covered his mouth and nostrils. Covered up to his chin with blankets, the skin on his face looked ashen gray. As Terry paused in the doorway, the old man opened glazed eyes and turned his head slightly in his direction. He attempted a weak smile, barely visible beneath the plastic of the mask. The nurse stepped around and pulled down the oxygen mask below his chin so he could speak.

"Jasper, you've got a visitor," she said in her soft voice.

Terry stepped into the room. "Hello, Mr. Higgins."

"Hello, son," Mr. Higgins replied, and then to the nurse, "Nurse, can you leave us alone for a bit?"

"Yes, of course." She stepped out and slid across the cubicle curtain, giving them some privacy. "I'll be near if you need me."

Mr. Higgins let out a labored breath and looked at the ceiling. "I'm dying ..."

Terry fought back tears. "The nurse told me that, but doctors have been wrong before."

"No ... I can feel it ... I'm going to see ... my Emma ... soon." He paused for a long second. "On the bedside table ... do you see a yellow writing pad?"

"Yes."

"I've changed my last will and testament ... I'm giving you the farm ... the oil leases ... mineral rights ... all my estate."

Terry picked up the writing pad from the table. On the page was a handwritten last will and testament. "I can't accept this."

"You're going to deny ... the request of a dying man?"

"No." Tears formed in Terry's eyes.

"Sell everything ... put the money in a college fund ... for yourself." Mr. Higgins shifted his eyes to look him in the face. "Will you do this ... for me?"

"Yes." He nodded as a tear ran down his cheek.

"Very good." Mr. Higgins returned his gaze to the ceiling. "Now call the nurse in here."

Terry moved aside the curtain. The ICU nurse was at the desk writing on a chart.

"He wants you," Terry announced.

"Very well." She came around the desk and into the cubicle. "I'm here, Jasper."

"I want you to witness ... my last will and testament."

"As you wish." She took out a pen from a pocket of her scrubs and signed the bottom of the note paper. "There. I've witnessed the will."

"Thank you," Mr. Higgins said and added in a weakening voice, "Terry, the number of my attorney ... listed on the paper ... call him Monday morning ... he'll handle everything."

"Okay."

"Just one more thing," Mr. Higgins replied. His arm came out from under the blanket, and he motioned weakly to Terry. "Come closer, son."

He stepped forward and took the old man's calloused hand. The skin on the inside of his palm felt as rough as sandpaper. "Yes?"

"Lean closer ... so I can tell ... you something."

He leaned down to where the old man's lips were close to his ear.

"The werewolf ... I shot ... had gray fur." He took a raspy breath. "The one that killed my Emma ... was larger ... black fur."

Terry's eyes met the old man's with an understanding of what his words meant. "There's more than one werewolf," he whispered.

Mr. Higgins attempted a weak nod. "It's still out there ... you must stop it ... before it kills others ... promise me you'll do that."

"I will. I promise."

"God be with you, son," The old man closed his eyes and let out one last breath. The grip in his hand went weak.

Terry stepped back from the bed and wiped tears out of his eyes.

The nurse put a comforting hand upon his shoulder and led him out of the cubicle. "It was so nice you showed up to see him in the end. I know it meant a lot to Jasper."

"Thank you."

"If his attorney needs to speak to me as a witness to his last wishes, you can have him call me. I wrote my number on the paper."

"Okay."

"Thanks so much for being there."

Terry nodded and left the ICU ward with tears flowing down his face. He crossed the hall and entered the small chapel. Light from the stained glass portrait of Jesus kneeling in prayer dominated the far wall giving the room a rosy glow. He took a seat in the first pew and stared up at the picture through his tears. His reality had taken a decided left turn this week. Finding out werewolves do exist, the death of Mr. Higgins, and the last will and testament he clutched in his hands made the world very unreal. Now, he had to deal with the revelation that there was more than one murderous beast running loose in the area. He promised Mr. Higgins on his deathbed that he would stop the monster. But how? Who was going to believe him? He wiped his wet eyes on the sleeve of his shirt. No more time for crying. It was on his shoulders now to put a stop to the terror. He would carry on the wolf hunt, alone, if need be.

He bowed his head and prayed for the soul of Mr. Higgins and, when finished, prayed for his own.

CHAPTER THIRTY-FIVE

"Something bad has happened," Roxie said from the passenger seat of her brother's truck. "I can sense it."

Collin took his gaze off his driving for a second to glance at his sister. "What did the sheriff tell you?"

"He was vague over the phone. I just know something's happened."

Collin returned to his driving down Route 23 toward Elmer Grosslin's farm. The headlights of the truck cut a yellow beam through the dark night on the road ahead. In the eastern sky, the full moon hung suspended above the first light of dawn. Dirt and gravel rattled under the body of the truck as he sped along the country road.

"I'm still pissed about you leaving me alone at the bar," Roxie stated. "Where did you go?"

Collin remained quiet for a second. "Out," he finally answered.

"You went to see Jess's little girl," Roxie stated, adding, "I know because she got a call from home that a big dog frightened her daughter."

"So what?"

"The sheriff isn't going to like it. He told you the little girl is off-limits."

Collin shot an angry gaze in her direction. "Why must we answer to him? He's only one of the Bitten and not a Pure Born. He should answer to us."

"He protects us."

"The fool still thinks he's human."

The truck rounded a bend in the dirt road. The headlights showed a parked patrol car in the drive leading to an abandoned oil lease sight. Collin slid the truck to a stop. Illuminated in the dusty light, Uncle Johnny's body lay stretched out in the dirt patch behind one of the rusting storage tanks.

"Oh, no!" Roxie cried, leaping out of the truck before it came to a full stop.

Collin put the truck into park but left the headlights on. Slamming shut the driver door; he rushed to his sister's side as she knelt beside the body. Shock and sadness welled inside at the sight of Uncle Johnny's corpse. Two centuries ago in the old country his name had been Dominic Nicolae. The

Wolfkin Clan he had lived in a cave hidden in the mountains of Romania. They fed upon the local peasantry. Toward the end of the nineteenth century, when the Clan chose to leave Europe for the primeval forests of British Columbia, Dominic served as a Clan elder whose wisdom and strength guided the hidden enclave for more than a century. He was one of the eldest Pure Born within the Clan.

"Who did this?" Collin looked up at Sheriff Sutton, who had stepped out of his patrol car.

"Jasper Higgins," he answered. "He forged silver bullets and used them to kill Dominic. I've confiscated the weapon so it is no longer a threat."

Collin's face distorted in anger. "He should pay for this outrage!"

"He already has. I just got word Jasper died in ICU from a bad heart."

"He didn't come up with silver bullets on his own. Somebody planted the idea in his head."

"Two teenage boys assisted him. Hopefully, I scared them enough to get off this notion of werewolves."

"And if you didn't?"

"Then I will deal with them if they continue being a threat."

"They should pay with blood for what they did to our elder."

Roxie knelt beside the body and stroked Uncle Johnny's gray hair. "Poor Dominic, I loved him like a father."

"This should have never happened," Collin snapped at the sheriff. "You serve to protect the Pack from such danger. How did you fail in your task?"

"I didn't," Sheriff Sutton responded. "It was you, running wild until someone suspected a werewolf in the area."

"Nonsense. No one saw me but two old farmers."

"My brother." Roxie rose to her feet with glistening tears running down her face in the early dawn light. "It is peasants who have been our worst threat over the centuries. They have hunted us beside our kin, the wolf, for years. You know that, and now Dominic is dead."

"Bah!" Collin turned to Roxie and used her old-world name. "My own sister, Reveca, would side with one of the Bitten and not her own blood."

"Dale is right. We were doing fine here and no one suspected our presence until you began your nightly prowls. You left me alone tonight at the bar."

"Sniffing around the little girl again?" Sheriff Sutton asked.

201

"Fuck you," Collin responded.

Roxie held up her hand. "Please stop. It is disrespectful to carry on such in front of the body of Dominic. Let's put his spirit to rest first."

Together, they removed their clothes to the sound of the noisy blackbirds in the nearby trees awakening to daybreak. When they had undressed, they stood over the body of Dominic and stared at the full moon.

"We must perform the Ritual of the Last Feeding," Collin announced. "We must devour his ancestral spirit so it will remain with us always."

In unison they shifted into their werewolf forms and fell upon the body. Ripping open Dominic's rib cage, they removed the dripping organ and shared it, each taking turns pulling apart the tough muscle with their canine teeth and swallowing it down hungrily. Once the heart was gone, the body decomposed to its true age of 183 years. Skin withered as bones cracked beneath the dried flesh. The corpse's face shrunk until it was a visage of leathery skin clinging to darkened bone. In a span of a couple of minutes, Dominic became a dried husk of his former self.

The remaining Pack howled in mournful harmony as the sun broke over the horizon.

The ritual was complete.

They returned to their human shapes again and dressed. Sheriff Sutton opened the trunk of his patrol car and removed a gas can. Pouring it over the remains, he lit the gasoline and stepped back. Crackling flames engulfed the corpse, sending oily black smoke into the brightening sky.

"Dominic told me something important before he died," Sheriff Sutton announced. "He said you two are the last Pure Born of the Clan. He wanted you to return to the north and mate to continue the bloodline. It was his dying wish."

"I am not ready to run and hide again," Collin replied.

"There is no place for you among the humans," Sheriff Sutton stated. "Their numbers keep increasing as does their technology. The time when they feared werewolves is over."

"Then they shall learn again."

"It is hopeless, Collin." Roxie touched his shoulder. "Our numbers are too few and our weaknesses too easily exploited. Dominic was right. We must hide in the north. I have recently inquired online about a hunting lodge in Alaska that is up for sale. It's a place where we can mate away from the eyes of the humans and regain our bloodline in secret."

"Dominic is dead, which makes me the new elder," Collin replied. "I'm leader of the Pack now."

Roxie bowed her head. "It is true."

"Then I'll make the decisions for the Clan." Collin turned to Sheriff Sutton. "The Feast of the Ebon Moon is tomorrow night. Once we have feasted, then we will leave this place and travel north to our new home. Until then, we wait."

"It's risky. The locals are becoming suspicious about a werewolf in their midst. We have to lay low and be careful."

"This is a time to remember the old ways," Collin replied. "During the Ebon Moon we must feed on the soul of a child. I want you to bring Jess and the little girl to me for the feast."

"You're crazy," Sheriff Sutton answered back. "Didn't you hear what I just said about being careful?"

Roxie stepped forward. "Dale, listen to me. Collin is right. We must remember the ways of our ancestors. If Jess and Megan disappear, everyone will believe they went back home. We will hide all evidence of the kill and leave this area to head north."

"I won't do it. There is no reason for us to kill a child. We've been lucky so far in having our kills go unnoticed. The murder of a child will only expose us. The locals will send out search parties into the area. More law enforcement will focus their attention on Hope Springs and drive us further underground. It is madness."

"Do you so easily forget the ways of our Clan?" Collin's rage erupted. He suddenly grabbed Sheriff Sutton by the throat. "You will do as I command, mongrel! Bring me the child so I can feast upon her flesh befitting a Wolfkin elder!"

He gripped the sheriff by the throat with one hand and lifted him off the ground.

"Collin, don't!" Roxie shouted.

"Shut up!" he snapped back as rage caused his body to start transforming into the beast again. "I have grown tired of this half-breed. He forgets his place and who his new master is." Collin's voice became hoarser as his emerging claws dug into the sheriff's throat. "You will do as I say."

"I refuse," Sheriff Sutton hissed.

"You'll do it!" Collin flung the sheriff away from him. He slammed against the side of the pickup truck before falling to his hands and knees. Once on the ground, Sheriff Sutton's facial features shifted into a semicanine form. Fangs extended from his mouth as his eyes flashed red in primal rage. He released an inhuman growl toward Collin and readied to pounce.

"Stop it!" Roxie stepped between the two. "We are already weak in numbers, and this fighting between us only weakens us more."

"Don't interfere," Collin said, pushing her aside. "He must learn his place."

"You will not harm the child," the sheriff snarled in a voice changing from human to animal.

He leaped full force and knocked Collin to the ground. Together they rolled through the powdery dirt, biting and mauling each other. Clawed hands grabbed each other by the throat and choked. Collin's rage increased, triggering a full transformation into his werewolf form. Howling in anger, he twisted and threw the sheriff away to crash against the side of the rusted oil storage tank.

"Stop!" Roxie raced to stand between the two.

Still in beast form, Collin looked down at his sister. She had always provided wisdom to his impetuous nature. He bellowed a roar toward the moon and fought back the animal rage boiling inside. He regained control and became his human form again.

Badly injured, the sheriff rose to one knee as his supernatural healing mended his clawed flesh and bite wounds. His hateful stare never left Collin.

"This fighting must stop," Roxie stated.

"It's the pull of the upcoming Ebon Moon," Collin replied. "Its influence affects us even now. As it grows near, it draws the beast out."

Roxie turned to Sheriff Sutton. "Dale, remember the Dark Gift was bestowed upon you. The ability to heal wounds and live longer than humans is in return for your servitude. You serve the Pack first. Don't forget that."

"What you call a gift, I call a curse." Sheriff Sutton stood shakily to his feet.

"Then what is it you seek? Is it to be human again?" Roxie laughed and continued. "Do you think your precious Jess and Megan would accept you once they knew what you really are? You bear the Mark of the Beast, and humans will only scorn and fear you. It is the reason we are standing over the ashes of Dominic now."

"I know what you say is true." Sheriff Sutton lowered his head. "It's just that the two of them remind me of my sweet Angela and little Elizabeth I lost so long ago."

Roxie shook her head. "Because you failed to protect your own wife and daughter, you're now going to protect Jess and Megan? Dale, there is no redemption for you. You cannot wash away your past sins by saving one mother and child. There is too much blood and death on your hands."

Collin stepped forward. "Put aside this foolish notion of protecting humans. They are nothing but cattle to us. Your duty is with the Pack."

"I can't." Sheriff Sutton pointed a finger at Collin. "On my watch there will be no killing a child, do you understand?"

Collin's eyes bore into the sheriff's. "Let me tell you what I do understand. You're only one of the Bitten and thus cling to your human side more than a Pure Born. You have feelings toward this mother and child and wish to protect them. So be it. But I also know we share the same hunger. Mark my words, Sheriff. When the moon goes dark tomorrow night, so will the beast inside. The hunger will take over and your beloved Jess and Megan will be nothing but meat on the bone to you." Collin laughed and added, "You will beg me to let you feed on them."

CHAPTER THIRTY-SIX

Terry Newman tried to call Sid from the hospital in Stillwater. No answer. Even though it was early in the morning and he had very little sleep, he decided to swing by Sid's place. The sun just broke over the horizon as he parked the old F-150 behind Sid's gray pickup in the drive to the garage apartment. He knocked on the door until it shook in its frame. Again, no answer. He found the door unlocked and entered.

Sid lay sprawled across a rumpled bed with iPod earphones blaring music so loud its muffled tones were audible from across the room. Dressed in a faded Rob Zombie T-shirt and a pair of white briefs exposing his skinny white legs, he slept with his head crooked to one side, leaving a pool of drool on his pillow. A tray with a bag of weed and papers sat on the bedside table. Terry shook Sid's shoulder, causing him to snap open his bloodshot eyes.

"What the fuck?" Sid yanked the earphones out and set up.

"You listen to that crap even when you're sleeping?" Terry Newman sat down on the edge of the bed.

"Yeah, so what?" Sid ran his hands through his greasy hair. "Man, I really should learn to lock the fucking door."

"You think you've got it bad. I'm the one who got to see you sleeping in your tighty-whiteys. Not a Kodak moment."

Sid blinked at the digital alarm clock next to the tray of pot. "Dude, it's fucking six thirty in the morning."

"I know."

"How's Mr. Higgins?"

"Dead."

Sid shook his head. "Oh, man, that's rough. I knew you and the old guy were close. I'm sorry. Are you all right? You need a hug, dude?"

"Not while you're in your underwear."

Sid rose from the bed and found a pair of jeans from the floor. "That old guy was tough. He fucking killed a werewolf last night," he said, sliding his legs into the pants.

"It still leaves us with a problem."

"Werewolf is dead," Sid said, sitting back down on the bed. He reached over and grabbed the pot tray. "Problem solved, right?"

"Oh, man, are you going to smoke weed this early in the morning?"

"Rise and burn is what I say."

"Well, our problem is that the werewolf Mr. Higgins shot last night wasn't the only one. There's still another one out there."

Sid stopped rolling a joint and looked at him. "You're shitting me."

"Mr. Higgins told me on his deathbed. The one he shot was gray, but the werewolf that killed his wife had black fur."

Sid put aside the pot tray and stood excitedly to his feet. He began pacing back and forth across the room. "I guess it's possible. In *The Howling* there was a commune of werewolves living together. A whole pack of the ugly fuckers could be in the area. You know how cool this is? If werewolves exist, then other supernatural shit is real, too. Vampires, ghosts, aliens, everything we thought as bullshit is real." He stopped and looked at Terry. "Fucking cool, man."

"That might be true, but who nearly crapped in his pants upon seeing the werewolf last night?"

"Dude, it scared me to death. Werewolves are some frightening shit."

"I promised Mr. Higgins right before he died that I would try to stop them." Terry looked down at his hands. "I'm going to do it, too."

"How do you propose to do that? The sheriff took the gun with the silver bullets. We got nothing."

"We warn people."

"Hey, dumbass, do you remember what Sheriff Dickhead said he would do if we started telling others about werewolves? He's going to throw our asses in jail."

"I have to do it," Terry replied. "Mr. Higgins made me promise. He wrote out his last will and gave me his entire estate. It's out in the truck. He wants me to sell his farm and put the money in my college fund."

"That's cool." Sid sat down again on the bed and grabbed his pot tray. "Let's celebrate with a toke."

"Dude, there's more werewolves out there and they're going to keep killing people."

"So what do you want me to do about it?"

"I came here for your help. Put the weed away and use some of your last remaining brain cells to help me think of something."

"Okay," Sid said, looking at the ceiling. "Obviously, we can't go to the sheriff, but we still got the picture Crazy Elmer took of the werewolf saved on my computer. We can use it to warn the locals. Make them aware of the danger. That way they can take up their pitchforks and torches and hunt for the monster, metaphorically speaking, of course."

"That's not bad, man."

Sid crossed to his computer and brought up the picture on his screen. Terry realized Mr. Higgins had been right. The fur of the werewolf in the picture was much darker than the one they saw the night before.

"We can put the picture on a flyer. Pass it around and tell others about the werewolf," Sid suggested.

"Kind of like when someone loses a dog."

"You got it."

Sid formatted the picture and hit print. The printer began spitting out the flyers one by one, and he grabbed them up. "I made twenty, man. That's enough to get the word out. But you know what?"

"What?"

"This is really going to piss the sheriff off."

Terry shook his head. "I don't care. We're doing this for Mr. Higgins."

"Where do you want to pass them out?" Sid asked as he slipped on his shoes and grabbed a hoodie jacket with an ICP logo of a hatchet man on the front.

"Hope Springs," Terry answered.

"Why there?"

"Deer season just opened up for bow hunting. My dad used to take me when he was around. Dottie's Café in Hope Springs is where most of the farmers and hunters in the area congregate and have breakfast this early in the morning. We warn them first."

"I was going to suggest the local Wal-Mart, but we'll do it your way."

*   *   *   *

Dottie's Café was busy when they arrived. A line of muddy pickup trucks complete with gun racks lined the parking spaces in front of the diner. A group of hunters dressed in ghillie suits huddled around the back of one truck discussing a freshly killed deer lying in the bed. The only parking left was across the street.

"Are you sure this is a good idea?" Sid asked as Terry shut the F-150 engine off.

"No," Terry replied, opening the driver door. "But we have to do something. There's another full moon tonight."

"Can't we just go to the paper?"

"The *Gazette* doesn't come out until Monday."

"We're going to get our asses kicked by a bunch of redneck crackers," Sid commented as he followed Terry across the road to the diner.

"Let me do the talking."

Terry's heart pounded as they made their way to the front door of the café. What he was about to do was going to take balls. He wouldn't have put himself in this position if it wasn't for Mr. Higgins and what he had seen last night.

Locals packed the place and occupied every seat. The air smelled of greasy fried bacon and hot coffee as waitresses ran to and fro attending to the noisy crowd. The place reverberated with the clatter of plates and a dozen conversations going at once. Terry knew he was going to have to shout to get everyone's attention.

Sid tugged on his jacket sleeve. "Did you ever think that one of them might be the werewolf? Hell, all of them could be werewolves. Let's get the fuck out of here."

"No." He shook his head. "I'm going to do this."

"Okay, it's your ass."

"When I start talking, you hand out those flyers." Terry swallowed hard and cleared his throat. "Excuse me," he called out above the noise level in the room. "Excuse me."

The place grew instantly quiet as all faces turned in his direction. Even the waitresses stopped to hear what he had to say.

"My name is Terry Newman, and this is my friend Sid Granger. We live over in Morris. Last night we encountered something that I think everyone needs to be aware of."

Sid slipped past him and started placing flyers on the tables.

Terry continued now that he had everyone's attention. "What I'm about to say is hard to believe but, please, bear with me. My friend and I saw something last night. The picture on the flyer should give you an idea of what it was."

"What the hell is it?" one hunter asked, peering closely at the flyer.

Terry answered, "It's a picture taken of a strange creature after it killed a cow."

"Who took it?" Another asked.

"Elmer Grosslin."

Sporadic laughter erupted through the diner.

"You mean Crazy Elmer?" More laughter.

"Listen to me, please," Terry replied. "Mr. Higgins came to us and asked for our help."

"You're talking about Jasper Higgins?" A large burly man interrupted. "The old drunk who makes signs by the highway?"

"Yes." Terry paused and added, "He died in the hospital last night."

"Serves him right for murdering his wife," the man replied.

"He didn't do it. The thing in the picture did." Terry felt he was losing control of the announcement. He plunged on in the same disastrous way as he did asking Becky Warren out the day before. "Last night we saw the creature break down the door to Elmer Grosslin's place."

"What is this thing you're showing us? The picture is pretty grainy and hard to see," an old man asked at the counter.

"A werewolf."

The entire diner erupted into laughter.

"It's true," Sid interjected. "We both saw it with our own eyes."

"What have you two boys been smoking this morning?"

"Last night Mr. Higgins shot it with a silver bullet before it ran off. The werewolf may still be alive and wounded. What's more, there are others. That's why I'm here to warn you. There's a full moon tonight."

"You hear that, boys? We better get home and make our silver bullets," a hunter shouted to the others in the restaurant. The place filled with raucous laughter and jokes about werewolves. Terry looked at Sid and shrugged.

"Hey, you stupid rednecks!" Sid suddenly yelled above the noise. "Pull your heads out of your asses and listen to my friend!"

The place went quiet again.

"Boy, what did you just say?" the burly hunter asked as he stood towering over Sid.

"I think he just called us stupid," another hunter chimed in.

"Did you say that, you skinny little fagot?" The large man crossed his arms.

"What I meant so say was …" Sid looked the big hunter up and down. "Shit!"

He threw the rest of the fliers into the air and ran for the door. Deciding it was also best to leave, Terry followed the fleeing Sid out of the café and into the street. Behind them the little diner roared with laughter.

"Let's get the fuck out of here!" Sid shouted over his shoulder while running for the passenger door of the F-150.

Terry unlocked the driver's side and hopped in.

"I don't think that went as well as I had hoped," he said to Sid, sliding in the passenger seat.

"No shit, Sherlock," he replied, and then his eyes went wide as he looked over Terry's shoulder to the diner. "Start the fucking truck! Here comes Farmer John. He's going to kick our ass!"

Terry glanced in the direction. A tall man dressed in blue bib overalls and a flannel shirt walked up to the driver widow of the truck. He tapped lightly on the glass.

"Dude, start the truck. Let's get the fuck out of here," Sid hissed.

"Let me see what he has to say," Terry replied, cranking down the window. To the man outside, he asked, "Yes?"

The stranger studied the two of them with his hazel eyes and held up the flier.

"My name's Sam Olson," he said. "And I believe you."

CHAPTER THIRTY-SEVEN

"Is that coffee I smell?" Jessica asked, sitting up on the couch where she and Megan had spent the night in the living room of the Olson farmhouse. The sunlight of dawn highlighted the front curtains with a gauzy kind of glow.

"I've got a fresh pot brewing," Nelda replied quietly from the next room.

"I'll be right there." Jessica slid from under the covers, careful not to disturb Megan. Tucking the blanket tighter around her daughter, she said, "I love it when she's sleeping like this. She looks so peaceful and calm."

"Megan's been through so much," Nelda replied. "She's a strong child."

Barefoot, she followed Nelda into the cozy farm kitchen. The older woman poured two cups of fresh steaming coffee while Jessica curled up on a wooden chair at the kitchen table and hugged her knees to her chest. The morning still carried the hint of a chill. Dressed in jeans and the tight black top from the night before, she knew her blonde hair was a slept-in mess but didn't want to deal with it until after coffee.

"There you go, dear," Nelda said, putting the filled cups on the table.

"Thanks, Nel." She picked up a cup and brought it to her lips. "Where's Sam?"

"He's gone into town to have breakfast at Dottie's. He tends to do that on Saturday mornings when he wants to catch up with the local farmers."

"So it's just us ladies, then?"

Nelda nodded. "Just us."

"Girl talk?"

"Sure." Nelda settled into the chair across from Jessica.

"Nel, you're a lucky woman. You've got a good man and a stable home here." Jessica sipped her coffee. "I can't seem to find either."

"You're young and pretty. There's still time to find the right man."

"Believe me, I have no luck with men. Every man I've ever had ends up being an asshole. I'm about to give up." Jessica chuckled. "I don't think there are any good ones left. Look at last night. Some creep follows me out of the bar and tries to assault me. I didn't even know the guy. That's the way it's always been, Nel. I'm a jerk magnet."

"You just don't know how to spot the good ones." She took a long sip of coffee and asked, "What about the sheriff?"

"Dale?" Jessica paused for a moment and then added, "He's handsome, and I feel a strong animal attraction to the man. It's the way he smells and carries himself, but there's something else, Nel. I don't know why, but an internal alarm goes off deep inside when he's around. Something I can't put my finger on. Maybe I'm just too paranoid after living with Blake for so long."

"You've only been here for a few days. Give things a little more time, and don't jump into anything."

"Good advice."

Nelda smiled. "You're right. I am lucky to have a home and a good man. But you're very lucky, too, Jess. You have something precious that Sam and I can never have."

"Megan," Jessica said, glancing over her shoulder to where her daughter slept in the living room.

"Precisely."

"I am thankful to have her."

"You should be. She's very special."

"She is."

Outside, a vehicle pulled up in the gravel drive beside the barn. The sound of a truck door shutting came next.

"Sam's back." Nedra put down her cup and rose from the chair to peer out the kitchen window. "It looks like someone followed him home."

"Who is it?" Jessica asked.

"Two teenage boys," Nedra answered. "Now what's he up to?"

*   *   *   *

Terry Newman closed the door of the F-150 as Sid exited the passenger side. Sam, already out of his truck, removed a hunting rifle from his gun rack in the back window.

"After last night, I don't go anywhere without this," Sam said, shifting the rifle to his arm.

"I understand," Terry replied

"Now listen to me, boys," Sam stated. "I've got two women and a little girl staying on the property. If we start talking about werewolves in the night, they're going to freak. The little girl has already been scared near to death. Let's just keep this between us until we get an idea of what we are dealing with here. Okay?"

"Okay," he answered, but Sid remained quiet. Terry shoved him in the shoulder. "Did you hear what the man said, dude?"

"Yeah, I got it." Sid responded by shrugging and putting his hands in the pockets of the ICP hoodie. "No talking about werewolves to the womenfolk."

"Fine," Sam said. "I'll take you to the trailer first."

As they started their walk around the barn, the back door of the farmhouse opened and an attractive older lady wearing gold-rimmed glasses stepped out on the patio.

"Sam?" she called out.

"Yes?"

"What's going on?"

"These boys are doing some work for me. I'm just showing them around."

"Oh," Nelda replied with a perplexed look on her face. "Did you want me to fix breakfast?"

"That would be fine, dear."

"Are your new friends going to be joining us?"

Sam sighed and turned to Terry and Sid. "You boys want breakfast?"

"Yeah," Terry answered.

"Breakfast would be cool," Sid piped in.

"They'd love to," Sam called back. "Give us a half hour and we'll be at the table."

"All right, then." The woman retreated into the farmhouse.

"This way," Sam said and headed around the back of the barn.

Following the farmer, Terry walked across a grassy lot leading to a double-wide trailer. Sid kept in step by his side. The sun had risen higher in the eastern sky but the air was still crisp and cold.

"I've been having a problem with something spooking my livestock the last few nights. Monday morning I found my old hunting dog, Rocky, torn apart in the woods bordering the creek over there." Sam pointed across a freshly plowed field toward a line of trees on the other side. "I also found some strange tracks in the field. Canine prints, by the look of them."

"What did you think it was?" Terry asked.

"I figured I got a couple of coyotes harassing the farm," Sam replied as he led them around to the back door of the double-wide mobile home. "But it wasn't coyotes that paid a visit to the trailer last night."

Sam stopped and nodded toward the back trailer door. Scratch marks crisscrossed the bottom half of the sheet metal. Terry felt a chill pass through his body.

"That's some scary shit," Sid commented.

"My sentiments exactly," Sam replied. "A little girl and my wife were inside when I came by for a visit. I had my rifle with me. While I was here, the little girl opened the back door and screamed. I came running to see what was happening. Something ran off into the darkness, and I shot at it twice. I'm pretty sure I hit it."

"What was it?" Terry asked.

The shadow of fear showed in Sam's weathered face when he answered. "I think it was the thing in your picture. I didn't get a real good look at it, but it had the same wolflike fangs and red eyes. One thing for certain, it wasn't a coyote. The creature was big and moved fast."

"Just like a fucking werewolf," Sid said.

"Son, I'm beginning to believe you're right," Sam replied, and added, "There's something else I want to show you boys. It's over across the field in the trees."

They trekked across the furrows of the plowed field and into the line of trees. Along the way, Terry filled Sam in about the events of last night, finishing with the death of Mr. Higgins in the ICU. He listened intently, and Terry got the impression he had found an adult who believed him. At the edge of the line of trees bordering the field, they stopped.

"At dawn's light, I came here looking for signs of the creature I wounded last night." Sam propped his rifle against a tree and knelt down on one knee. "The first thing I found was this."

He pointed to an object laying in the dead leaves and grass.

"Binoculars?" Terry asked, confused.

"That's right." Sam nodded. "They weren't there yesterday because I didn't see them. Since I found my dog dead back here in these trees, I walk through here every day."

"Werewolves don't use binoculars," Sid commented. "But their human side can."

"It could've been dropped by a hunter," Terry suggested.

"It's possible, I guess, though hunters are not allowed on my property without permission and would be trespassing," Sam said.

"Who do you think needed binoculars?"

"Somebody watching the farm." Sam stood again and motioned for them to follow. They walked for another twenty-five yards deeper into the wooded area until they reached the bank of a creek. Sam pointed to the leaf-covered ground. "Here's another thing that baffles me."

An aluminum baseball bat lay nestled in the undergrowth beneath the trees.

"A baseball bat?" Sid asked, surprised.

"That wasn't here yesterday, either." Sam picked it up out of the wet leaves.

"Who would have brought it back here?" Terry asked.

Sam shook his head. "I don't have a clue, but take a look at this." He presented the bat so they could see it closer. Bite marks had left deep pits in the aluminum. "Something with big powerful teeth made those."

"This is seriously scaring the shit out of me," Sid stated.

Terry felt it, too. Something was very wrong. "So someone was back here watching the farm before transforming into a werewolf. From there they went and scratched up the back door of the trailer. Why?"

"Werewolves are hungry," Sid replied. "That's what they do. They eat people."

"Why didn't it just break down the door like it did at Crazy Elmer's? If it wanted to eat somebody, why bother with this place? It could just grab somebody out of a car or wait in the bushes for someone to leave their house? Why here?"

"I don't know what the reason is, but the damn thing's been coming back every night. There's something it wants," Sam said.

"Can you think of anything causing the creature to pay attention to your farm?"

"Well, everything's been quiet until Jess and Megan moved into the trailer."

"Jess and Megan?" Terry asked.

"Jessica is the mother and Megan is her five-year-old daughter. They started renting the trailer this week."

"That has to be it."

"There's something wrong with your theory, guys," Sid interjected. "The werewolf bit the baseball bat for no reason? I think there was a second person back here. This guy was using the binoculars and carried the bat with him. He got attacked by the werewolf and used the bat to defend himself. Thus, the bite marks."

Terry smiled. "I knew there was a reason to drag a stoner like you along."

"We need to bring the sheriff in on this," Sam stated. "We're in over our heads."

"Bad idea," Terry said in unison with Sid.

"Why not? The only reason I haven't reported it to Sheriff Sutton was because he wouldn't believe me about a werewolf. Hell, I still find it hard to believe myself, and I wouldn't, if I hadn't seen something with my own eyes."

"To convince the sheriff, you're going to need more evidence than a pair of binoculars, door scratches, and bite marks on a bat," Terry replied. "So let's look around and see if we can find the half-eaten body of our mysterious stranger."

"Please, I haven't had breakfast yet," Sid stated. "If I see that I'll fucking hurl."

"I thought you like all that horror movies and slasher stuff," Terry replied.

"Yeah, I do, but that shit's fake."

They walked up and down the creek bed finding no trace of anyone, living or dead. Walking the fence running along the edge of the property, they came across one section of barbed wire torn completely down.

"Goddammit!" Sam shouted upon seeing the damage. "Now I got to rewire the broken fence before my cows get out!"

Terry knelt to examine the strands of broken fence wire. Black fur and spots of blood still clung to the barbs.

"A different werewolf did this from the one we shot last night," he said to the others. "Look at the pieces of black fur."

"So Mr. Higgins was right. There is a black-furred werewolf running free," Sid stated.

"Yeah, the one that killed his wife," Terry replied.

"Now I can call the sheriff and report this as vandalism," Sam said.

"Please wait until we've had breakfast," Sid spoke. "I've got the munchies real bad."

"Better not tell the sheriff you talked to us first, either," Terry added.

CHAPTER THIRTY-EIGHT

Collin swung up the wooden door to the storm cellar where he intended to keep Jessica and her daughter prisoner until the Ebon Moon. The morning sun, highlighting specks of dust flying in the air, cast a golden light down the dirty stairs. The cellar sat a few yards from the old wooden hay barn. Two years ago, Roxie purchased the abandoned property behind the roadhouse when they moved from British Columbia to Oklahoma. It was the first time he had ever looked inside the dingy cellar.

Collin descended the dirt-covered stairs. Hanging cobwebs from the low ceiling brushed against his hair when he reached the bottom. The place was small, cramped, and empty of furniture. Just dirt and spiders made a home here. Rusted water pipes jutted out of one wall, which Collin surmised were part of the well system leading to the barn.

"Brother?" Roxie called as her long shadow stretched down the stairs.

"Here."

Roxie descended the steps. "What are you doing?"

"I'm preparing a place for Jess and her daughter."

She studied the small room. "In this dirty cellar?"

"It is no worse than the cattle pens we kept humans in back home," Collin answered. "They will stay here until the Feast of the Ebon Moon."

"The sheriff isn't going to like this."

Collin showed Roxie an icy stare. "So what? He will do as I say."

"Brother, why must you provoke him so?"

"He has yet to learn his place."

"Our bloodline is so few now. We need unity in our ranks and not contention."

Collin stepped forward and embraced his sister. "Reveca, let's not forget our past and who we are. For centuries the humans feared going into the woods of the Old World because of us. Now we must fear them because we are afraid to provoke the wrath of those who have hunted us to near extinction?"

"Is it not wiser to slip quietly away and return to the north?"

"I'm tired of running, sister." Collin pulled away from her embrace and stared deep into her eyes. "I'm tired of living afraid when it us they should fear. I want a return to the old ways, a time when we hunted freely. Look at the humans, Reveca. They kill each other without regard many times over the number we slay per year. We cull small numbers from their herd—the undesirables, the sick and frail, the forgotten who fall through the cracks in their pitiful society."

"I understand."

"Then say no more about it and support my decision," Collin said, leading her back up the stairs. He closed down the cellar door and slid a padlock through the hasp. "That will hold Jess and her daughter until the feast."

"What will you do with the sheriff if he resists this plan?" Roxie asked.

"Show him the error of his decision." Collin took her by the hand. In the bright morning light, her dark eyes glistened. "I may have to kill him if he continues to thwart the feast and protect Jess and her daughter."

"Then there will be no one to serve us." Roxie's eyes turned downcast toward the ground.

Collin touched her chin. "There may be another."

"Another?" She looked up again.

"Last night I came across a human stalking outside the farm where Jessica is staying. He managed to escape but not before I bit him deeply. If he survives the transformation, he will seek us out."

"What was he doing there?"

"I do not know." Collin took her hand and headed back the quarter-mile toward the roadhouse. "Whatever the reason, we may soon have another to protect us. You inquired about the hunting lodge in Alaska?"

"Yes." She nodded. "I have told the sellers I want to buy. I will begin the transaction Monday morning."

"Good. After the Feast of the Ebon Moon, we will slip away from this accursed place and travel north to mate." Collin stopped their walk and pulled his sister close to him. "I love you, Reveca, more than life itself, for we share the same wolf blood. It is a bond stronger than any foolish sentimental emotion that the humans pretend is love. Wolfkins mate for life. Never forget that. Not long, my love, and we will be far from here and surrounded by Wolfkin children."

Roxie laughed. "It is what I want, too, my love."

"Then tonight let us run free under the full moon, as we did in the old days. We will find prey and devour them without fear of retaliation since we will soon be gone from here. What do you say to that, sister?"

"Yes."

"You must do something first. Call Jess at her home and ask her to come back to work again at the bar. We must not lose contact with her until I can figure a way to capture both her and the child. They're too protected on the farm. I'll have to use some other ploy. Once we have them both here, we will use chloroform to put them asleep. You still have some, don't you?"

"I have one bottle hidden away in the bar."

"Good. Once we put them under, we can hold them until the moon is dark. Now make the call and bring Jess back here. Will you do that for your brother?"

Roxie nodded. "As you wish."

CHAPTER THIRTY-NINE

"We're having two teenage boys over for breakfast and you know what that means," Nelda said, handing her a flannel shirt from a closet.

"Raging hormones," Jessica chuckled as she slid it on over her tight top. "Did Sam say why the boys followed him home?"

"They're helping him with something."

Jessica tucked the shirttails into her jeans and tied back her blonde hair. "I should probably go back to the trailer and clean up. My hair smells like cigarette smoke from last night."

"You're fine," Nelda replied. "Come help me with breakfast."

Jessica followed her into the kitchen. Watching Nelda cook was like observing one of those professional chefs on television. In no time the woman had eggs frying, bacon popping, and biscuits browning in the oven. Jessica was given the task of stirring the white gravy. Soon the smell of cooking roused Megan, and she padded into the kitchen on bare feet.

"There you are, sleepyhead," Nelda remarked.

"Hi, Mommy." She rubbed her eyes. "Hi, Aunt Nel."

"Did you sleep well, baby?" Jessica asked as she poured gravy into a ceramic container.

"I had some bad dreams," Megan replied.

"You know they are just dreams and nothing else?" Jessica placed the gravy bowl on the table.

Megan nodded. "Yes, Mommy."

"Are you hungry, sweet pea?" Nelda asked with a smile as she removed a tray of biscuits from the oven.

"Uh huh."

"Well, go wash your hands and face and then come back and help your mommy set the table," Nelda replied. "We're having guests for breakfast."

"Okay." Megan bounded off toward the downstairs bathroom.

*   *   *   *

As if by some male instinct, the men came in from the field as soon as breakfast was on the table. Sam entered the kitchen first, taking off his ball cap and leaning his rifle against the wall. The two teenage boys stood behind him hesitating at the door.

"You can hang your jackets up here," Sam told them as he took off his own and put it on a set of pegs on the wall. They followed suit.

"Boys, come on in and take a seat," Nelda called out.

Sam took his place at the head of the table. Jessica studied the two youths as they pulled out chairs and sat down quietly. One was brown-haired and chubby around the middle with a boyish cuteness to his face. The other was thin with a face full of unfortunate acne and a chestnut-colored mop of greasy hair desperately in need of brushing. A faded Rob Zombie T-shirt clung loosely to his bony frame.

"Sam, dear, why don't you introduce us to your new friends?" Nelda asked while filling a cup with coffee.

"I'll let the boys do that."

"Sid Granger," the skinny boy said.

"Terry Newman," said the other. He smiled shyly to Jessica and glanced briefly down at her bust.

Sam cleared his throat. "That's my wife, Nelda, and these two are our guests, Jessica and her daughter Megan."

"Hi," Megan replied with a wave.

"Hello," Jessica echoed. Terry showed her another shy smile before looking away.

"Are you boys old enough to drink coffee?" Nelda asked, putting a full cup in front of Sam.

"We're seventeen," Sid replied, holding up his cup. "So fill 'er up."

"I'll take a cup, too, Mrs. Olson," Terry added.

Nelda laughed. "You make it sound like we're in a coffee commercial." She filled their cups and sat the pot back on the stove. "Just call me Nelda."

"Are you from Hope Springs?" Jessica asked while fixing Megan a plate of eggs and biscuits.

"We're both from Morris," Terry answered.

"Well, there's plenty of food, so help yourselves." Nelda sat in her chair at the other end of the table. "Terry, are you related to a Clara Newman who works as a cashier at Wal-Mart?"

"She's my mother," he replied, shoveling eggs and bacon on his plate. "She's been there a long time. Sixteen years. She got the job when I was a year old."

"A nice lady. She's waited on me several times. Tell her I said hello."

"Okay."

A long pause followed while everyone focused on the meal. As was typical with teenage boys, they proved to have ravenous appetites. Sid devoured his first plate as if he hadn't had any food for days.

"These biscuits are fu-freakin' awesome, Mrs. Olson," Sid announced with his mouth full.

"Thank you."

"Dude, don't talk with food in your mouth," Terry said, elbowing Sid in the side. "Show some manners at the table."

"Sorry," Sid replied around a half-eaten biscuit.

Megan laughed. "You're funny."

"He's a real clown," Terry commented.

"So what grade are you in?" Jessica asked while buttering a biscuit.

"I'm a junior in high school," Terry answered.

Sid remained quiet, and Jessica guessed he was a dropout.

"What work are you going to do for my husband?" Nelda asked.

Sam shifted in his seat. "They wanted permission to deer hunt on my land. Bow hunting season just opened, and they were here to look over the property. I told them they could." Sam nodded toward Terry. "You boys are coming back tonight to hunt, aren't you?"

Terry glanced at Sid for a second and then said, "That's right. I'll be back after dark with my bow."

Jessica sensed something rang untrue about the conversation. The two gawky teenage boys across the table didn't look like hunters to her. She decided not to ask questions and wait for Nelda to fill her in.

"All done, Mommy," Megan announced to the table.

"Good girl. Put your dirty plate in the sink."

"Okay."

Megan slid out from the table and picked up her plate.

"You got a cute little girl there," Terry observed.

"I like to think so."

"How old is she?"

"Five."

The phone on the wall rang, causing Jessica's heart to jump.

"Goodness sakes," Nelda said, rising from the table. "Who could that be at this time of morning?"

Picking up the receiver, she spoke for a second to the caller.

"Jess, it's for you," she announced.

"Who is it?"

"Roxie," Nelda replied.

Jessica took the phone. "Hello."

"Hi, Jess, this is Rox."

"What's up?"

"I'm sorry we got off on the wrong foot last night. I don't want you to think I'm upset. I need you to come back tonight."

Jessica paused. "I don't think I can leave Megan alone again."

"You can bring her. She can stay in the back room while you wait tables."

"I don't know if I want to take my daughter into a bar."

"It's Saturday night and I need the help, Jess." There was a pause. "I'll pay you ten dollars an hour plus tips."

Jessica sighed. She so needed the money. "All right, I'll be there."

"Good. See you around seven, then."

The line went dead.

CHAPTER FORTY

Sheriff Dale Sutton had enough problems to deal with before he parked at Dottie's Café for breakfast. An Oklahoma Highway Patrol cruiser sitting in front of the diner was the first hint he was about to have a very shitty day. His problems doubled when he went inside.

"Good morning, Sheriff." Dottie nodded from behind the register as he entered. The breakfast rush had died down and the few customers left were chatting over coffee in the lull before lunch.

"Morning, Dot," he replied, removing his cap. He spotted the two OHP officers seated in a back booth. "Bring me my usual. I'll be at the back table."

"Sure, Sheriff," she replied with a flirtatious smile.

He walked up to join the two patrol officers laughing among themselves. One of them, Ted Allison, noticed his approach and motioned to the other. The second man turned to look over his shoulder. He recognized him as David Walker.

"You got a werewolf problem in this town, Sheriff?" David asked, showing a toothy smile.

Sheriff Sutton felt the blood in his veins turn to ice.

"Why do you ask?"

Ted produced a paper with the printed picture Elmer Grosslin had taken two nights ago.

"Found this sitting on the table when we got here," he said and chuckled. "Seems someone's trying to warn the local hunters there's a werewolf running loose. Stupidest damn thing I ever heard of."

Sheriff Sutton settled into the booth and studied the picture. "Who passed these around?" he asked, knowing the answer.

Dottie put an empty cup on the table and filled it. "Two teenage boys came in about three hours ago, Sheriff. Started talking nonsense about werewolves and gave the flyer to everyone here. One of them got mouthy with big Bob Holsten and he ran them off. I've opened this diner for the last twenty-three years and never seen anything like it."

"Thanks, Dottie," Sheriff Sutton replied as she walked away. He looked down at the flyer and fought back his anger. The two boys ignored his warnings, and now they would pay for it.

Pay dearly.

"You can't smoke that much crack to come up with something this stupid," Ted said. "Or are they trying to get a jump on Halloween?"

"A little early for a Halloween prank since it's still a month away," David commented.

"Who knows?" He slid the paper back across the table. "They can photoshop this shit easy off the Internet. I've encountered these two potheads before. They're a couple of delinquent punks living over in Morris."

"I would have a word with them about trying to scare people in your town," Ted suggested.

"I will."

"But that's not why we're here, though," David stated.

"I was wondering what brought you into my neck of the woods."

David reached into the front pocket of his uniform and removed a folded piece of paper. "OHP got a call from the governor's office about a missing hitchhiker. Seems he's a wounded Iraq war vet suffering from posttraumatic stress. The kid's got a purple heart and a couple of other combat medals. His mother's a friend of the governor. He called her from OKC and said he was hitching to Wichita a couple of days ago. No one's heard from him since. Mother is all worried and reported him missing to the state attorney's office. His name is Russell Norris."

Taking the paper, Sheriff Sutton studied it for a second. A picture of Russell Norris in full military dress occupied one corner of the missing person's report. Statistics such as height, weight, age, military service, etc., filled the rest.

"I haven't seen him," Sheriff Sutton lied.

"We're thinking he may have gotten off the interstate and might end up in one of these small towns. He was last dressed in dirty army clothes and a backpack," Ted replied.

"Might be sleeping under a bridge somewhere," David added.

"If you see him, Sheriff, give us a call." Ted stuck a toothpick between his teeth. "Come on, Dave, let's hit the highway."

"I'll let you know if he comes around," Sheriff Sutton replied and stood to let David out of the booth.

Both officers grabbed their uniform hats and paused before leaving.

"Good luck with your werewolf problem. By the way, there's a full moon tonight," David said with a smirk.

"I know."

"How-o-o-o-o! Werewolves of Hope Springs," Ted sang, doing a lame imitation of the classic Warren Zevon song.

"Very funny," Sheriff Sutton replied.

Both men laughed and left the diner.

Fighting back his rage, Sheriff Sutton stared at the flyer left on the table. Violent images of ripping out the throats of Sid Granger and Terry Newman filled his mind. The intense anger triggered his lycanthropy. His fingernails elongated as the hair on the back of his hands thickened.

"More coffee, Sheriff?" Dottie asked, breaking his thoughts. The woman stood beside the table holding a glass coffeepot.

He forced back the transformation and put his hands under the table. "Just half a cup, Dot."

As he watched the coffee pour into the cup, Sheriff Sutton thought about his dilemma with the two teenagers. They were going to have to die now. Maybe he could salvage the situation by offering the boys to Collin for the Feast of the Ebon Moon and keep Jess and Megan off the menu.

*   *   *   *

"So who do you think is spying around the Olson farm?" Terry Newman asked, driving the F-150 back to Sid's house in Morris.

"A Peeping Tom," Sid replied. "Did you see how hot that Jessica chick is? I'd want to peep in her windows any day."

"You would." Terry shifted gears and added, "I have to admit she's even hotter than Becky Warren."

"She's a definite milf."

"Milf?"

"Mother I'd love to fuck," Sid clarified.

Terry laughed. "Now I get it."

Leaving the Olson farmhouse after breakfast, they now reached the outskirts of Morris. The mid-morning sun blazed brightly through the windshield, forcing Terry to put down the visor to shadow his eyes. Sid picked up the yellow notepad from the truck seat with Mr. Higgins's last will written upon it.

"He left you fucking everything," Sid said, reading the writing.

"I was the only friend he had when he died," Terry replied. "I'm calling his attorney Monday morning. It's what Mr. Higgins wanted."

"The old man was innocent all along."

"And we're the only ones who know it."

"Sad."

They drove the rest of the way in silence until they pulled into the drive of Sid's grandmother's house. Terry shut off the truck and turned in the front seat.

"I've been thinking. Mr. Olson suggested that we come back to the farm tonight and help him hunt for the werewolf. I've got all kinds of hunting junk my father left me."

"So we're really going back?"

"There's something going on there with the werewolf making a visit every night. Plus there is the Peeping Tom with the baseball bat. I think Jessica might be in danger."

"Let me guess. You want to be Jessica's knight in shining armor and protect the babe from the big bad werewolf?"

"Yeah, she's so hot."

"I fucking knew it."

"Come on, you have to admit the girl is fine."

"You're going to get yourself killed over a girl you barely met?"

"I think I'm in love."

"Why don't you make a move on her then?"

Terry paused for a moment and thought. "Dude, did you see her wedding ring?"

"That don't plug no holes."

"You're disgusting. She's at least seven years older than me."

"Yeah, and an older woman always got a thing for a younger man. Especially a woman that's married. A guy your age is just reaching his sexual prime, and she knows it. She's probably fantasizing now about how she's going to fuck your legs off."

"You think?" Terry turned to Sid in the front seat. "If you're such an expert, why don't you come on to her?"

"I get all the fucking sex I want."

"Beating off in front of a computer doesn't count."

"Okay, dude, you're on. Pick me up when you go back. I want to see if you've got the stones to make a move on Jessica or if you're going to pussy out. I have to be there for that."

"You got a deal. I'll be back before sunset."

"You're going to pussy out." Sid opened the passenger door and slid out of the truck.

"No I'm not."

"Fuck yeah, you are," Sid commented, shutting the door before walking toward his apartment.

CHAPTER FORTY-ONE

"Mommy, the sheriff's at the door," Megan said, standing in the entrance to the trailer bathroom.

Jessica stuck her head out of the shower. "What, baby?"

"The nice sheriff is at the door."

Jessica held her arm out. "Hand me the towel, sugar."

Megan placed a plush towel in her hand. "Mommy, what do I say?"

"Tell him I'll be right there."

Megan left as Jessica stepped out of the shower and vigorously dried her body. She couldn't imagine what he wanted this early in the morning. Without owning a bathrobe, she had to slip back into her jeans and throw on a T-shirt. Wrapping the towel around her dripping hair, she walked barefoot into the front room, leaving water spots on the carpet. Through a window she saw Sheriff Sutton standing on the wooden deck, his patrol car parked next to the Camaro in the front grass.

Opening both the door lock and dead bolt, she stuck her head out the door. "Hi."

"Did I come at a bad time?" he asked.

"I just got out of the shower," she replied.

He glanced down at her wet breasts sticking to her T-shirt.

"I guess it depends on who's looking if this is a bad time or not." He smiled.

She covered her chest with her arms. "Very funny."

"Sam called me to come out here. He wasn't very clear about why when he talked to dispatch. I just wanted to make sure you and Megan were all right."

"We're fine after last night."

"Last night?" The sheriff's eyes hardened.

"Yeah, some big dog tried to scratch its way into the back door. It scared Megan to death. That's the reason I had to leave the bar early."

Sheriff Sutton's eyes hardened. "Why didn't you tell me?"

"I guess in all the excitement, I forgot."

"Is that what Sam wants to talk to me about?"

"I have no idea. It's been a strange morning. Two teenage boys dropped by for breakfast. Said they were deer hunters, which I didn't buy for a second. To me they were just a couple of nerdy boys. One kept ogling me."

"I bet." Sheriff Sutton stepped off the wood deck. "I'm going to find Sam. Nelda told me he's out fixing his fence. I'll drive out to meet him. Talk to you later, Jess."

"Next time you drop by, I'll be dressed."

"Don't do it on my account."

"Why, Sheriff Sutton, are you flirting with me?"

He flashed his white smile. "Yes, ma'am, I do believe I am."

As the sheriff walked toward his patrol car, Jessica called out, "Oh by the way, thanks for talking to Roxie about me returning to work. She called this morning and asked me to come back."

"She did?"

"Yeah, so I'll be going in tonight. Is your offer still good about dropping by at closing time?"

"It is. I've got to assist the police over in Morris, but I'll be there by the time you get off work."

*　　*　　*　　*

Sheriff Sutton fought back more anger as his patrol car bounced along the rutted cattle road running along the south fence line of the Olson property. The shitty day he was having just got worse. Now he had those two meddling teenagers visiting the Olson farm. He knew it had something to do with the big dog Jess claimed tried to get in the trailer last night. The perpetrator involved was no mystery, either.

Collin.

He's out of control and screwing everything up over a little girl. The whole town is about to explode into werewolf hysteria if I don't stop him soon.

He spotted Sam digging a post hole in the hard dirt where a broken barbed wire fence section lay curled on the ground. Sheriff Sutton halted the patrol car, slid out, and put on his cap.

"Morning, Sam. You wanted to see me?"

"Sure did, Sheriff." The tall farmer wiped his brow and nodded. "Look what happened to my fence last night."

"Somebody cut your wire?" Sheriff Sutton asked, spotting Sam's hunting rifle leaning against a nearby tree stump.

"They didn't cut it. They tore it the hell up. I got to a rewire a whole section plus put in two fence posts."

"Did you lose any cattle?"

"All are accounted for. I did a head count this morning. They've been refusing to come back here lately." Sam picked up a fence post and planted it in the freshly dug hole. "Who do you think tore my fence up?"

"I don't know, but they drove a motorcycle to get here." Sheriff Sutton kneeled and pointed to some tire treads in the red dirt. He sniffed the crisp air and detected the familiar scent of something he had come to know so well over his years as a Wolfkin. Human blood. Faint but still noticeable. His stomach rolled with hunger from the smell. "I followed these tire tracks in the dirt all the way up here."

"I heard a loud motorcycle last night," Sam replied.

"I think it was a trespassing hunter who broke down your fence."

"Why? He could have just as easily slipped through it." Sam picked up a broken strand of barbed wire. "Check this out, Sheriff. What left these pieces of black fur on my fence?"

Sheriff Sutton studied the broken barbed wire. Tufts of black fur still clung to several of the barbs. The undeniable odor of a Wolfkin wafted in his nostrils. He knew the scent. It was Collin's.

"Is that dog fur?"

"Could be."

"You had a problem here last night? Something about a big dog?"

"How did you know?"

"I just talked to Jess."

"We had more than a big dog sniffing around last night," Sam replied, removing his work gloves to pick up his rifle. "I'll show you."

Sam led him into the wooded area on the other side of the fence.

"How long has this been going on?" Sheriff Sutton asked as he walked through the dead underbrush and leaves.

"Something's been spooking the livestock the last few nights. It's why I carry the rifle." Sam stopped and pointed to the ground. "I found this here."

A pair of field binoculars lay in the dead leaves. Sheriff Sutton crouched. "I've seen deer hunters use those, Sam. Your trespasser probably dropped it when chased by the dog."

"Then maybe you can explain this, Sheriff."

Sam led the way another twenty-five yards through the underbrush toward the banks of Skeleton Creek. He stopped and pointed to an aluminum bat lying in the brush.

"Found that here this morning, too."

Sheriff Sutton adjusted his gun belt and knelt to get a closer look.

"I have to admit this is strange, but teens like to party along the creek bed. I have found all kinds of weird stuff—beer cans, pot pipes, used condoms, anything you can think of."

"They brought a pair of binoculars with them as well?" Sam shook his head no. "I think someone was watching the farm last night."

"That could be. Jess might have had a stalker follow her home last night. She was assaulted leaving the bar by a drunk Brody Carlson acting stupid again. After she left, someone nearly bashed in Brody's brains. The same person could have followed Jess home and dropped the bat here. This could be the weapon used in that attack."

"Did he leave the tooth marks in the aluminum, too? Can you explain that?"

He leaned closer to take a better look. Deep fang marks pitted the aluminum of the bat.

"What do you think made those tooth marks, Sam?"

Sam gave him a hard look. "Is there such a thing as a werewolf, Sheriff?"

Sheriff Sutton stood. "You've been talking to Terry Newman and that Granger kid out of Morris? I know they were passing out some stupid flyer at Dot's."

"They said Jasper Higgins shot a werewolf last night at the Grosslin farm. He used silver bullets, too. They also claim the one that killed Emma Higgins is still running around loose in the area."

"A couple of stoner kids pass the idea to Mr. Higgins that a werewolf killed his wife. The old man is so desperate to convince himself he's innocent of murder he'll jump on any story. That's how this werewolf thing got started. Next it'll be Bigfoot and alien abductions responsible. No wonder they all were at Elmer Grosslin's last night."

"I saw something last night scratching at the back door of the trailer. I shot at it while it ran away."

"Was it a big black dog?" Sheriff Sutton removed a pair of latex gloves from his back pocket.

"It was hard to see in the dark, but I caught a flash of it when the rifle fired. It was big and moved fast."

"I've heard reports of a rogue black bear over in the next county."

"I've farmed for twenty-some years on this land and never caught wind of a bear in these parts," Sam replied. "What's with the gloves, Sheriff?"

"The bat could be linked to a possible assault. I'm taking it as evidence." Sheriff snapped on the latex gloves. "Is that the rifle you shot last night?"

Sam nodded. "This is my old trusty 30-30 Marlin. Dad gave it to me."

"Good-looking rifle, Sam. Can I hold it?"

"Sure," Sam replied, handing it over. "She's cocked and ready, but the safety is on."

He hefted it to his shoulder. "Nice firearm. Not too heavy. Good clean sights." Sheriff Sutton's finger slipped down to the trigger and hesitated. He could kill Sam now. Make it look like a terrible hunting accident. The Pack would be protected from exposure, but for how long? One day? Two days? Thanks to Collin's obsession with Megan, everything was beginning to unravel beyond his ability to fix. He fought down the temptation to commit another murder and returned the rifle to Sam's hands. "She's a beauty."

"Thanks, Sheriff. Do I have your permission to shoot anybody snooping on my land?"

"Just make sure it's Jess's stalker and not some teenage kid."

"I will."

Sheriff Sutton picked up the aluminum bat. "I'm going to have this dusted for fingerprints and run it through the system. Find out who it belongs to."

"Okay."

Together they walked back to the broken fence. Sam put down his rifle against the stump and slipped on his work gloves.

Sheriff Sutton said, "I'd keep this between us at the moment, Sam. I wouldn't get the others all worked up until we know what we're dealing with here."

"Okay, Sheriff."

"I'll talk to you later."

Crossing to the trunk of his patrol car, Sheriff Sutton opened it and threw in the aluminum bat. Next he stripped off the latex gloves and slammed it shut. His shitty day was getting worse. Much worse. He started the engine and waved to Sam before turning toward the blacktop. Picking up the radio, he called dispatch.

"Wanda here."

"It's Sheriff Sutton."

"Hello, Dale."

"Wanda, I want you to find out what you can on Chicago Police Officer Blake Lobato."

CHAPTER FORTY-TWO

Blake Lobato's body was on fire. Every nerve screamed in agony. He thrashed around on sweat-soaked sheets to the tune of a Mexican radio thumping through the thin motel walls from the room next door. He had no idea how much time passed in his feverish delirium. The waking world competed with vivid dreams, giving him no bearing on reality. Sometimes he opened his eyes and stared at the ceiling fan going in circles overhead. For how long, he could not even guess. Once, he tried to stand, but waves of disorientation forced him to fall back on the bed.

He closed his eyes and succumbed to the intense dreams again. Visions came of running through a deep forest with trees so massive they stood like towers against a starry sky. Shadowy mountains, unrecognizable and alien, loomed in the distance. He had never seen such a landscape before. A huge full moon, bright and magnificent, shone silver through the leaves overhead and lit the forest floor. He was running close to the ground, scanning left and right. Hunting for something, but what, he couldn't fathom. His breath came in deep panting grunts. Stopping to lean against a tree, he noticed his fur-covered hands ending in black hooked claws.

He continued through the primeval forest, but not alone. A pack of wolves had joined in, beautiful creatures with coats of gray, white, and silver in the cascading misty moonlight. They ran along his side, and he seemed to be joined with the canines deep within his soul. The beauty of this realization brought tears of joy to his eyes, replacing the years of violence, pain, abuse, and addiction he had suffered throughout his life. His restless spirit had found home.

The pack stopped.

A large elk stood in a moonlit clearing. Displaying a full rack of antlers, the beautiful animal bent its head to munch on the undergrowth. It paused. Its nose quivered as it sniffed the night air for danger, unknowing that in the shadow of the great tree, death waited. Blake sensed the fear coming in waves from the animal and heard the thunder of its heart, the blood pulsing through its veins. The pack of wolves gathered silently about him. One with fur was as white as snow and looked in his eyes. He comprehended an unspoken message from the ancient wolf.

Kill!

He pounced from the shadows, leaping through the air to come down upon the animal's back. Claws and fangs ... *his claws and fangs* ... tore flesh and muscle. The elk tried to bolt, but his maw sunk deep into the animal's throat and hot blood spurted into his mouth. The great elk collapsed to the forest floor. He continued mauling the creature as it trembled and gasped its last breath. Pulling bloody strips of sinew and raw meat from the carcass, he swallowed it down. The other wolves moved in to join the feast. On a nearby tuft of grass, the white wolf raised its head and howled against the full moon.

Blake snapped opened his eyes. The dream had been so real he was once again unsure of his surroundings. He focused on the revolving ceiling fan overhead and realized he was still in the cheap motel room. Licking his chapped lips, he tasted salt from his sweat; his mouth parched to the point his throat burned when he swallowed. He was thirsty but too weak to rise from the bed to get a drink from the bathroom sink. How much time had passed? Morning sunlight blazed against the curtains of the picture window in the room signaling he had survived the night. The incessant Mexican radio from the adjoining room added a surreal touch to his surroundings, as if the motel was actually someplace south of the border.

He turned his attention to the crude towel compress pressed against the bite wound in his shoulder. Something moved beneath the bandage like a thing alive. He lifted the bloody cloth to check the wound. The bleeding had stopped and the trauma wasn't as severe as the night before. The skin throbbed and pulsed around the bite marks.

What is happening to me?

He laid his head back on the pillow. Somehow his shoulder flesh had knitted together. Though, he knew it was impossible, his mind was too fatigued to ponder the fact. He breathed slowly and sensed the room around him. On the edge of his perception, whispering voices and vague shadows shuffled about the room. Again he was too tired to deal with these new phenomena. He closed his eyes and wavered on the edge of sleep.

"Blakey," a strong voice spoke a name he hadn't heard since childhood.

He reopened his eyes and gasped. His father dressed in his police uniform sat in the cigarette burn-pitted chair beside the bed. He stared at him with dead white eyes. Blood leaked from the bullet hole in the side of his head and dripped on his blue dress shirt.

"Blakey," he repeated.

"Dad?" he choked out in shock.

"Do you remember what fun we used to have?" His head tilted one way causing more blood to leak out. "The game I used to play with your mother? Put one bullet in the pistol and spin the chamber. It was fun, wasn't it, son? Do you remember, Blakey?"

"Go away."

"Your wife's a backstabbing whore, Blakey. You know what you do to a whore like that?" He tightened his dead fists. "You teach her a lesson. A severe lesson. Just like I did with your mom. You force her to play the game. That's what you do, son. Put one bullet in the chamber and spin. Show her what the old man taught you, Blakey."

"Leave me alone. You ruined my life."

The figure and the voice faded like mist in the dim light.

Blake closed his eyes and tried to calm his pounding heart. He wasn't certain if he had dreamed the apparition or not. More voices whispered to him, and he sensed movement coming from the bathroom. He gazed toward the door where a shadowy figure formed. The stranger stepped forward into the dim light. Again, Blake froze in shock and blinked his eyes in disbelief. Tyree Williams, the black teenager he had murdered last year in a back alley on the south side of Chicago, now stood in the motel room wearing his gang colors and sporting bling of pure gold around his neck. Three bullet exit wounds were still visible in his chest. His dead white eyes contrasted against the dark color of his skin.

"You know who I am, don't you, pig?" the apparition asked.

"You're not real," Blake replied.

"Yeah? I'm this way 'cause you busted a cap in me from behind. Shot me in the back."

"Get the fuck out of here."

Tyree stepped closer to the bed. "I got killed so you can steal my snort. You remember, pig?"

"You don't frighten me, Tyree. You were always a two-bit hood hustling dime bags on a corner. I did the world a favor by killing you."

"Just 'cause you got this supernatural shit in your blood, why you going to dis the dead?" He crossed his arms and slowly faded into nothingness. Blake let out a nervous breath. His meeting with Tyree seemed almost comical, but he wasn't laughing.

He knew what was coming next.

The bed covers moved as if pulled by invisible hands. He watched in horror as another apparition slowly formed at the foot of the bed. Passion, the black stripper he had murdered two days ago in Chicago, was barely recognizable. Her face had become a misshapen pulp with the skull cracked open exposing gray brain matter, one white pupil-less eye opened, and the other mashed and leaking down the front of her battered face.

"Look at what you did to me, motherfucker." She grabbed the blankets and crawled on the bed. "You did this to me."

"Get the fuck away!" he shouted but was too frozen in fear to move.

"Motherfucker." She moved closer with her destroyed face hovering near his. "You did this shit to me."

The apparition faded away.

His scream was drowned out by the blaring mariachi music next door.

CHAPTER FORTY-THREE

After dropping Sid off, Terry Newman went straight home and parked the F-150 in the drive. Picking up the yellow notepad with the last will, he went inside. There was so much he wanted to tell his mother, but he knew it had to wait due to her working the day shift at Wal-Mart. A note on the refrigerator said there were egg salad sandwiches for lunch. Still full from breakfast, he settled for only one sandwich before going to his room and lying on the bed. He tried to go to sleep, but the incredible events of the last twenty-four hours prevented him from drifting off. Instead, he stared at the ceiling and thought of Jessica, his new love he met only this morning.

She was older than him, but not by much. Not really. Besides, he was tired of immature girls like Becky Warren. He needed someone equal to his own maturity, and Jessica was a total babe—blonde hair, blue eyes, nice boobs, the perfect package he had dreamed of. She smiled at him over the breakfast table, or at least he thought she did. If she was married, where was her husband? If the man wasn't in the picture, how was he going to get her to fall for him?

The words Sid said repeated in his mind.

"You want to be Jessica's knight in shining armor and protect the babe from the big bad wolf?"

That's what he needed to do. Protect her from the werewolf coming around the farm. Slay the monster and get the girl. Kill two birds with one stone. Keep his promise to Mr. Higgins and win Jessica's love. Isn't that how it works in the movies? Aragorn got Liv Tyler in the end of the *Lord of the Rings* trilogy. James Bond always got the girl after saving the world. It should work for him, too.

But how?

He jumped off his bed and crossed to the closet where he pulled out a large metal trunk unopened since his father had left four years before. He flipped the latches and swung up the lid. Inside was the hunting gear his dad had bought him when he was thirteen. He removed the items: a ghillie suit that didn't fit anymore, a pair of walkie-talkies with a seven-mile range, a camouflage poncho, and hiking boots that were too small. At the trunk bottom, he found the thing he was looking for. His buckshot deer-hunting crossbow still looked as new as on the Christmas morning he unwrapped it. Along with the bow, there was the quiver that held four arrows. He removed the bow and returned to his bed.

When he was younger, he had to have his father's help to cock the weapon. He was much older and bigger now. This time he was able to pull back the string and cock it in place. He put the bow aside and turned his attention to the four arrows in the quiver—broad-tipped with razor-sharp edges designed to penetrate deer flesh and drop the animal quickly.

But would they stop a werewolf?

Terry leaned back on the bed and pondered his question. Remembering the silver bullet Mr. Higgins gave him the day before, he removed it from his pocket and studied it. What he needed was something equal to bring a werewolf down. In an instant he knew the answer. He grabbed up the Ford F-150 key ring from the bedside table and loaded the hunting gear in the back of the truck.

To save Jessica he was going to need the right weapon to do the job. He imagined himself holding the bow over the slain werewolf as Jessica rushed into his arms. Then he would get the blonde babe just like the heroes in the movies do.

His heart swelled at the prospect as he pulled out of the drive to his house.

*　　*　　*　　*

Roxie's Roadhouse was dark and empty when Sheriff Sutton let himself in. The major light source came from the dim neon glow of the jukebox in the corner. Crossing to the bar, he tossed the baseball bat upon the wooden countertop, making a loud clattering.

Roxie stepped out of the back room wearing nothing but a T-shirt and bikini underwear over her lithe body.

"Quiet," she hissed. "Collin's still asleep."

"I bet," Sheriff Sutton replied, fighting back the anger in his voice. "He was busy last night."

"What are you saying?"

Sheriff Sutton pointed to the bat on the bar. "I found this at the farm where Jessica and her daughter are staying."

"A baseball bat?"

"This one's got Collin's teeth marks on it."

She picked up the bat and her nostrils flared. He knew she identified her brother's scent as the perpetrator of the bite marks.

"So what?" Roxie asked.

"Is that all you can say?" He reached across the bar and took her hand. "What's going on, Rox? We had a good thing set up here, but Collin is throwing it all away. I've kept you two safe and hidden from those who would do you harm. I've provided good kills over the last two years. We were making it work and now everything has gone to shit. Those teenage boys are passing around flyers warning of a werewolf in the area. I got OHP officers snooping around and asking questions. It might have been Jess's husband that Collin bit at the farm last night."

Roxie's eyebrows arched. "Jess's husband?"

"I think he's the one that clubbed Brody from behind. After that, he followed Jess home and ran into Collin. It's the only person I can think of who would be stalking her. He's a cop from Chicago and may have tracked her to Hope Springs."

"We'll just have to deal with it. If he survives the bite, he will seek us out to join the Pack. With Dominic's death, we have an opening for a new member."

"Not this one. I checked with Chicago. The man is already wanted for arson and the murder of a stripper. He's very dangerous and unstable."

"If he refuses to join and serve us, then Collin will kill him."

Sheriff Sutton shook his head. "Very risky. It's only a matter of time before the police will find him here. We should dispose of him now."

"We're preparing to disappear after the Ebon Moon. The buy is in the works for our new home in Alaska. We just have to keep up this ruse until then. If the new Bitten isn't controllable, Collin will dispose of him before we leave."

"Did I hear my name?" Collin stood naked from the waist up at the entrance to the back room. His muscular frame highlighted the various tribal tattoos across his chest. "What's the situation?"

"You bit someone last night?" Sheriff Sutton asked.

"I got shot in the chest and lost it for a bit. A human was watching the farm as well." Collin stepped into the room and pulled a cold beer from under the bar. He glanced down at the baseball bat. "He had that."

"Dale thinks it was Jess's husband," Roxie stated.

"So?" Collin popped the top from the bottle with a church key. "He may not even survive the transformation, and if he does, he will learn to serve the Pack."

"His name is Blake Lobato and is a felon wanted for murder and arson in Chicago," Sheriff Sutton replied. "He's also an abusive asshole and very dangerous."

"We need someone strong to join the Pack. This Blake sounds like he fits the bill." Collin took a sip from the longneck. "We're preparing to move away and leave Oklahoma nothing but a bad memory behind us for our new hunting grounds in the north. We will take the new Bitten with us."

"I'll agree to this under one condition." Sheriff Sutton picked up the bat. "You spare Jess and Megan. I've got somebody else for the Feast of the Ebon Moon tomorrow night."

"Who?" Collin asked.

"Those two teenage punks out of Morris. They're causing trouble again by spreading rumors about werewolves in the area."

"The same ones responsible for the death of our beloved Dominic," Roxie interjected.

Collin nodded. "Very well, I will agree but only because they helped kill Dominic. They need to pay with their flesh and blood."

"I'll bring them to you for the feast." Sheriff Sutton walked toward the door. "I promise."

Collin put down his bottle. "If you don't, then Jess and her daughter will take their place. Understand?"

"Very well," Sheriff Sutton answered before closing the door behind him.

*   *   *   *

After the sheriff left, Roxie turned to Collin.

"You're feeling generous this morning," she said with a smile. "Allowing someone else for the feast besides Jess and Megan."

"I lied." Collin took her into his arms.

"Why?"

"To keep him busy while we continue with our plans to capture Jess and her daughter."

"And what happens when the sheriff finds out we've taken his precious human mother and daughter?"

Collin put his forehead against hers and looked deep in his sister's eyes. "Reveca, I'm afraid our sheriff has outlived his usefulness to us. We have a new Bitten to join our Pack. I've sensed that he has survived the transformation. He will replace the sheriff and won't have any problem with killing and devouring Jess and Megan."

CHAPTER FORTY-FOUR

"There's something bothering Sam," Nelda said softly.

"What do you think it is?" Jessica asked while pouring another cup of hot tea. The two women sat in patio chairs on the back porch of the farmhouse while Sam and Megan tended to Princess in the stock pen. Since the morning's frost, the sun had done little to heat up the day.

"It's not anything I can put my finger on. It's just after so many years of marriage, I know the man." Nelda picked up a sugar cube from a saucer on the patio table and plopped it into her tea. "You get a sense about things."

"I understand." Jessica nodded.

"It's something to do with what scared Megan last night. I think it scared Sam, too. The strange thing is that I've never seen him afraid of anything."

Megan left petting Princess and ran up to the back porch. Her cheeks were nearly as red as her new coat bought at the Dollar Store yesterday.

"Can I have some more sugar cubes, Aunt Nel?" she asked breathlessly, her eyes wide with excitement.

"Sure you can, sweat pea." Nelda picked out a few sugar cubes from the saucer and put them in her hands.

"Princess loves these," Megan said and took off running back down to the pen.

"I wish I had her energy." Nelda laughed.

"Don't we all. That reminds me. Roxie called and wants me to come back to work at the bar. I told her I didn't think I could leave Megan, especially after what happened last night. She said to bring her along and she'll put her up in the back room so I can work and watch her at the same time."

"What are you going to do?"

"I don't want to take Megan there, but she offered me ten dollars an hour." Jessica put her cup down on the table. "I do need the money. I owe you."

Nelda touched her arm. "Normally, dear, I'd tell you to forget paying me the money, and I would mean it. In this case, I don't get the impression charity is what you're looking for. I think you want to prove to yourself that you can make it on your own. If you want to go back to work, feel free, is what I say."

"Thanks, Nel."

The phone rang from inside the kitchen.

"Lord sakes, again?" Nelda rose from the patio chair. "Now who could it be?"

She entered the house as Jessica turned her attention to Sam and Megan. Love swelled in her chest at the sight of her beautiful daughter feeding the horse sugar cubes. She was growing up so fast, and the farm was much better for her than the stress-filled home they left. Sipping on the hot tea, she whispered a silent prayer of thanks.

Nelda stepped back out on the patio. "Sam!" she called out.

Sam looked up. "Yes?"

"It's the nursing home calling about your mother," Nelda answered with a worried look on her face.

"Coming," Sam replied, hurrying toward the patio.

"Is something wrong?" Jessica asked as Sam entered the house.

Nelda gave her a nervous look. "Sam's mother is in an extended-care nursing home in Bartlesville. She's eighty-two years old."

Jessica sipped at her tea and waited in silence. Nelda stood in the door and stepped aside to let Sam back out.

"What's wrong, dear?" Nelda asked upon seeing the sad face of her husband.

"My mother's had some sort of stroke. She's been rushed to the hospital."

"We have to go see her," Nelda stated.

Sam nodded his head. "As soon as possible. I've already fed the livestock this morning and I'll call Chuck Ramsey to come over and check on the farm until I get back."

"Can I help?" Jessica asked, standing to her feet.

"I'm just going to throw a few things in a suitcase and go," Nelda replied. "Jess, I hate leaving you and Megan alone on the farm like this."

"Don't worry about us. We'll be all right."

"If you don't want to sleep in the trailer, you're welcome to stay here in the house while we're gone."

"I'll be fine, Nel. I'll have Sheriff Sutton come by and check on us."

"Very well." Nelda rushed into the house to pack for the trip.

Megan left feeding Princess to join her on the patio. "Is something wrong, Mommy?"

Jessica put her hand on her daughter's shoulder. "Sam's mother is very sick. They've got to go out of town to see her in the hospital."

"Is she going to die, Mommy?"

"I don't know, baby."

*　　*　　*　　*

Within a half an hour, the Olsons were ready to leave. Jessica waited in the drive with Megan by her side as Sam threw a suitcase in the truck bed and turned toward them with a concerned look. He attempted a warm smile at Megan.

"You take good care of your mother while I'm gone, Meg," Sam said.

She ran forward and gave him a hug. "I will, I promise."

"I'll see you when I get back." Sam returned the hug before sliding behind the wheel of the truck.

Jessica stepped up to the open passenger window to speak to Nelda, already sitting in the truck.

"I'm going to miss you guys."

"We will probably be gone overnight and back in the morning," Nelda replied. "Hopefully, you'll be fine out here for one night."

Jessica nodded. "We'll be all right. You worry about Sam's mother now."

"I will."

Sam started the truck.

"Got any special instructions for me?" Jessica asked.

"I've got a man coming over in the morning to feed the livestock, so don't be surprised if he's around for a while. Oh, and I almost forgot, those teenage boys, Terry and Sid, are going to drop by tonight for some hunting. They might show up around dark."

"I'll probably be working at the bar when they're here," Jess commented.

"Okay."

"Good-bye." Jessica stepped back from the truck as Sam put it in reverse. With Megan by her side, they waved one last time as the truck pulled out of the yard and onto the road. A dull fear settled in Jessica's stomach watching the truck disappear. She walked toward the trailer, realizing that tonight she would be alone with Megan on the farm.

CHAPTER FORTY-FIVE

Blake Lobato opened his eyes to find he was still in the motel room.

Above him the ceiling fan revolved in its continuous cycle to the tune of the Mexican music playing next door. This time, though, it was much louder and clearer than before. Other sounds drifted in from outside: the roar of a truck on the highway, a man and woman arguing in Spanish somewhere in the motel parking lot, and a television on in some other room. His sense of hearing seemed more acute and sensitive to his surroundings.

He sat up in the bed and looked back. The blood stain had dried into a crusty reddish brown blot upon the sheets where he had slept. The crude bandage on his shoulder was equally dried. Removing the cloth, he stared in disbelief.

The bite was completely healed. Only the scar left by tooth marks remained in his flesh.

How long have I been asleep?

A late afternoon sun lit the curtained front window. He had slept through most of the day and barely remembered the haunted events of the previous night. Feeling energized and alive, he slid off the bed to stand on strong legs. Gone was the wracking fever and disorientation. Naked from the waist down, he studied his physique. The hair across his chest was thicker and darker. His muscles were more defined and tighter, complete down to a washboard six-pack of abs that he could never accomplish before, no matter how hard he worked in the police gym. He tested his speed and reflexes by throwing a few shadow punches. The air reverberated by the power of his quick jabs.

He was not only healed, but improved.

Rushing to the bathroom, he switched on the dirty light bulb, sending roaches scurrying across the floor. Blake studied his reflection in the mirror. He was a changed man. Gone from his pallor were the ravages of years of cocaine abuse. His complexion was youthful and clearer, the dark circles under his eyes no longer present. Running his tongue over his teeth, he felt two sharp points. He lifted his lip to study his canines in the mirror. They were much sharper and prominent.

Am I a werewolf? he asked his reflection.

His stomach rolled with a deep hunger, and he had no recollection of his last meal. Another pang wracked his body, almost causing him to double over. He needed badly to eat. He threw on the long duster jacket over his bare torso and buttoned it in the front. The one shirt he brought with him was too blood-stained and ripped to wear in public. He would have to go out like that. Lastly, he slid on his black sunglasses before stepping outside.

With his sense of hearing much more acute and clear, he heard every sound in sharp detail. A cacophony of noise assaulted him when he left the motel room into the afternoon sun. As he stood in front of his room door, he realized his sense of smell had also undergone the same upgrade. Blake sniffed the air, detecting odors from various sources: an oil spot beneath a parked car, a bag of rotting trash placed outside a door several rooms down, and the body odor of a Mexican man talking on a pay phone at the corner of the lot. The most prominent was that of meat cooking. He turned toward the smell and noticed a barbeque diner in a strip mall on the other side of the highway. The name of the place was Lou's Pig Shack.

Deciding to walk instead of taking the Harley, he started across the highway and stopped in the middle of the road. His attention was suddenly drawn back down the two-lane blacktop toward Hope Springs.

Jess was back there.

His hatred returned again. Tonight he would find and kill her.

A slight smile played across his lips. *What will she think of the new me?*

Continuing to the barbeque place, he found the small diner almost empty when he entered. One couple sat at a table, and he guessed they were regular customers since both were well in excess of three hundred pounds. The layout of the place was similar to a deli with patrons choosing their meat selections from behind a glass counter. Blake spotted an entire rack of ribs broiling beneath a heat lamp.

"Can I help you?" a teenage girl asked from behind the counter.

"How much is the rack of ribs?"

"Fourteen dollars," she replied.

"I'll take it to go." He stomach twisted again, causing him to wince. "Now."

"Sure."

She cut the ribs apart and stacked them into a Styrofoam container. "You get coleslaw and baked beans with that."

"Just the ribs, please."

The girl started to ring up the purchase. Blake placed a fifty-dollar bill on the counter.

"Keep the change."

He took the container and rushed out the door with the hunger tearing at his insides. Unable to wait until he returned to the hotel room, he squatted in a parking space and placed the Styrofoam container on the tarmac. Opening the lid, he devoured the stack of cooked ribs with his new set of canines. In less than a minute, he had finished the meal, leaving bones scattered about. Meat juice covered his chin and bare hands.

He sensed someone watching him and glanced back at the diner. The obese couple along with the teenage girl stood staring through the front window. Deciding he was drawing too much attention, Blake ran back across the highway to the motel.

The rest of the afternoon he paced the small room as nervous anticipation grew with every passing minute. There was a full moon tonight, and he had no idea what to expect. At one point, he pulled out the bag of coke and contemplated snorting a line but flushed it down the toilet instead. He didn't need coke anymore. He had found something better. Repeatedly, he pulled aside the curtains of the one window to watch the setting sun only to return to pacing back and forth. As the afternoon wore on, his agitation grew to the point the blaring music next door became unbearable. He pounded his fist against the wall.

"Shut that shit off!" he shouted at the top of his voice, but the music continued unabated.

The hunger also returned, and this time he knew it was going to take more than a tray of ribs to appease it. A lot more. As the sun slipped toward the horizon, he stripped off the rest of his clothes and pounded again on the wall for the music to stop, but to no avail. Every nerve tingled with energy as his breathing and heart rate increased. Sweat broke out in beads across his naked flesh. Stepping once more to the window, he pushed aside the curtain to stare at the skyline above the last light of sunset. A huge golden full moon hovered in the sky above the horizon, and as he looked upon it, his body began to transform.

Blake stepped back from the window and stared at the back of his hands. Thick hair pushed through the pores of his skin. He raised his right hand and watched in awe as black nails extended below his own fingernails. A wave of burning pain caused him to fall on the carpet at the foot of the bed. Curled into a fetal position, he screamed in agony and kicked about as the femur bones of his legs elongated in length. Multiplying at an incredible rate, coarse hair covered his naked flesh in a coat of dark fur. His spinal column popped and snapped as the painful transformation continued. He tried to scream out but his tongue thickened as canine teeth descended from an elongating jawline forming the face of the wolf. Within a minute, the shape-shifting was complete and he stood looming over the bed on new canine legs. Saliva dripped from his maw in streams.

He was still Blake, but now joined with a beast.

Next door the blaring Mexican music hurt his ears. Animal rage boiled at the sound.

Kill!

His eight-feet-tall form charged the cheap wall of the motel. Black claws ripped a hole through the wood and Sheetrock as he broke through in a cloud of plaster dust. A Hispanic man, dressed in blue jeans and a white tank top, lay on the bed with a boom box blasting from a nightstand. He gawked in speechless terror at the sudden monster in his room. Blake smelled his fear and the bottle of tequila by his side. Panic-driven, the Mexican tried to run for the door, but Blake slapped him back with his claws ripping deep bloody gouges in the man's chest. He fell on the bed screaming as the beast pounced upon him. Trying to block the attack, the man lifted his arm, but Blake severed it below the elbow with one bite. Warm blood rushed down his throat in a hot torrent. The taste of it spurred him on and he continued his attack, mauling and clawing the hapless victim. Blood splattered the walls as he ripped out chunks of meat and organs. The note of a dozen trumpets blasting out of the boom box drowned out the man's dying screams.

Blake and the beast fed then. Using his canine maw, he pulled up sinewy meat and swallowed it down. He reduced his victim to a mass of severed limbs and mutilated flesh upon the bed mattress. Once the kill was complete, he tore the boom box from the wall, raised his bloody snout toward the ceiling, and emitted a loud howl.

CHAPTER FORTY-SIX

It was late afternoon when Terry Newman pulled up in the old F-150 in front of Sid's house. After working in Mr. Higgins's workshop, he wanted to show his friend the result. Sid emerged from the house and walked down the drive to meet him with his hands in the pockets of his ICP hoodie.

"Oh, man, you got to see the stuff I've brought with me," Terry stated as he slammed the truck door.

"Didn't you get any sleep, dude?"

"Are you kidding? I'm too excited." Terry threw aside a tarp in the truck bed and lifted out his Buckshot crossbow. "I'm going to kill me a werewolf tonight."

"With a toy crossbow? Not fucking likely."

"This is not a toy. It'll take down a deer, so it will do the same for a werewolf."

"You tell it that when it's chomping on your ass."

"I got something else." Terry reached back into the truck bed and removed the quiver of flanged arrows. He pulled one and handed it to Sid. "Silver-tipped arrows."

"You're shitting me," Sid replied.

"I worked all afternoon dipping them into molten silver and grinding the points sharp again."

Sid studied the arrowheads. "Holy shit, you're as crazy as Mr. Higgins."

"I only got four arrows, though." He threw off more of the tarp. "I found this in Mr. Higgins's work shed."

Sid peered at the jangle of collapsible steel pipes. "What the hell is it?"

"A deer hunter's tree stand. You erect this thing up against a tree and it gives you an elevated place to spot deer. I figure you can get up there and watch for the werewolf and alert me when you spot it." He picked up the pair of walkie-talkies and handed one to Sid. "That's what this is for. You radio me when you see the monster."

"You got this all figured out."

"Sure do."

"What's the range of the radio?"

"Five miles."

"I've been busy, too. While you're acting like fucking William Tell with your little crossbow, I'm going to shoot the werewolf with this, if he shows up." Sid reached into the pocket of his hoodie and removed a Sony digital minicam. "My grandma bought it for me and it's got night vision and everything. I'm going to capture a werewolf on video this time. We can sell the footage to *60 Minutes* or the Discovery Channel. How fucking awesome is that?"

"Coolness," Terry replied.

Sid chuckled. "Plus, I want to record you asking that Jessica girl out and falling on your ass."

"Oh, man, I've been thinking … you know … Jessica is a lot older."

"I knew you were going to pussy out of it."

"No, dude, I'm going to ask her out." Terry opened the door to the truck. "Hop in and let's get going. The sun's setting and the moon will be up soon."

*　*　*　*

Jessica received a shock when she and Megan exited the front door of the trailer to leave for Roxie's. Terry Newman and Sid Granger stood in the front yard beside the Camaro. Normally she would have been suspicious finding teenage boys standing beside her car, but not these two. After living within the shadow of Blake, she didn't fear two geeky teenagers. Besides, she had the .357 in her purse.

"Hi," said Terry, who shyly looked down at his shoes. Sid stood quietly off to the side.

"Hello," she replied.

Terry slipped his hands in the pocket of his jeans. "We were looking for Sam. Do you know where he is? We knocked but got no answer at the farmhouse."

"His mother had a medical emergency, so he and Nelda had to leave." Jessica helped Megan down the three steps of the wooden deck. "I don't know when he'll be home."

"Did he say something about us coming back tonight?" Terry asked.

"He told me you two were going to hunt deer."

"You're going to kill a deer?" Megan's eyes went wide. "Like Bambi?"

"Not like Bambi, little girl." Terry laughed and added, "We'll probably end up going home empty-handed."

"You guys ever hunt deer before?" Jessica asked, glancing toward Sid standing a few feet away. He smiled back at her.

"Oh yeah, lots of times," Terry answered.

"Well, I'm off to work, and I'll be back late." She unlocked and opened the Camaro passenger door. Megan hopped up into the seat, and Jessica buckled her in.

Terry cleared his throat. "By the way, you look real pretty tonight, Jessica."

She straightened and shut Megan's door. "Thank you, but call me Jess."

"Jess," Terry repeated. He stepped a little closer and looked again at his shoes. "I was just wondering … Jess … if you would like to … you know … go out and do something sometime. Like go get a chili dog … or something," he stammered and added, "I got a truck now."

Jessica crossed in front of the Camaro. "You're asking me out on a date?"

"Not like a real date … but sort of like one."

"How old are you?"

"Seventeen."

"I'm ten years older than you."

"I know, but Natalie Portman was older than Anakin Skywalker in *Star Wars* and they fell in love."

Jessica tried to keep from laughing. The boy was so shy and sweet, she didn't want to hurt his feelings. "Don't you have any girls your own age to ask out?"

"They're too immature. I want a girl who can match my maturity."

"I see," Jessica replied, unlocking the driver door. She raised her hand to show her wedding ring. "Sorry, but I'm already married. I'm sure if you ask a girl a little closer to your age, she would say yes."

Terry bobbed his head. "Okay."

"Well, I got to get to work now. Good luck, guys, with your hunt."

"Thanks, Jess."

"Yeah," Sid piped in.

Sliding into the Camaro, she started the engine. She held back her laughter until she pulled out of the farm and onto the road to Hope Springs.

"Mommy, you're laughing again," Megan observed.

"I know, baby," she replied with a chuckle. Would her bad luck with men ever end? Either they were violently psychotic, emotionally distant, or in the case of Terry Newman, way too young.

"Wow, Mommy, look at the moon," Megan announced, breaking her thoughts.

Jessica looked ahead in the night sky. A magnificent golden full moon hovered over the horizon.

"It's beautiful, baby," she said.

"It's big."

"Tomorrow night there's an eclipse. Do you know what that is, sweetie?"

Megan shook her head no.

"Well, that's where the moon gets covered in shadow." Jessica turned onto the highway leading to Hope Springs.

"In shadow?" Megan asked, perplexed. "What does that mean, Mommy?"

"Tomorrow night the moon will go dark."

*　　*　　*　　*

"Natalie Portman was much older than Anakin Skywalker and they fell in love." Sid broke into laughter so hard he doubled over. "You're such a dumbass."

"Screw you," Terry replied with his cheeks burning red with embarrassment. *Why did I act like a dork in front of Jess?*

Sid showed him the Sony minicam. "I got every bit on tape, and it so going on YouTube."

"You're a prick, Sid." Terry turned and started walking back to his truck. "Let's get the hunting gear," he called back over his shoulder.

Wiping the tears out of his eyes, Sid followed. "That was some funny shit."

Once they had the gear loaded out of the truck, they carried the collapsible deer stand across the freshly plowed field to the line of trees bordering the south side of the Olson farm. The sun had set and the first stars appeared in the darkening sky. Hovering over the horizon, the moon shone like a giant gold ball.

"Would you look at that moon?" Terry said. "What werewolf wouldn't want to come out on a full moon like that?"

"Let's hope you're right. I hate to think we hauled this fucking deer stand all the way out here for nothing."

They entered the line of trees at the spot where Sam had found the baseball bat and binoculars earlier in the morning. With the sun down, the air grew colder and the trees loomed over them, dark and foreboding. Terry switched on a flashlight to show the way and spotted the binoculars laying in the leaves.

"Hey, look what's still here," Terry said, shining the beam on the field glasses. "Sid, take those so you can use them to spot the werewolf for me."

Sid picked the binoculars up and stuffed them in the pocket of his hoodie. "Fucking A."

"This is the place where all the action has been the last few nights." Terry pointed to a nearby tree. "Let's set the stand up there."

Over the next few minutes, they erected the steel deer stand against the tree trunk and secured it in place. With a set of climbing rungs in the front, the stand provided a platform for a hunter to sit fifteen feet above the ground.

"Okay, Sid, get your ass up there," Terry said.

"Where are you going to be at?" Sid looked around the clearing in the trees.

"About twenty-five yards over there hiding in the brush by the creek bank," Terry said while unfolding his camouflage poncho and slipping it on.

"I'm going to feel like a piece of raw meat up there," Sid replied, grabbing hold of the rungs.

"I won't be far." Terry handed him the walkie-talkie. "Radio me if you see something."

"You fucking know it."

Sid climbed up to the platform. At the top, he sat and looked down at Terry. "Just tell me one fucking thing," he said.

"What's that?"

"Tell me this isn't the stupidest thing we've ever done."

"Okay, it's not." Terry brought up his crossbow and pulled back the bowstring, locking it in place. Next, he removed one of the silver-tipped arrows from the quiver and loaded the weapon. He turned and started across the clearing toward the creek bed.

"Yes, it is," Sid called after him.

CHAPTER FORTY-SEVEN

Stepping out of the dollar store in Hope Springs, Debbie Miller spit out her gum and climbed into the waiting black pickup. Steve Kiegler, the latest hopeful who wanted to get in her pants, smiled as she climbed in. Slamming the door behind her, she grabbed a pack of Marlboros off the dash.

"I've wanted to get a smoke all goddamn day," she commented, putting a cigarette between her lips.

Steve reached over with his Bic lighter and lit the end. "What now?" he asked.

"Let's go see Brody," she replied after taking a long drag.

"Is he out of the hospital?"

"We're going to go get him out." She exhaled a cloud of smoke. "He's over at County Regional in Stillwater."

"I thought we were partying at the lake tonight. You promised me, Deb. I got the tent, sleeping blankets, and beer packed in the back. Just me and you tonight."

She reached over and put a hand on the thigh of his blue jeans. "A little detour first. Then you can have me all to yourself."

He threw up his hands. "All right."

As the truck pulled away from the curb, Debbie puffed on the Marlboro pondering what she wanted to do next. Sheriff Sutton had stopped returning her calls, and she knew it was because of Jessica. It was time to teach the bitch a lesson.

Brody needed in on this. Someone had nearly brained the guy when he followed Jessica out of Roxie's. She had no doubt the person who clubbed Brody was a friend of hers. The stuck-up slut from out of town needed to learn you don't come into Hope Springs, screw with her man, and beat up her friends. Payback's a bitch, and Debbie knew she was the right bitch for the job.

*　　*　　*　　*

Jessica walked Megan through the front door of Roxie's. The place was nearly deserted. One couple occupied table six, and two old farmers sat at the bar talking to Roxie.

"Hi, Jess." She looked up and smiled. She reached around and turned on the light in the back room. "Bring your daughter and come on back."

Jessica continued around the bar, guiding Megan into the room. Once inside, she helped her daughter up on the sleeping cot.

"There you go, sweetie," Jessica said, straightening up. "Now you have to stay back here, baby. You can't go running around."

"Okay, Mommy." Megan looked about the room and spotted Collin's sketches taped to the wall. "Ooooh, pretty pictures."

"Roxie's brother, Collin, drew those."

"Would she like a pop to drink?" Roxie asked from the door.

"A Sprite would be fine," Jessica answered, opening a locker. She put her purse with the .357 magnum inside. Because of Brody's assault the night before, she felt safer with the weapon near. Closing the locker door, she smiled at Megan.

"You'll be all right while Mommy works?"

Megan swung her legs over the cot edge and nodded.

Roxie came into the room popping open a can of cold Sprite. "There you go, baby."

Megan took it and said, "Thank you. Your hair is pretty."

Roxie laughed. "So is yours, sweetheart."

"I'm ready to start," Jessica stated to Roxie. "Ten dollars an hour was our agreement, right?"

"That's right," Roxie replied, adding, "I know you're worried about bringing your daughter, Jess. I tell you what, I'll work the tables and you run things behind the bar. That way you're close and can keep an eye on her."

"Thanks." She glanced toward Megan sipping a Sprite. "That will be fine."

"Come on. I'll show you how to run the register."

She followed Roxie out into the serving space behind the bar. She didn't see her brother anywhere.

"Where's Collin?"

"He's gone into Morris to pick up some beer. He'll be back before long. Things are slow because of the OU–Texas football game. Once the game is over, the place is going to fill pretty quickly. Another full moon tonight, so expect anything."

"You don't have to tell me."

"I heard you had a problem with Brody Carlson last night. After you left, someone nearly beat his head in. I had the sheriff, ambulance, everyone out here. I'm not going to let anything happen tonight. If Debbie Miller and her white trash posse show up, I'll have Collin run them off."

"Thank you."

"You better take this," Roxie stated, handing over her bottle opener on a string. "You're going to need it."

Roxie was right. Within an hour, customers crowded the honky-tonk, and it soon became a noisy smoke-filled place. Jessica took beer orders and put money in the register as the bills steadily increased in her tip jar. Even as busy as it was, she kept an eye on Megan sitting on the sleeping cot in the back room. At the slightest break in the chaos, she went into the room to talk to her.

In time, Collin rolled in a stack of beer cases on a two-wheeler. He stacked the boxes in the cooler while Megan watched with curious interest. He didn't say anything to her or Megan in the process.

At around eight, Pearl showed up. She walked into the back room to put her purse in a locker. After a minute, she came back out.

"Jess, is that your daughter?" she asked with a smile above the noise.

"Yes," Jessica answered while opening a line of cold beer bottles with her church key. "Megan's her name."

"She's an absolute doll," Pearl replied, getting a bottle of cold water out of the cooler behind the bar. "She's got her mom's eyes."

"Thanks," Jessica replied.

Pearl nodded toward the stage. "Time to fire up the karaoke machine and get this party started."

The next couple of hours became a whirlwind rush of serving cold beer, bad karaoke singing, and boisterous drunks arguing back and forth about the OU football game score. One old man at the bar peaked down her top every time she bent over to pull a beer out of the ice boxes below the counter. Jessica wished he would put a dollar in her tip jar each time he got a free show. She looked in on Megan, but the time between checks got longer. The smoke became so thick her eyes started to burn. At about ten, she glanced into the back room and her heart went cold.

Collin sat on the cot next to Megan. She had an art pad in her lap and concentrated on drawing a picture with her tongue sticking out of the corner of her mouth.

"What are you doing?" she called out, completely forgetting about her customers.

"I noticed she didn't have her coloring book, so I gave her something to draw on," Collin replied, looking up with his cold gaze. "She looked bored."

"How did you know she had a coloring book?"

"Lucky guess," Collin said with a shrug.

"Mommy threw my coloring book away," Megan said and continued drawing on the pad. "It had scary pictures."

Jessica stepped into the back room. "Thank you, but she's not supposed to talk to anyone."

"I was just being nice." Collin stood to his feet. "You're the boss."

He brushed past and went into the serving area behind the bar.

"Can you take over for a bit?" she asked behind him. Collin's only response was to start taking money for beer.

Jessica sat on the bed next to Megan. "What are you drawing, sweetie?"

"The Bad Wolf." She passed the art pad over for her to see. Drawn in crude pencil lines, the picture showed something bestial with big teeth and wild eyes.

Jessica fought a chill down her spine. "Is this what you saw last night?"

"Uh huh," Megan said with a nod and went back to drawing. Her pink tongue stuck out again.

Jessica spotted the empty can of Sprite. "You got to go pee, baby?"

"Uh huh."

Not wanting to take her daughter out through the crowded bar to use the restroom, she nodded toward the back exit door. "You can pee outside."

"Outside?" Megan blinked.

"Come on, I'll show you."

Taking Megan's hand, she helped her off the cot and opened the back door. The cool night air blew into the room replacing the smoke. With her daughter by her side, she stepped out on the deck and let the door close behind her, cutting off the noise of the bar. A short distance away stretched the winding footpath through the wall of dark trees. Under a full moon, the silhouette of the large wooden barn stood in the distance.

Jessica took a second to breathe deeply.

"Where do I go, Mommy?" Megan asked.

"We'll use the trail through the trees," she answered, helping Megan down the steps to the ground.

Once off the deck, she led her daughter across the moist grass to the mouth of the path. Dark tree limbs stretched overhead like spiny fingers interlocked together.

"You can go here, baby."

"No, I can't, Mommy."

"Why not?"

"I don't have anything to wash my hands with."

Jessica sighed. "I've got some baby wipes in the car." She took Megan by the hand again. "Let's go get them."

They walked along the back wall of the bar and rounded the corner. Twenty-five yards away, the Camaro waited in its parking space in the crowded lot. She was about to cross the distance when a black pickup truck slowed to a stop behind her car. Jessica stepped back around the corner of the building bringing Megan in close to her. Holding her breath, she prayed the black truck wasn't driven by Blake.

"What's wrong, Mommy?"

"Quiet, baby," she whispered.

Peering around the corner with her heart thumping, she watched the passenger door open and Brody Carlson climb out. In the garish neon light provided by the bar, he sported a white bandage on the side of his skull, making his head look misshapen. Debbie Miller sat inside the cab smoking a cigarette beside a man she didn't recognize.

"It's the bitch's car," Brody announced. "She's here."

"Good," Debbie replied, tossing out the lit cigarette butt on the gravel. "Let's go inside. I want to see her face when we show up again."

Brody produced a knife out of his pocket. The blade glinted in the light of the full moon. He knelt beside the back tire of the Camaro. "Let me slash the tires first."

"You idiot, it's too obvious to do it while we're still here. Wait until we leave."

"Fuck it." Brody stood, put the knife back in his pocket, and climbed back into the truck. The passenger door slammed shut as the pickup rolled away to find a parking space.

"I got to go pee, Mommy." Megan tugged on her hand.

Jessica undid the front of Megan's jeans and yanked them down. "Go now, baby. Quickly."

Megan squatted. "Is something wrong, Mommy?"

"We need to get back inside."

While her daughter urinated in the shadow of the wall, Jessica considered her next course of action. She had maybe two minutes before the black pickup parked and unloaded everyone. Enough time to get to her purse and pistol. She came to the stark realization she had made another stupid mistake bringing her daughter to the bar. She should've known better. Now she had to get Megan safely back home.

"All done, Mommy," Megan said, standing from her crouch.

Jessica pulled up and fastened her jeans. "Good girl."

Grabbing her by the hand, she rushed to the back door with Megan trying to keep up. Once inside the back room, she put her daughter back on the cot.

"Stay here, baby, until Mommy gets you."

"Okay," Megan replied, sensing her mother's fear.

Glancing out at the bar, she spotted Roxie picking up a tray full of beer at the end of the counter. She motioned for her to come back. Collin was busy ringing in money to the register.

"What's up?" Roxie asked.

"Debbie Miller and Brody are on their way in here." Jessica opened the door of her locker and reached into her purse. Roxie's eyes went wide as she removed the .357 pistol." I saw them out by my car. Brody wanted to slash my tires with a knife."

"Whoa! What are you doing with that pistol?" Roxie asked with eyes wide.

"Protection." She tucked it in the waistband of her jeans and covered it with her shirt. "I won't let them vandalize my car."

"Just stay back here and I'll have Collin handle it."

"What's up?" Collin asked from the bar.

"Debbie Miller and her friends are back to cause more trouble," Roxie answered.

Collin slammed shut the register drawer and grabbed up the sawed-off end of the pool stick from under the counter. "I'll take care of it."

"Be careful," Jessica stated. "Brody has a knife."

Debbie, Brody, and the third man Jessica didn't know entered through the front door. They stood in the entrance scanning the interior until they spotted her behind the bar. Immediately, Brody headed in her direction tailed by Debbie and her companion.

"Bitch, who did this to me!" he screamed at her above the noisy crowd and pointed to the side of his bandaged head. "I got forty stitches in my skull."

Collin showed the makeshift club. "Brody, get your ass out of here, and take your friends with you."

"Fuck you, Collin," he snapped back, his bruised face livid with anger. "We ain't leaving until that bitch tells me who fucked my head up last night."

From over Brody's shoulder, Debbie looked straight at her and grinned. *The little skank set this up,* Jessica realized.

The crowd began to take notice of the shouting. Even the karaoke singer on the stage stopped her rendition of a Shania Twain song as everyone focused on the drama. The old man who had looked down her cleavage all night moved out of his bar stool and stood to the side.

"Tell me who did this, bitch!" Brody shouted again.

"If you don't get out of my bar I'm going to fuck up the other side of your head," Collin said in his gruff voice.

"I ain't afraid of you, Collin." Brody produced the knife from the pocket of his jacket. "You want some of me, big boy? Come and get it!"

Jessica wasn't sure what took place next because it happened so fast. One second, Collin stood on the other side of the bar; the next, he cleared it in an amazing leap. He landed on his feet next to a surprised Brody, who reacted by stabbing him with the blade in his hand. Jessica gasped in shock as the point of the knife sunk deep into Collin's abdomen. An instant later the brawny bartender had his hand around Brody's throat.

"Get out of my bar," Collin said in a voice almost animal-like as he shoved him up against a wall.

Brody's eyes went wide as he struggled against the hold. "Okay … okay, man." His knife dropped to the floor.

Collin released his hold and shoved him out the front door. He next turned to Debbie. "You, too," he growled.

"You tell that two-bit whore hiding behind the bar this isn't over," Debbie replied, pointing toward Jessica. "This isn't over by a long shot, bitch."

The other man who came in with Debbie put his hands on her shoulders. "Let's go, Deb. We don't need this shithole place to party. We can go to the lake and do that."

"Fine," Debbie said, storming out of the bar.

After she left, Jessica rushed for the front door to make sure none of them vandalized her car.

"Jess, wait!" Roxie called out after her.

Jessica stopped in the open door watching the black pickup tear out of the parking lot, kicking up gravel in its wake. Exhaling a breath of relief, she turned to Collin standing behind her.

"My God, are you all right? Do you need to go to the hospital?" she asked.

"I'm fine," he replied. "Why?"

"I saw him stab you—"

"I'm fine," he interrupted.

Jessica glanced down at the bloody knife on the floor. "He cut you."

"He didn't cut me," Collin replied, picking up the blade. "Don't worry about it."

"Somebody needs to call Sheriff Sutton," one of the customers suggested. "Brody Carlson is as crazy as he is stupid. He might come back here with a gun."

With that announcement, the bar cleared out as people left in a hurry. The fight had put a damper on the mood in the place. Jessica returned to the back room.

"Mommy, are you okay?" Megan asked on the verge of tears.

"We're leaving, baby," she replied, opening the locker and removing her purse. "Come on."

Jessica emptied out her tip jar.

Roxie was on the phone apparently to Sheriff Sutton. "Are you going, Jess?" she asked, pausing her phone conversation.

"Yes. I'm sorry, Rox, this isn't working out. I won't be able to work here anymore." She faced Collin, who blocked her way to the door with a fierce look in his dark eyes.

"You're going to run out just like that?" he asked. "I just protected your ass from Brody."

"I've got to think of my daughter."

"I think you should stay here."

"I'm done with this place."

"Why don't you and your lovely daughter return to the back room?" His dark eyes glinted.

"Get out of my way, Collin." The way he looked at Megan made her stomach knot. Jessica reached into her waistband for the grip of the .357 pistol. "Now."

"She's got a gun," Roxie stated from behind the bar.

Collin smiled, stepping aside. "Okay."

She left with Megan in tow. With hurried footsteps, they walked to the Camaro while the parking lot emptied of cars and trucks. She unlocked the front door and helped Megan inside. Starting the engine, she glanced toward the front of the tavern one last time. Roxie and Collin stood in the doorway watching her leave. A strange chill went down her spine at the sight. She gunned the motor and tore out of the parking lot.

Two miles down the highway, Jessica broke down in tears. She pulled over to the grassy shoulder and wept.

"Mommy, don't be sad." Megan undid her seatbelt and hugged her mother tightly.

"I'm sorry, baby," she sobbed against her daughter's blonde locks. "I'm so sorry."

Through her tears, she noticed headlights growing brighter in the rearview. Blue and red lights suddenly flashed as a patrol car pulled behind the Camaro. She wiped her eyes as Sheriff Sutton got out, walked up to the driver's side, and tapped on the glass.

Cranking down the window, she asked, "Are you giving me a ticket?"

"I heard what happened at the bar," he said with a grim face. "I'm escorting you home."

CHAPTER FORTY-EIGHT

Terry Newman leaned his crossbow against a tree and shifted his body to keep from falling asleep. Cramped from squatting in the same place for too long, he checked his watch. Four hours had passed since he hid in the brush by the creek with no sign of a werewolf or any other creature moving about the dark trees. Deciding to join Sid for a few minutes, he pulled the walkie-talkie off his belt and pushed the send button.

"Hey," he radioed.

"Anakin?" the speaker hissed back. "Is that you?"

"Very funny," he sent back. "I'm coming over."

He picked up the crossbow and walked to the deer stand. Fifteen feet above him, Sid perched with his legs hanging over the edge of the platform.

"I feel like Tarzan up here," he said, putting aside the binoculars.

"Have you seen anything yet?"

"Not a fucking thing," Sid replied. "Dude, how long are we going to stay out here?"

"All night, if we have to," Terry replied and turned his attention toward the quiet farm under the light of the full moon. Both the house and trailer were dark. "We have to make sure Jessica is safe."

"I don't know how much longer I want to freeze my ass off."

"Just a few hours more," Terry stated. "You can last that long."

"Wait," Sid said, grabbing up the binoculars and pointing them toward the farmyard. "A car is pulling in."

Headlights of two cars drove around the back of the barn and parked in front of the trailer. From the distance across the dark field, he recognized Jessica's Camaro but not the other car.

"What's Sheriff Dickhead doing here?" Sid asked, watching with the field glasses.

"Is that his car?"

"It sure as fuck is," Sid answered.

Car doors slammed. Terry spotted Jessica, Megan, and the sheriff walking to the trailer. They disappeared inside as lights went on throughout the house.

"What's he up to?" Terry asked.

"Probably going to get him a piece of tail off that fine mama," Sid remarked.

"You don't know that."

"Dude, don't get jealous. You're just pissed because she turned you down."

"Jessica can do so much better than that creep." Terry exhaled a long, weary breath. "I'm going back to my hiding spot. Radio if you see anything."

"I just wish I could see through the trailer windows," Sid remarked with the binoculars glued to his eyes. "Dude, I sure would like to peep in on Jessica taking her clothes off."

"Quit being such a perv. You're looking for a werewolf. Remember?"

"If you say so."

With a heavy heart, Terry returned to his spot under the brush of the creek bank. He had hoped to impress Jessica by slaying a monster for her. Now his fantasy lay shattered, thanks to the stupid sheriff. If anything happened now, Sheriff Dutton would be there to protect her. Still, he promised Mr. Higgins on his deathbed that he would kill the werewolf, and he meant to carry it through until the end.

*   *   *   *

"Jess, we need to talk." Sheriff Sutton stood just inside the door of the trailer with his uniform cap in his hands.

"Have a seat while I put Megan to bed," Jessica replied.

"Do I have to?" Megan pleaded. "Can't I stay up?"

"Not tonight, baby." She took her daughter by the hand and led her to the restroom. After Megan washed her face, Jessica tucked her into the bed.

"You sleep in your bed tonight, baby."

"Okay."

"I'll leave a light on." She knelt by her daughter on the mattress. "I'll be right outside if you need me."

"Good night, Mommy."

"Good night." She kissed her on the forehead.

"Is the sheriff spending the night, too?" Megan asked innocently.

Jessica paused. "I'm just going to talk to him for a while."

"I don't like to see Mommy cry."

"I know, sweetie. Sometimes Mommy is sad that things aren't better for us."

"Things will get better."

"I hope so. Now go to sleep."

She softly closed the door and walked back down the narrow hallway into the living room. Sheriff Sutton sat on the recliner leaning forward with his elbows on his knees. He looked up when she entered and showed a thin smile.

"Megan's gone to bed," Jessica stated, adding, "Thanks for following us home. Would you like some coffee?"

"Let's talk first." He nodded toward her to sit on the couch adjoining the recliner.

"Fine." Jessica settled into the divan. "You're the sheriff."

"I noticed a pickup parked in front of the barn. It's driven by Terry Newman."

"Terry and his friend are deer hunting. Sam gave them permission to do so."

Sheriff Sutton chuckled. "If I know them, they're probably doing more pot smoking than deer hunting. I guarantee it. Those two slackers have been a thorn in my side lately."

"Those kids?" she responded and laughed. "They seem pretty harmless. Terry asked me out, by the way. What do you think? Maybe the best way for me to get a man is to train him from puberty."

"I can't believe the nerd had the balls to ask anyone out, but I can't blame him for having good taste in women."

"Thank you. He was so sweet, too. I hated turning him down. Is that what you wanted to talk to me about?" Jessica asked, surprised he wasn't asking about the events with Debbie Miller at the bar.

"I want you to stay away from Roxie's. It's not safe for Megan and you."

"I'm not going back. Collin creeps me out, and I've had enough of Debbie Miller's drama. You should arrest Brody Carlson, though. He pulled a knife on Collin and stabbed him. I saw it from behind the bar even though Collin denied he was hurt."

"Collin can take care of himself." Sheriff Sutton's face tightened. "It's you I'm worried about. I want you to be extra careful, Jess. Where's your pistol?"

"It's in my purse. Do you think Debbie will come after me?"

"It's not Debbie I'm worried about." He reached out and took hold of both her hands.

"Then who?" Jessica felt a knot of fear growing in her stomach.

"Your husband."

His name hit her like a cold slap in the face. "Blake?"

"I know you've been through a lot tonight, and I'm sorry to dump more on you." He took a deep breath and continued. "I checked with Chicago PD. Blake Lobato is wanted for the arson of your home in Chicago and the murder of a stripper going by the stage name of Passion."

"Passion? Oh my God, I knew her. We worked together in the same club."

"You were a stripper?" His eyes widened with surprise.

"Yes." She looked down at her hands held by the sheriff. "Blake forced me into it. He has a terrible cocaine addiction. I used to make over a thousand dollars a night stripping. You have to understand, I lived in absolute fear of my husband for years. He's crazy when he's high. Megan and I are both lucky to be alive." She looked up and met his eyes. "Passion was a dealer in one of the clubs I worked. Blake used to score coke off her after hours."

"Your hands are shaking," Sheriff Sutton said, clasping her hands tighter.

"Please tell me they arrested him," Jessica asked, turning her gaze to the dark front windows of the trailer.

"Illinois law enforcement has put out a statewide canvass to find him. So far, no luck. He could be anywhere."

"Like outside waiting for you to leave," she said, feeling panic rising inside. "He's an ex-cop with a lot of connections. Maybe he found out where I am."

"Not likely, but until he's caught, I want you safe. He committed a homicide and is on the run. That makes him desperate and dangerous." Sheriff Sutton released her hands and stood. "Stay here in the trailer and don't go anywhere. I'll keep a close watch for strangers in the town and drop by to check on you when I can."

"You're leaving?" she asked, trying to hide the fear in her voice.

"I've had a rough day. I'm tired."

She reached up and took his hand again. "Then stay here tonight."

"Jess, what are you asking?"

"If Blake is in the area, he will find us and not hesitate to kill me or my daughter. That much I know." She paused before adding, "I'm not asking you to sleep with me. I may have been a stripper, but I'm not a whore. I'll make you a bed on the couch. You can sleep there."

"You're asking a lot of my self-control to stretch out on a couch when one of the most beautiful women I've ever met is sleeping alone in the next room."

"You can come to my bed if you have to," she replied with a tremor in her voice. "Just don't leave."

"You don't really mean that, Jess. You just want me to stay here to protect your daughter." Sheriff Sutton sighed and unzipped his uniform jacket. "Taking advantage of a desperate woman is not my style. I can't believe I'm saying this, but I'll sleep here on the couch."

"Thank you." She kissed his hand and stood. "I'll get you a blanket and pillow."

She went to a closet and took out the bedding. When she returned, Sheriff Sutton had removed his gun belt and pulled his Glock semiautomatic pistol from the holster. She placed the blanket and pillow on the end of the couch.

"The doors and windows are all locked?" he asked, taking the pillow and hiding his pistol underneath.

"Yes," Jessica replied, removing the .357 from her purse on the dining room table. The sheriff watched her stuff the pistol in the waist of her jeans. "This will be under my pillow, too."

"Do you know how to use that?" he asked.

"I trained for two months at a pistol range in Chicago. It's a little heavier than what I'm used to, but I do know how to shoot."

"Just don't put a bullet in me in the middle of the night if I go to the bathroom."

"I won't."

He put his boots up on the couch and pulled the blanket over him. "I'm not taking off my boots. I hope you don't mind. I want them on in case something goes down outside."

"That's fine." She reached over to turn off the living room lamp. "Good night, cowboy."

"I don't even get a good-night kiss?" he asked with a smile.

"You're no Marshal Dillon, are you?"

"Why do you say that?"

"I was told Marshal Dillon never kissed a girl in all his years on *Gunsmoke*."

He chuckled and took her hand. "I'm no Marshal Dillon."

He drew her down on top of him covering her mouth in a deep, wet kiss. His intoxicating smell sent her pulse racing as their tongues interlocked. Hands caressed gently up her back.

"Is that a gun or are you happy to see me?" he asked, ending their kiss.

"What?" she breathed against his face.

"Your pistol." He winced. "It's sticking me where it hurts."

"Oh God, I'm so sorry." She sat up and removed the .357 and placed it in her purse on the coffee table.

"Much better." He drew her once more to him. They shared another long kiss. His hands slid up her top, moving along her bare skin and stopping at her black bra. His powerful aroma made her dizzy. Breathless, she separated from his embrace.

"Okay, cowboy, come with me." She grabbed his hand and pulled him up from the couch. "This is a onetime offer and you better take it before it expires."

"Sold," he replied, following her from the living room and down the hall. She peeked into her daughter's room to find Megan fast asleep. Closing the door, she led him into her bedroom, shutting off the light switch.

In the moonlight from the one window, they undressed each other with reckless abandon. He pulled her top off over her head as she unbuttoned the front of his uniform shirt. Baring his chest, the muscular build of his torso surprised her. Sheriff Sutton had the body of a professional athlete. Her hands ran over his defined chest muscles and down to the chiseled abs. On his left side just above the hip, she spotted a strange scar that reminded her of bite marks. She wanted to ask how he got the wound, but his mouth covered hers before she could get the words out. The waves of intense male aroma emanating from his moonlit flesh made her forget everything but their impending passion together.

The sheriff unclasped her bra, freeing her breasts for his hands to hold. Jessica fumbled with the front of his slacks, undid his pants, and let them fall. He responded in kind by sliding down her jeans and underwear. Picking her up easily, he dropped her naked upon the bed. She studied his perfect body while he stood by the bed admiring her nudity. Something about his gaze caused Jessica to nearly gasp in shock. His eyes seemed unnaturally dark. She decided it was just a trick of the moon and shadows. The next second he was on top of her, and she embraced his naked flesh with her own.

"Jess," he breathed hot against her neck.

"Don't stop," she whispered back.

He pushed himself deep inside her. Jessica clung to him as each thrust increased her pleasure, drawing her closer to an explosive climax. She had never known such wanton lust with a man. Animal-like grunts escaped from his throat as their lovemaking increased in its intensity. Grasping his back, her fingernails dug into his shoulder blades as she rode the pounding of his body against hers. Their passion ended in a shared ecstasy that left them both spent and collapsed together. Too weak to move, he lay panting against her neck while her hands slid along his sweat-slick back. Finally, they separated and he brushed the loose strands of blonde hair out of her face.

"How was it?" he asked in a whisper.

"Incredible," she replied with tears of joy forming in the corner of her eyes.

"For me, too." He smiled, pulling her close. He softly kissed her tears. "Thank you."

They caressed and explored each other's body until they became aroused again. The second round of lovemaking was much more systematic and controlled compared to the frenzied lust of the first. When finished, Jessica snuggled against him as he wrapped his arms around her.

"Where did you get that scar?" she asked, touching the spot above his left hip.

"Oh, that?" He took a deep breath. "A few years back I was part of a narcotics bust up north. We broke down a meth dealer's front door, but unfortunately he had a shotgun. The vest absorbed most of the blast saving my life."

"It looks like a shark or something bit you."

He laughed. "I guess it does. I never thought about it."

"Dale, where do we go from here?"

"Honestly, I don't have a clue. Get some sleep and we'll worry about it in the morning." He kissed her lips. "You're safe now."

CHAPTER FORTY-NINE

"Hurry, my brother, I don't know how much longer I can fight it," Roxie said from the passenger seat of Collin's truck, which was racing down a two-lane blacktop eleven miles west of Hope Springs. She hung her head down and clutched the dashboard with both hands, attempting to stave off the transformation. Collin glanced at his sister. The nails on her fingers started to extend and dig into the dash. He understood her stress. With the full moon tonight and the Ebon Moon twenty-four hours away, the urge to become a werewolf raged against his control to stay human.

"Just a bit longer," Collin replied. "You won't be disappointed, I promise."

"Where are we?"

"Grover Lake," he answered.

"Just tell me we're going to feed?" she asked in a thick voice, starting to turn animal-like.

"Yes."

Collin turned in to the Grover Lake recreation area. He switched off the headlights. Due to the recent cold snap, the camping area consisted of deserted picnic tables and unused outdoor grills standing in the dark. No campers or vehicles were present. The lake stretched across the horizon with the full moon glistening on the black water, like a spotlight.

"I'm burning up," Roxie stated, sliding off her T-shirt. "I have to get out of these clothes." She stripped naked in the dim light from the dashboard.

Collin rounded a bend on the access road winding through the empty lake area. He scanned the campgrounds looking for any sign of someone else. Ahead, he spotted the orange glow of a flickering campfire near some trees by the water's edge.

"I think I found them," he said, stopping the truck.

"Who?"

"Debbie Miller and her friends," he replied. "One of them said something about going to party at the lake. This is the closest lake to Hope Springs." He shut the engine off. "I bet they're camping over by those trees. What makes this more perfect is there's no one else around."

"A midnight snack." Roxie smiled, showing her thickening canines. "I love it."

*   *   *   *

After leaving Roxie's, Debbie Miller rode out to Grover Lake, sitting between Steve Kiegler and Brody Carlson. She was in a foul mood and chain-smoked Marlboros the entire way. The events at the roadhouse had not gone as she had planned. Collin's interference ruined her wish to teach Jess a lesson. Now she would have to think of some other way to get even.

Arriving at the lake, they chose a spot by the water's edge where tall trees bordered one side. Together they unloaded the tent, ice cooler, Coleman lantern, and sleeping bags from the back of Steve's truck. Only after they pitched the tent and started the fire did her mood improve. Sitting in a folding chair by the campfire, she took shots from a bottle of Wild Turkey and smoked another cigarette. The whiskey and the moonlit night helped her to forget about getting even with Jess. She sat listening to the lapping of the waves against the lakeshore and the popping of twigs in the fire.

"I'm enjoying this." She blew cigarette smoke into the air.

"Not me." Brody Carlson leaned forward, holding his bandaged head. "My fucking head hurts."

"Take another shot." Debbie Miller handed him the bottle. "It'll make you feel better."

"Maybe we should've left him at the hospital," Steve Kiegler stated, tossing another dried branch on the campfire. "He don't look so good."

"Shut up." Debbie watched Brody take a long swig of whiskey. "He'll be fine."

He put the bottle down and rubbed his temple. "Fuck, I hurt."

"You okay, baby?" she asked, getting up from her chair. She crossed over and sat on his lap. "Let mama show you some love."

"It's just my head." He wrapped his arm around her thin waist. "It hurts like hell."

"Are you in too much pain for some pussy tonight?"

"No way," he chuckled.

"Hey, what about me?" Steve stood up from his chair. "I paid for the whiskey, cigarettes, and food for this outing."

"You'll get yours, too, Stevie, if you quit whining and play your cards right," Debbie replied. "I just got to take care of my wounded homie first.

You can have seconds."

"Okay," Steve said, taking the whiskey from her hand and laughing. "Sloppy seconds is better than none."

"You know it," Brody echoed the sentiment.

Debbie brushed back her blonde highlights. "Brody goes first because he was the one who stood up to Collin at the bar. It sure as hell wasn't you."

"Excuse me, didn't I see him running like a little girl after Collin tossed him out the door?" Steve asked.

"Screw you, man. I stabbed that sucker right in the gut. There's something crazy about the guy. He had this crazy look in his eyes, like he wasn't human. I swear the guy's high on something. It scared the shit out of me."

"If you stabbed him, how come he didn't go down?"

"I guess he was so juiced up he didn't even feel it."

An owl hooted somewhere in the nearby stand of trees. Debbie's gaze sought the dark spaces where the flickering firelight didn't reach. A chill passed over her body. The woods at night always spooked her. She remembered being thirteen again and hiding from her liquored-up stepfather in the trees outside her family's trailer. She would wait for hours until he passed out. Back then, the disgust of having the drunken asshole crawling into her bed each night overrode her fear of the dark trees. Waiting in the woods worked well until the night her stepfather found her hiding place.

"Are you cold, baby?" Brody asked, rubbing his hand down her bare arms.

"Why do you ask?"

"You got goose bumps all over you."

"Let's take our party inside," she said, putting her arms around his neck.

"Sure thing, babe."

She got off his lap and grabbed the bottle of Wild Turkey from Steve. "You can come in after he's done."

Steve chuckled. "That'll be in about a minute."

"Fuck you," Brody replied.

Debbie Miller took Brody's hand and guided him to the front of the tent. He staggered and nearly fell against her.

"Are you drunk already?" she asked.

"Just feeling a little dizzy."

She unzipped the front of the tent and bent down to go inside. Brody followed and stretched out on a sleeping bag in the light of the Coleman lantern hanging overhead. He looked terrible. The hospital had shaved the swollen left side of his head and taped a bandage against his scalp. His left eye was extremely bloodshot and his pale skin felt clammy. In the lantern light, he reminded Debbie of a zombie from one of those stupid movies Steve liked to make her watch. She zipped up the entrance and turned down the Coleman lantern, allowing the fire outside to glow against the fabric walls of the tent.

"I feel like shit, baby," Brody muttered in the dim light. "So go easy on me."

She knelt and reached for the fly of his jeans. "I know a way to make you feel better."

The entrance suddenly unzipped. Steve stuck his head inside.

"Man, wait your turn," Brody shouted.

"There's a big animal moving through the trees," Steve said with panic in his voice. "It's a bear or something."

Debbie looked up in shock. In the glow of the firelight, a large shadow of something hunched and inhuman loomed against the tent wall behind Steve. She wanted to scream but it stuck in her throat. Steve turned and screamed instead as black claws grabbed him by the head and yanked him out of the tent door. Animal growls drowned out his pitiful screams for help.

"What the fuck?" Brody asked, raising his head off the sleeping bag.

Debbie was too frightened to say anything. Frozen in terror, she watched another dark shape appear in the entrance blocking the firelight. Black claws reached in and snagged Brody's tennis shoe. She tried to hang on to him, but the thing ripped him from her grip and out the front of the tent. Screaming obscenities, he struggled against the shadowy horror just outside the door. A second later he fell back inside with the entire left side of his face torn open in bloody gashes. Desperately, Brody reached for her hand and their fingers touched briefly.

"Debbie ... run," he muttered before the thing dragged him outside again.

She knew her only chance to survive was to get away as fast as she could. If she stayed in the tent, the nightmares would come in and get her. She rushed out the front opening. To her right, a horrid hunched beast ravaged a screaming Brody with its teeth and claws. His blood-curdling screams died away. Beyond the campfire, Steve's black pickup truck waited like a beacon to safety. She ran full speed toward the vehicle. Halfway there, she nearly tripped over the body of Steve lying in the dirt. His ripped-open chest and throat revealed a red wetness in the shifting firelight.

Debbie screamed and reached the driver's side of the pickup. In her panic, she forgot the truck would be locked. She pounded against the driver window as if some angel inside would hear her pleas and miraculously open the door. None did. Close behind her came a low-throated growl. Her gaze shifted to the dark trees standing tall beyond the firelight. Her only thought was to seek the safety of the woods, as she once did as a frightened thirteen-year-old child.

She fled into the woods and hid behind a tree. Her back pressed against the rough bark as she held her breath to listen above the jackhammer of her heart. Low growls and the sickening noise of ripping flesh came from the campsite. She didn't want to see what fed upon her two friends. Instead, her eyes peered ahead into the dark between the trees where firelight did not reach. Too scared to even breathe, she watched as something darker than the shadows filled the space. The crunching of footsteps in the brush accompanied its arrival. In her terror, she imagined her drunken stepfather had found her again.

"Please, Daddy, no," she pleaded in a childlike voice barely audible. Urine ran down the inside of her leg.

But something else emerged from the dark into the flickering light, a creature from a nightmare she never dreamed would exist in her world. Covered in bristling black fur, it stood over her with a wolflike face and blood-red eyes. The beast licked its tongue across a maw of sharp fangs and stepped forward on canine legs. Due to the horror movies she had watched with the now-dead Steve, Debbie recognized the monster.

A werewolf!

"Please, don't kill me," Debbie begged the horror looming over her.

The creature paused. Hot slaver dripped upon her face. It sniffed her for a second and emitted a rumbling growl.

"Don't kill me," she repeated in a weak voice.

Wet lips pulled back as if the werewolf attempted to smile. She looked up into its hungry eyes but saw only savage death. "Oh God, please forgive—"

The teeth of the beast latched on to her throat and ripped it open. Her prayer ended in a gurgling croak. The monster wolfed down the torn flesh as she slid down the trunk of the tree with blood soaking the front of her shirt. Her last sight was of the werewolf bending over her to continue feeding.

CHAPTER FIFTY

Blake Lobato awoke to find himself lying on a dirty carpet in someone else's motel room. Blood and plaster dust covered his naked body. Confusing images of changing into something beastlike, smashing through the wall, and savagely murdering a man played through his mind. The memories were alien and surreal, like seen through the eyes of a stranger's nightmare.

He rose to check out his surroundings. Broken chunks of plaster littered the floor from a huge gaping hole in the Sheetrock. Splattered blood covered the walls and furniture as if done by the hand of a demonic painter. What waited for him on the bed made him recoil in revulsion. Stretched across the blood-soaked sheets were the mangled remains of a decapitated body. A Hispanic male's head rested on a pillow with his mouth open wide in a last silent scream of terror. A wave of nausea threatened Blake's stomach. Staggering over the broken plaster, he entered his room and barely made it to the toilet in time to throw up the contents of his last meal—raw human flesh and blood. He heaved a second time, filling the porcelain bowl with more gore.

His stomach lurched once more from the horror of what he had done.

He had eaten a man alive!

What's happened to me? What have I become? I'm not human anymore!

From somewhere deep inside came another voice.

You're more than human. You're the new improved Blake Lobato.

Wiping his bloody mouth, he stared at his reflection in the mirror, feeling a cold resolve. It was true. He wasn't the same Blake Lobato; he was something more. He had come to Oklahoma to kill his wife and get his revenge before the police found him. But now his focus had changed with his new physiology. He wasn't going to stop with Jess. He was going to keep killing. He loved it too much. Destiny had granted him the power to release his inner savagery onto the world.

Flushing the toilet, he watched the contents disappear along with the last threads of his humanity.

He smiled.

Mexican food had never agreed with his stomach.

Leaving the bathroom, Blake found his clothes scattered about the floor. He quickly dressed and donned his black duster. With the vicious murder he committed in the next room, he needed to get away from the crime scene as fast as possible. Stuffing the wad of stolen drug money in his coat pocket, he grabbed the Harley keys. He stepped out the front door and surveyed the parking lot of the cheap motel. The full moon shone overhead above the glow of the streetlights. By his guess, it was still the dead of night. The motel was dark, and no one watched him leave.

He crossed to the Harley, kick-started the engine, and pulled away. The highway was an empty asphalt ribbon stretching back to Hope Springs. He drove with the wind whipping his coat and reached the deserted downtown where the bank clock blazed 3:04 in the morning. Blake gritted his teeth in a grim smile.

It was time to pay Jess a visit.

CHAPTER FIFTY-ONE

Sleeping naked next to Jess, Sheriff Sutton snapped awake. Every nerve ending of his body seemed on fire. He raised his hand into the moonlight coming through the trailer window. The sharpened points of black claws pushed out below his fingernails as the hair thickened on the back of his hand.

Not now! his mind screamed. *Not here!*

He had put off the beast for too long. Now, it wanted out.

Slipping quietly out of the bed, he stood in the light of the silvery full moon shining through the window blinds. Hair multiplied down the length of his arms and across his bare back. He glanced over to where Jess slept peacefully. He needed to keep her safe from the beast fighting inside to be free.

Using all of his will, he stalled the transformation, but he knew it wouldn't be for long. He grabbed up his clothes from the bedroom floor and went barefoot down the hall. There was no time to dress. Picking up his gun and holster in the front room, he opened the back door and rushed naked out into the night.

Another wave of uncontrollable change swept through him. He unlocked the door to his patrol car and climbed in the driver's seat with the upholstery sticking to his buttocks. He glanced once again at the trailer. The back door hung open as if to beckon him to return inside. The beast raging within spoke.

Why should Collin get to eat the mother and child? You should feed on such a feast.

No! his human mind screamed back.

He had to get away before the beast took over completely with its hunger and rage.

Sheriff Sutton started the car engine with clawed hands barely able to turn the ignition key. Putting the patrol car in reverse, he backed out of the yard and turned onto the blacktop in front of the farm. Remembering the rutted cattle road used to meet Sam Olson earlier in the morning, he swung the patrol car down the broken trail.

Bouncing along the ruts and potholes, he brought the car to a sudden stop. The silver orb of the full moon high in the night sky triggered an uncontrolled transformation. Popping open the door, he threw himself out of the vehicle. On his hands and knees in the dirt, his naked body quaked under the full moon. Bone and muscle shifted, transforming him into the cursed thing he carried inside.

The beast stood up to its full height. No longer answering to the human mind, the creature turned its attention back to the dark trailer. It remembered the two innocent females sleeping within. A ravenous hunger burned in the pit of its belly. Ears twitched and nostrils sniffed the night air. Someone else was nearer. It turned its attention to the trees bordering the edge of the recently plowed field. A human's scent wafted from the dark woods. Leaping over the barbed wire fence, the beast landed on all fours and licked its dripping lips. Other prey was out tonight.

It was time to feed.

*   *   *   *

"This is so fucking lame," Sid Granger said aloud to no one but himself. Sitting on the elevated deer hunting platform through the night had proven boring to the point that both his butt and mind were numb. His back ached from the cold metal of the stand, and he hadn't heard from Terry in over an hour. The poser had probably gone to sleep, hiding in the brush by the creek. Sid wanted to go home but decided to maintain his post. He owed Terry that much because of all the shit he put up with by being his only friend.

"Time to bring out the peace pipe," he chuckled.

Removing the one-hitter from his hoodie pocket, he lit the end with a lighter and inhaled deeply. He held in the pungent pot smoke and stared up at the stars overhead. Movement caught his attention out of the corner of his eye. He glanced toward Jess's dark trailer and coughed in shock. A naked Sheriff Sutton, carrying his clothes, ran from the back of the house. Snapping up the binoculars, he caught a glimpse of the lawman's bare ass before jumping into his patrol car.

"What the fuck?" Sid muttered.

He grabbed up the walkie-talkie and pushed the button.

"You won't believe what I just saw," he radioed. "Sheriff Dickhead running naked out of the trailer. The dude's ass is really white, by the way." He continued watching through the glasses as the patrol car started and pulled out of the yard. "He's leaving in a real fucking hurry."

Sid released the button waiting for a reply but got nothing but a static hiss.

"Come back, Anakin," he said into the walkie-talkie.

More radio silence.

"Shit," he cursed, putting down the radio. Standing up, he searched the surrounding darkness but saw nothing but trees and shifting shadows caused by the full moon high in the sky. No sign of Terry. A few more minutes passed before he finally decided to climb down and look for his hunting partner. Using the metal rungs, he descended to the leafy floor. Once on the ground, he removed the Sony minicam from his pocket and flipped out the small LCD view screen on the side. Set on night vision, the camera allowed him to see better through the darkness. A cursory scan of the immediate area still showed no sign of Terry's location.

"Hey, man, where the fuck are you?" he asked aloud in a hoarse whisper.

Quiet.

Sid watched through the video camera screen while walking toward the creek bed. Tree trunks looked ghostly through the greenish gray colors of the night-vision mode. To his left a twig snapped. He swung the camera toward the noise and froze in place. Something big moved through the trees.

"Fuck," he gasped. "Is that you, Terry?"

The only answer was the rumbling growl of a large animal.

"Okay, you're not Terry." Swallowing in fear, Sid pushed the record button with a shaking hand while focusing the camera on the spot where he last saw the movement. *This is the chance of a lifetime,* he reminded himself. *I could be the first person to get actual footage of a real werewolf. The last thing I want is to blow it by running away like a pussy.*

"Come out and smile for the camera, you ugly shit," Sid said in a shaky voice, holding the camera steady at the same time.

With a horrendous growl, the monster leaped in the clearing. In the little view screen, Sid caught a glimpse of a beast with sharp fangs, bristling hair, and glowing eyes caused by the night-vision effect. The record light flashed red in one corner of the display. A deep growl caused Sid to look up from the video screen at the beast before him. The huge creature hunkered down in the beams of moonlight. Red eyes glared back at him while its mouth opened showing a dripping maw of canine fangs.

"Fuck me!" Sid screamed throwing the camera to the side. He sprinted toward the deer stand with the growling beast closing in behind him.

*　　*　　*　　*

Without any real sleep in the last twenty-four hours, Terry Newman had dozed off in the brush. He shook himself awake to see a screaming Sid run past headed toward the deer stand. Something large and hairy chased after him. Terry grabbed his Buckshot crossbow, rolled out of his camouflaged hiding place, and raced behind the pursuing beast.

"Shit!" Sid cursed, reaching the base of the deer stand. He half-climbed, half-ran up the rungs to the metal platform.

Behind him, the monster leaped in the air to grab Sid with its claws. Terry reacted without thought and pulled the trigger of the crossbow. The silver-tipped arrow flew straight and impaled the thigh of the beast in mid-leap. The creature howled and crashed to the ground with the arrow sticking through its leg.

Terry ducked behind a tree and grabbed up another silver arrow from his quiver. With his heart thundering, he pulled the drawstring and locked the arrow in place. He steeled his nerves and swung around the trunk ready to fire the crossbow again.

The creature was nowhere in sight.

"Where did it go?" Terry yelled up to Sid.

"It ran off," he gasped back and pointed south. "In that direction."

"Are you all right?"

"Fuck no. I think I shit and pissed at the same time," Sid stated, still trying to catch his breath.

"Gross," Terry replied.

"Where were you, man? I tried to call you."

"I fell asleep. I'm sorry."

"Some werewolf hunter you turned out to be. It shows up and you're sleeping on your ass."

"Did it have black fur?" Terry kept his eye on the trees.

"Why do you ask?"

"Its fur seemed lighter. Like a brown color."

"You got to be fucking kidding me." Sid shook his head. "How many werewolves are out there?"

"I wish I knew. I only got three arrows left."

Terry pulled a flashlight out and trained it on the ground where the werewolf had fallen. A trail of fresh blood led through the trees.

"I'm going after it," he announced with his heart thumping in his throat.

"Not me. I'm staying right here," Sid replied.

"Fine, just keep the walkie-talkie handy. Let me know if you see it."

Terry took off tracking the blood trail by flashlight while keeping the loaded crossbow at the ready. Somewhere nearby was a wounded werewolf. Fear clutched his gut. The fanciful notion of a heroic monster hunter didn't seem too smart now faced with a dangerous supernatural werebeast in the dark woods. He swallowed and kept on going.

Something metallic on the leafy ground caught his flashlight beam to the left. He stooped to pick it up. It was the Sony minicam Sid had brought with him. Terry checked the view screen and saw the camera still on record. He shut it off, stuck it in his pocket, and returned to the blood trail. The flashlight beam cut an eerie arc through the misty woods. The track of the monster turned toward the barbed wire fence where Sam had taken them earlier in the day. He heard the shutting of a car door. He rushed forward until he came out of the trees. Twenty-five yards beyond the fence, the patrol car waited with a naked Sheriff Sutton standing beside it pointing a pistol straight at him.

CHAPTER FIFTY-TWO

Naked and wounded, Sheriff Sutton staggered out of the tree line. The arrow stuck in his thigh had caused him to return to his human form. Only a wound by a silver weapon affected a Wolfkin in such a way. Rage boiled inside at the realization. One of those stupid teenagers had shot him with a silver-tipped arrow, aborting his natural lycanthropic healing ability. Blood poured down his leg leaving a trail behind him, but there was nothing he could do. He needed to get away before he bled out completely.

He slipped through the barbed wire fence and hobbled the distance to his patrol car. The driver door stood open. Reaching inside, he grabbed the Mag flashlight from his gun belt lying in the passenger seat, turned it on, and examined the arrow wound.

The tip had completely pierced his leg. Blood pumped out in a red stream around the fiberglass shaft. The arrow needed to be removed before he could drive. Gritting his teeth, he broke off the feathered shaft and yanked the arrow tip from his flesh on the other side. The pain and the sudden loss of blood nearly caused him to pass out. He fought against unconsciousness and limped to the back of the patrol car. Popping the trunk, he reached in and grabbed up a portable trauma kit in a plastic case. From the kit, he quickly stuffed gauze dressing into the puncture wounds and wrapped a tight bandage around his thigh. It was the best he could do at the moment, but at least it managed to slow the blood loss.

Heavy footsteps moving through brush sounded from the woods on the other side of the fence. He realized one of the boys tracked him through the trees. His anger at the two teenagers, who had caused him so much trouble and pain, reached a boiling point. He pulled the Glock from his gun belt and waited. Terry Newman emerged holding a hunting crossbow in his hands. Their eyes locked for a second before he ducked back behind a tree. Sheriff Sutton didn't shoot the boy. He needed Terry and Sid Granger alive. He had offered the teens for the Feast of the Ebon Moon in the place of Jess and Megan. Without the boys, there was nothing to stop Collin from abducting Jess and her daughter. He was too wounded now to fight for them.

Blood continued to ease around the bandage and down his leg. He needed time to recover and come up with a plan. Retreat was his best option. Keeping the gun trained on the trees, he eased himself into the driver's seat and started the engine. He dropped the car in gear, backed out, and turned around. The drive back down the cow trail sent jarring pain up his leg with every bump in the road.

Before reaching the blacktop highway, he glanced at the dark trailer where Jessica slept oblivious to the events outside her door. She had touched something deep within him, a memory forgotten by his human side. Feelings of another woman and child lost long ago surfaced when he met Jess. He couldn't let Collin devour them.

Not this mother and child.

He would stop him or die trying.

*   *   *   *

Terry pressed his back against a tree hearing the patrol car engine turn over and the vehicle leave. His knees shook from having a gun pointed at him. He looked around the trunk. The sheriff's car bounced along the rough cattle trail toward the highway.

Terry grabbed up the walkie-talkie. "Sid?"

"Yeah?"

"Sheriff Sutton's the werewolf. I just saw him climb naked into his car. He had a bandage on his leg where I shot him." Terry took off running toward the farm.

"You're fucking kidding me," Sid came back.

"He's getting away in his car. We've got to follow him. Get to my truck. Now!"

He put away the radio and pushed his chubby body to move as fast as it could across the furrowed field toward the farmhouse. Behind him, Sid followed, a sprinting black silhouette in the moonlight. Together they reached the old F-150 parked in the front of the barn. Terry tossed in the crossbow and hopped behind the wheel. Sid climbed in the passenger seat and shut his door. Slamming the truck in gear, he pulled out of the drive in a cloud of dust. A mile ahead, the taillights of the patrol car turned right on Highway 71 toward Hope Springs.

"Sheriff Dickhead's a werewolf?" Sid shook his head. "I should've known. It makes sense. Who better to help keep a secret?"

"He always gave me the creeps," Terry replied.

"Dude, turn your headlights off. Don't let him know we're following."

He shut off the truck lights and turned on Highway 71. A Harley motorcycle with a rider dressed in black roared past them going the other way. Terry kept his focus on the patrol car ahead, which had now reached the outskirts of Hope Springs. Sid brought up the binoculars.

"Where's the sheriff going?" Terry asked.

"Not to the police station," Sid answered. "He just drove by it."

"Okay, we're still following him." Terry increased his speed. He was in the thrill of the hunt, now feeling more alive than he could remember.

"He's turning down Highway 133 toward Morris." Sid put down the binoculars and pulled out his cell phone from his hoodie. He started dialing a number.

"What are you doing?" Terry looked over at him.

"I'm calling the fucking highway patrol."

"What are you going to tell them?" Terry turned on the Highway 133 junction at the traffic light.

"The sheriff's a fucking werewolf."

"It's not going to work, bro." Terry shook his head. "No one's going to believe us. We're on our own, dude."

"Fuck it." Sid put away the phone and grabbed the binoculars again.

The truck raced down the dark highway past the Higgins farm where the homemade signs stood stark and morbid against the night sky and full moon. Terry pondered for a moment what had brought him to this point of chasing a werewolf in a sheriff car. Mr. Higgins was the reason. If it hadn't been for the old man's determination to prove his innocence in his wife's murder, none of this would be happening.

"The sheriff's turning," Sid said with the binoculars trained on the road ahead.

"Where?" Terry asked.

"Roxie's."

CHAPTER FIFTY-THREE

Blake Lobato wasn't sure what to make of it.

While riding the Harley down Highway 71, the sheriff's patrol car rushed past going the other way to Hope Springs. A minute later, an old Ford F-150 followed with its headlights off. He knew both vehicles came from Jess's place. *Something must have happened there,* he realized. *But what?* He watched in the bike's rearview to see if any of them turned around to come back his way. None did.

Deciding to let nothing stop his deadly rendezvous with his wife, he continued down Highway 71 atop the thundering bike before turning on the blacktop running in front of the farm. A half-mile from the property, he shut the bike engine off and walked it the rest of the way in. He didn't want the Harley's noisy pipes to alert anyone of his approach. The farm looked empty and dark with no lights showing in the windows of the house. The only hint anyone was present was the one lit window in the rear of the trailer home. He rolled the bike slowly down the gravel drive and kicked down the stand in front of the barn.

In the shadow of the building, he paused. He listened and smelled for any danger using his new acute senses. Everything seemed quiet. Moving cautiously along the barn wall, he reached the corner and went around. The slight scent of propane gas hung in the air while he crouched in the shadow of the large cylinder-shaped tank and studied the trailer. His Camaro sat parked in front of the house. Jess and Megan must be inside. With eyes now accustomed to the dark, he scanned the home and spotted something unusual.

The back door hung open as if to invite him in.

Could it be a trap?

His pulse quickened. He had come so far and been through so much to reach this point. He couldn't stop now. Leaving the shelter of the propane tank, he moved quietly for the open door with senses on alert.

* * * *

Jessica awoke in the dark bedroom.

After the intense lovemaking, she had slipped into a deep and untroubled sleep. Gone was the paranoia that had gripped her for the last few months. The reassuring presence of Dale Sutton lying next to her had erased her fears. She sensed movement in the bed and slid her naked body closer to his. In response, he tenderly stroked her bare arm while leaning in to lightly kiss her ear.

"Hello, love, did you miss me?" Blake whispered.

Jessica gasped and tried to scream, but a black-gloved hand clamped down hard around her mouth. Her eyes widened in shock. This time it was no nightmare. Blake was in the bed next to her! In the moonlight streaming from the window, his gaunt face hovered an inch from hers.

"Been playing hide-the-sausage with the local yokel sheriff, haven't you, Jess? Don't lie to me, love." He sniffed. "I can smell him. His scent is on the bedsheets and all over you. You're such a naughty, naughty girl."

Panic flooded Jessica's thoughts. She had to get Blake away from Megan sleeping in the next room. Her hand grasped under the pillow for the .357 pistol before realizing it was not there. She had put it in her purse while making out with the sheriff on the couch.

Stupid!

"Don't think about screaming for help, Jess. Your boyfriend ran off. I saw him heading back to town in his patrol car," Blake hissed in her ear. "Nice of him, though, to leave the back door open."

She struggled against his hold over her mouth and tried to speak.

"I'm going to take my hand off now," he whispered. "You better not scream. You wouldn't want to wake our lovely daughter, would you?"

She nodded.

He removed the glove over her mouth.

"Blake, listen. Don't hurt Megan, please," she gasped. "It's my fault. Not hers. She's innocent. Please, she's our daughter."

"Shhh." He placed a finger against her lips. "Don't beg, Jess. It only makes you look weak. It'll be over soon, I promise." He squeezed her arm hard. "Get out of the bed and put some clothes on."

Slipping off the mattress, she contemplated her options. Blake would kill her, she had no doubt. Her only hope now was to save Megan. Trembling with fear, she slid on her jeans and pulled down a T-shirt over her naked chest.

"You always were a beauty, Jess," Blake whispered while his dark eyes studied her like a snake. "I have to give you that. It's too bad you turned out to betray me. I want to thank you for ratting on me to Internal Affairs and telling them I was a dirty cop."

"I didn't." Jess shook her head, fighting back tears. "It wasn't me."

"I'm supposed to believe a backstabbing whore?" He stood in the moonlight of the window. There was something different about her husband, she realized. His eyes seemed darker, his face more virile than she remembered. He grabbed her by the arm. "Into the front room," he ordered.

Stepping out into the dark hall, Jessica glanced down at the light coming from under her daughter's bedroom door. Tears flooded her vision. She wanted nothing more but to look upon Megan sleeping one last time but couldn't risk waking her daughter. Instead, she whispered a silent good-bye.

Sleep tight, baby. Mommy loves you.

"Keep moving." Blake pushed her from behind.

Jessica staggered and nearly fell before his strong hand caught her by the arm. The grip caused her pain, but she knew it was just the beginning. They entered the shadowy living room illuminated by the moon glow coming through the bay window.

"Take a seat," Blake demanded and shoved her toward the dining room table. He pulled out a chair and forced her in it. Releasing his hold, he stepped back and turned on a table lamp. Dressed in his long black coat and gloves, he appeared an ominous figure standing beyond the glow of the lamp. His eyes studied her with an animal-like stare showing no hint of a cocaine glaze.

"You should've killed me in Chicago, Jess," Blake commented as he crossed to the kitchen window and yanked out the curtain cord. "Neat trick with the baseball bat, though. That hurt like hell. I was going to return the favor when I found you, but I lost the bat along the way. You wouldn't believe what I've been through to get here."

Jessica trembled in fear. Tears blurred her vision as he stepped before her holding the curtain cord in his hand.

"Blake, promise me one thing. Spare Megan. Please." She wiped her face with her hands. "Don't hurt our daughter."

"Like the promise you made to love me forever on our wedding day?"

"I did love you then. I promise. But you treated me like shit. You abused me. Hit me in front of Megan."

He smiled a wolfish grin. "Sorry, but I'm a little sick in the head, love. I guess you've figured that out by now. I blame my old man. He taught me to do it. But that was the old me. You're looking at the next evolution of Blake. No more drugs, Jess. I don't need them anymore. I found something better. What would you say if I told you I've been given a second chance?"

"A second chance?"

"That's right, Jess. A second chance at a new me."

"What are you talking about?"

"You're going to find out soon enough," he replied. "Hold out your wrists."

She hesitated.

"Don't make me get ugly," he said with a low chuckle. "You won't like it if I get ugly."

Jessica raised her trembling hands. "What are you going to do?" she asked in a voice choked by fear.

"There's a little magic trick I want to show you." Blake wound the curtain cord around her wrists. "You're not going to believe it." He smiled. The lamplight glistened on his prominent canine teeth. "Trust me. It'll be a surprise. You haven't seen anything like it."

"Mommy?" Megan's quiet voice spoke from the hallway.

They both turned to see their daughter, dressed in a T-shirt and pajama bottoms, standing in the dark hall. She rubbed her sleepy eyes.

"There you are, baby," Blake said, holding out his arms. "Come to Daddy."

"No!" Jessica screamed.

Panic for her daughter's life overwhelmed her. She threw herself out of the chair while driving her shoulder hard into Blake's stomach. The impact didn't move him. Instead, he responded by twisting and throwing her body across the room. She flew over the couch before crashing atop the coffee table, which broke beneath her weight. Stunned by the sudden speed and force of Blake's response, she shook her head to regain her senses. He had never been so strong before. Spotting her purse amid the wreckage of the table, she clutched for her one chance to survive. She yanked the handbag to her, snatched the pistol out, and leaped to her feet. The stainless steel .357 magnum filled her hands still bound by the curtain cord.

"Stay away from her!" she screamed, pointing the gun directly at Blake.

"Jess, what are you doing?" he asked, narrowing his dark eyes on the pistol.

"Finishing what I should've done in Chicago." Her voice was calm and certain as she pulled back the firing hammer. To Megan, she said, "Baby, run out to the car and wait for Mommy there."

On bare feet, Megan darted past her and out the front door into the darkness.

Standing on the other side of the couch, Blake smiled. "You can't kill me, Jess. I'm going to keep coming back."

"Bullshit."

Jessica pulled the trigger. The large gun bucked in her hand. The first bullet caught Blake in the right eye, blowing chunks of skull and brain matter out the back of his head. He staggered against the dining room table as she fired again. The second round caught him dead center of the chest, punching a hole through his black duster. An animal-like growl emitted from his throat as he collapsed to the floor. She continued firing until the pistol was empty. Each shot caused his prone body to twitch from the bullet's impact. Only when the firing pin struck against empty cartridges did she stop. Blake lay sprawled on the carpet in a spreading pool of blood. The shot to his eye had nearly blown off the right side of his face.

Jessica dropped the pistol to the floor and used her teeth to unwind the curtain cord around her wrists. Grabbing up her purse, she exited the trailer into the cool morning air. Megan stood at the passenger door of the Camaro with tears streaming down her face. Seeing her mother, she ran to her arms hugging her tightly.

"Is Daddy dead?"

"Yes, baby," she replied with her voice surprisingly calm. "Get in the car."

Megan remained quiet as they climbed into the Camaro. Starting the engine, she looked over the trailer. Both the front and back door to the home hung open now. She would leave it like that. Jessica knew her next course of action. Report the shooting death to Sheriff Sutton.

She had no reason to run scared anymore.

Blake was dead.

SUNDAY

CHAPTER FIFTY-FOUR

"So what do we do now?" Sid asked from the passenger seat of the F-150 parked on the shoulder of the highway running in front of Roxie's Roadhouse.

Terry rubbed his tired eyes. The rush of confronting and chasing the sheriff to Roxie's had dissipated. His energy level was about to crash. He turned his attention back to studying the outside of the roadhouse. In the dark before dawn, the place was quiet and dimly lit by low interior lights. The sheriff's patrol was the only vehicle visible in the parking lot.

"I don't know," he replied. "Get a closer look, I guess."

"Dude, you're not going over there?"

Terry grabbed up his crossbow from the floorboard. "You stay here and keep the walkie-talkie handy if anything happens."

"Did you forget there's a fucking wounded werewolf in there? There might be others, too. Roxie's could be their lair."

"I have to find out." Terry popped the door latch. "I'm just going to scout around."

"You're nuts." Sid shook his head and glanced toward the bar. "Leave the truck running."

"I'll leave the truck running in case I need a quick getaway. Just don't drive off and leave me."

Terry shut the truck door quietly and stepped out in the cool night air. Hanging low in the night sky before dawn, the full moon lit the landscape in a silvery hue. He hefted the crossbow, kept to the shadows of trees running along the edge of the parking lot, and headed toward the darkened roadhouse.

*   *   *   *

In the gaudy glow of a neon light, Roxie quickly spread a plastic tarp over the top of the bar as Collin lifted the wounded sheriff and eased his naked body down upon the makeshift bed. The gauze bandage wrapped around his thigh was soaked with blood.

"What happened?" Collin asked, turning on an overhead light.

"One of those damn teenage boys … shot me with a silver-tipped arrow," Sheriff Sutton replied, grimacing in pain.

Roxie pulled apart the wad of gauze and examined the wound. "It's bad," she announced. "The arrow must have nicked an artery. It's still bleeding."

"Damn!" Collin cursed. "You let those two teenage punks do this to you?"

Sheriff Sutton laid his head back on the tarp. "I had no idea they … would be this big of a threat."

Roxie felt his forehead, which was clammy and cold. "He's suffering from silver poisoning. There's no way he can heal the damage."

"Unless he transforms and feeds again."

"He's too weak."

"He won't be when the Ebon Moon takes place tonight," Collin replied. "If he feeds during the shadowing of the moon he can regain his strength and power."

"If he does not, he will die when the eclipse passes."

"Either way, he is of little use to us in this condition." Collin patted the sheriff on his bare leg. "Did you hear me, Sheriff? You have to feed tonight, and I have just the person in mind."

"Please … leave Jess and her daughter … alone," Sheriff Sutton pleaded.

"Sorry," Collin replied. "You had your chance to bring us the two teenagers. You failed miserably. We continue with my plans for the feast tonight."

"The wound needs another bandage," Roxie stated. "I have nothing to use."

"There's a trauma kit … in the trunk of the patrol car," Sheriff Sutton said.

"I'll get it," Collin said, stepping for the front door.

"My clothes, too … in the front seat," Sheriff Sutton added.

Collin exited out the front door into the night. He sniffed the air and detected the wafting scent of a human nearby. Judging by the scent of fear mixed with the odor of junk food permeating the breeze, Collin surmised it was one of the teenage boys who had followed the sheriff. He smiled to himself. Any true hunter would have known not to sit downwind from the prey.

Reaching the driver's side of the patrol car, he leaned in and took the keys. He popped the trunk, pulled the trauma kit, and grabbed the sheriff's personal belongings from the front seat before returning to the inside of the bar. Once back inside, he put a finger to his lips, motioning for Roxie to be quiet while he locked the door.

"What's wrong?" she whispered.

"Someone's outside." He placed the trauma kit, clothes, and gun belt on the bar. "You were followed, Sheriff."

"Those punk-ass teens," Sheriff Sutton grimaced through his teeth. "Take my gun ... and shoot them."

Collin shook his head. "Too noisy, and I only spotted one. If I shoot him, the other could still be out there and get away. Then this place will be crawling with cops and OHP in no time."

"Brother, what do you propose to do?"

Collin went behind the bar and removed the aluminum baseball bat that the sheriff had brought in from the Olson farm. "I'll use something a little quieter instead. You stay here and keep working on his wound. I'm going to go out the back door and sneak around the front to catch the kid by surprise."

*   *   *   *

When the tall man with shoulder-length black hair appeared at the front door of the roadhouse, Terry crouched in the brush with his heart hammering with fear. The man went to the sheriff's patrol car, removed some items, and returned inside. Terry breathed easier after he shut the roadhouse door.

He pulled the walkie-talkie from his belt and pushed the send button. "Sid?"

"What's up?"

"Someone just came out of the bar and went back inside," he whispered into the radio. "The guy was the baddest-looking dude I ever seen."

"Are you coming back?"

"I'm going to get a closer look. Keep the truck running and the radio open. I may need you to come and get me real fast."

"You're a crazy fucker, you know that?"

"I know. Out."

Terry put away the radio and moved across the parking lot to crouch at the rear of the patrol car. He spotted a neon glow coming from behind the blinds of one of the front windows. Fighting back his fear, he crossed to the side of the building and peeked inside. A black-haired woman bandaged the leg of the sheriff stretched out on the bar. Terry studied the young woman in the neon bar light. She was slim and sexy with raven-colored hair cascading down over her shoulders. The top of her round breasts jutted out of the low neckline of her tight shirt.

A sudden shadow caught the corner of his eye.

Terry ducked. An aluminum baseball bat swung with a whoosh above where his head had been a heartbeat before. He staggered back in surprise. The badass biker man he had seen exit the building earlier now stood before him holding the familiar aluminum baseball bat. His eyes showed dark rage.

"You should learn to mind your own business, punk," the man growled in a low voice.

Terry snapped up the crossbow at his assailant, but the man charged forward swinging the bat again. He fell back while pulling the trigger. The arrow missed and disappeared into the night sky. He had no other arrow to load. Another bat swing whisked across the front of his face barely missing him by an inch.

"Sid!" he screamed at the top of his voice. He ducked another swing and took off running.

The large man followed behind swinging the bat at the back of his head. The headlights of the F-150 turned into the parking lot entrance as the truck barreled toward both of them. A spotlight mounted on the driver window blazed suddenly, hitting the large stranger in the face. In the last second, the truck turned sideways and fishtailed to a stop in a cloud of white dust. Terry reached the back of the truck and threw himself in the bed. The blinded man swung the bat, shattering a taillight instead.

"Go!" Terry shouted.

The truck tires spun and threw a rocky spray of gravel in the man's face.

"I'll be coming after your ass!" the man raged and threw the bat. It bounced in the truck bed beside Terry as the F-150 shot forward in a squall of white dust and gravel rocks. "Next time you're dead!"

The truck pitched onto the asphalt highway and sped away, leaving the roadhouse behind. Bruised and shaken, Terry lay in the truck bed staring up at the stars while trying to catch his breath and slow his heartbeat. After a half a mile, Sid brought the F-150 to a stop and leaped out of the cab. He peered at Terry over the rim of the truck bed.

"Dude, are you all right?"

"I'm too fat to run like that," Terry answered.

Sid chuckled. "I was there for you, man."

"You saved my ass." Terry sat up. His back and legs ached. Picking up the crossbow, he eased his exhausted body over the side.

"Who was that dude chasing you?"

"It had to be the black-furred werewolf in human form," Terry answered. "I'm sure of it."

"You nearly got your fucking head bashed in."

"I know."

"Did you see anyone else inside?"

"A dark-haired woman was tending to the sheriff on the bar. She was definitely hot-looking." Terry tossed the crossbow in the front seat of the truck. "We have to assume she's a werewolf, too."

"A whole fucking pack of werewolves," Sid replied. "You know how cool that is?"

"Yeah, and no one is going to believe us."

"I wish I hadn't lost my fucking minicam. I shot some great footage before the wolfie sheriff came after me. It was proof. We need to go back and see if we can find it."

"No need." Terry reached into his coat pocket. "I picked it up but forgot about it in all the excitement."

"No shit?"

Terry pulled the camera from his coat and handed it to Sid, who flipped out the view screen and rewound the footage. Together in the LED glow of the screen, they watched the short thirty-second clip of the werewolf stepping out of the trees and roaring at the camera. Even though it was shaky and shot in night vision, the footage clearly showed the beast.

"Fucking A!" Sid exclaimed. "You can tell it's no guy in a suit or some computer-generated bullshit. We got the bastard now."

"Congratulations," Terry stated. "What do we do with it?"

"Sell it," Sid answered. "Call the major news stations and offer the video for sale. Discovery Channel, *Sixty Minutes*, you name it. I'll do that first thing Monday morning."

"That's smart," Terry said. "Until then what are we going to do about our problem?"

"What problem?"

"Our werewolf problem." Terry glanced back down the dark highway toward Roxie's. "They know who we are and they know where we live, thanks to Sheriff Sutton. They're going to come after us and won't stop."

"What do you propose?"

"We go after them first. Tonight. During the eclipse. Catch them off guard."

"Count me out of it." Sid shook his head. "I've had enough of fucking werewolves trying to eat my ass."

"I'll do it alone then."

"You want to take on a pack of werewolves solo?" Sid shook his head. "You're going to get yourself killed."

"It's either them or me," Terry sighed. "I've only got two silver arrows left, and they haven't been too effective so far. I need something else to battle werewolves with."

"Fire," Sid suggested.

CHAPTER FIFTY-FIVE

Collin slammed the door to the bar behind.

Roxie looked up from tending to the sheriff's wound. "Brother, what's wrong?"

"The punk got away. I almost had him but he managed to escape."

"It's not so easy ... stopping this kid," Sheriff Sutton said.

"Screw you!" Collin snapped back. "If you had done your job he wouldn't be a problem now."

"What are we going to do about it?" Roxie asked while winding a fresh bandage around the sheriff's thigh. "He could warn others, bring them here."

"Who would believe him? One of our greatest defense is that humans still don't believe we exist. As long as they're in the dark, we're safe. Besides, we're set to abandon this place after tonight. Tomorrow we will be on our way to Alaska. How are things going with the relocation?"

"All I have to do is make one phone call and we're in."

"Good. Do it. We'll just keep up our vigilance if he comes sneaking around again. Tomorrow we just slip away."

Roxie helped the sheriff off the bar and eased his uniform pants back on over the bandaged wound.

"Collin ... listen to me," Sheriff Sutton said, fastening his pants. "Your sister is right ..." He winced in pain as Roxie helped him slip on his shirt. "We should leave now ... before others come to ... find us."

"We're not leaving until after the Feast of the Ebon Moon tonight."

"You're putting ... all of us in danger."

"You fool," Collin snapped back. "You are only a Bitten and don't understand anything. To devour a human child during the Ebon Moon gives our race power. It strengthens our bloodline and has done so for centuries. We don't partake of such a feast out of a cruel taste for a child's flesh. We do so out of necessity. Our extinction hangs over us. The need to perform this ritual is greater than ever."

"I must stop ... you," Sheriff Sutton responded weakly.

"Idiot!" Collin struck him across the face. "You dare to defy me!"

The sheriff staggered back from the blow and fell against the bar.

"Brother!" Roxie cried out. "He's hurt. You'll reopen his wound."

"Bah!" Collin raged. "He betrays us for a human woman and child! We have no more use for this half-breed."

"What do you propose we do with him?" Roxie asked.

"We'll lock him in the storm cellar until the Ebon Moon tonight. That should curb his tongue. Then we go find Jess and her daughter. Give me your bottle of chloroform. I can use it to capture our human guests for tonight's feast."

"I refuse to … be a part of this … madness," Sheriff Sutton said.

Collin grabbed the sheriff by the front of his uniform shirt. "What did you say, Sheriff? Are you so human now you would refuse to feed on them? I think not. When the moon grows dark tonight, you'll be begging me to let you feast upon the child."

"I … won't."

Roxie reached under the bar and pulled up a brown bottle and a washrag. "This will put Jess and her daughter asleep. They won't know a thing."

"Good." Collin grabbed the bottle and poured out some on the rag. "It's time to give it a test. Let's see if it works on the sheriff."

"Don't …" Sheriff Sutton protested a second before Collin clamped the rag down over his mouth and nostrils. After a few moments of struggling, he collapsed unconscious to the floor.

"That should keep him quiet," Collin commented as he hefted the sheriff's sleeping body over one shoulder. "Let's lock him in the cellar and …"

The cell phone clipped to the sheriff's gun belt abruptly rang.

*   *   *   *

Jessica's hand shook as she dialed the number Sheriff Sutton scrawled on the napkin at Dottie's Diner three days before. Fighting to keep her composure, she turned her attention from the pay phone to the dark windows of the closed Jiffy Trip. She gave up smoking while pregnant with Megan, but now she craved a cigarette to calm her nerves. She'd have to wait. The town's only convenience store was still two hours away from opening.

The call rang on the other end of the line.

"Come on, Dale, pick it up. I need you now," Jessica muttered into the receiver. "Please."

The ringing continued until it went to voice mail. "This is Sheriff Sutton. I'm currently not able to answer the phone at this time. If you have an emergency, call 911; if not, leave a message at the sound of the beep."

Beep.

"Dale, this is Jess. Where did you go? You just disappeared." She fought back the tears in her voice. "Blake broke into my trailer. I shot him. He was going to kill Megan and me. He's lying dead on the floor. I want to turn myself in. I'm waiting in the parking lot at the Jiffy Trip in Hope Springs. Please come quickly. Please."

Jessica placed the receiver back in the cradle and bowed her head. Tears formed in her eyes as she thought about her situation. With very little money, she had no place left to run. Her only option was to throw herself on the mercy of the court and let the legal system sort out the details of the shooting.

"Mommy?"

Jessica straightened up, wiping her face. "Yes, baby?"

Megan had climbed out of the parked Camaro and was now by her side. "It'll be all right. Don't cry, Mommy."

She crouched down to hug her daughter close. "You're safe. That is the most important thing." Jessica kissed her on the cheek. "I love you so much."

"I love you, too, Mommy."

"We better get back in the car where it's warmer, sweetie. We'll wait for the sheriff there."

"Okay."

Jessica led Megan back to the Camaro and shut the door. She glanced down the deserted street hoping to see the patrol car. This early on Sunday morning, Hope Springs was an empty ghost town. The lone traffic light buzzed, going from red to green in a continuous cycle. Clearly heard a block away due to the lack of residual noise, the sound did little to ease her sense of total isolation.

Where the hell is Dale?

"Mommy, what's going to happen to us now?" Megan asked.

The very adult question surprised Jessica.

"I don't know, baby." She reached out and held her close. "Mommy may have to go away for a while. I hope only for a short time. Maybe Nel and Sam can watch you. Would you like that?"

"I don't want you to go away," Megan sobbed.

"I know, baby. I know."

Jessica let out a deep breath. Surely, the court would recognize Blake was a murder suspect and killing him was an act of self-defense by a battered wife and daughter. At least, she hoped they would see it like that.

The aftershock of the violence in the trailer caused her hands and knees to shake. Minutes passed while she held Megan close. The adrenaline rush of the shooting fled her body, and a growing panic took its place. She closed her eyes and attempted to calm her shaky nerves.

Bright headlights pulled up behind the Camaro. Jessica looked up and recognized the sheriff's patrol car.

Finally.

Wiping her wet face, she ran hands through her unkempt hair in the rearview as a dark silhouette walked along the driver's side of the car. A hand knocked on the window and she rolled it down.

"Out of the car," Collin said in his deep voice while sticking the barrel of a Glock pistol against the side of her head. "Now."

"What the hell?" Jessica sputtered in surprise. "Collin?"

"You heard me." He opened the driver door. "Get out."

In shock, Jessica glanced toward Megan. On the other side of the car, Roxie opened the passenger door.

"What's going on?" Jessica asked in a voice broken by rising panic.

"You're coming with us," Collin replied, grabbing her shoulder and yanking her from the driver's seat.

"Mommy!" Megan cried out as Roxie pulled her kicking from the car.

"Get your hands off my daughter, you bitch!" Jessica screamed.

"Shut up, Jess!" Collin slammed the pistol barrel down on the back of her head.

White stars splayed across her vision. Jessica groaned. Her knees gave out and she collapsed against the side of the car. Desperately, she clung to consciousness but her vision swam in and out of reality. Too weak to fight, Collin dragged her to the back of the patrol car and threw her inside. As if in a dream, she heard Megan crying.

From there everything went black.

*　　*　　*　　*

Jessica opened her eyes.

The first thing her fuzzy vision focused upon was a pencil sketch of a forest and full moon in the sky. She recognized it as one of Collin's sketches and realized she was on the cot in the back room of Roxie's. Pain throbbed in her head as if someone twisted a knife in her skull. She raised her hands to feel the wound but discovered her wrists tightly wrapped in duct tape.

On the cot next to her, Megan slept soundly. Jessica lifted her aching head to check her daughter. Both her wrists and ankles were bound in duct tape. Megan's blonde hair was a disheveled mess covering her face. Jessica attempted to move but found her ankles were taped as well. She twisted in the cot the best she could to embrace Megan.

Her mind tried to grasp her situation. How had this happened? What did she miss to put Megan and her in such danger? She had suspected Collin was a junkie. Her gut warned her about the man, but she never expected this threat. Dealing with Blake had consumed her thoughts. Why were Collin and Roxie driving the sheriff's patrol car? Where was Dale? The ache in her head made it hard to focus.

Shifting in her bound status, Jessica glanced around the room. The overhead light was off, but a gray glow filtered in from the main area of the bar. Just after dawn, she guessed. *I must have been out for a couple of hours. Where are Collin and Roxie?*

"Hey," she said aloud.

Roxie stepped into the open entrance to the back room. Dressed in tight blue jeans and a black tank top, she held the Glock pistol in her right hand.

"Quiet," she replied.

"What the hell is going on? What did you do to my daughter?"

"I used chloroform to put her asleep. She wouldn't stop crying."

"Why, Rox? Why are you doing this?"

"It's nothing personal, Jess."

"Nothing personal!" Jessica replied. "You kidnapped my daughter, and your fucked-up brother hit me in the head!"

"If you're not going to be quiet, I'll put duct tape over your mouth next."

"Okay … okay," she said. "You at least owe me an explanation, Rox. What did I do to you and Collin?"

"Like I said, Jess, it's nothing personal. Remember all the times you sat down to eat a turkey on Thanksgiving? Think of it like that."

"So what are you saying?"

"We have a hunger that forces us to eat human flesh."

"You're going to eat us?" Jessica couldn't believe her words. The ache in her head made it hard to focus. It all seemed surreal. "What are you and Collin up to? Some freaky cannibal cult bullshit?"

"We're not human, so eating you won't make us cannibals."

"You're not human?"

"No."

Jessica leaned her head back and stared at the ceiling for a moment. *Obviously the girl is as whacked as her brother. I have to keep her talking. Figure some way to get Megan away from here.*

"So you and Collin aren't human? Then what are you? Let me guess. Vampires?"

Roxie smiled. "Hardly."

"Listen, Rox, I don't give a shit what you think you are. Cut me and Megan free and I'm gone. I won't talk to the police or anything. I'll just disappear."

"I can't do that. It would make Collin very angry."

"Then let my daughter go. I'll play along with your sick fantasy. Just set Megan free."

"Can't do that, either. You're just a side dish, Jess. She's the main course."

"Fuck!" Jessica cursed.

The back exit to the storeroom opened, letting Collin into the room. His dark gaze centered on Jess.

"Such language, Jess. I'm shocked." He smiled coldly. "I'm glad your daughter is asleep and couldn't hear it."

"Asshole," Jessica replied.

Collin squatted next to the cot. "I must apologize for hitting you with the pistol, Jess. I didn't mean to knock you out that way, but you were making a lot of noise. I should have used the chloroform instead. I acted rashly. I tend to do that sometimes." He reached out and ran his fingers through Megan's hair. "You have such a lovely daughter, Jess."

"You sick perverted bastard!" Jessica hissed. "Don't touch her!"

"You think the reason I have you here is because of some sexual perversion?" Collin chuckled and stood. "Don't flatter yourself, Jess. I have no desire to have sex with any human. Your species is below me. You and your daughter are just food for my kind."

"Your kind?" Jessica asked. "What the fuck are you?"

"You'll find out tonight when the moon goes dark."

"The lunar eclipse?"

"Yes. It happens this evening after dusk. Until that time, however, I think it would be easier on both of us if you slept."

Collin stepped aside, revealing Roxie behind him holding a white rag. She leaned forward forcing the cloth over Jessica's nostrils and mouth. She struggled and tried not to breathe in the pungent fumes but her fight became weaker. A cloudy veil of white filled her mind and soon gave away to darkness.

CHAPTER FIFTY-SIX

Collin stood in the center of the old wooden hay barn. The rising sun brightened the dusty interior through gaps in the roof. Tonight he would view the magnificent Ebon Moon through the same missing timbers and devour the human child.

He had parked Jess's Camaro inside the barn to hide it from the outside world. The sheriff's patrol car he left outside in case he needed a getaway vehicle. Sheriff Sutton lay handcuffed to a pipe in the storm cellar while Jess and Megan slept unconscious in the roadhouse as his prisoners. The pieces were all in place for tonight's festivities. He had only one loose end to tie up. One guest had yet to be invited.

Blake Lobato.

Collin closed his eyes and cleared his mind. Unlike Sheriff Sutton, he had a special psychic bond to the new Bitten. He was the one who had passed the Dark Gift of lycanthropy to Blake. The voice mail on the sheriff's phone said Jess had shot and killed her husband. Since she had not used silver bullets, Blake was not dead, but Collin sensed his wounds were severe. It could take many hours to heal such extensive damage. In such a suspended state, Collin could speak to Blake's mind over distance.

He concentrated, shutting his eyes. *Blake, my name is Collin. I'm the Wolfkin who bit you. You are one of us now and serve the Pack. Tonight the moon will be dark and a feast will be held. Come to the barn behind the roadhouse to join your new family.*

"Brother?" Roxie's voice broke the silence and his thoughts.

Collin returned his focus to his surroundings. His sister stood at the open door.

"How are our prisoners?" he asked.

"Sleeping." Roxie joined his side and embraced him. "The chloroform will put them under for hours. I will keep administering it until darkness."

"Good." Collin returned her embrace. "Do you not feel it, my love? The pull of the upcoming Ebon Moon is growing within."

"I do."

"I've been trying to mentally contact the newest member of the Pack."

"Jess's husband?"

"His name is Blake. He sleeps in a stupor as his body heals. When he awakens he will be hungry and need to feed."

"But can he be controlled? Will he join the Pack?"

"It remains to be seen."

Roxie pulled away. "Should we not go to him and bring him back?"

"No, we stay and watch over our prisoners. We don't know if those damn teenage boys aren't going to come snooping around again. Blake will find us."

"Then there's nothing do but wait."

Collin nodded. "All we do now is sit until the moon rises tonight."

CHAPTER FIFTY-SEVEN

When he got home, Terry crashed in his bed and had no idea how long he had slept. He vaguely remembered talking to his mother before she went to work at noon. Afterward, he fell back in a deep sleep driven by exhaustion. Strange dreams plagued his slumber, but they were too obscure and disjointed to remember. Sometime in the afternoon he awoke. He stared at the bright sunlight pouring through his bedroom windows and contemplated the bizarre events over the last few days. Everything was dreamlike and unreal. He rolled over and caught sight of the lone silver bullet Mr. Higgins gave him sitting on the bedside table beside the old man's scribbled will and testament.

The whole thing is real, he realized.

Sitting up in bed, he picked up the bullet and turned it over in his hand. *Am I really thinking about going back to the roadhouse to fight werewolves tonight?*

The plan seemed insane in the light of day.

He put aside the bullet and grabbed the yellow pad. Mr. Higgins's scratchy handwriting filled the page, and he read through it. The old man had given him the entire estate on the assumption that he would continue the werewolf hunt after his death. Terry knew he had to carry it through. He was the only one who could. It would be dangerous—of that he was sure—but he had to try.

Terry Newman, badass monster hunter, had become a reality.

Lying back in bed, he thought about his strategy for fighting the creatures tonight. A better weapon was what he needed. The silver-tipped arrows didn't have much stopping power, and he only had two left.

"Fire," Sid had suggested.

He slipped the bullet in a pocket of his shirt. So far it had brought him good luck.

Terry jumped out of bed and crossed through the house and out the door leading to the garage. A full five-gallon container of gasoline sat on the floor next to the lawn mower. His mother had put it there because he was supposed to mow the lawn this weekend. He would use it to kill werewolves instead.

A few minutes later, he poured the gasoline into two empty wine bottles in the kitchen and ripped up a wash towel into strips. These he soaked in gas, as well, and stuffed each piece of cloth tightly in the each bottle's mouth. The thick smell of raw gasoline choked his nostrils and throat before he had the task completed. He packed the bottles in a plastic milk crate with more rags as a cushion and put them in the back bed of the old F-150. Rummaging through an old cabinet drawer, he found a charcoal lighter his dad had used to fire up the grill in the backyard for summer afternoon cookouts. This he stuffed in a jean pocket.

He now had fire in his arsenal of werewolf-fighting tools.

Before he left to go to Sid's place, he looked over his room he had from the time he was a child. The posters on the walls reflected his gradual age change. Where once the walls were covered with posters of Teenage Mutant Ninja Turtles and Spiderman, they were now replaced with Megan Fox, Jessica Alba, and other media hotties. He smiled and picked up the home phone.

It was almost five in the afternoon. His mother would be on break. Terry waited until she was paged to come to the phone.

"Hello?" she asked on the other end.

"Mom."

"Terry? Is everything all right?"

Terry paused. "I'm going to be home late tonight."

"You've got school tomorrow, young man."

"I know. I'm going to watch the lunar eclipse with Sid."

"When do you plan on mowing the yard?"

Terry thought for a moment. "Later this week, I promise. Mom, I just want to say ..." He choked back the emotion in his voice. "I don't blame you for Dad leaving us. I love you."

There was a moment of silence. "I love you, too, son."

"Good-bye."

"Bye."

The line went dead, and Terry replaced the phone in the cradle. At least he had said what he wanted in the case he didn't make it back tonight. A weight had lifted off his heart. He left the house, climbed in the F-150, and pulled out of the drive to head for Sid's house.

CHAPTER FIFTY-EIGHT

Blake ran naked through an endless forest of giant trees. His bare feet crossed over mossy tree roots and grassy undergrowth in footfalls so light he barely sensed stepping on the ground. All about him a mist floated between the tall trunks and obscured the treetops in a white haze. The great forest seemed to stretch forever, and he continued his run unabated, racing toward what he couldn't fathom, but he didn't care. Gone were the shackles of addiction, pain, hatred, and violence that had ruled his life. In this place there was only a oneness with the primeval forest around him.

He breathed in the clean air and took in the sickly sweet aroma of lush green growth coupled with the odor of decaying foliage. The damp air left a wet sheen on his naked flesh, but he was not cold. There was only the simple joy of running naked without care or worry. He slowed his step and paused to drink in the wonder and magnificence of the great trees stretching upward until lost in the fog.

"Blake," an unfamiliar voice said his name.

Not sure if he heard the voice in his ears or mind, he turned toward the sound. A large man stepped from around a moss-covered tree trunk. A mane of shoulder-length black hair reached down to his shoulders, and equally dark eyes bore into his. The naked stranger bore intertwining tribal tattoos down his defined biceps and forearms. The uneasiness of looking upon another man's nudity made him want to look away, but he couldn't.

"I'm Collin, the one who bit you," the stranger said with no emotion. "You are one of us now and serve the Pack. Tonight the moon will be dark and a feast will be held. Come to the barn behind the roadhouse to join your new family."

"I don't serve anyone," Blake replied. "I don't want to leave this place!"

The man's image started to fade to nothingness.

"I don't want to go back!" he screamed at the empty space where Collin had stood.

As if on cue, the vision of the magnificent forest faded to a dark void filled with searing pain.

Blake opened his left eye. Something kept him from seeing out the other. Reaching up, he touched the gaping hole in his face where Jessica had shot him. An empty socket remained where his right eye had been. Head to toe his body ached. All its resources focused on healing. Stretched out on the carpet in the front room of Jess's trailer, his mending flesh painfully pushed the lead fragments from the multiple bullet holes. He twitched again in agony as wracking pain passed through him like a jolt of electricity. Too weak to move, he remained still to conserve his strength.

"Get up, Blakey," the voice of his dead father haunted him. "Your work's not done, son. You let the bitch get away."

Blake shifted his one-eyed gaze. His father, decked out in his blue police uniform, stood a few feet away with blood leaking from the bullet hole in the side of his head. His dead white eyes looked down upon him.

"Go away," Blake responded and winced as another wave of agony shook him.

"Don't lay there like a pussy, boy. Get up and teach the backstabbing whore a lesson. The bitch shot you, son. You got to do what your old man taught you." The apparition tightened its fists. "You got to make her play the game. Pay her back for hurting you."

"Leave," Blake demanded. "You're the reason my mind's fucked up."

"Your mind's not fucked. It's pure in its purpose." The dead face of his father leaned close. "You're the perfect instrument to carry out what I taught you. Now rise, son, your work's not done." The ghost faded into sunlight shining through the flowered curtains of the front room windows.

Blake sat up. Another storm of devastating pain made him cry out. Staggering to his feet, he stripped the black duster off and hobbled down the hall into the trailer's restroom. Switching on the light, he faced his reflection in the medicine cabinet mirror. The .357 magnum bullet had bore a hole through his face, leaving him with the visage of something out of a hellish nightmare. Nothing human could have survived such a wound. He was glad to be more than human now.

He gazed down with his good eye at another bullet wound in his chest. As he watched, his super healing slowly expelled a blob of lead from his flesh. It fell into the bloody sink with a clinking sound. Once rid of the slug, the hole closed, leaving no scar. He returned to his reflection. The terrible hole shrank with red tissue and bone forming in the void of the wound. He watched with ghoulish interest as supernatural forces went to the painful work of reforming his destroyed face and eye. His body quaked with pain, but he managed to stay standing at the mirror. In minutes, the pain subsided and the physical trauma he suffered from the gunshots disappeared.

His fully healed face smiled back at him in his reflection.

He had learned to cheat death so he could dispense it to others.

New hunger gnawed in his stomach. The regenerative process had drained him of his physical resources. The beast needed to feed again to regain strength. Blake stripped naked and stumbled back to the front room where he fell to his hands and knees. The transformation began, and he howled as his body shifted into its bestial form. Newly grown claws tore holes in the carpet as the bones of his spine popped to form a hunched shape. The monstrous mind of the beast pushed Blake's human persona aside.

Kill! the creature bellowed internally. *Feed!*

Driven by a primal hunger for flesh and blood, the creature leaped out of the trailer and onto the front deck. It sniffed the afternoon air. The smell of young horse flesh came from the stables. Growling, the beast bounded across the farmyard. Reaching the stock pen, it cleared the fence to land on two legs in the pitted dirt of the corral. From inside came the scent of fear and the frenzied cries of panicked animals sensing the hungry werewolf outside the stable door. The monster tore the lock off with one swipe of its claws and threw aside the entrance.

The beast's long shadow fell across the dirt floor. Trapped in a stall, the young foal whinnied and kicked at the doors to escape. The beast licked its maw, preparing to pounce upon the terrified animal ... but paused. Something else had caught its attention.

Truck doors slamming and human voices.

*   *   *   *

"I don't like this," Sam said in a tense tone as he exited his truck.

Nelda had suspected something bothered her husband for several days now. Since they had left Bartlesville, the man had been quiet most of the way back. She sensed there was something more on his mind than his mother's poor condition. Now upon returning to their farm they found a parked black Harley motorcycle in the drive.

"I wonder who's here," Nelda said.

"The person who vandalized my fence drove a motorcycle." Sam reached in and pulled the Marlin rifle from the rack in the back window. "It could be the same trespasser."

"Sam, what's been going on?" Nelda asked with her eyes focused on the rifle. "You've been spooked for the last couple of days. That's not like you."

"Something has been snooping around the farm."

"Something? You mean the big black dog?"

Sam cocked the rifle. "It wasn't a dog, Nel."

"Then what was it, Sam?"

"Something very bad."

"Tell me."

"I can't because I don't believe it myself."

"Sam Olson, you tell me what's going on."

Sam pushed back his hat. "I think the dog Megan saw the other night was ..." he hesitated, his eyes glancing toward the horizon. "... a werewolf."

The term caught Nelda by surprise. She suspected some sort of bear or mountain lion. She looked deep in her husband's eyes and knew he believed in what he was saying. A cold chill embraced her spine.

"You're kidding me, right?"

Sam shook his head. "Those boys who were here yesterday had seen it, too. That's the reason they dropped over. The monster's been coming around since Jess moved into the trailer."

She could tell he spoke the truth, and it frightened her even more. "I'm going to check on Jess and Megan." She headed toward the trailer.

"Wait, Nel," Sam responded. "Let me go first."

With rifle at the ready, Sam led the way with Nelda following close behind. They rounded the barn and paused by the propane tank. The trailer looked empty in the late afternoon light. Jess's Camaro was not parked in front of the home.

"Sam," Nelda whispered. "The trailer doors are wide open."

At that moment a horrible racket came from inside the stables fifty yards away.

"Something's in the barn," Sam stated. "You check the trailer, Nel. I'm going to see what's scaring the livestock."

"Be careful," she replied.

Sam took off, trotting toward the horse stables. A gnawing fear ate at the pit of Nelda's stomach as she watched her husband race toward the building. Something was terribly wrong, as if she had stepped into a waking nightmare. Fighting panic, she crossed the distance to the trailer and up the steps of the wooden deck. The front door hung open, revealing the dim interior.

"Jess?" she called out.

Silence.

She stuck her head inside. A pool of fresh blood stained the carpet beside the couch. Her heart turned to ice.

Where are Jess and Megan?

The crack of a rifle went off in the horse barn.

"Sam!" Nelda cried out and raced off the deck. "Sam!"

A terrible growling noise accompanied her husband's desperate cries from inside the stable. Reaching the fence, she stopped. The double door flew open and Sam staggered out. He no longer held the rifle. Blood spewed from a gaping hole in his throat. He took a few steps toward Nelda before collapsing in the dirt. Another horrific bestial noise came from inside. Shocked beyond fear, she looked from her dead husband to the thing poised in the open barn door. It stood on two canine legs with bristling black hair covering its hunched form. Red eyes stared back at her. The horror emitted another inhuman snarl revealing a maw dripping with bloody slobber before it pounced upon her fallen husband. Sinking fangs into his back, it ripped up a bloody chunk of meat and cloth.

Nelda screamed.

The monster howled in response.

Panic gripped her as she raced for the farmhouse. Reaching the patio door, she slammed it closed behind her in the desperate hope to lock the nightmare outside. She charged for the telephone on the wall by the refrigerator as a hunched shadow loomed in the sunlight shining through the glass.

Call 911!

Nelda's hands yanked the phone from the cradle as the glass patio door shattered behind her. She turned. The huge werewolf had leaped through the broken door and roared at her in rage. The horrid creature stood so tall its elongated ears nearly brushed the ceiling. Wolflike paws moved across the broken shards of glass on the floor.

"Oh, God," Nelda muttered as her fingers sought to dial the phone.

The monster shoved aside the kitchen table and bellowed another horrible snarl.

Backing up, Nelda glanced around the room and spotted a large butcher knife lying on the counter. She snatched it up.

"Stay away!" she shouted, brandishing the knife and dropping the phone.

Its evil eyes studied her as it licked bloody lips with a red tongue. A low monstrous growl came from deep within its throat. Nelda backed away with the kitchen knife before her. The beast followed.

"You killed my Sam!" she screamed with tears forming in her eyes. "You want some of me. Then come on, you ugly bastard!"

The werewolf snarled again. In an instant it lunged and Nelda stabbed the knife deep in its furry chest and yanked it out. It slapped her aside, ripping away the flesh of her left shoulder. Wounded and bleeding, Nelda staggered back but still held the knife. She slashed again as the creature drew closer. In response, its black claws ripped open a bloody swatch across her abdomen. The force of the blow sent her backward, where she tipped over the kitchen table. She lay stunned amidst the debris on the floor and tried to regain her senses. Blood pumped from the gashes in her flesh. The werewolf stepped closer and growled. Nelda turned her head and spotted the dropped knife just in reach of her hand. With weak fingers she clutched the handle one last time.

"Go to hell!" she screamed as the horrid beast savagely fell upon her, ripping and tearing her apart.

CHAPTER FIFTY-NINE

"Check this shit out," Sid said, letting Terry into his garage apartment. "It's badass."

"The video footage you shot last night?"

"Yeah." Sid nodded and crossed over to his computer. "I transferred it over to the hard drive. It looks a lot better in hi-def. Just watch."

Sid touched the mouse and a video began playing across the monitor screen. Terry watched with fascination. Even shot through night vision, the frightening image of the werewolf stepping out of the trees and growling at the camera was more real than anything created by Hollywood using CGI technology.

"What do you think?" Sid asked when the thirty-second clip finished.

"Badass," Terry replied.

"You know it." Sid smiled. "I'll start e-mailing television producers tomorrow and shop the story around. See who wants to cover it: Larry King or Geraldo. We're going to be so fucking famous."

"That's great."

Sid stepped back from the computer, and his smile evaporated. "You're not going back to the bar tonight."

"I've got to," Terry replied.

"Bro, you don't have to. This video footage will help convince others these monsters are real. We can let them deal with hunting them."

"In the meantime, the one who killed Emma Higgins might get away. I promised Mr. Higgins on his deathbed I would stop him."

Sid let out a sigh. "This doesn't have to do with Jess, does it?"

Terry looked away toward the door. "I only wish she knew her sheriff is a werewolf and I stopped him last night. Then maybe I wouldn't look like such a dork to her. She probably doesn't have a clue."

"Are you still thinking about her?"

"Yeah. I guess so."

"So you're going back to fight a pack of werewolves alone? Dude, you haven't even kissed a girl yet and you want to go off and get yourself fucking killed."

"You've never kissed a girl, either. You're just as big a virgin as I am."

"I know, and that's why I'm staying right here. I don't want to die before losing my cherry to some fucking hot babe."

"Yeah, like that's going to happen in your future anytime soon."

"It might." Sid shrugged. "It sure as fuck ain't going to happen if I get chewed to death by some werewolf. So why don't you stay and forget about it?"

"I can't."

"Why the fuck not?"

"I don't know. Call it destiny or fate. I just feel it in my bones. I've got to do it, you know." He paused for a second. "It's important. Maybe this is what it means to finally grow up and be a man."

"Then I'm not ready to grow up."

"I understand." Terry turned toward the door to leave. "By the way, I took your suggestion about using fire as a weapon and cooked up a couple of Molotov cocktails. I also have two silver-tipped arrows left. Listen, man, I'm not looking to get killed. I'm going to scope the place out during the eclipse tonight. If I get a chance to take out the black werewolf, I will. If I don't, I'll just sit tight and observe."

"You're a crazy son of a bitch," Sid replied.

"You may be right." Terry put his hand on the doorknob. "It's going to be moonrise soon."

"The eclipse starts at about seven thirty tonight, and the moon should be totally dark by nine thirty."

"They'll be out then. I better get going."

Sid suddenly embraced him with his skinny arms. "Don't get yourself killed, man. You're my only friend, and I don't want to look for another."

Terry returned the awkward hug. "I'll be all right, bro."

"Okay," Sid replied, letting him go. "By the way, it's not a gay thing."

Terry laughed. "I know."

He left the garage apartment and walked out to the old F-150 in the drive. Climbing into the front seat, Terry paused and contemplated what he was about to do. He didn't really want to face a bunch of werewolves alone. On the other hand, he couldn't let the monsters kill other innocent humans. Besides, Jessica was in danger of the beasts. According to Sam Olson, one had returned to the trailer several times and even tried to claw through the back door.

Why? What was it after in the trailer?

Behind the steering wheel, Terry stared at the door to Sid's place and contemplated the question.

It wasn't Jessica. She was gone at the time.

A realization struck Terry with the force of a hammer.

They had it all wrong. It's the little girl.

Megan.

The door to Sid's place opened, and he stepped out wearing his ICP hoodie. He carried a pump shotgun in one hand and a box of shells in the other. Terry watched, speechless, as he climbed into the passenger seat of the F-150.

"What the hell?" he sputtered in surprise.

"Just drive," Sid replied, putting the shotgun across his knees.

"You're coming, too?"

"I've saved your ass this far. I'm not going to stop now. It's destiny, like you said. It's just something I got to do."

"Okay." Terry started the pickup and backed out of the drive. "Where did you get the shotgun?"

"It was my grandpa's 12 gauge. I had it hidden under my bed." He reached into the box of shells and began loading the gun. "I never told you why I just upped and dropped out of school, did I?"

"I figured it was to get stoned," Terry responded. Driving through the neighborhood around Sid's house, he spotted people setting up lawn chairs in their front yards in preparation to watch the full lunar eclipse tonight.

"No, man." Sid shook his head. "I was getting picked on a lot by the jocks. Brandon Harrison and his bunch of fags treated me like shit. I had to drop out." Sid loaded another shotgun shell. "It was fucking terrible. One day I came close to returning to the school with this shotgun to kill as many of the fuckers as I could before I got taken out by the cops. I couldn't do it so I put the barrel in my mouth instead. I wanted to go out like Kurt Cobain. Bang! It would all be over and the whole shitty world could kiss my ass."

"But you didn't do it."

"Naw, I didn't because I found a friend." He slapped another shell into the shotgun. "You saved my life, man." Propping the shotgun between his legs, he glanced over with tears glistening in his eyes. "We're in this fucking thing together."

"Thanks, bro."

*　　*　　*　　*

Blake awoke naked on the blood-soaked linoleum.

He lifted his head off the kitchen floor and looked around. Not far away, the body of a half-eaten woman lay sprawled out like the remains of a grisly buffet. In the last rays of sunlight streaming in through paisley curtains, she stared at nothing with dead eyes and a mouth open in terror. Blake rose to his feet and stood in the center of a wrecked kitchen. Slick blood covered his body. He realized with a grim satisfaction that he had fed again. The kills came easier and quicker now. He just wished he could remember the savage killings instead of waking up to their bloody aftermath. Perhaps over time he could learn the skill.

Blake left the farmhouse and stepped onto a patio. The sunset had turned the western sky into a smear of red and gold. The smell of another kill tickled his nostrils. He glanced at the stock pen and saw more of his internal beast's handiwork. This time it was a man laying sprawled out face-first in a puddle of bloody mud within the corral. Blake smiled. He had really let himself go this time.

But he had also lost Jess. How could he pick up her trail now?

Disappointed, he crossed the distance to her trailer. A thought crossed his mind when he reached the front door.

Why hadn't she gone to the police?

She had shot him in the early morning hours, and it was now sunset of the same day. There was plenty of time to report the shooting. Why wasn't the farm crawling with deputies and homicide detectives? Did she just run away leaving everything behind? It didn't make sense. As far as she knew, he was dead. Jess had no more reason to run.

Something must have kept her from reporting the shooting.

But what?

He decided it would be best to leave, as well, before someone showed up at the farm.

Taking a quick shower in the trailer bathroom, he washed the blood off his body and watched it swirl down the drain like red watercolor. His dream of running through the woods and encountering the naked stranger haunted his mind. The dark-haired man had said his name was Collin and invited him to join the Pack during the eclipse tonight. The proposed meeting was to be held in an old barn behind Roxie's Roadhouse. Blake pondered the invitation. Did he really want to join? He had found a new power and freedom. Serving as a lapdog for a pack of werewolves didn't appeal to him.

Blake found his clothes lying on the living room floor. Sliding on his long black duster, he reached into a pocket for the Harley keys and felt the rolls of hundred-dollar bills inside. He had money and a sweet ride. Fuck the others. He wanted to roam the open road. Ride. Kill. Eat. Sleep. Repeat. Be an Angel of Death roaring across the highways of America.

Night had fallen when he left the trailer for the last time. Overhead the full moon showed the first signs of the oncoming eclipse. Blake crossed to his Harley and kick-started the powerful bike. Settling things with Jess would have to wait until he picked up her trail again. He had no idea where she had gone. Somehow, he knew they would cross paths again. Staying in the area with the two murders he left back at the farm would be stupid. It was time to hit the road.

Blake left Hope Springs behind and traveled south on Highway 71 under the darkening moon. The beast inside, satiated by the recent kills, slumbered peacefully as the bike thundered down a black ribbon of asphalt. After an hour on the road, Blake slowed the Harley and looked up at the eclipse. The shadow covered half the moon's face. The strong sense of leaving unfinished business behind tugged at his gut.

Jess was still back there, he realized.

He knew it in his soul.

The Pack wanted him to join them. He should at least hear what they had to offer. Maybe they could help him find Jess. If he drove fast, he could make it there before the full eclipse.

Blake swung the bike around and raced back the way he came.

CHAPTER SIXTY

How much time passed in chloroform-induced sleep, Jessica had no clue. A white fog filled the corners of her mind, giving no bearing on time and space. She had a terrible dream of running after Megan through trees and shadows but was unable to catch her, even though she called her name several times. Finally, Megan disappeared into the dark and was gone.

Jessica jolted awake. A powerful aroma burned the inside of her sinuses. She opened her eyes to a white light and Roxie bending over holding a bottle of smelling salts.

"Showtime," Collin said from someplace beyond her fuzzy sight.

"What?" Jessica sputtered.

"Time to get up," Roxie stated.

Jessica attempted to move but found she was still lying on the cot with her hands and feet bound by duct tape. Megan slept next to her, equally taped. Standing by the bed, Collin and Roxie looked down on them with dark emotionless eyes. Jessica's heart turned cold with the realization that her dream of chasing Megan through the shadows wasn't nearly as bad as the reality she now faced.

"The Ebon Moon draws near," Roxie said to her brother. "I can feel its power growing."

"We must prepare the feast," Collin replied.

"Feast?" Jessica asked. "Ebon Moon? What does that have to do with my daughter?"

"Our kind has traditionally feasted on human children during a lunar eclipse. It strengthens our bloodline," Collin answered.

"What kind of monster are you to eat an innocent child!" Jessica screamed in desperation and struggled against her bonds.

"You're soon going to find out." Collin smiled while pulling a large hunting knife from one of the nearby lockers. "As I said before, it's nothing personal, Jess. We're doing this to survive. You would do the same in our place."

At the sight of the knife, Jessica felt a wave of panic but fought it back. She needed to keep a clear head and buy some time until she found a way to get her daughter to safety.

"What are you going to do with that?" she asked.

"Nothing sinister, I assure you," Collin replied. "I'm going to cut the tape holding your legs so you can walk." He bent and sliced through the duct tape. "There."

The instant Jessica's legs came free she decided to act. Kicking Collin's hand, the knife flew from his grip to land on the floor next to the cot. In desperation, she threw herself off the bed and grabbed it up with her bound hands. She pointed the blade toward Collin.

"Stay the fuck away from my daughter, you sick bastard!" she screamed.

Collin straightened up. His dark gaze centered on Jessica.

"Or what?" Collin asked, stepping forward.

"I'll kill you if you don't."

"Give the knife back, Jess," Roxie demanded. "You haven't got a chance."

"I'm warning you to stay away."

Collin sighed. "Cooperate with us and I'll let your daughter sleep through the feasting. If you don't do as we say, I'll make sure she's awake and screaming when we devour her. It's your choice, Jess."

"Fuck you!"

Jessica's rage and fear reached a boiling point. Screaming like a mad woman, she stabbed viciously with the knife at Collin who held up his right hand to block. The blade pierced through the back of his hand. In response, he shoved her back hard against the metal lockers.

Stunned, Jessica slid to the floor.

Standing over her, Collin studied the knife sticking through his hand. "Now look what you've done," he stated in a calm voice as he pulled the bloody blade from his flesh. "That hurts, by the way."

My God, Jessica thought with disbelief. *He's whacked out on PCP or meth and can't feel pain.*

"Look at this, Jess." Collin held up his wounded hand to show light shining through the hole in his flesh. "You can see right through it."

"You're crazy," Jessica replied.

"Oh, the fun isn't over yet. Keep watching."

The light through the hole grew smaller as the wound closed together and healed in a matter of seconds. Jessica's mouth hung open in shock. What she had just witnessed was impossible and threatened the shaky hold she had left on reality.

"Much better," Collin commented, working his fingers.

"What the fuck are you?" she asked in amazement.

"A Wolfkin," Collin answered. His eyes changed to dark pools and his smile displayed unnatural canine teeth.

"Wolfkin?" Jessica responded in a weak voice as she looked at his terrible visage in disbelief.

"A werewolf to you."

She paused for a second, trying to grasp the concept. Images tumbled through her mind, like an old tint-type movie running on high speed.

Full moon. Silver bullets. Men turning into animals.

"A werewolf?" she repeated the term as if doing so would help her believe.

"Now you know." Collin bent down and picked her up easily from the floor. Holding her by one clawed hand, his horrid face loomed before hers as he licked his tongue across sharp teeth. "We're the real deal, Jess," he added. "We've lived alongside your useless species for many centuries. In darker times, we fed at will without fear of reprisal. Now we must hide our kills and feed only on those who fall through the cracks of your worthless human society. On special occasions we still feast on the flesh of a child. Guess what, Jess. Tonight is a very special occasion."

"What are we going to do with her?" Roxie asked, nodding toward Jessica.

"We'll put her in the storm cellar with the sheriff," Collin answered.

"Dale is here?" Jessica asked. Shock had caused her mind to disconnect from the situation, as if she observed what was happening through someone else's eyes. With the mention of Dale's name her mind returned to focus on the reality with a desperate hope. "You locked him in a cellar?"

"I had to. He's supposed to be one of us, but somehow you gave him the notion he wanted to be human again." Collin showed a grim smile. "Now you're going to help me remind him of his Wolfkin legacy." He shoved her toward Roxie. "Take her and I'll get the child."

Roxie grabbed her by the arm. "I'm sorry, Jess, but this is the way it has to be. We do this to survive."

Jessica glanced back over her shoulder as Collin lifted her sleeping daughter from the cot. Megan's face looked serene and beautiful, unaware of the danger holding her in his arms. An immense sadness coupled with helplessness swept through Jessica. She had fought so hard to keep her safe from Blake. But for what? In the end, she'd put her daughter in the clutches of these two monsters.

Oh God, please don't let her wake up.

Roxie took a flashlight off the hook on the wall near the exit door.

"Outside," she commanded, pushing Jessica toward the back door of the roadhouse.

Jessica exited through the door. The cool night air embraced her as she stood on the back deck.

"Keep going," Roxie demanded, showing the flashlight beam down the trail leading through dark trees.

Tears formed in Jess's eyes. "Roxie, please … think about what you're doing. Let Megan go. Please. You can have me, but not my daughter."

"I said to keep moving." Roxie shoved her toward the dark trail.

"Bitch!" Jessica snapped back.

She started down the wooded trail with Roxie behind her. Collin followed carrying Megan. An eerie silence hung in the cool air as they made their way through the patch of woods. Jessica followed the path illuminated by the flashlight and felt as she did under Blake's cruel control. There was no avenue of escape. No way to get her daughter away to safety. Even though she had fled one cruel fate, she was the victim of another.

They emerged from the trees at the edge of an expanse of open grass lit by the moonlight. Jessica glanced up at the dark moon hanging in the starlit sky. The entire orb was nearly eclipsed in shadow.

"Look upon its magnificence, my sister," Collin announced. "Observe the beautiful face of the goddess veiled in darkness."

"I can feel her power growing inside," Roxie replied. "It won't be much longer, my love."

Jessica scanned the open area of ground leading to the large two-story wooden barn standing in the pale moonlight. One door hung partially open to reveal a dark interior. She shifted her gaze to the grounds before the barn. Her heart jumped at the sight of the sheriff's patrol car parked fifty yards away.

Dale is here!

"Keep walking," Roxie said, shining the flashlight toward a storm cellar door between the patrol car and the wooden barn.

Jessica stumbled on. Grass and dead leaves crunched beneath her feet as she crossed the distance to the cellar. Reaching the wooden plank door of the underground shelter, Roxie shone the light on the hasp bolt.

"Open it," she ordered.

Jessica knelt down and slid the bolt aside. Grabbing the rope handle, she swung up the cellar door. The flashlight's glow illuminated dirty stone steps leading down to blackness. A damp smell rose up to her from the dark.

"Who's there?" Sheriff Sutton's hoarse voice asked from below.

"Jess," she answered.

"Oh, God … Jess … don't come down here. Stay away."

"We wouldn't want you to get lonely," Collin shouted in response. "You should be thankful I found someone to share the Ebon Moon with."

Roxie placed the flashlight in Jessica's hand. "Go on down the steps."

"Wait," Jessica replied. "Let me say good-bye to my daughter."

"Very well." Roxie stepped aside to allow her to reach Megan in Collin's arms.

Tears blurring her vision, Jessica kissed Megan's face. "I'm sorry, baby. Mommy wasn't able to save you. Sleep tight and wait for Mommy in heaven. I love you so much."

"Touching," Collin stated.

Jessica wiped the tears from her eyes and met his dark gaze. "I'm going to kill you for this."

"I think you have more important things to consider. Like your boyfriend waiting for you at the bottom of those steps."

She touched Megan's blonde curls one last time. "Good-bye, baby."

"Get down there," Roxie demanded.

Jessica stepped on the first step and directed the flashlight beam into the dark below. She caught sight of the sheriff's khaki uniform pants for a brief second before he moved his legs from the light.

"Don't come down here," his rough voice warned.

"Keep going," Roxie ordered behind her.

The sudden haunting howls of coyotes pierced the quiet of the night. Their eerie mournful cries called out from the shadows of the trees surrounding the edges of the barnyard.

"They sense the Ebon Moon," Roxie spoke to her brother.

"Time is running out. I better get the child to the barn," Collin replied and headed toward the open doorway of the dark structure.

Jessica descended a couple more steps into the cellar as Roxie prepared to shut the door behind her. She turned to face the dark-haired beauty in silhouette with the eclipse behind her.

"If I get out of this cellar, you're dead."

"Good-bye, Jess."

Roxie slammed the door down, causing a cascade of dust and dead leaves. She next clicked a padlock through the hasp before walking away. Feeling panic rising, Jessica turned the flashlight down the steps where the animal-like breathing echoed in the empty dark.

What am I locked in here with?

"Dale?" she asked in a voice cracking in fear.

The labored breathing continued.

She descended the steps on trembling legs, the flashlight cutting a yellow beam through the dust hanging in the air. Someone or something huddled in one dark corner. She swung the light toward the figure. Sheriff Sutton, still dressed in his khaki uniform, crouched with his face hidden from the light. Blood stained one leg of his uniform pants.

"Dale?" she asked again.

He looked up showing a face half-human and half-bestial. Jessica screamed in horror and dropped the flashlight, which rolled across the floor. In the erratic light, the half-human Sheriff Sutton growled and reached for her with a clawed hand. She fell back against one wall, fighting another scream rising inside. Due to his other wrist handcuffed to an iron pipe, she managed to stay just out of the reach of the horrid thing.

"Don't look at me," he stated, pulling back to huddle once again in the corner. "Keep away."

Anger tempered with frustration filled Jessica's heart. Her trust in Sheriff Sutton saving her and Megan from danger evaporated. Now she realized the truth. The sheriff was part of the monstrous nightmare.

"You bastard!" Jessica shouted. "You're one of them! I trusted you! I brought you into my home. I even made love to you. Now they've got Megan!"

"Jess," he replied between labored breaths. "I tried to stop them … because you reminded me of my own wife … and daughter … the ones I lost so many years … ago." Pulling on the handcuff attached to the pipe, he added, "They died during a snowstorm … I couldn't … get to them in time. When Collin wanted your daughter … I turned against the Pack …

that's the reason … they chained me down here."

Jessica ran hands through her blonde hair and tried to come to reason with the insanity of it all. "What can I do to save Megan?"

"Escape … get out of the cellar." The sheriff's body twisted as if in pain. "I can't hold back … the changing much longer."

"I can't. They've locked me in here."

"You must." The sound of popping bones resonated in the cellar. "I can't prevent …the transformation … much longer … if I shape-shift … then you will be … killed … I can't control … the beast inside."

Jessica picked up the flashlight from the floor. "You must fight it."

"The pull of the Ebon Moon … too strong," he replied. "Can't stop it."

Jessica swung up the flashlight beam and gasped. The sheriff's body started to change into something even more nightmarish. The buttons on his uniform shirt ripped open to make room for his expanding chest. Thick hair bristled on the back of his hands as black claws extended from the ends of his fingers. In a voice barely recognizable as human, he snarled, "Get out … Jess! Can't hold it back … in the glove box of the patrol car … pistol with silver bullets … if you reach it … kill the others."

The sheriff twisted in the throes of his bestial transformation. Tilting his head back, he released a terrible howl of torment as his handsome face shifted to the visage of a monstrous canine. It licked out with a long tongue and eyed Jessica with a savage hunger. Dale Sutton was no longer present in the horrendous body; only the beast now remained. Howling again, the thing yanked on the cuff and pulled the pipe an inch from its mounting in the cement wall.

Jessica raced up the cellar steps. "Dear God, help me!"

Using the butt of the flashlight, she pounded against the wood planks of the door while the beast growled and fought to free itself in the darkness below.

CHAPTER SIXTY-ONE

"Man, you ought to check the moon out. It's almost completely dark," Sid stated, sticking his head out the truck's passenger window while training the binoculars up at the sky. "The eclipse is fucking cool."

Terry kept his attention out the windshield toward the rear exit of the roadhouse. Deciding the werewolf pack would leave the bar out the back door, they parked the truck in the abandoned farmland behind Roxie's. When they pulled onto the property, they spotted the sheriff's patrol car near an old abandoned wooden barn. They parked the F-150 along a tree line and watched the back of the bar as the eclipse progressed overhead through the night sky.

"I was thinking earlier," Terry announced. "Maybe we got this whole thing wrong. I don't think the werewolf is after Jess."

"Why?" Sid asked, dropping back into the cab.

"She wasn't home the night it tried to get in the trailer. Jess was at work."

"Who was it after?"

"The little girl," he answered.

"Megan?"

"Yeah." Terry nodded. "Do werewolves do that? I mean, do they go after little children?"

"Not so much in the movies," Sid answered, adding, "but I read a book once about myths of the Old World. Werewolves were reported to snatch children away in the night. It's a scary fucking image. Running off under the moon with a child in its jaws like a bloody doll."

"What do they do with the children?" Terry asked, still keeping his watch on the back of the bar.

"Eat them."

A light showed at the door.

"Let me have those," Terry said, reaching for the binoculars.

"What's up?" Sid asked, putting the field glasses in his hand.

"I saw something."

Focusing the binoculars, Terry spotted three dark figures emerge from the back of the bar. One carried a flashlight. Together they cut a path through the trees heading toward the barn and the sheriff's patrol car.

"Something's happening," Terry relayed to Sid.

"What?"

"I can't tell much from this distance, but some people just left the roadhouse."

"The werewolves are on the move," Sid replied.

Terry grabbed up his crossbow and popped open the driver door. "I'm going to get a closer look." Reaching into the bed of the truck, he slipped on his hunting poncho. "You stay here and keep the walkie-talkie open just like before. If I get into trouble, I'll radio you."

"Don't get yourself killed."

"I won't, dude." Terry patted his front pocket. "I brought Mr. Higgins's silver bullet with me as a good luck charm."

"I hope it fucking works."

"Me, too," Terry replied, pulling two Molotov cocktails from the milk crate in the truck bed. He slipped them into pockets in the poncho along with the lighter. "Just sit tight. I'll be back in a minute."

"Okay, Rambo." Sid slid over behind the steering wheel and pulled his shotgun to him. "Just radio when you're coming back so I know it's you. I see anything else getting near this truck I'm going to shove this shotgun up its ass."

Terry nodded. "Okay."

He took off toward where he had seen the others trekking through the woods, and he soon discovered moving through the brush in the dark was too slow and noisy. Deciding to continue along the edge of the tree line, he headed toward the barn in the distance. At the halfway point, Terry crouched, pulled out the binoculars, and spotted the shadowy shapes of three people walking past the sheriff's parked patrol car. The group stopped before an underground storm cellar door. One bent to open it. Even through the binoculars, it was hard to determine details of the dark figures. Low voices floated through the night air to him, but he couldn't make out the conversation.

The sudden howls of coyotes caused his skin to turn to ice. He scanned the surrounding area to find the source of the haunting cries. The animals were hidden in the trees beside him. Glimpses of their eyes reflected the fading moonlight. The eerie howling increased in intensity. Something supernatural had drawn them to this site. He glanced up. The eclipse now covered the moon's face. With his heart pounding in fear, Terry put down the binoculars, grabbed up the crossbow, and contemplated returning to the truck.

Fifty yards away, someone slammed down the cellar door with a crash.

He snapped his attention back in that direction. Two shadowy figures headed toward the barn. The third person was still inside the cellar.

Why?

He swallowed back the fear caught in his throat and decided to take a closer look. Keeping a low profile, he jogged the distance to the back of the patrol car and squatted beside the rear bumper. The howling of the coyotes had risen in volume like the mournful wails of lost souls. Yellowish eyes watched him from the dark. Terry gripped the crossbow with sweaty hands and risked a glance around the back of the car. The two figures had disappeared in the barn. He turned his attention to the storm cellar.

A woman's scream came from inside.

*   *   *   *

Collin placed the sleeping for of Megan in the soft dirt of the barn floor. He looked up through the hole in the roof at the eclipsing moon overhead. The shadow had grown to cover its face. From deep inside, the beast spoke to him.

Feed me.

Yes.

He cut away the tape binding the hands and feet of the sleeping child and studied Megan in the dim light. Clad in a T-shirt and pajama bottoms, the sight of the little girl's tender flesh caused his stomach to rumble. Very soon she would be ripped apart to satiate his hunger and feed his soul with her life energy. He breathed in the aroma of her succulent body. Saliva flooded his mouth at the thought of the forbidden feast he was about to partake.

"Something's wrong," Roxie whispered, breaking his thoughts.

Collin turned to his sister waiting by the Camaro parked in the barn. She was half-crouched with senses focused on the open door to the outside.

"What is it?"

"Someone's moving about," Roxie replied. Her long raven hair splayed across her shoulders as she glanced at him with dark, bottomless eyes. She sniffed the air again. "Hunters."

"Those damn teenage punks," Collin snapped back. "They must be back."

Roxie slid off her shirt and undid her jeans. "I'll stop them."

"Be careful," Collin said. "They may be armed with silver weapons."

She slipped out of her jeans and stood naked in the dim light of the barn. "Stay with the child, my love. I'll be back to feast."

"Make it quick. We only have a few minutes more before the Ebon Moon is gone," Collin stated.

Roxie fell to her hands and knees and transformed to her Wolfkin form. Once completed, she gave him a last look before emitting a low growl and darting in a loping gate out the door of the barn.

*   *   *   *

Terry raced from the patrol car to the storm cellar door. On the other side, a woman shouted and pounded against the wood to get out. He thought he recognized her voice. Laying aside the crossbow, he crouched and reached for the padlock on the hasp of the door.

"Jess," he said, "is that you?"

"Yes," she answered through a space between the wood planks. "Oh God, who is that?"

"Terry," he replied. "The door's padlocked. I have to find something to break the lock with."

"Hurry," she said. "I'm down here with a monster! It'll be free soon!"

"Okay."

He searched the ground around the cellar looking for a brick or a two-by-four to break the lock. He found nothing in sight.

Without warning, the coyotes grew eerily quiet.

Terry turned toward the barn.

A dark blur raced toward him.

Driven by reflex and fear, he twisted to the side as the growling shape flew past, shredding his camouflage poncho with its claws. The attacking beast landed in the grass a short distance away. Terry spun to face his attacker. This time the werewolf was female, signified by her fur-covered breasts. In the fading moonlight, it hunkered down on all fours and glared at him with burning red eyes. He glanced at the crossbow that lay near the cellar door. It was too far away for him to reach.

"Nice girl," he muttered, pulling the two gasoline-filled bottles from the poncho. Crouching, he placed them on the ground. "Don't want any trouble, girl."

The creature growled but kept watching him with her evil red eyes.

"You don't want to eat me, do you, girl?" He removed the lighter and ignited the ends of the gasoline-soaked rags. "That wouldn't be nice."

He grabbed both burning bottles and stood while the creature rose up on its two legs.

"Eat this instead!" he shouted and pitched the first bottle at the monster.

Faster than he could follow, the she-creature ducked to the side, causing the Molotov cocktail to shatter against the side of the barn wall. The splash of flaming gas ignited the old wood planks.

"Oh shit," Terry blurted out.

The werewolf raced toward him and he threw the second Molotov cocktail. In midair, she caught the bottle and prepared to throw it back at him.

"Oh shit!" Terry repeated louder.

Suddenly, Sid appeared at his side with the shotgun leveled at the beast.

"Catch this, bitch," he said, pulling the trigger.

The shotgun boomed. The blast shattered the bottle, showering the creature in burning gasoline. She howled in agony as her fur caught fire. Engulfed in a billowing inferno, the monster fled for the barn and collapsed just inside the door.

"What are you doing here?" Terry turned to Sid in shock.

"I knew you'd get your ass in trouble, so I followed you." Sid jacked another round in the shotgun, ejecting the smoking cartridge. "Who's in the cellar?"

"Jess," Terry answered.

"Should have known," Sid replied.

*　　*　　*　　*

Ear against the cellar door, Jessica strained to hear the events happening outside. Below her in the dark, metal grated against cement as the horrid thing fought being cuffed to the pipe in the wall. Any moment it would be free to maul her to death. Time was running out.

She heard the boom of a firearm, more voices, and something howling like a wounded animal.

"Jess," Terry said again through the space in boards of the cellar door.

"I'm here."

"Step back. Sid's going to shoot the lock with a shotgun."

"Make it quick," she replied and squatted on the steps as the rending sound of the metal pipe tearing free from the wall echoed in the cellar behind her.

The shotgun went off, blowing chunks of wood splinters in her hair. Out of the corner of her eye, the dark shape of the freed werewolf appeared at the bottom of the steps. It snarled up at her with hungry red eyes and dripping maw. Jessica threw open the cellar door, causing Terry and Sid to stand back in surprise.

"Run!" She slammed down the door behind her. "Run like hell!"

"Where?" Terry asked.

"The sheriff's car," she answered, already sprinting toward the vehicle twenty-five yards away. "There's a pistol with silver bullets in the glove box."

"I know that gun," Terry replied, running at her side. "It's Mr. Higgins's pistol."

Jogging with the shotgun, Sid lagged behind them both.

The cellar door burst open again. From the subterranean darkness, the beast leaped out to the surface and roared in rage.

"Fuck!" Sid cursed, turning around.

With the erratic beam of the flashlight bouncing in front of her, Jessica reached the side of the patrol car. Behind her, the shotgun boomed followed by screams mixed with growling. She flung the flashlight against the driver window, shattering a hole through the safety glass. Reaching in, she unlocked the door and lunged into the front seat.

"Sid's in trouble," Terry stated at the open car door. "I've got to help him."

He turned and disappeared back the way they came.

Jessica fumbled with the latch on the glove box. "Come on ... open, goddammit," she muttered in desperation.

The compartment popped down and she groped inside for the pistol. Her hand wrapped around the grip as Terry shouted somewhere outside. Pistol in hand, Jessica dived out of the car, rolled to her feet in a firing stance, and took in the situation before her. Half the distance back to the cellar, the huge werewolf loomed over Terry's prone form sprawled out on the ground. One crossbow arrow jutted from its left shoulder.

"Hey!" she shouted at the horror.

It turned its attention toward her with rage-filled eyes. Jessica blinked in disbelief at the full sight of the horror. Covered in thick brown fur, the creature stood eight feet tall with a wolflike face showing a maw of canine teeth. The nightmarish sight caused Jessica to freeze. Her finger hesitated against the trigger.

"Shoot it!" Terry screamed.

Suddenly, the monster jumped toward her as she pulled the trigger twice in rapid succession. The pistol flashes illuminated the horrid beast in mid-leap before it knocked her to the ground. Jessica lay pinned beneath its weight with the werewolf's wet maw and hot breath against her neck. Before its bite sank into her flesh, it let out a gasping moan and collapsed heavily atop her. Shocked, Jessica rolled it off and scrambled to her feet. The creature was dying. Blood pumped from two bullet holes in its chest. She watched amazed as the beast's fur and claws retreated, leaving nothing but the naked body of Sheriff Sutton.

"Jess," he whispered in a rough voice while reaching a hand toward her. "I'm finally free."

He coughed a last breath and died.

"Rest now in peace," Jessica said, tenderly stroking her hand through his sandy brown hair, the way she had when they made love the night before.

Terry reached her side with a look of concern.

"Are you bit?" he asked

She wiped a tear from her cheek and shook her head. "No."

"Thank God," he replied.

"What about you?"

"Another second and I would have been. I'm glad you know how to shoot a pistol."

"What about the other werewolves?"

"The female is dead."

"Roxie, which leaves only Collin now," Jessica stated and asked, "How's your friend?"

"Sid!" Terry turned. "Are you all right?"

"Oh man, that fucking werewolf kicked my ass," he replied in a weak voice from where he lay sprawled out on his back in the grass.

"Oh, no!" Terry rushed to kneel by Sid's side. "Oh, hell no!"

Jessica followed, realizing for the first time the wooden barn was now ablaze. Rolling flames engulfed one wall and spread across the rotted wood shingles on the roof. Her heart sank at the sight.

Megan's in there!

In the firelight, blood gushed from ragged gashes on the side of Sid's neck and head. He looked up at both of them with glazed eyes.

"I'm all fucked up," he stated.

"I'm here, bro," Terry replied, lifting the skinny young man and holding him in his arms. More blood spurted from Sid's torn neck. "Hang on. I'm going to get you to the hospital."

Jessica glanced again at the burning barn.

"I've got to save my baby," she said, dropping open the cylinder on the pistol and counting her live rounds. Only three silver bullets left.

"I know," Terry replied with the glitter of tears in his eyes. "But I can't leave Sid like this. He'll die. I have to get him to the emergency room. I'll bring help as fast as I can."

"You do that." Jessica slapped the cylinder back. "I'm going to go get my daughter."

She sprinted toward the fiery structure of the barn.

*   *   *   *

Collin heard the Molotov cocktail shatter against the side of the barn wall. He turned his attention from the sleeping girl to concentrate on the events happening outside. A shotgun blast sounded followed by the agonizing screams of his sister.

Her horrible screech of agony grew louder. Seconds later, her flaming body collapsed inside the open barn door. He rushed to her. Fire had immolated her skin to a sickening black, and the smell of burning flesh and gasoline nearly forced him to wretch. Scooping handfuls of dirt from the earthen floor, he tossed it on her in a desperate hope to put out the fire. Flames spread from her burning form along the hay on the floor, but remorse for his sister blinded him to the fact that the barn was also on fire.

"Sister!" he bellowed in shock. "No!"

He threw on more dirt and managed to smother her flames, but he knew it was too late. Her beautiful body had been reduced to a blackened mass of smoking charred flesh. Deep loss filled his heart, and Collin turned his face up to the eclipse showing through a hole in the roof.

"Not her!" he screamed, unheeding of the flames raging behind him.

Reveca was dead. Nothing could bring her back now. Tears formed at the sight of her burned body. His rage and sorrow brought on an instant transformation. Clothes ripped away as the body of the beast replaced his. In horrible torment, the monster howled. Everything was lost now, his dreams and hopes as dead as his sister lying before him. Without Reveca nothing mattered. The beast clawed open the blackened torso and ripped the heart from her chest. It swallowed the organ whole and howled mournfully again toward the sky.

The face of the Ebon Moon was in complete shadow.

Licking sharp teeth covered in gore, it turned toward the sleeping child.

Time to feed, Collin spoke inside.

*   *   *   *

Terry held Sid while running to where the truck sat parked near the trees. Thanks to the adrenaline surging though his muscles, he seemed to carry a hollow plastic mannequin instead of the weight of his friend. Sid's wounds bled profusely with each step he took. Only another fifty yards to reach the truck, but it seemed miles away.

"Put me down, man," Sid said in a soft voice.

"No," Terry replied. "We're almost there."

"I'm not going to make it."

"Oh, man."

Terry lowered his dying friend to the ground. More blood spewed from the bite wound in his neck.

"Fuck." Sid winced.

Terry started to weep. "I'm so sorry."

"Don't be." He showed a weak smile. "I saved your ass, didn't I?"

"You did." Terry held tightly one of Sid's bloody hands. "You're a good friend," he added, choking back emotion.

"You got to help Jess now," Sid said and coughed a rattling wheeze. Bloody foam colored his pale lips. "Just promise … you'll kiss her … one time for me."

Sid's grip went weak as his eyes rolled back in his head. Swiping the tears from his vision, Terry stripped off the torn poncho and covered his friend's body.

"I will, brother," he said, standing to his feet.

*   *   *   *

Megan coughed awake to smoke in the air.

It burned her nostrils and made it hard to breathe. She sat up to take in her surroundings. She didn't know where she was but saw fire burning everywhere. Crackling flames ran along the walls, and burning bits of hay dropped down on her like fiery snowflakes. She spotted her mother's car through the thickening smoke.

"Mommy!" she shouted above the roar of the fire.

She clamored to stand. Something growled like a big dog nearby.

Megan turned.

A short distance away, the Bad Wolf stared at her with eyes the color of the burning flames. The terrible beast snarled low in its throat. Megan sprinted for the Camaro in the hope that her mother would be waiting inside. She saw no one when she reached the passenger window.

"Mommy!" she cried out again.

The Bad Wolf's reflection appeared in the window glass. Screaming, Megan ducked and crawled beneath the Camaro as the beast grabbed at her. The monster howled in anger and bent down to snatch her out from under the car. Scooting back along the dirt floor, she pressed her small body farther under the chassis. Black claws groped blindly for her, but she managed to stay just out of their reach. The horrid face of the Bad Wolf bent low to see her location with evil red eyes. It pulled back its lips in something resembling a grimacing smile and grabbed her foot.

"Mommy!" Megan screamed again at the top of her lungs.

*   *   *   *

One quarter of the barn was aflame when Jessica reached the building. The hundred-year-old wood of the structure was going up like a matchbook, and the entrance had become a wall of flames. The heat from the blaze was hot on her face as she continued down along one wall looking for another way in. Jessica paused and listened. She heard something above the roar of the inferno consuming the barn.

Her daughter's muffled cry.

"Megan!" she screamed back and desperately searched for a way inside. Just above ground level, she noted one piece of siding looked rotted and weak. She tore at the old wood. The board gave way and she flung it aside. Smoke poured from the hole as she wriggled in on her belly through the narrow opening.

"Mommy!" Megan screamed again, this time louder and nearer.

Jessica sat up on her knees and peered in the direction of her screams. She spotted the Camaro and the huge form of a black-furred werewolf kneeling by its side.

"Collin!" she shouted. "Get away from her!"

The monstrous creature turned toward her and growled.

Jessica snapped up the .38 pistol and pulled the trigger. The beast threw itself to the side as the gun went off. The bullet winged the fur on one shoulder and knocked through the passenger window in a spray of glass. The creature bounded over the top of the Camaro and disappeared.

Jessica crossed to the car with pistol ready. Very little visibility prevented her from seeing far in the thick smoke.

"Megan?" she called out.

"I'm here, Mommy," her daughter said from under the car.

Jessica knelt on one knee and reached down.

"Baby," she said. "Take my hand."

Small fingers wrapped around her palm, and Jessica pulled Megan out from beneath the Camaro. Grease and grime covered her torn T-shirt and face.

"Mommy, you came for me." Megan hugged her tightly around the waist.

"I promised I would protect you," Jessica replied, opening the passenger door. "Get in the car, baby, and lay on the floorboard. The air will be easier to breathe down there."

"Okay, Mommy," Megan said and slid onto the floorboard of the passenger seat.

Jessica coughed from the smoke and contemplated a way to escape. Embers of burning wood and hay floated through the stifling air. The fire consuming the old wooden roof had turned the hayloft into a hellish inferno. Burning timbers overhead cracked under the relentless flames. The structure would not remain standing much longer. She needed to get Megan out but had to deal with the werewolf first.

"Collin!" she screamed above the roar of the fire. "I'm waiting, you son of a bitch."

She caught movement beneath the hayloft. A dark shape growled and leaped aside. Jessica fired the .38, but the smoke in her eyes made it hard to focus on the target. The bullet missed and kicked up splinters from one of the support pillars holding up the fiery loft. The werewolf retreated once more into the thick pall.

It's baiting me, Jessica thought. *It's trying to get me to use all my ammo.*

Jessica glanced inside the Camaro. The keys were in the ignition!

Oh God. I can drive out of the barn!

She leaped inside and slid over the console into the driver's seat.

"Keep your head down, baby," Jessica said to her daughter. "It's going to be a bumpy ride."

She reached for the ignition key.

The werewolf attacked then. Its dark shape loomed in the smoke outside the driver window. Claws shattered the safety glass and hooked onto the car door. Jessica screamed and threw herself back as the beast ripped off the door and flung it into the fire. The violence of the motion caused her to drop the keys to the floor. The werewolf growled, attempting to grab Jessica. She dodged back but not before the creature snagged her hair with its black claws. Yanking herself free, she twisted into the passenger seat and brought up the pistol in the hope of getting a good shot. The beast was now halfway into the car and nearly upon her. In fear and desperation, she kicked out against its horrid face and slobbering maw.

"Stay away!" she yelled.

The impact of her kicks caused Jessica to slide out the open passenger door where she landed on her back in the hard dirt. The beast made a grab for her daughter crouched in the floorboard.

Jessica fired the .38 pistol. Blood and fur erupted where the bullet hit the monster's arm, reaching for Megan. Howling in pain, the werewolf pulled itself out of the car and disappeared once again into the smoke.

Jessica struggled back to her feet, feeling a badly bruised hip.

The fire had now spread everywhere inside the barn. Unbearable heat and black smoke made it impossible to breathe. Overhead, the barn roof had turned into a broiling furnace consuming the old rafters. One wooden beam cracked and tumbled from the inferno above, its flaming end shattering through the back windshield of the Camaro.

"Mommy," Megan choked. "I can't breathe."

"Get out of the car, baby."

"The Bad Wolf will get me," Megan protested.

"No, it won't," Jessica replied, wiping away smoke-caused tears. She shifted the pistol and reached a hand toward Megan. "I won't let it. We can't stay in here. There's a hole in the wall where Mommy crawled inside the barn. You have to help me find it so we can get out."

"Okay." Megan nodded and exited the Camaro.

"Crawl on your hands and knees, baby." Jessica pointed with the pistol toward the wall. "I think the hole is over there."

More burning wood fell from the roof and crashed in a spray of embers, blocking the way to the hole.

"No!" Jessica cried out in desperation.

"Mommy." Megan wrapped her arms around her waist. "Hold me."

Jessica picked her up and hugged her close while keeping the pistol in her other hand. "I'll carry you out."

"Okay."

The ceiling creaked overhead from the relentless onslaught of the fire. Jessica tried to determine which direction to go in the suffocating smoke and heat.

Oh God, show me the way out.

A deep growl sounded close.

She spun around with pistol ready. Under the burning hayloft, she spotted the werewolf form of Collin through the thick pall. Blood poured from the bullet hole in its arm. Jessica brought up the pistol and pulled the trigger.

Click.

No more silver bullets.

The werewolf's red eyes showed satisfaction as a cruel smile parted to reveal its fangs. Unleashing a primal growl, the beast charged.

"Mommy loves you," Jessica whispered, burying her daughter's face in her chest so not to see the horror about to befall them.

The next instant, a flaming wall exploded inward, revealing an old red Ford F-150 crashing its way into the barn. The front grill rammed the werewolf in mid-charge and sent the beast hurling back under the hayloft. Before coming to a stop, the truck knocked out one of the loft's support pillars, causing a mountain of burning hay to fall upon the monster. The horrendous screams of the beast rose above the roar of the fire.

"Get in," Terry shouted, swinging open the passenger door. "Now!"

She rushed to the truck and hefted her daughter into the front seat before throwing herself inside. A thunderous crack sounded overhead, signaling the roof's collapse. Terry slapped the truck in reverse, sending the F-150 shooting backward out of the burning building as the roof crashed down in a massive avalanche of wood and fire. Buried beneath the blazing ruins, the beast that was Collin released a final dying howl of agony and went silent.

In stunned silence, the three sat in the front seat watching the flaming mass of the collapsed barn send embers spiraling up into the night sky.

"Are you okay, baby?" she finally asked Megan.

She coughed. "I got all dirty, Mommy."

Jessica smiled. "It's all right, sugar." Realizing she still held the pistol, Jessica dropped it to the floorboard and hugged her daughter close. "You're safe and that's all that matters."

"Is the Bad Wolf gone?"

"Yes."

She turned her attention to Terry looking out the windshield.

"Sid?" she asked.

"Dead," he replied.

"I'm so sorry."

"So am I. He was a good friend," Terry stated and started to laugh.

"What?" Jessica asked, surprised.

"I just remembered something, and if Sid were here, he would be laughing right alongside me." Terry reached into his front pocket and pulled out a bullet. "This is the silver bullet Mr. Higgins gave to me. I've carried it as a good luck charm all this time. I guess it did work."

Jessica chuckled. "I could've used it a couple of minutes ago."

"You can have it." He dropped the bullet is Jessica's palm. "I don't need it anymore."

The driver door of the pickup flew open. A shadowy shape grabbed the teenager and yanked him out of the cab. Next the dark figure snatched Megan. Jessica gasped in shock and tried too late to hold onto her daughter.

"Come to Daddy," Blake said.

CHAPTER SIXTY-TWO

Jessica jumped out. On the other side of the truck, Blake held Megan before him with the hooked nails of one hand hovering above her throat. His cruel eyes showed pure evil.

"Surprised to see me, Jess?" he asked in a low inhuman voice. "Since you shot and left me for dead the last time we met."

"Nothing surprises me now," she replied. "Let me guess. You're a werewolf."

"Go figure." He smiled, showing extended canines. "Funny thing happed outside your trailer the other night. I got bit. Believe me, no one was more surprised than I was. I do consider it an upgrade. The rush it gives is so much better than coke." Blake nodded toward the burning building. "What happened to the others?"

"They died in the fire."

"Too bad." He shrugged. "I was supposed to join their little pack tonight. I guess that makes me a lone wolf now, if you'll pardon the pun. After we finish our business, I'm hitting the road. I won't have any qualms about who I feast upon, either. Women and children are just walking pieces of meat to me. I'll paint this country blood red before I'm done. What do you think about that?"

"You still have to deal with me." Jessica reached down to the floorboard of the truck, grabbed the .38 pistol, and picked up the lone silver bullet Terry had handed her.

"True." Blake nodded. "Who's your teenage friend? Are you fucking them that young now, Jess?"

"He's ten times the man you'll ever be," she replied. "Did you kill him?"

"No." Blake shook his head. "I just knocked him out. Sorry about the couple who lived with you on the farm, though." He chomped his teeth together. "Your friends were quite tasty."

Jessica's heart turned to ice. Blake murdered Sam and Nelda. She glanced at Megan, who stood motionless with his sharp nails pressed against her throat. He wouldn't hesitate to kill their daughter, either.

"This ends tonight, Blake." Jessica brought up the pistol.

He tilted Megan's head back. "Put the gun down, Jess. I'll tear her throat open before you can pull the trigger."

"It's not Megan you want. It's me."

"Oh, but it is so much fun watching you try to protect her."

She spotted movement over Blake's shoulder. Terry stood to his feet and motioned for her to be quiet. Jessica returned her focus on her husband, knowing she needed a ploy to keep him occupied so he wouldn't know Terry was behind him. She opened the pistol cylinder and shook out the spent cartridges. They rolled across the hood of the truck.

"What are you doing, Jess?" Blake asked

Jessica showed the silver bullet. "One bullet." She dropped it into the chamber and snapped up the cylinder. "Isn't that how you play the game?"

He laughed a dry chuckle. "You won't do it."

Jessica spun the chamber, put the .38 against her temple, and pulled the trigger.

Click.

"Does that answer your question?" she asked, trying to keep her voice calm.

"Now that's more like it, Jess."

"You used to love this game, or are you too big a pussy to play now, Mr. Werewolf?"

His tongue licked across his lips. "Fuck no."

"Then let go of Megan so we can play."

Blake shook his head. "I'm not stupid. I let her go and you'll shoot me." He pushed his nails harder against Megan's throat. "You already shot me once."

"I'm serious, Blake."

"Prove it to me, Jess. Pull the trigger twice and I'll let her go."

"Okay," Jessica replied with a tremor in her voice as she placed the barrel against her head. She had lost sight of Terry.

Did he run away?

Oh God, I hope not.

She closed her eyes and pulled the trigger.

Click.

Her finger tightened once more against the trigger. With her heart pounding in her ears she felt the chamber slowly turn as the hammer pulled back. On the other side of the truck hood, Blake watched with a psychotic glint in his dark eyes.

Oh God, please.

The hammer dropped.

Click.

Blake let out an excited growl. "I have to admit I like this new Jess better. The old one would just cry and whine. You really did grow a set of balls."

"So what do you say?" she asked as the rush of still being alive coursed through her body. She placed the .38 on the truck hood and slid it toward her husband. "Do you feel lucky?"

Blake focused on the pistol. She knew he contemplated the offer. His grip on Megan's throat loosened.

Pick up the gun, Blake.

"What the fuck?" He released Megan and grabbed up the .38.

Jessica motioned for her daughter to step away. Blake's gaze fixed hers as he spun the chamber and put the barrel against his temple. "You tried to kill me once, Jess. I came back, didn't I? I'm immortal now. The Angel of Death." He put the barrel against his head.

Do it. Pull the trigger, she prayed. *Please God.*

Instead, he laughed and pointed the pistol at her.

"Did you think I was that stupid? You had a chance when you still had the gun."

"I knew you didn't have the balls to pull the trigger. You're a coward just like your father."

"You fucking backstabbing whore!" His eyes grew darker as spittle flew out of his mouth. "You're going to pay for saying that about my father!" The bones on his face started to pop and shift. "I won't shoot you." His voice deepened into an animal's low growl. "I'm going to rip you apart!"

A sudden impact caused Blake's head to snap forward. He dropped the gun and it skittered across the hood where Jessica snatched it . Terry now stood behind him preparing to swing the aluminum baseball once more against the back of Blake's skull. Screaming in rage, Blake turned toward the teenager and caught the swing in a clawed hand. With the other, he gripped Terry by the throat and lifted him off the ground.

"You punk!" he snarled in an inhuman voice.

"You forgot about me, Blake," Jessica called out, taking a firing stance.

He threw Terry aside and turned, showing a face transformed into something half-canine, half-human. Blake's dark eyes met hers a second before she pulled the trigger. In that instant, she realized the beast and her husband had become more terrifying than just a werewolf. Together they formed an unholy union fueled by Blake's savagery, an abomination ten times worse than Collin.

The gun went off. The silver bullet hit him between the eyes, plowed through his brain, and blew out the back of his head in a spray of blood and bone. Blake fell over backward upon the ground.

"Now you're dead," Jessica stated.

"Mommy," Megan cried out, rushing to her side.

Jessica swept her beautiful daughter up and embraced her with more love then she had ever known. She looked up at the Ebon Moon to say a silent prayer of thanks. A rim of silver light had now emerged from the shadowed edge of the eclipse.

"I love you, baby." Jessica kissed her daughter's face.

A low moan came from where Terry lay in the grass.

"Are you okay?" she asked.

"Yeah." He sat up holding his side. "I got the wind knocked out of me." Standing shakily to his feet, he tossed aside the aluminum bat. "I'm glad I kept this in the back of the truck."

"So am I," Jessica replied.

The wail of fire truck sirens sounded in the far distance.

Jessica patted Megan on the back. "Get in the truck, sweetie."

"Okay." Megan hopped in the truck cab.

Crossing over to Blake's body, Jessica knelt by his side. His dark eyes stared lifelessly up at the sky as brain matter leaked from the hole in his head. She dropped the empty pistol on his chest and noticed something sticking half-out of the pocket of his black duster. She pulled out two thick stacks of hundred-dollar bills.

"Consider this child support," she said to his corpse while stuffing the bills in her jean pockets.

Terry limped over to her side. "Tell me he's dead."

"He is." She turned to face him. "Fire trucks are on the way. There's going to be a lot of questions I don't want to answer. I need to get out of here. Can I buy the truck?"

"You can have it." Terry handed her the keys. "It was a gift from Mr. Higgins, and I give it to you. He would want you to have it."

"Thanks."

"Where are you going?"

"I've always wanted to see Colorado."

"I'll stick around here, but what am I going to tell the cops?" Terry asked, looking around at the scene of carnage. "Werewolves are going to be a hard story to sell."

Jessica thought for a moment. "Tell them Blake did it. He went crazy. He's already wanted for multiple murders, and his fingerprints are on the gun that shot Sheriff Sutton. Tell them he set the barn on fire. Everything else they'll just have to guess."

Terry nodded. "Okay."

The sirens grew louder.

Jessica studied the teenager's face in the glow of the fire. He met her eyes before looking down at his feet.

"I know there is no way to repay you for saving me and my daughter." She leaned his head up and kissed him full on the lips. "Thank you for being there."

"You're the first girl I ever kissed," he relayed as she stepped back toward the driver door of the truck.

"I'm honored," she replied. "But for the record, I kissed you."

"In that case," he grabbed her by the hand and drew her to him, "this is for Sid."

His lips pressed expertly against hers. Jessica felt the warmth of his kiss, and the surprising passion made her forget for a second he was a teenage boy. She released herself from the embrace and stepped back to catch her breath.

"Keep that up and you'll have a lot more girls to kiss in your life."

Terry showed a broad smile. "I will."

Jessica slid behind the steering wheel and started the truck.

"I guess this is good-bye," she said.

He leaned forward and shut the driver door. "Good-bye, Megan."

"Good-bye," she replied.

He stepped back as Jessica put the truck in gear. "Bye, Jess."

"Bye and thank you.." She drove away and headed for the exit onto the country road.

Before pulling off the property, she caught one last glimpse in the rearview mirror of Terry silhouetted against the backdrop of the burning barn. She smiled inwardly with a sudden revelation. If a teenage boy could be so brave and passionate, there was hope for the male gender after all. She wasn't going to give up hunting for a good man.

"Mommy?" Megan asked in the dark silence of the cab.

"Yes, baby?"

"Monsters are real, aren't they?"

"Yes." Jessica nodded. "I guess they are."

She turned onto the dirt road and pointed the truck west toward Colorado.

THE END

Complete the trilogy of terror
with

13 Nightmares

and

Undead Flesh.

Both available on Amazon.

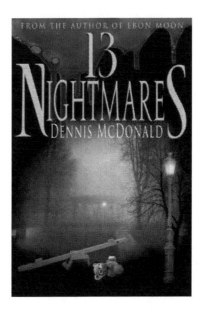

HORROR IS BEST WRITTEN IN THE DARK.

Thirteen tales of original terror penned in the dead of the night with only the glow of a computer for light. The collection of short stories runs the gamut of horror. Within its bloody pages you will find a slasher clown, a blood red church, a little girl locked in a closet, a haunted sex doll, etc. 13 Nightmares is a fine collection of terror for the short story lover, but be warned. Some of these stores are not for the faint of heart. Do you dare enter a world where the supernatural, the macabre, and the horrific collide?

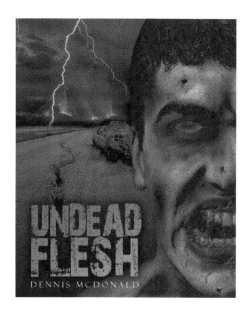

What would you do if the zombie apocalypse happened tomorrow?

Meet Jack Garret. Wishing to reconnect with his family, he takes them on a much-needed vacation to the Grand Canyon. While driving through Oklahoma, a massive earthquake strikes and shatters the landscape. However, this is no natural phenomena, for in its wake, the sun turns dark and the dead crawl from their graves. Uncertain what has happened, Jack leads his family on a desperate journey through a devastated countryside to find an escape from the nightmare. On the way, he will face hordes of zombies, brutal rednecks, crazed religious fanatics, and the darkest fear in his heart.

I hope you enjoyed Ebon Moon. Please feel free to write a review and post it. Or you can email it to me. I'd love to hear from you. If you liked this novel, don't hesitate to check out my other books. I'm sure you'll enjoy them too. You can find me at the following online locations.

Email: dragonmac007@yahoo.com

Website: dennismcdonaldauthor.com

Blog: hauntedfunhouse @ blogger

Twitter: Nightmarewriter

All the best,

Dennis McDonald

Made in the USA
Columbia, SC
06 November 2021